Jesse McMinn is a Canadian writer and lover of fantasy raised on a healthy diet of Brian Jacques, David Eddings, and Terry Pratchett. He currently lives in Toronto with his wife Nicole and their family mascot, Pickle the crested gecko.

I0748075

Jesse McMinn Titles by IFWG Publishing

Tower series (epic fantasy)
    Loria (Book 1)
    Trials (Book 2)
    Archsage (Book 3)

Mero and the City of Ghosts

Mero and the City of Ghosts

a novel by
Jesse McMinn

IFWG Publishing International
Gold Coast

www.ifwgpublishing.com

For the goddess.

Part I

1

When the traveler first came upon the encampment nestled in the shadow of the ravine, he thought his eyes were playing tricks on him. He had seen no signs of life, intelligent or otherwise, in over twenty days—not a footpath, not a hoofprint, not even a buzzard wheeling through the sky. His water had run out four days ago, his food five days before that. His horse trembled with fatigue; he felt it through his legs. He himself was so tired he could hardly stay awake. He dozed in the saddle, the horse's reins wrapped around his wrists. He had drawn his scarf up over the bones of his cheek to protect his face from blowing dust. Even so, his eyes had nearly gummed shut.

The traveler's view of the encampment was poor. It was yet some miles away, down across the yellow dunes, at the far end of a rocky valley sheltered from the wind. Though the floor of the valley was in shadow, the air above it shimmered with heat. The desert sun was merciless. It burned through the thick fabric of the traveler's hat, cooking his brain inside his skull.

His horse nodded its head, pawing at the burning ground. It smelled water; it wanted to find the hidden spring and drink. The traveler tugged lightly on the reins. That his horse wanted to make for the encampment was a good sign. If there really was a spring somewhere in the valley, it would explain the presence of men so deep into the desert.

Even so, the traveler was wary. He couldn't seem to make his eyes work properly. Every time he tried to fix them on the far side of the valley, they would close, or slip away, or the sight would simply melt into a wash of yellow and red. He thought he saw tarpaulins stretched among the rocks—perhaps even a wooden hut or two—but could not be sure. And even if there were men here, he had no reason to believe they would welcome a stranger.

For some time the traveler sat upon his shaking horse, debating whether or not to enter the valley. The answer should have been obvious, but like his eyes, his brain was not working as it should.

A great scholar had once told him the brain was full of water, and that a man's thoughts needed this water to move about and come together. 'Medium' was the word he used: 'Water is the medium for thought!' he would say, as an explanation for why he never drank alcohol or ate salted meat.

The traveler did not know if the scholar's claim was accurate. If it was, the waterways of his own mind must have been clogged with foundered thoughts, thirsty as he was.

His horse whickered; he caught movement in the corner of his eye. There, on a rocky outcrop not ten yards from his horse's flank, sat an old man upon a thick blanket. His skin was black and wrinkled; what curls of hair he had were gray. He was naked but for a strip of cloth around his groin and had no possessions other than the blanket on which he sat. The blanket had once been red, though now it was the color of dust.

The old man had gathered a small pile of beans or seeds on the blanket before him. Every now and then he reached down, took one in his fingers, lifted it to the side of his mouth, and crunched it between his teeth.

The traveler was perturbed. He must have been more exhausted than he realized if he couldn't even see an old man sitting next to him, black against the hot white sand. He wanted to ask the man who he was, and how he had come to be here among the dunes with nothing but a scrap of blanket to sit on, but could not make his tongue form the words.

The old man, of course, had noticed the traveler long before the traveler noticed him. He brought another bean to his mouth and cracked its shell, then nodded at the traveler and said, "Your horse."

The traveler blinked. That was a mistake; it was several seconds before he could open his eyes again.

"What about it?" he asked.

"She will die soon," the old man said.

The traveler considered this. "Yes, it might."

The old man shook his head. "Not might, *will*. You should stay here and wait for her to die. Then we can eat her together."

The traveler understood why the old man might want to eat his horse. Horsemeat would certainly be easier on his teeth than a handful of dry seeds. But to think of eating it was to concede it was destined to die, which the traveler was not yet willing to do.

He cast his eyes towards the encampment he still couldn't be sure was there. "What is that place at the far end of the valley?"

The old man was shaking his head before the traveler had even finished speaking. He swung it in wide, sweeping arcs, his whole body swinging with it.

"That is a bad place," he said. "You cannot go there."

"Why not?" the traveler asked.

"Menahem lives there. He is a terrible man. If he finds you, you will wish you could die."

That was unwelcome news, but the traveler, in his exhaustion, could not muster the strength to be afraid. "He is a bandit?"

The old man sat and chewed for a moment, slipping another seed under his lip. The traveler wondered if perhaps he didn't know the word "bandit".

"He will kill you, in the end," he said at last. "But first he will make you suffer. There is poison in his heart. It makes him happy to cause other men pain."

The traveler was silent for a while, giving the old man time to take his measure. The newcomer was skinny as a knife, his limbs even more slender than those of a woman. All that showed of his face was a single dull eye, peering out from under the brim of his hat. The oddest thing about him was the sword on his hip. Its blade was naked to the air, curved and white, a sliver of the desert moon.

Finally the traveler asked, "If Menahem kills every man he sees, how are you still here?"

The old man chuckled and fed himself a bean. "I hide when I hear his men coming."

"Hide? Where?" As far as the traveler could see, there was no shelter to be found for miles, except down in the valley itself.

"I hide under the sand. Menahem is clever, but he is not so clever as to go looking for me there."

"Under the sand?" the traveler said, incredulous.

The old man grinned, showing four yellow teeth. "It is a good trick. I learned it from the snakes that swim in the desert."

A moment went by. Then the old man said, "You should not linger here. You are lucky you came to this place in daylight, when Menahem is asleep. If you are still here when the sun sets and his men leave the valley, they will find you and kill you. You must leave, and soon," he said again, for the stranger showed no sign he had heard. "It will take time for the wind to hide your tracks."

Still the traveler did not answer. His horse's nose was pointed at the valley below, towards the rock and the shade, and the promise of water.

"Is there a spring in the valley?" he asked the old man. "Is that why Menahem camps there?"

The old man shook his head, big swinging shakes. "No water."

"No?" The word was steeped in distrust.

"Menahem will find you before you drink your first drop. It would be better to die free, out in the desert. Or else you could cut your horse's throat and drink her blood, if you are thirsty. I will help you, if you promise to share."

"I need my horse," the traveler said. "I have many miles to go yet."

The old man was vexed. "Menahem has many ways of torturing the men he captures. Sometimes he locks them in tiny cages and leaves them out for the buzzards to eat. Sometimes he cuts off their arms and cooks them, then makes them eat their own arms. Sometimes he pushes cactus needles under their skin, until they are all red and swollen like a berry."

"Where can I go, if not the valley?" the traveler asked.

"Back," came the answer. "Away from here."

"I have no water or food. I will die if I go back."

"You will die either way."

Something in the traveler hardened. Sunlight licked the edge of his blade. The old man froze in the act of bringing a seed to his mouth, suddenly aware of the weapon's closeness.

"Thank you for warning me about Menahem," the traveler said coldly. "I promise to keep you a secret from him." He kicked his horse, and it started down the valley with a tired sigh.

"Wait," the old man said.

The traveler half-turned in his saddle. "Yes?"

"What is your name? A man ought to spread his name far." He waved a hand over the empty dunes, as though scattering seeds.

The traveler seemed surprised by the question.

"Mero," he said, before turning his back and nudging his horse onward.

2

The old man was soon proven wrong about at least one thing: when death finally came for Mero's horse, it was not from exhaustion, nor from lack of water.

Mero never saw the spear fly. He felt a *thump* by his leg and looked down in puzzlement. Some sort of large quill was sticking out of his horse's shoulder. A moment later, its forelegs buckled, and Mero pitched forward, tumbling over its neck and onto the ground.

His horse began to kick, the spear in its side a quivering flagpole. Dust rose in a cloud around it, and blood oozed from its neck.

Mero staggered to his feet. He could see nothing but dust. He waved a hand in front of his face, but that only made him cough. The spear had probably come from one of the dark crags lining the canyon wall, but as to who his attackers were or how many, he had no idea. His chest ached from his fall. He might have cracked a rib.

Drawing his sword, Mero crept away from his dying horse. Ahead of him, the canyon walls closed in, forming a narrow pass. Shelter beckoned among the rocks, but before Mero could reach it, two shapes grew out of the darkness to meet him. It was a pair of men, filthy and half-naked, their skin baked by the sun. One carried a spear and the other a stone axe. Their teeth were bright against their dark skin.

Mero swept his bleary eyes to either side. A third man emerged from the rocks on his left, and a fourth approached from a narrow path by his right arm. And though he did not dare turn around, he was certain there were more behind.

A familiar lassitude settled on Mero's shoulders. He was surrounded, outnumbered, exhausted and half-blind, his throat raw and dry, his stomach cramped, horseless and hardly able to keep his feet. His arms shook, and the point of his sword wavered.

A low chuckle cut through the air. It came from the frowning rocks above. There, seated on a stony plate overlooking the canyon floor, was the old man of the desert.

Mero blinked, his confusion deepening. What was the old man doing here? There was no doubt in his mind it was the same man he had spoken to not half an hour before. The wrinkled skin and wiry hair were unmistakable. He even had the same faded blanket, though now he wore it across his shoulders like a mantle.

The man on the rock flashed a grin when he sensed Mero's eyes on him. Mero realized his teeth were not yellow after all, but solid, glittering gold.

"Greetings, traveler!" he cried. "I am Menahem, king of the desert. You stand within the halls of my palace. The men you see before you are my courtiers."

Mero squinted up at the wrinkled old man. "So," he said, "you were Menahem all along."

"Yes?" said Menahem. "Who else should I be?"

Mero almost answered, then thought better of it. Could it be this was *not* the same man who hid under the sand with the snakes? More probably Menahem was mocking him, or was simply mad. Either way, Mero had little to gain from indulging him.

Instead he said, "Why have your men killed my horse?" Of course they hadn't killed her, at least not yet; he could still hear the churning of her hooves.

Instantly Menahem's fury erupted.

"You do not ask questions of me!" he bellowed from his perch.

"Why not?"

"I am king," Menahem cried. "And you—you are nothing—you are less than shit. These are my halls; this is my kingdom. Every rock, every sheep, every cactus plant, every puff of air in this desert belongs to me, to do with as I wish. Your horse was mine to ride or eat or kill, as it pleased me, and it pleased me to kill her." He pointed a gnarled finger at Mero. "You too belong to me, stranger."

"Is that so?" Mero said.

"It is," Menahem answered, with deep satisfaction. "All that you are, all that you have been, all that you will become—this is mine. Your sweat and blood belong to me. Your arms, your brain, your asshole— all these are mine, too. Even your death is mine, now. You are not a man anymore. You are a goat, a donkey, a spear in my hand, a coin I can keep or trade away."

Despite everything, Mero felt like laughing. *Old fool, my death is not yours*. He decided to goad the mad old man. If he could whip Menahem into a rage, the so-called king of the desert might order him to be killed. That was certain to be a kinder fate than becoming his prisoner.

"I have no intention of giving you anything," he said. "I have little enough as it is, less now that you've killed my horse. Besides, I don't believe you are a king at all. Your halls are open to the sun, and your robes are nothing more than a filthy blanket. Your courtiers are little better than beasts. I have dealt with kings before. You are nothing like them."

Menahem laughed. It came from low in his gut, making his belly shake. He bent forward, leering.

"Foolish man," he said softly. "I was a king from the moment I came into this world, and pissed and shit myself in my mother's arms. But *you*—were you to wrap yourself in golden robes, and sit upon the tallest throne, and wear the heaviest crown—you would *still* be less of a king than me, a baby covered in his own shit."

That suits me fine, Mero thought. *I never wanted to be a king.*

Pivoting on the ball of his foot, he turned and slashed at the man who had been creeping up behind him. His attacker held a large hoop of rope, and had been caught in the process of dropping it over Mero's head. Mero's cut severed the hoop and drew twin lines of red across the man's wrists. The man fell screaming, but another was already advancing from the right, swinging a heavy club. Mero managed to turn the blow aside, but the man bowled into him, knocking him face down into the sand.

The man landed on top of him, forcing the air from his lungs. Mero tried to draw a breath, but dust poured down his throat. Coughing, he slashed wildly over his head. His attacker grunted, but his arms still wormed their way around Mero's chest, meeting under his chin.

The man stood, lifting Mero off his feet. A third man reached for him and he kicked with all his strength. Mero's boot struck his chin, and his teeth snapped shut on his own tongue. Mero thrust his head backwards and was rewarded with a *crunch* and a warm trickle of blood down the back of his neck. The arms around his chest loosened. He fell to his hands and knees, gasping for air. Shouts sounded behind him. Gripping his sword in shaking hands, he spun and stabbed at the man who had been holding him, a bear with dangling arms and a long face, now covered in blood. But before Mero's blow could land, a rope slipped around his neck, jerking him off his feet. He struck the ground with his shoulders and then with his head. Pain overcame him and the strength left his arms. He dropped his sword and with it, the last of his hope.

The man holding Mero's rope dragged him backwards, away from his sword. Mero clawed at his throat. More men came running; one of them picked up the fallen weapon. Someone grabbed a fistful of Mero's hair and hauled him to his knees. Mero felt his scalp was being torn free. His eyes focused long enough to see the man with the stone axe approaching from the front, a look of bestial cruelty on his face.

The first blow from the stone axe took him in the chest. Mero heard his ribs crack. He would have screamed but the rope around his neck was too tight. The man raised his axe again. Mero struggled, but someone twisted his hands behind his back. The second blow came, catching him in the side of the hip. His legs turned to jelly, and he hung limply by his hair.

The third blow struck him full in the face. Mero's nose shattered and his mouth filled with blood. A tooth, hard and rough, landed on his tongue, and he swallowed it reflexively. As it scratched his throat on its way down, he thought, *One more. Just one more and I'll be dead.*

"*Enough!*" Menahem roared from up high. "Bring him to me."

Mero was dragged forward by his hair and neck and arms, his knees bouncing on the hard ground. Every beat of his heart brought excruciating pain, as though it were straining against his shattered ribs.

"Look at me," Menahem commanded.

The blood was wiped from Mero's eyes, his head jerked back to point at Menahem. The king sat smugly upon his rock, his golden teeth flashing in the sun. His eyes burned with malice.

"Did I not tell you that even your death was mine?" he crooned. "I thought I might keep you, and make you my slave. But now I think you shall be my plaything instead. I will show you what it means to wield true power, here in this world with no gods but man. For what is a king but a god made flesh?"

Menahem's face grew sly. "You ought to thank me, traveler. Perhaps the lessons I teach will be of some use to you in the next world. You will find your way there, in the end—but not too soon. Not too soon." He nodded to his men. "Take him inside and clean his wounds. And mind that he does no harm to himself. Our guest must not be allowed to slip away before his time."

3

They dragged him deeper into the canyon, letting his hands and feet and knees bang and scrape against the rocks. Mero, too weak to take his own weight, hung limply between his captors. His shoulders throbbed, and his chest was on fire. His nose and mouth were clotted with blood; he was certain he would choke on it and die. The thought that he might defy Menahem after all was a pleasant one, but he couldn't bring himself to believe it. He knew from experience just how tenacious a life could be.

They passed under the canyon's shadow, and it grew cold enough to shiver. Weakly, Mero lifted his head. He saw tarpaulins stretched into crude shelters, hints of life scattered about: a pair of baskets, a fire pit dug out of the red earth. Then pain lanced up his neck and lodged in his head, and he fell limp again.

He was carried through a narrow doorway and dropped to the ground. He rolled onto his back, and his swollen tongue filled his mouth. Suddenly he could not breathe at all. He gagged, clawing at his throat. A shadow loomed over him and a foot kicked him onto his side. Sour-tasting fingers thrust into his mouth, grabbing hold of his tongue and nearly yanking it free. Mero coughed and gasped for air.

His vision shrank to a single point of light in the distance, as though he stood at the end of a long tunnel. The cold air was like water on his skin. Mero floated away from himself, borne by the gentle lap of the waves.

They brought him a drink. He was too weak to support his head, so they had to cradle him upright and dribble the water past his cracked lips. It was warm, but sweet as nectar. *Perhaps Menahem is a king after all*, Mero thought, *if he has such fine water to drink.*

Mero's next memory was of shivering against the cold. He had lost his clothes and lay naked against the wall, clutching his hands to his bruised chest. To shiver made his wounds ache, but he couldn't stop himself.

Figures moved in the darkness, but he couldn't tell if they were real, or figments of his fevered mind.

"Please," he appealed to the shadows, over and over. "Please, I'm cold."

That night lasted an eternity. Mero ached and shivered, shivered and ached, curled on his side with his back pressed against the cave wall. He considered crawling out in search of warmth or help, but was afraid of the yawning darkness before him. His tongue kept finding the empty space where his tooth ought to be. The ground beneath his head was dusty. When he coughed, his chest exploded with pain, until he feared even to draw breath. But he couldn't stop himself from breathing any more than he could stop himself from shivering. His will to live was simply too strong.

Mero woke to a scratching against his cheek. His limbs were stiff. He tried moving them one by one, testing the empty space in his mouth with a finger. It hurt, and so did his head, and neck, and chest. His mouth, at least, was wet, and he was no longer cold—in fact he was baking under the cover of a rough woven blanket. Letting the hand fall from his mouth, he slid it down across his bruised chest to his groin. He was naked. Sometime in the night they had taken his shirt and pants and belt and boots and hat and everything else.

A hunched figure approached, its footfalls soft against the stone floor. Mero shied away, but it was only an old woman with a wrinkled face. She was accompanied by another, as wrinkled and bent as the first. One of the women took Mero's chin and tipped it back, pressing an earthenware jug to his lips. A trickle of water struck his tongue, and he drank greedily. Meanwhile the other woman peeled back his blanket and pressed her fingers into his ribs. He moaned in pain, but she kept working, speaking under her breath in a language he did not know.

A curtain was thrown back, and sunlight flooded the cave. The women cried out, scattering like spiders. Mero whimpered, frightened and confused, the light stabbing his darkled eyes.

A shadow filled the doorway. It was soon followed by another, and another after that.

"Take him," said one of the men, and the others closed in. They took him under the arms and hauled him upright. His blanket fell away, exposing his naked body. They tried to stand him on his feet, but his knees buckled under the weight.

"Hurry up," a man said.

"He can't stand," another answered.

"Then drag him," said the first.

So they did, hauling Mero between them like a sack of grain, drawing him away from his night of torture and into the blinding sunlight.

Mero's captors walked him down the length of the canyon, under awnings of stretched canvas, past wooden lean-tos and fissures in the rock like the one in which he had spent the night. A few scrawny chickens crossed their path, clucking softly. An old goat was tied to a post outside one of the caves. There were people here, too, but they flickered like ghosts in the corners of Mero's sight, keeping well out of the way of Menahem's men. Too exhausted to look around, Mero never saw so much as a single face, never found out if the furtive people of Menahem's camp were men or women or children. None of them spoke so much as a single word. The air was silent and hot.

The canyon narrowed, and their path, strewn with loose stones—some no larger than a fist, some taller than a man—started to wind upwards. Once again Menahem's men tried to set Mero on his feet and get him to walk, but he would not, even when they twisted his penis and told him they would tear it off if he didn't get moving. In the end one of them grabbed Mero by the waist and slung him over his shoulder. His clavicle gouged into Mero's ribs. The pain was unbearable, and Mero soon fainted again.

By the time he came to, they had emerged onto the plateau beyond the canyon. Mero's carrier threw him to the ground, where he arched his back in pain, hissing through the gap in his teeth. There was no shelter from the beating sun, and the red surface of the plateau shimmered in the distance.

A face eclipsed Mero's sight. It was Menahem, wearing a beatific smile.

"Welcome, traveler!" he said gaily. "I trust you are well-rested and ready to learn."

"Go to hell," Mero rasped.

Menahem only laughed. He signaled to his men, who grabbed Mero's arms and drew him into a sitting position.

"There is no such place," Menahem said, folding his hands behind him. Today he wore his blanket slung across one shoulder like a wise man's robe. "Hell is a story told by weak men to free them from shame."

"Shame?" Mero said.

"Yes, indeed. Why should a man believe in hell, if not to free him from the burden of striking down evil by his own hand? That is why I make sure to torture my enemies before I kill them. Pain is fleeting, and death is freedom. It is a short time we share together on this earth."

"I am not your enemy," Mero said.

Menahem ignored him. With a snap of his fingers, he retrieved Mero's curved sword, balancing it on his palm so it glowed white in the sun.

"This is a most wonderful blade," he said. "Is there magic upon it, perhaps?"

"There is," Mero said.

Menahem looked amused. "Oh?"

Mero nodded, meeting his eye. "The blade carries a powerful enchantment. When you cut someone with it, all of their blood spills out, and they die."

An ominous silence fell. The men holding Mero tightened their grip, ready to punish him for his joke. Menahem looked on a moment, then smiled broadly, his golden teeth agleam.

"Powerful indeed," he said. "I see you carry no sheath for such a deadly weapon."

"The sword has none," Mero said, "nor would it suffer one."

Menahem nodded sagely. He handed the naked blade to one of his men, who, Mero noticed, accepted it with a look of apprehension.

When Menahem turned back around, he held another of Mero's belongings. It was a simple clay whistle, such as a child might carry, dangling from a thin leather thong.

Mero's heart began to race.

"And this?" Menahem swung the whistle on its cord. "Is this magic, as well?"

"Yes," Mero said. "It is a magic whistle, one that only I can play."

Now Menahem laughed. "A camel could play this, if I stuck it up her ass."

"Go ahead and try. You won't make it sing."

Menahem's brow bunched down until his eyes were in shadow, his broad smile becoming a snarl.

"Ah, but what if this is a trick?" he said. "There might be a scorpion or a spider inside, that will sting me the moment I bring it to my lips."

"Let me play it, then, if you're so worried," Mero said.

Menahem's scowl deepened, his air of affability crumbling with alarming speed. He tossed the whistle to one of his men. "Play."

The man's eyes bulged, but he was clearly more afraid of Menahem than of the whistle. He tried to peer inside it as he brought it to his mouth. Wetting his lips, he kissed the mouthpiece and blew.

No sound came out. The man tried again, and again, until his veins popped and his cheeks blew out, but the whistle refused to play.

"Enough!" Menahem snapped. He pointed at Mero with his chin. "Now him."

The man shoved the whistle into Mero's mouth. It knocked against his aching teeth, bringing tears to his eyes. Blinking them away, he drew a deep breath and blew.

A sound rang out across the plateau, mournful and clear like the cry of a hunting bird. It reverberated through the empty air, doubling and redoubling until the sky itself had come alive. It continued long after Mero had run out of breath. By then Menahem's men had begun to mutter and curse, covering their ears against the sound.

Mero let his chin fall to his chest. Relief washed over him like rain, drawing away the fear, the dirt, the pain. He had done all he could. Now he was in the hands of the goddess.

4

As the echoes of the whistle died away, Mero wondered how Menahem would react. With his head bowed, all he saw of the king was his feet. They were bunioned and bare, the soles white, the bridges black, the toes like beetles burrowing in the sand.

Most likely Menahem would have him beaten. He might even order his men to smash the whistle and cut off Mero's lips, to destroy the source of the sound if not the sound itself. But here Menahem surprised him.

"Take him," he said to his men, turning from Mero with a sweep of his robe. And that was all: no violence, no rage, not even an acknowledgement of what had just happened.

Clever, Mero thought, as rough hands once again seized him by the arms and hair. Really, it was little wonder Menahem was king.

They dragged him a short distance across the plateau, the very ground aglow with light reflected from the sun. It burned the soles of Mero's feet, his ankles and knees, any part of him that touched it. Naked and weak, he had no defense against the heat above or below. He couldn't even sweat, as not a drop of water remained in his body.

A blotch of darkness grew before him, a single black bean in a sea of white grain. Next to it stood Menahem, his arms folded and a smile on his face. The bean came up to his shoulder; Mero realized it was much larger, and closer, than he had thought. It was, in fact, a slab of black stone, round and flat as a river rock. Four wooden stakes had been hammered into the ground around it, giving it the appearance of a gemstone set in an enormous ring.

Ropes were tied to each of the four pillars.

"What do you think of my stone, traveler?" Menahem asked, looking fondly at the smooth rock. "When I first came to this valley and found it here alone, I decided that this, above all others, was my sign that I belong in this place. How do you suppose it came to sit upon this height, so far from others of its like? Do you suppose some passing giant lifted it from the sea floor and dropped it here for my own use?"

He seemed to be expecting an answer, so Mero indulged him. "I suppose they did."

Menahem's grin broadened. Uncurling his fingers, he held out his palm for Mero to see. The skin was warped and bubbled like wax.

"That day, my curiosity got the better of me, and I was taught a lesson I will never forget. I lost my palm, but my curiosity remained. Can you guess, traveler, what I was so curious about?"

Mero said nothing. Rather than answer his own question, Menahem stepped around the rock, reaching out though never quite touching it.

"Each day it sits here and bakes in the sun, drinking heat like a plant drinks water." Menahem stroked his beard, his eyes lost in recollection. "The first man I tied to this rock burned for a while, but it started to cool while he was still screaming, and I was forced to cut him down and finish the work elsewise. After that, I had my men light fires and shovel coals beneath it, but it still wasn't enough. Then one of the women in my camp came to me with a thought. She wondered if the stone got cold at night, just as a man would. Bless the hearts of women! They think themselves mothers of all, and see the world full of babes for them to swaddle. So while you shivered in the dark, we wrapped this stone in blankets and furs and shoveled in fresh coals throughout the night. All this, so that my curiosity might at last be satisfied. And what I am curious about, traveler, is this: can I burn a man to death with nothing but the touch of a stone?"

A shiver climbed Mero's spine. The old man of the desert—perhaps Menahem himself—had warned him of the king's obsession with pain. But Mero hadn't listened, and now his death was staring him in the face, a death even stranger and crueler than most.

For an instant, Mero wished he was foolish enough to pray. But his prayers had already been sent. There was nothing else to do but wait.

Menahem waved to his men, who spun Mero around and dragged him backwards towards the rock. He already felt its heat between his shoulders. It radiated warmth like an iron stove.

Goddess, please…

"I will let you lie on your back," Menahem said, "so you can spend your last moments watching the sun. Me, I will watch your face. You are nice and thin, and there's not much water in you, so I think you will burn well."

While Menahem spoke, his men got to work, lifting Mero off the ground and hoisting his feet in the air so they could bind his ankles with rope. A pair of men, each holding one of Mero's wrists, skirted the rock on either side, so that he was soon stretched across it, hovering inches from the surface. It took his every last drop of strength to arch his back away from the hideous heat. Even so, his tailbone grazed against the rock, and he screamed as the burn settled into his skin.

"Careful!" Menahem snapped. "Don't let him touch. Today is an auspicious day; everything must be perfect." In a show of surprising nimbleness, he leapt at one of the pillars to which Mero's ankles were bound, digging his toes into the notch where the rope was tied. Wrapping his arms around the top of the post, he hovered over Mero like a vulture.

"I never thanked you, traveler," he said, "for delivering yourself to me. It's been so long since anyone came to my camp. I hope my stone can kill you. If not, who knows how long I will have to wait for the next traveler to arrive?"

Mero didn't answer. He was holding his breath. His stomach burned with the effort of keeping himself suspended over the rock. His wrists were tied along with his ankles; he wouldn't have been able to free himself even if he weren't exhausted.

His vision was nearly gone. The sun filled the sky. Just as he spotted a wink of black among the blazing yellow, Menahem gave the signal, and Mero was dropped onto the stone.

His back struck hard, followed by his head. For a second he barely felt the heat.

Then it grew.

Mero screamed. He screamed with his mouth to drown out the screaming of his back. He screamed and yanked on the cords that bound his ankles and wrists, knocking his head as hard as he could against the stone, wishing he could crack open his skull and dash out his brains and die now, now, *now*. He screamed as the heat blossomed and spread and burrowed deep into his flesh, the pain growing with every instant, though it was already more than Mero ever knew he could feel. He did not know if Menahem was still there. He did not know if anything existed other than him, him and the hellish black stone.

Then something heavy struck Mero's chest, and the sun was eclipsed by a pair of outstretched wings. A fearsome eagle, half as tall as a man, had alighted on his ribcage. Its claws punctured Mero's flesh as easily as if it were the skin of a fruit. Turning its head sideways, it stared down at him with a golden, unblinking eye.

"Kill me," Mero croaked. "Please."

The eagle blinked. Then it thrust its head into the wound in Mero's chest, the hollow left by the stone axe. It slashed at Mero's skin with its wicked beak, plucking out shards of bone and tossing them aside with flicks of its head. Mero screamed again as the beak plunged deeper and deeper, the eagle's bright feathers soon matted with blood, its head a red executioner's hood. He thought he heard Menahem screaming as well—cursing at his men to chase the bird away—but all that was distant to him now. Blood poured from his ruptured chest, sizzling as it touched the burning stone.

Mero no longer felt any pain. It was with a strange detachment that he watched the eagle at its work. Whenever it emerged from his chest with a piece of him held in its beak, he only thought, *that was a part of me, and now it's not*. Blood covered him from his neck to his knees. It was warm and comforting, a blanket made of himself.

A throbbing filled his ears. The corners of his vision faded, patterns in the sand washed away by the tide. His cheeks prickled, and so did his toes. He was getting lighter with each piece the eagle ripped away; soon he would be light enough to float into the yawning sky. Only Mero could not see the sky anymore; all the colors and shapes that had once made the world around him were melting and merging and running together. The throbbing in his ears changed to ringing. The sound came from all around, as though Mero were the clapper of a bell.

Everything was slipping away. He had no possessions, no wants, no hopes or fears. No arms, no legs, no voice, no pain. No future, no past.

Nothing at all.

5

Here was a place of gentle contradiction.
It was nowhere and everywhere.
It contained nothing and everything.
It was amnesic, yet brimming with memory.
It was alien, yet familiar.
It was, and was not.
A sea of endless cloud, awaltz in the firmament.

Twin strips of silver, stretching as far as they could in either direction, arcs so long they appeared as straight. They would meet again, somewhere on the other side of the infinite expanse: a pair of silver arms to embrace the universe. The air was suffused with the gentle patter of millions of billions of raindrop voices, every sound that any tongue had ever uttered blending into a single, harmonious chorus.

The goddess was nowhere and everywhere, too. She could not be found, and she could not be lost. She was, just as everything else, and everything else was her.

Everything was so clear. So smooth and flat, a trillion disparate grains of sand pressed and baked into a single, featureless sheet of glass. A simple image, perfect in its unity, an ocean untouched by the slightest breeze. A silver mirror, its own reflection.

Every moment here was an eternity, and eternity lasted only a moment.

There were so many things this place was not. But like a dream in the moments after waking, all memory of what had come before soon melted away, dissolving in the golden light. Lies peeling back, exposed as mere shadows of the truth.

It was calm, this place. Nothing ever changed, because nothing was left to change. Everything was everywhere, containing and contained by everything else. It was neither dark nor light. Heat and cold both were gone. Motion was a memory. All was still.

Until it was not.

An intrusion, a sliver of otherness thin as a razor's edge: a slice, a cut, a division where unity had reigned. All of a sudden there was a *NOW*, and in that *NOW*, a fishhook pierced, snagged, caught—seized hold and began to pull. A gossamer thread, so thin as to be invisible yet strong as an iron chain, pulled *down, down* through the nothingness.

It hurt, not in any physical way, but in a way that was breath-stealing and heart-breaking and close: a lover's hand slipping free of one's own, curtains drawn over a glimpse of paradise.

The fall began slowly, but soon accelerated to terrifying speed. His sight narrowed, and his horizons shrank. He lost and lost and lost again, and the worst part of it all was that he didn't understand just what he was giving away each minute, each second. Wind throbbed in his ears, and the earth rose up to swallow him. He was cold and afraid. He didn't understand why the goddess was casting him out, and entreated her silently:

Please, can't I stay? Must I go there again?

And she answered in his own words, mocking:

Again.

Mero breathed.

His collapsed lungs strained and swelled, sucking air past his cracked lips and down his ruined throat. It burned like ice, and cut all the way down, a mouthful of swallowed glass.

The pain that breath ignited in Mero's chest was so intense that he opened his eyes and screamed it back out, throwing his head back like a jack-wolf howling at the desert moon. Every part of him was on fire. Even his mind was white-hot, overspilling with impressions and memories, half-formed thoughts and boiling emotions, inclinations and fears, the flicker of his five senses. He didn't understand who or where or why he was. It was all too much yet somehow, paradoxically, it was too little. Behind it all was a memory delicate as a soap-bubble, distant as a whispered song. It shone, a silver egg, in the farthest corner of awareness, then slipped away.

Mero was so consumed by his howl, he never noticed it was gone.

As the last of his scream died in his throat, Mero started to cough. Wherever he was, it stank of feces and rot. The smell was so overpowering it was like being strangled. Every breath made him want to heave, and every heave was like slicing his stomach open all over again. As he heaved and coughed, coughed and heaved, a rope of yellow bile trickled out. It was all Mero's stomach had to give.

Desperate to move, Mero tried to find his feet. He was lying face-up on a dark mound that was in some parts soft and in others sharp enough to cut. When he jerked his legs to one side, his thigh was sliced open by an edge he couldn't see. Mero sucked air through the hole in his teeth; warm blood dribbled down his ankle.

He tried moving his hands next. The left came easily to his face, but the right would not budge no matter how hard he tugged. The smell of rot intensified, and waves of nausea rolled over him. Mero thrashed like a snared rabbit, yanking and yanking until he felt his shoulder popping out of its socket.

Finally, with a hideous ripping sound, his arm came free. Mero's relief only lasted an instant. Then his stomach swooped, and the stars overhead started to wheel. He realized he had pulled his arm free with such force that he had thrown himself off some unknown edge. He struck something hard and began to tumble, rolling down an uneven slope, colliding painfully with jutting rocks and unseen obstacles into the darkness.

SLAP, his fall came to an end, face-first against hard stone. Galaxies burst before Mero's eyes. The ground under his hands and cheek rolled away from him, as though he were stuck to the face of a spinning coin.

Finally the spinning stopped. Mero tried to push himself up, but something was wrong with his right hand. He brought it to his face to examine it.

The hand dangled lifelessly from its wrist.

It must have been caught under something sharp. In yanking it free, Mero had ripped it halfway off. The gash started under his thumb; he could barely move his two smallest fingers. The tendons to the other three had been cut.

Mero stared at the hand for a long time. It looked like his own, but the weight pulling at his wrist was the weight of a stranger's hand. Struck with a sudden revulsion, Mero came close to seizing the foreign hand and finishing what he had started. He balked only when he realized how painful that would be.

He put his good hand under him and stood. He was still naked. The ground under his feet was firm and stony, and cold air blew between his legs. Night had fallen over the desert; the moon hung low and full. Mero could clearly make out the canyon walls around him, rippled pillars standing silhouetted against the sky.

The wind changed, and the foul smell returned. Mero's gaze was drawn by a dark mound behind him—the same mound, he realized, whose sides he had just tumbled down. It was a large black mass tall as two men, clinging to the sides of the canyon.

Mero crept towards the mound on wobbling legs. His eyes, he found, were working perfectly—better than they had in days. Soon he could make out the smaller shapes within the pile.

A wooden post. A stretch of canvas. A heap of compost and human waste.

Two white bones, stark against the darkness.

A nest of rats, squeaking softly, brown bodies asquirm.

Then, peering even closer: maggots and fleas, millions of them, tiny white bodies crawling and hopping over every inch, even coating the whiskers of the rats the way frost might settle on the branches of a tree—

Mero turned and staggered away, the insides of his cheeks prickling though nothing, nothing, nothing was left for his stomach to throw up. Of course this was where Menahem had dumped Mero's corpse: the same place he threw all of his garbage.

Clenching his teeth, Mero put his good hand against the canyon wall and followed it as far from the garbage heap as he could. It wasn't far; after some twenty paces the fissure narrowed to a palm's width, so that even skinny Mero didn't have a hope of squeezing through. This was no canyon, he realized—it was a pit. Menahem had likely chosen it for his garbage dump especially for this reason. No doubt some of the corpses within that heap had not been corpses when they were thrown in.

Mero slid to his knees, then rocked back onto his rump, letting his head dangle between his shoulders. His back burned, the skin stretched and aching. Sludgy blood still oozed from the wound in his chest, though most of it, by now, had pooled in his feet. He itched as well as hurt, and for a while he scratched absently at his legs and at the base of his skull. Then he began to notice tiny brown insects hopping out from under his fingers, crawling through the hairs on his legs. For a second he froze in place, his skin rippling with revulsion. Then, gathering up fistfuls of sand in his good hand, he scoured himself from head to toe, rubbing his already burnt skin raw, not caring how much it hurt, preferring agony to impurity.

Finally the fever cleared. Mero collapsed against the canyon wall, too tired even to weep. This was punishment, he knew—the goddess's own brand of justice. He couldn't argue it was unfair, couldn't claim it was undeserved. All he wanted was for it to be over.

As if the mere thought had summoned her, Mero felt the goddess draw near. She spoke to him as she always did: in his own mind, his own words, rearranging his thoughts from the inside out.

Over, she echoed, and painted a vision using the colors that whirled along the insides of his eyelids: a vast plain, a black lake. Sparkling pillars set against a dark sky. Twisted roadways filled with nonsensical patterns of shadow and light.

Mero knew the vision well. The goddess had shown it to him many times before. He didn't know where it was meant to be, or even if it was a real place at all. He'd never heard of any place where the mountains grew tall and thin and sparkled like stars. Still, he knew she expected him to follow it. He had even let himself believe that if he somehow found that place—that glittering range beyond the black lake—his torment would be over, and the goddess would consent to lift his curse. Of course, he couldn't know that for certain. The goddess was nothing if not reticent.

Mero rose to his feet. He felt thin, depleted, a husk of a man. Gingerly he put a hand to the wound on his chest. No heartbeat came from inside.

Still, when he looked beyond the garbage heap and into the valley beyond, he felt a faint silver thread like a fishhook tethering him to this world, tugging him gently but irresistibly forwards. He knew what he would find at the hook's other end; this was not the first time he had dangled on its line. With a sigh and a cough, he carried on.

6

Escaping the pit turned out to be a simple matter, so much so that Mero was forced to retract his theory that Menahem used it on living victims. Over years of use, the mound of garbage had risen and risen until it was nearly level with the rocky ledge from which it was fed. All Mero needed to do was scale the filthy pile—swatting away fleas, stumbling over old bones and beams of rotting wood while wads of human excrement squidged between his toes—and leap from the top. Menahem would never have been so lax as to allow a living prisoner such an opportunity.

Lucky for Mero, then, that he had been dead.

After crawling to the top of the pile, it was the work of a moment to locate some old planks and sink them into the mound to create a springboard. Gauging the distance with a bob of his head, he took two quick steps and vaulted towards freedom.

He hit the ledge with his stomach; it struck against his hollow gut. Curling his legs under him, he dug his toes into the sandstone wall, reaching out with his good hand to pull himself up. It came back with a fistful of dust, and he slipped backwards. Gritting his teeth, he jammed his chin against the ground, reaching out further, digging in harder. Inch by inch he gained height, puffing tiny clouds of sand into the air with each breath. At last his balance shifted. He dragged himself onto the ledge belly-first, leaving behind a trail of half-hardened blood.

Free of the pit, he rested for a minute or two, rolling onto his back to watch the stars. The night took on a ghostly quality, as though the moon had leached the world of its color. Mero found himself staring at the moon, struck by a feeling somewhere between nostalgia and regret.

He'd forgotten something important. It dangled tantalizingly just out of reach. He felt he might remember it if he could only look closely enough at the sky—past the distracting moon and stars and into the deep darkness beyond. But the more he tried to chase the feeling down, the more distant it became, until it was little more than a faint pang of loss.

Mero rolled onto his stomach and pushed himself up, then turned in place, gathering his bearings. In the direction of the pit, the valley opened up, a few crooked columns giving way to open sand. In the other direction, the walls rose and closed in. There were no signs of habitation—no sentries or lights to reveal the location of Menahem's camp—but even so, he knew it lay somewhere among the rocks. The silver fishhook tugged at him, drawing him towards the purple crags.

Yes, Menahem was there. And so was Sheathless.

Mero's tongue touched something rough. He realized that, either while escaping the pit or being thrown in, another one of his teeth had come loose. He plucked it from his mouth with forefinger and thumb, glanced at it for a moment, then tossed it aside and began to walk.

Menahem's camp was much as Mero remembered it. Long and thin, it lined the valley floor and walls, a strip of hovels and caves chiseled into the stone. Cold desert wind howled down the valley's throat, rattling the driftwood roofs and making the curtains in the thresholds ripple and snap. Not a soul was outside. Mero might have thought it abandoned, were it not for the lone goat that still stood tied to its post some fifty paces away.

The camp had multiple levels; in places where the valley walls allowed, two or three caves stood one on top of the other, linked by sandstone paths worn smooth and flat by the tread of hundreds of feet. Creeping along the canyon wall, Mero took one of these paths up and off the valley floor. He soon reached a threshold curtained by a threadbare blanket. Mero crouched before it, waiting for a dip in the wind. The moment the flapping curtain settled, he dashed past the opening. On the far side of the doorway, he squeezed himself into a shadow and waited breathlessly. The moon was bright, and anyone watching from inside would have seen his feet scamper past. But the camp remained silent, and Mero unstuck himself from the wall and carried on.

The fishhook pulled more strongly now. That meant Sheathless was close—and he would likely find Menahem wherever he found his sword. The tugging came from the other side of the valley. Hunkering down, he peered across the way to see if he could catch a glimpse of the desert king's palace.

Mero wasn't sure what kind of home Menahem would keep. The man insisted he was a king, yet dressed himself in rags. Quite possibly his home was no different from any other in this camp. Yet when Mero glanced across the valley, something caught his eye and held it, and the longer he looked, the more his certainty grew.

Opposite his vantage point was a cluster of dwellings three stories high, carved into a natural amphitheater where the river must have pooled thousands of years ago. A dozen doorways faced Mero across the canyon, blind eyes with tattered lids. All were roughly the same size—large enough to let a man through stoop-backed, and no larger. All except one. This one was twice as wide as the others, and high enough that even a tall man could pass through without bowing his head.

Yes, that was Menahem's door. Mero was sure of it.

He followed the path from the threshold with his eyes, marking the place it met the valley floor. It wasn't far—some forty paces—but it was on the opposite side of the canyon, and there were no shadows to hide him along the way. He would have to risk a dash through the center of the camp.

There was nothing for it. Mero needed to reach Sheathless before his time ran out. Already the pull of the hook was painful, reality distant and flat. He didn't know what would happen if he ignored the summons. He had never dared to try.

The path on which he stood was only eight feet off the ground. Glancing around to make sure no one had stepped out to pass water, Mero sat, swung his legs over the edge, then dropped to the valley floor and ran. He kept low to the ground, setting his feet down softly, watching the dark doorways for signs of movement. There were none.

The closer Mero got to Menahem's abode, the more his senses quickened. His own breaths sounded like waves crashing on the shore; the blood trapped in his veins was heavy and cold. He moved smoothly past the rippling curtains of the other valley-dwellers, keeping to the shadows when he could and boldly crossing patches of moonlight when he could not.

He arrived at Menahem's door. It was curtained against the wind by several different patches and strips of cloth all quilted together.

Mero crept up to the threshold and flattened himself against the canyon wall. Reaching over with his good hand, he peeled the curtain back an inch. Was Menahem likely to keep a guard? Mero thought not, but he had been wrong about Menahem before.

"If you're coming to kill me," said a voice, "then you'd best come in and do it, before my servants find you."

Mero froze, too late realizing his mistake: by pulling the curtain back, he'd let a strip of moonlight into the house. The voice had been Menahem's—but if he thought Mero was an assassin out for his life, why would the king invite him inside?

There was no time to ponder it further. The pull of the silver hook was too strong to ignore. Mero could no more delay this moment than night could resist day.

He flipped back the curtain and stepped inside.

7

It took Mero's eyes a moment to adjust to the gloom. The first thing he saw was Menahem himself, sitting cross-legged on his pallet with his blanket wrapped around his shoulders. His hairy stomach protruded past his chin. His teeth twinkled in the dark.

"Who's there?" Menahem demanded, squinting. "Come closer so I can see you."

Mero found himself obeying the command. As he crossed the beam of moonlight the curtain let in, Menahem's eyes grew wide, and he leaned back with a sigh of astonishment. He did not seem the least bit afraid; in fact he looked like a man who had just seen an angel. He started to laugh, his belly jiggling with mirth.

"Ah!" He wiped his forehead and mouth with a corner of his blanket. "You are not who I was expecting."

"Who were you expecting?" Mero asked.

"I thought you might be Hajesh. He has hated me for a long time, ever since I made him kill a woman he was fond of." Menahem leaned forward, a hungry look in his eyes. "But you are *alive*, traveler."

"No," said Mero, "I'm not."

Menahem chuckled again, dropping his chin to his chest. "Then you are a spirit from the land of the dead, here to prove to me that hell is real after all."

"No," said Mero, "I'm not that either."

"But you *are* here to kill me."

This time Mero nodded. "Yes."

"I see." Menahem wrapped his blanket around him. He drew a deep breath, then blew it out through his lips.

"Good," he said. "I would be happy to be killed by one such as you. How do you plan on doing it?"

"What?" Mero said.

"You ought to drag me through the valley and tie me to that rock." Menahem said, tracing a path with his finger. "I never got to see if it would kill you all the way. That was very rude of you—I was angry for a long time. I thought I might have to burn one of my own men, just to satisfy myself. But now you can burn me instead. That would make all of us happy."

Mero drew back, trying to make sense of what he was hearing. "I don't plan on burning you."

"Then what?" Menahem said, annoyed. "Remember that I am a king among men. My death ought to be fitting."

"Where is my sword?" Mero asked.

"You would kill me with *that*? Me, who has been a student of death since before you were born?" Menahem made a noise of disgust. "Cut holes in the soles of my feet and string me up above the valley, so my blood leaks out one drop at a time. I would suffer much to die that way."

"Return my sword to me," Mero said, "and I will give you a death unlike any other."

It was not a promise he normally would have made, but he was desperate to have Sheathless back in his hand. His time was running out; the silver hook twisted in his gut. He only hoped Menahem didn't notice his discomfort.

The old man's eyes came alive at the promise of an unusual death. With a grunt, he reached under his pallet and drew out Mero's glittering sword. He blew some dust off the handle, then offered it to Mero with open hands.

Mero was reaching for Sheathless even before Menahem presented it. He could no longer disguise his hunger for it, his need to feel its weight in his palm. As soon as his fingers closed around the hilt, relief washed over him like a tide. He pointed the blade at the ceiling, dividing Menahem's face into two vertical halves.

"Well?" said the bandit king. "I have upheld my promise. Now you, traveler, must uphold yours."

Mero nodded. It was difficult to think; the silver hook was tearing him apart from the inside. "Do you remember what I told you about this sword, before you tied me to that rock?"

Menahem wrung his hands. "Yes, of course."

Mero thrust the blade into the old man's heart. It was as easy as dipping a hand into water. Menahem gasped. Mero took a step forward, bringing their faces closer together. He put his ruined right hand on Menahem's shoulder, where it flopped onto the king's back.

"I only told you about the first part of the enchantment," Mero said softly. "Here is the rest. When your blood spills out, it doesn't go to waste. I'm the one who drinks it. I'm the one who picks up your fallen life and wears it like a mantle. Look."

He glanced down. Menahem did the same. Something strange was happening where the curved blade disappeared into the old man's chest. Dark blood leaked from the wound—but instead of dribbling to the ground, it fell up the length of Mero's blade, each droplet a tiny red fish swimming against gravity's current. The droplets soon gathered into a river, staining the cool white of Sheathless's blade, pushing against the dam of the cross-guard. Soon the sword was red to the pommel, and still blood gushed from Menahem's wound, draining out of him faster than seemed possible for such a small cut.

The droplets slipped between Mero's fingers, swam past his knuckles, squeezed through the hairs on the back of his hand. Somewhere between the tips of his fingers and the crook of his elbow, they sank under his skin, seeping into his flesh like water soaked up by the roots of a tree.

Soon Mero's arm was as bloody as his blade. Streaks of red crept up his shoulder and spidered across his chest.

He began to *fill*.

It started slowly, with a thickening of his arm and a fulling of his cheeks. His collapsed stomach flattened, then swelled. Then: *CRACK*, went Mero's ribs, the shattered bones snapping back to their rightful place. Menahem jumped at the sound.

CRACK, CRACK, CRACK, Mero's ribs made room for his new heart. White tendons wormed free of his wrist, seeking their counterparts on the far side of the wound. Lashing together, they dragged Mero's hand back into place. Muscles re-knit and bones clicked together, then all was covered by fresh new skin.

Menahem watched Mero's restoration in silent awe. His jaw trembled, and so did his hands. His eyes showed white all the way round. Every so often a groan escaped his lips. Already his cheeks were sunken, his skin waxy and tight. His legs shook, and his knees actually knocked together with the soft *pat-pat-pat* of flesh on flesh.

He reached for Mero's face with palsied hands. At first Mero thought the old man wanted to fight him off. Then he realized Menahem was trying to stick his fingers in his mouth.

"Teeth," he whispered. "Let me see your teeth."

Mero peeled back his lip. As Menahem watched, the two missing teeth pushed their way out of Mero's gums, sliding down to join their neighbors.

"Ah," Menahem said. "Ah. Ah!" It started as a laugh, but ended in a wheeze. His arms dropped to his sides. He stared drunkenly at them, his head wobbling on his neck. With difficulty he looked back at Mero, an expression of hurt confusion on his face.

"You're dying, Menahem," Mero told him. "A kinder death than the one you chose for me—and many others, too, no doubt. I wish I could say that was why I chose to kill you. The real reason is much simpler. I had to. If it hadn't been you, it would have been someone else—the first person who crossed my path. I would have regretted it, but I would have done it all the same. So I suppose I should be thanking you. For letting me take you, instead of someone less deserving."

Menahem said nothing. His face puckered like an old lemon left out in the sun. More and more of his weight rested on Sheathless's blade.

"I have a question for you, before you die," Mero said. "Who was the old man of the desert? Was it really you, warning me about yourself? Why did you give me that chance to escape? Was it just to give me a false sense of hope—would you have sent your men after me if I had turned away? Are you really just insane, or is there something more?"

Menahem's eyes were pointed at Mero, but they were glassy and unfocused. With his brows stretched tight against his skull, his expression was almost pitying. Then, with a sigh, he fell sideways off Mero's sword and collapsed to the ground. His bones clattered as they struck the hard-packed floor, his skull rolling on a stick-thin neck.

For a minute Mero stood over the corpse, cursing his bad luck. He'd waited too long to ask his question, and now Menahem had taken the answer to his grave. For all he had taken from the desert king, he had no way of seeing into Menahem's mind. The mystery of the old man would haunt him forever.

As he stood in the fusty silence of Menahem's cave, Mero's new heart pounded in his ears. *WHUMP, WHUMP, WHUMP*, it went, the pressure in his skull much greater than normal. Swapping Sheathless to his dominant hand, he examined his restored body with the other. His ribcage was intact, his mangled hand restored, the burns on his back nothing more than scars.

Warm blood suffused his cheeks and lent a red cast to his skin. His fingers were swollen with it—it was hard to make a fist. Even his penis was semi-erect, hanging heavy and full between his thighs.

He'd done it again. The sand had fallen up.

Mero crossed over to the doorway and used Sheathless's point to peel the curtain back. The sword was still drenched in blood, dark red from pommel to tip. Mero couldn't see much through the narrow gap he had opened, but silence reigned beyond it. He was safe.

Stepping back to Menahem's corpse, he knelt and tugged off the old man's blanket, wrapping it around his own shoulders. After a moment's thought, he reached into the corpse's mouth and pulled out the four golden teeth. Menahem's gums were withered and dry, and the teeth dropped readily into Mero's palm. Wherever his travels took him next, gold was likely to be useful.

Realizing he had nowhere to put them, Mero went searching through the corners of Menahem's house. The king, however, hadn't been the kind for worldly possessions. There wasn't even any food or water inside the cave, and no clothing other than the threadbare blanket Mero already wore. He did, however, find his clay whistle in the same place Menahem had kept his sword. Slipping the leather thong over his head brought a measure of relief. Tearing a square from Menahem's blanket, he fashioned a simple pouch, dropped the teeth inside, and hung them from the whistle's cord.

Mero took a steadying breath, savoring the swelling of his chest, the way the cool air slipped down his throat without causing the faintest twinge of pain.

He had to escape the camp, and soon. There was no telling how Menahem's men would react to the death of their king. And yet, striking out for the desert in his current state would be nothing short of suicide. He needed food, and water, and clothes to protect him from the sun. Having a mount would be better still, but the chances that Menahem kept a secret stable were slim.

Mero thought about the old goat tethered outside. If he filled some packs with food, he could bring the goat along to carry them.

The prospect of food made Mero's stomach growl. His body didn't care that it had been well-fed in blood; it wanted to chew, swallow, and digest.

There was no sense in staying here any longer. Mero spared a last glance at Menahem before he left. The bandit king was smaller in death—a huddled, naked, toothless corpse. For an instant Mero saw him as the old man of the desert, the jolly, bean-eating sage who hid under the sand with the snakes. Had that life, too, been snuffed out by Sheathless's touch?

With a shake of his head, Mero threw back the curtain and stepped outside.

8

He found the camp exactly as he had left it: silent, bathed in milky moonlight. An old life had ended and a new one begun, all in the space of a couple minutes, but the wider world was utterly ignorant of the exchange.

Mero stuck to the canyon wall as he had before, checking every doorway and footpath for signs of movement. Confident as he was in his newfound strength, he would rather avoid further bloodshed tonight. He had nothing to fight with other than Sheathless, and did not like to feed it any more than necessary.

He came to a threshold, narrow and small. He hesitated only a moment before pulling back the curtain and squeezing inside. He needed supplies if he wanted to cross the desert, and this was as good a place to find them as any other. If he was quiet enough, he might be able to slip in and out without waking anyone.

This cave was smaller than Menahem's, and was almost utterly dark once the curtain fell into place. Blotted shapes crouched in the edges of the room, but Mero couldn't tell if they were people or pots or empty beds.

He heard a gasp just as his vision resolved a shape squatting a few paces away. It was a woman's gasp. Before she could cry out, Mero strode forward and clapped a hand over her mouth, driving her back against the wall.

"Quiet," he hissed. "Don't make a sound."

He had no idea if the woman understood him. She was little more than a dim outline and a pair of wide, terrified eyes. She began to sob, her hot breath slipping between his fingers. Mero hardly blamed her. She probably thought she was about to be raped.

"I'm not here for you," Mero said. "Just stay quiet. Do you understand?"

He didn't think she did, but he had no more time to waste. Gently he released his grip. The woman slid to the ground, clasping her hands under her chin. From the darkness near Mero's feet came a soft, muttered prayer. He turned from the sound and went searching through the room.

First he found a half-dozen earthenware pots that sloshed when rocked from side to side. They were sealed with pats of mud and straw. Using Sheathless to break one open, Mero poured some liquid onto his hand and licked it.

It was water. Mero could have cried. Without hesitation he threw Sheathless down and grabbed the jug with both hands. Throwing his head back, he drank and drank and drank some more, splashing water down his front, letting it spill down his cheeks and into his ears. He only stopped when his lungs were ready to burst, and even then it was merely to take a few sucking breaths before tipping the jug back again. Once he had drunk his fill, he upended the jug on his own head, letting the rest of its contents soak through his hair and Menahem's blanket. It was as the cool water trickled down his back that he realized he *was* crying, his eyes and nose running with water, possibly for no other reason than to celebrate the fact that they could.

The woman in the corner was quiet now. Frozen in place, she watched Mero from behind the bars of her fingers. She whimpered when his eyes landed on her and tried to push herself even further away. Mero returned to his search.

The next jar was full of dried beans, hard and black. Mero felt a bitter irony as he considered them. They would have made the perfect provisions, if only he had had some way to cook them. As it was, they were worthless. He set the pot aside and kept looking.

Here was another jar, the same size as the last, only lighter. Mero broke the seal and peered inside. A multitude of small, dark shapes twinkled in the meagre moonlight. At first Mero thought they were more beans. Then, after picking one up and turning it over, he realized they were beetles: dark brown, desiccated, the size of the last knuckle of his thumb.

He stared at the beetle a while. Was it food? He had known places where the people ate insects, where the grazing was too scarce for cattle. But he had no idea what kind of beetle this was, or whether it was fit to eat.

Pinching the insect between forefinger and thumb, he stepped over to the woman in the corner. She moaned when he drew close. He hunkered down and held the beetle up to her face.

"What is this?" he asked. "Is it food? Can you eat it?"

The woman stared in confused horror. Mero's eyes had adapted to the dark; though the cave was written in smears of brown and gray, the whites of the woman's eyes and teeth stood out against the backdrop. There were wrinkles on her face.

He opened his mouth and mimed putting the beetle inside. "Eat?" he said. "Can you eat it?"

She looked at the beetle, then back at him. Finally she nodded.

"Eat," she said. "Eat, yes."

Mero was satisfied. He doubted the woman would lie. Her words awakened a thrill of joy in his heart. He had water and food — he might make it out of the desert after all.

A scream erupted behind him. It was ear-piercing, the kind of sound a person makes when they are terrified beyond anything that has terrified them before. The woman in front of Mero screamed as well, and for a moment he was stunned. Dropping the beetle, he stood and brandished Sheathless in one fluid motion.

There was another woman in the cave. Now that his vision was better, Mero could see the second cot tucked in the corner. Its occupant must have slept most of the way through his burglary, waking only to find a stranger in her house. She had scrambled out of bed and now stood between him and the doorway, paralyzed with fear.

Mero held out a hand. "Wait."

It was too late. The woman bolted, pushing through the curtain and disappearing outside. Her screams echoed through the valley.

It was time to go.

Mero knelt before his precious jugs, realizing he had no way of carrying them without filling both his hands. Desperately he glanced around. The flapping curtain caught his eye. Jumping to his feet, he grabbed the curtain in both hands and ripped it from the threshold. Moonlight flooded into the cave. It fell squarely upon the woman cowering in the corner, who screamed and covered her eyes.

Shouts came from down the valley, some belonging to women, others to men. Even the old goat was bleating. Mero worked furiously, tearing two long strips out of the curtain. Taking a strip by the middle, he wrapped it around the neck of the water jug, then knotted it to his waist. The jug slapped his thigh when he moved, but it was better than nothing.

He had just finished tying the second jug next to the first when a man appeared in the threshold, his silhouette carved out of moonlight. Mero grabbed Sheathless and the remainder of the curtain and rose to meet him. The man's fists were balled and his lip was pulled back, but his anger abandoned him the instant he saw Mero. His expression turned to one of horror, and he began to back away, stumbling over his own feet.

Mero could guess why. This man must have witnessed his death on the plateau; perhaps he had even been the one to twist Mero's penis on the way there. No doubt he had thought Mero well on his way to the land of the dead—but now that same traveler he had seen beaten and burned and devoured by an eagle stood before him, Menahem's kingly mantle draped across his shoulders.

"Menahem," the man croaked.

"Menahem is dead," Mero said, letting Sheathless play in the light. "I killed him. I would rather not kill anyone else tonight, but I will if I have to."

He advanced without waiting for an answer, watching his opponent's face. His gamble paid off. The man, though broader than Mero and taller by half a head, threw up his hands and backed out of the threshold. Mero followed him outside, Sheathless pointed at his heart.

By now the entire camp was awake. Across the valley, curtains were thrown back, and the walkways between the dwellings were dotted with shapes. Every so often a cry or curse split the air.

Two more men came down the path to Mero's right. Their pace slowed as they approached, but Mero didn't want to give them time to find their courage. Holding Sheathless before him like a talisman, he skirted the edge of the camp, taking the path down towards the valley's mouth. As he passed a threshold, a dark face poked out then instantly vanished back inside. A snatch of prayer drifted up from somewhere nearby.

Soon Mero had gathered a crowd of onlookers—men and women, old and older, watching him silently and following at a safe distance. On bare feet they shuffled along, matching Mero's cautious pace. He no longer sensed any hostility from them, only fascination and awe.

As he passed a group of women, one of them reached out and stroked Menahem's mantle. It was over before he could react. The woman pulled away, her knotted old fingers shaking. She moaned once, as though she'd been struck.

Finally Mero reached the camp's entrance. The crowd massed behind him in a half-circle, as though seeing him off on his journey. From here they did not look the least bit threatening. They were not bandits or torturers, just a huddle of confused old men and women, hungry and sad. Some were skinny as rails and others had bellies swollen from constipation. There were welts on their knuckles and wrists and their hair was matted with dirt. Even the larger men who had served as Menahem's guard now only looked stupid and lost.

Mero didn't know why they had followed him all this way. He felt he ought to say something, but had no idea what. Just as he turned to leave, a man's voice cut through the silence. It was the man who had shattered Mero's ribs with the stone axe.

"Please!" he bellowed. "Please do not leave us without a king!"

Mero turned back. The man was not looking at him, but at the ground, shifting his weight from one foot to the other.

Disgust rose in Mero's throat. It was so sudden and so strong that he actually brought Sheathless to his ear, ready to dash forward and strike the man's head from his shoulders. Then the mist cleared, leaving him with an awful emptiness. He shook his head and let the sword fall. With a sweep of his mantle, he put Menahem's kingdom at his back and stepped into the desert.

Part II

9

The bazaar sat at the intersection of three roads: those which ran to the north and south, marking the border between desert and grasslands, and that which ran into the east, into the heart of the grasslands themselves. It was a place not unlike the desert, ever shifting yet never changing. It was a crossroads, a nowhere place, a castle built on sand. A place where travelers drew together and came apart, after they had purchased what was needed and sold what was not.

There were no streets here, only spaces between. Tents, pavilions, wooden stalls and mud huts jostled and pushed, canopies shading, colored pennants snapping in the hot breeze. Everywhere one looked there were people and things: wrinkled men who sucked blue smoke out of long wooden pipes and stallholders who hollered and beckoned and clapped. Veiled women who glittered with jewels and men in long, dark robes. Bags of rice, corn, beans, and peas. Barrels of raisins, dates, apricots, persimmons, currants, olives, and plums. Meat, dried, raw, cooked, and live: clucking chickens, bleating goats, lowing cattle, and grunting, snuffling pigs. The smells were sweat and spice and smoke, paprika and tobacco, curry and anise. There were bolts of cloth and casks of wine. Filthy children ran underfoot. The sandy ground was churned by feet and hooves and wagon wheels, and scavenger birds circled the sky.

Between all this noise and life walked a man with a slow, unsteady gait. He was naked except for a pair of blankets, a red one wrapped around his waist and a blue one covering his shoulders and head. His feet were bare, and he was covered in burns from head to toe: flaking, bleeding, radiating heat. His skin crackled like that of a roast chicken, and his belly and cheeks were sunken with hunger. Some who saw him laughed, while others sucked air through their teeth in sympathy. Most simply ignored him. The bazaar was no stranger to disfigurement and disease, and besides, the man carried a sword—not wore, but carried naked in hand, the blade catching so much sun that it looked more like a beam of light than a piece of metal.

It had been six days since Mero escaped Menahem's camp—six days of soul-scorching heat and five freezing, interminable nights. His water had run out by the end of the first day. He had spent most of it in flight, putting as much distance between himself and the bandits' camp as he could. By the time he realized how quickly he was using his precious water, it was gone.

He hadn't regretted it at the time. Rather, it had been with great satisfaction that he unhooked the heavy clay jug from his waist and let it drop to the desert floor. No, the regret had come later, when his spongy tongue filled his mouth and the beetles he had brought along for food scraped his throat all the way down. He had given up on them, too, after the second day, dropping the jug at his feet still three-quarters full. He couldn't eat without water, and besides, the jug had been slowing him down. He used the two stretches of curtain to bind his feet, instead.

He walked in the morning and rested during the day, burying himself under layers of sand. He thought of Menahem as he did, then hated that the old man had taken up residence in his mind without his asking. Not for the first time, he wondered if Sheathless didn't steal more than blood.

When the sun set and the air began to cool, he emerged and carried on his way. He only had a few good hours of walking before the wind started to sting. Soon it was freezing cold, and Mero was faced with the choice of waiting for dawn or pressing on through the night. The first two nights he had managed to find shelter among some outcroppings of rock. After that, he decided to walk. If he was going to die, he might as well die following the goddess's mandate.

The goddess had not come to him at all in the desert. Though he talked to himself constantly, she never echoed so much as a single word. Instead, it was the scholar's face that swam out of memory to meet him, he of the twinkling eyes and cloud of cottony hair.

"Water is the medium for thought!" he proclaimed, over and over as Mero stumbled along on burning feet.

So you've said. But I don't see any water here.

Now at last Mero was close—so close he could smell it. The promise of water pulled him down the winding streets of the bazaar, past the watching eyes and clouds of spiced smoke. He didn't know where he was going, only that he was sure to find what he was looking for sooner or later. Places like this only bloomed near water. Pennants or palm leaves—to the lost traveler, they meant the same thing.

A shadow eclipsed Mero's vision. It was a man in a long red coat, with a waxed moustache and a black headwrap.

"*Alun hen hadach?*" he said, or something like it.

Mero stared blankly.

The man scowled and pointed at Sheathless. "*Dak?*"

Mero shook his head. The man's scowl deepened, and he stepped close enough that Mero could smell his breath. It was sour, like rancid yogurt.

"No weapons in the bazaar," he said, slow and angry.

Mero blinked and looked around. "I see others wearing swords."

"In a sheath!" the man barked, waving his own saber under Mero's nose. The hilts were golden, the pommel cast in the shape of a flowering lotus.

"I have none," Mero said calmly, looking at the ground.

"Is that my problem?" the man said.

"I don't want trouble. Please. I'm very thirsty."

The man reached out. "Give me your sword."

Mero weighed his options and found he only had one. This man wouldn't hesitate to kill him if he resisted, and winning Sheathless back from Menahem had been a stroke of luck. He wasn't likely to have such an easy time again. So he reached into the pouch he had made with Menahem's blanket and drew out a golden tooth. He pushed it into the man's hand, saying, "Please. I only want somewhere to drink and wash."

It was a knife-edge moment. The man glowered furiously, reaching for his sword even as he opened his palm to see what Mero had placed there.

The golden tooth caught the sunlight. The man's expression changed, from surprise to disbelief to greed and at last to curiosity. Closing his fist, he searched Mero's face, his dark, bushy eyebrows modulating with thought.

"From where do you come, traveler?" His voice was lower but no less harsh.

"The desert," Mero said.

The man snorted. "No one crosses the desert."

Mero didn't answer. His strength was fading; he had already lost all of the weight he had gained from killing Menahem. It was all he could do to put one foot in front of the other, and now this man had broken that vital rhythm. He wasn't sure he would be able to start walking again even if he got the chance.

The man eyed him shrewdly, smoothing his mustache with fore-finger and thumb. Finally he tucked the tooth away in his coat.

"Come."

He swept away without waiting to see if Mero was following. Mero, breathing heavily, put his left foot in front of his right, his right foot in front of his left. But the man's strides were long, and at the end of five seconds he was already twice as many yards behind.

"Wait." He couldn't raise his voice above a whisper.

The man turned. His scowl deepened into a snarl.

"Hurry up!" he barked.

I can't. Mero stared at his feet, struggling to remember how to walk. Yellow pus oozed between the threadbare bindings.

Pushing his way back through the crowd, the man grabbed Mero's wrist and yanked. Mero allowed himself to be driven along, hanging on to the outstretched arm like a child clutching his mother's skirts.

He knew he ought to pay attention to where the red-coated man was taking him, but he couldn't muster the energy. His knowledge of the bazaar was written in half-formed impressions, bursts of color and noise imprinting on his senses. A bug-eyed man with a wide, toothy grin; a frying pan throwing up clouds of greasy steam; a mass of twittering birds in golden cages, their tiny bodies glistening like jewels. Then: a long, silent line of people, mostly women, each carrying a pot or pitcher or bucket.

Mero's escort dragged him towards the front of the line, ignoring the odd look or muttered remark aimed their way. Judging from the way people melted out of his path, Mero figured the red-coated man for a guardsman or peacekeeper.

The line was interminable. Mero was in no mood to count, but it must have comprised over a hundred people. It snaked between two rows of stalls, then turned right onto a long, narrow staircase carved into the rock. Mero took the stairs two steps to one, arranging both his feet on one step before venturing down to the next. His escort swore at him more than once, but he kept his head down and shuffled along.

The air cooled as they descended. The stair curved to the left, and Mero realized they were entering the mouth of an enormous well. A pool of clear water, round and still, waited at the bottom. On the far side of the pool another stair wound its way up, walked by a procession of women balancing sloshing jugs on their heads. Mero's tongue tingled, and he quickened his pace.

Two steps later, he caught his heel on the edge of a stair, and his knees buckled under him. He tumbled headfirst down the hard stone steps, sweeping several other people along with him. In an instant the orderly line erupted into a chaos of tangled clothes, smashed pots, and shouting voices.

"*Idiot!*" the mustached man screamed. He pulled Mero off the ground by his hair and slapped him hard on the cheek. "Do that again and I will cut your throat and leave you for the buzzards to eat!" He threw Mero towards the well, kicking him in the backside to drive his point home. Grabbing a bucket, he thrust it into Mero's hands, saying,

"Now drink. *Only* drink. No washing here. Touch that water with your filthy hands and I will cut them off."

Mero was too entranced by the shimmering water to care about anything else—about the pain in his backside, about the insults being hurled at him from the stairs above. Using the bucket as a crutch, he crawled towards the well on his belly, stopping just shy of the pool's lip. The level of the water was perfectly flush with that of the stone around it, and when Mero peered over the edge, his eyes fell into a perfect, cylindrical shaft, plunging deep into the earth. Even in his addled state, he recognized the shaft for what it was.

"Hellhole," he whispered.

Hellhole, the goddess confirmed.

"Hurry up!" Pain exploded in Mero's groin as another kick landed.

Arms shaking, Mero skimmed the bucket along the surface of the water. He wanted to fill it to overspilling and plunge his head inside, but knew he wouldn't have the strength. Gathering his legs beneath him, he rocked back into a seated position, then raised the bucket to his lips and drank.

It was a moment of bliss, over too soon. In seconds the bucket was empty and the red-coated man snatched it away. Mero cried out, chasing the bucket with outstretched hands, collapsing in a heap when he realized no more water was coming.

"Please," he said to the ground. "Wait, please. Just a little more."

"I see your tongue is working better." The man's boots creaked as he hunkered down. He fetched the golden tooth from inside his coat and waved it under Mero's nose. "Now you will tell me where you are from, and how you got this."

10

It was hours later—two, or four, or eight. Mero was alone, hunkered in a cramped sandstone cell. A fist-sized vent near the ceiling let in a beam of moonlight. Otherwise, it was entirely dark.

They had taken Sheathless, the clay whistle, and the remaining golden teeth. All Mero had left were his blankets and the bindings on his feet, which he had removed by the simple expedient of picking at the threadbare cloth until it fell apart. His feet were little more than lumps in the darkness, which was probably for the best. They ached when he curled them and stung when he stretched them out. When he hovered a hand over them, he felt their burning heat.

It was cool in the cell, for which Mero was grateful. He dozed for some time, waking to find the window dark. His stomach cramped—a half-dozen mouthfuls of water had been enough to upset it. He wrapped his arms around it and wished for sleep.

The scholar joined him, as he sometimes did when Mero was tired or ill.

"I've got a question for you," he said. "What is the most terrifying monster man has ever created?"

"The sphinx?" Mero guessed. The scholar was fond of talking about the sphinx.

"Her, the poor dear?" The scholar laughed. "Heavens, no! *Her* worst crime was asking a question to which men didn't have the answer."

"Then who?"

The scholar leaned close, a conspiratorial twinkle in his eye.

"*Dracula*," he said, before melting into the darkness.

Mero mused about this for some time. The monster's name meant nothing to him; he had never encountered it in his studies. He resolved to ask the scholar about this the next time they met, though when that might be was anyone's guess.

The next thing he knew, he was waking to the sound of an iron key rattling the bars of his cell. Pale yellow light slanted through the vent in the wall, the unripe light of a new day.

The man doing the rattling was the same frowning, mustached man who had led him to the well in the bazaar. Mero still didn't know his name, though he and his fellow guardsmen had spent the better part of the afternoon questioning him—slapping his face, tugging his hair, rubbing sand into the burns on his shoulders and back. They had asked him where he came from, where he was going, how he had gotten Sheathless and the golden teeth. They had called him all sorts of names and made plenty of dark promises about his future, but in the end they had come away frustrated. Mero had heard it all before— questions, insults, and threats alike—and his was a meatless bone of a story, a truth so bare and indigestible that his lies were easy to swallow by comparison. He gave both away indiscriminately, not caring what the men believed or didn't believe.

Now the man scowled at him as though he were a dog that had just relieved itself on the carpet. Squatting down, he pushed a small clay pot through the gap in the bars.

"Eat," he said. "If there's broth in that bowl when I come back, I will pinch your nose and pour it down your throat—and if there is any on the floor, I will stand and watch while you lick it up."

He swept away. Mero, after waiting to see if anything else was forthcoming, uncurled and crept towards the pot. Steam billowed onto his face when he lifted the lid. He blew it away to reveal a thin yellow broth, a few dried currants floating on the surface and a handful of white bones clunking around the bottom.

Mero sniffed once, then took a tentative sip. The sweetness of the fruit mingled with the earthy heartiness of meat. Mero was struck by an overwhelming hunger. He forced himself to savor the broth, knowing he would just throw it up again if he drank too quickly. Though his stomach twisted and his brow broke out in sweat, he managed to empty the bowl without incident.

In the hours that followed Mero sat with his back to the wall, thinking of the questions he would put to the red-coated man upon his next visit. The meal had put him in good spirits—not only did he feel clearer and stronger than he had in days, he now knew that these men did not intend to starve him to death. A small consolation, but a consolation nonetheless.

When the guardsman did return, he was accompanied by another man in sweeping robes of red and yellow. The newcomer had a handsome, clean-shaven face, and smelled strongly of wine and floral perfume. Boots clicking, he strode up to Mero's cell and peered down at him, hanging his forearms through the bars to bring his face closer.

"Is this him?" he asked, eyes walking up and down Mero's body.

"Yes," answered the guardsman. He carried a brass lamp that burned with a soft, steady flame, and his mood was even fouler than usual.

"He looks like shit." The newcomer wrinkled his nose. There were rings in his ears that twinkled when he moved. "He *smells* like shit. What have you been feeding him?"

"Nothing until today. He was too weak to eat."

"He needs cleaning up," the newcomer declared. "Sanja is sick of waiting for him to get better."

"Who is Sanja?" Mero asked, before the guardsman could answer.

The newcomer treated him to a smile, as though it were a great trick that he had figured out how to talk.

"Sanja Al-Sat is he who holds your life in his hands," he said. "If I were you, I would drop to my knees and pray in his name."

"What business does he have with me?" Mero asked.

"That is for him to decide." The newcomer turned to the guardsman. "But first we must do something about that smell. Sanja would lose his lunch if you brought him up now. Take him to the baths and let him soak for an hour or so."

The guardsman nodded curtly. The newcomer shot Mero one more glance, grinned, and withdrew, leaving the two of them alone.

"So you work for Sanja," Mero said. "What sort of man is he?"

The red-coated man gave him a scowl. Mero wasn't cowed; the man probably scowled at his reflection when he shaved.

Finally the guardsman said, "He is a merchant prince from the south, one of the wealthiest men alive. He owns the oasis and he owns this bazaar. Everything in it—you, me, this lamp, these walls—belongs to him."

That sounded familiar. "And is he kind to the people he owns?"

"He is…generous. If he makes you an offer, traveler, you would do well to accept."

Mero spread his arms, showing off his tattered blankets. "What could I possibly offer him?"

"He will think of something," the guardsman said. "He always does."

11

Shortly after, the guardsman returned with two of his fellows, and the three men escorted Mero out of his cell. They led him down a maze of sandstone corridors, plain but expertly cut, oil lamps burning at steady intervals. Servants in plain yellow robes brushed past their procession, carrying tools or linens or baskets of food. Mero, trying to keep stock of each turn they took, was astounded at the scale of the place. If these corridors were any indication of the structure above, it must have been truly palatial.

The guardsman opened a door, and the narrow sandstone tunnels gave way to a wide, sumptuous hallway, richly carpeted and tapestried, lit by tall, glittering lamps. The air was hazy and smelled of ambergris.

The walls, lined with channels of water on which floated candle bowls and lotus flowers, were carved in relief, every inch covered with figures. There were men and women and animals, too, and every last one was pleasuring or being pleasured by those around them. A man and a woman knelt side-by-side before a third man with an enormous erection; that man, in turn, had one of his hands wrapped around a donkey's shaft and the other inserted into the cleft of a reclining woman. A boy poured a stream of stony wine between the reclining woman's breasts, which was lapped from her stomach by a dog who was busy mounting yet another woman of his own. On and on and on it went, figures bending, writhing, folding, spreading, kissing, caressing, engorging, inserting.

"Your master is quite the patron of the arts," Mero said.

"Be quiet," the guardsman snapped. One of his men sniggered.

At the end of the hallway, twin doors of blushing metal yielded under the guardsman's touch, revealing a cavernous space sectioned off by screens of finely-wrought gold. The air was thick and cloying, and distant splashes and peals of silvery laughter echoed off the walls. The chamber

Jesse McMinn

was not entirely unnatural; in some places the ceiling spiked down, and in others it opened three stories high.

A woman greeted them at the entrance. Her dress was gossamer and her breasts were bare, and her ears, arms, fingers and toes were covered in jewels that twinkled and winked. She wore a golden collar around her neck and golden shackles around her ankles. Her skin was like bronze, her eyes smoldering—but the expression she wore was more hassled than seductive.

She shot Mero the briefest of glances, then spoke to the guardsman in a low, worried voice. Though he understood her tone well enough, the language she used was not Mero's own. Based on the guardsman's face and the way the woman's eyes kept flicking to him, he figured he was the subject of conversation.

The guardsman answered roughly, and the woman started talking again the second he was done. Finally he threw up his arms in disgust and the woman spun and stepped off, jewels atwinkle.

"Is there a problem?" Mero asked.

"The problem is you," the guardsman growled. "You are too ugly. Shareen is worried you will scare away the other bathers."

Mero came closer to laughing than he had in months. "I won't get any prettier if I can't bathe."

"She is fetching linens." The guardsman's face was a thundercloud. "Once you have covered yourself, she will take you to a private bath."

Shareen returned with a pair of towels, white as cream and soft as eiderdown. She made Mero stand in a corner to wrap the first around his waist, then pulled the second over his head like a hood. Though her face revealed that she was not entirely pleased with the effect, she allowed Mero and the guardsmen to follow her around the perimeter of the baths. Curtains and screens kept most of the chamber from sight, though every so often Mero caught a snatch of conversation or a flash of soft, sumptuous flesh. He knew there would be trouble if the ugly traveler was caught peeking at Sanja's more beautiful guests, so he kept his hood up and his chin to his chest.

They turned down a short passage and Shareen pulled aside a curtain of midnight blue. Beyond it was a small grotto lit from above by a shaft of natural sunlight. The light fell on a steaming pool twice as wide as Mero was tall. The smell was a heady mixture of bath salts, perfume, and fresh desert air.

Shareen shared some words with Mero's guard, then swept past him and disappeared through the curtain. As she passed by, Mero noticed that she had folded one hand under her breasts—as though she was sick to her stomach—and was pinching her nose with the other. That struck him as bitterly funny, and he had to bite his knuckle to keep himself from laughing.

The guardsman jabbed at the pool with his chin. "Get in."

"While you stand there and watch?" Mero said. His escort was sweating in the humid air.

"My orders are to have you bathed. I mean to see them carried out."

Mero sighed and pulled off his hood. "Suit yourself."

12

If Mero thought he would be taken to meet Sanja after his bath, he was mistaken. After lowering himself into the too-hot water and scrubbing the worst of the grime from his raw, peeling skin, he was marched back to his cell and put under lock and key for the rest of the day. That evening another bowl of broth arrived, a few scraps of meat and skin floating on the fatty surface.

The pattern repeated itself twice more, with four more meals of increasing solidity and two more trips to the cavernous bathhouse. Mero grew restless as his detainment wore on. Something deep in his sternum nagged at him, pushing him forward like a bird trapped in the cage of his ribs. His palms itched for Sheathless, and his feet, calloused and sore as they were, yearned to walk the roads of the world. When he slept, he dreamed of mountains covered in stars, lit from behind by the rising sun. *East,* he would think, *I have to go east,* and the goddess would echo the word in his mind, *east, east,* a drum beat compelling him to march.

On the morning of the third day, the newcomer with the grinning face and glittering earrings returned. He hung his arms into Mero's cell just as he had days before, scuffing his soft leather boots on the floor. The red-coated man was there, of course, looking as dour as ever.

The newcomer closed his eyes and sniffed. "He smells better. Not good, but better."

"Does Sanja care that much how I smell?" Mero asked.

"Sanja's constitution is delicate," the newcomer said. "He is sickened by anything ugly or base."

"He must be sick often, then."

The newcomer's eyes grew distant, and his nose wrinkled as though he'd caught a whiff of rotting fish. Whatever he was thinking of, it was enough to twist his handsome features into a mask of disgust.

"You have no idea," he said softly, "how much pain it causes him to live in such an imperfect world. Imagine! All the riches a man could have, but still he must walk the same earth as all these—these—"

He waved a hand vaguely, and Mero realized the object of the newcomer's hate. It was the bazaar itself: the bazaar, with all its hot, filthy, sweating, swearing people.

Mero couldn't help but find that funny.

"It's lucky for Sanja all those people exist," he said, "or else he wouldn't be so rich."

The newcomer looked at Mero, surprised he had spoken. His expression bubbled like the surface of a pot. Then he turned to the red-coated man and said,

"Get him out of there."

The guardsmen complied, turning the heavy key in its lock. He grabbed Mero by the arm and pulled him into the hallway. There the newcomer took his chin and turned his head this way and that, as though examining a horse he was thinking of buying. He ran his fingers through Mero's hair, then stepped around him in a circle, his boots clicking softly.

Finally he heaved a rather overwrought sigh and said, "Give him another bath before you take him up. Make sure they use perfume this time. And dress him in some proper clothes." He thumbed Menahem's kingly mantle, a fresh look of contempt on his face. "He looks like an animal in those rags."

In preparation for his meeting with Sanja, Mero underwent the longest grooming session of his life. It started with another bath, after which a pair of silent men in loin-wraps held him down and scrubbed the flaking skin from his body. His burns were not fully healed, and the rough touch of the pumice was agonizing. Mero screamed and screamed until the guardsman—who was supervising, as always—swore at the men to shut him up. They stuffed a wooden basket handle between Mero's teeth and kept working. By the end of it all, Mero was red as a newborn babe and delirious with pain. They stood him on jellied legs and half-walked, half-carried him to the next chamber.

After the scrubbing came an endless procession of ointments, balms, and perfumes, applied to his arms and legs and back and face by an equally endless procession of stony-faced women and men. They rubbed oil into Mero's burning skin and daubed his face with ocher greasepaint. It was a kinder treatment than the scrubbing had been. The oil leached away some of the pain from the burns, and Mero even allowed himself to doze as a small woman with a round face, round belly and round breasts circled him with a pair of golden tweezers, pulling errant hairs from his ears and the nape of his neck.

At last it was all done, and Mero was clothed in a loose-fitting shirt and pants dyed a brilliant blue. He was ushered out of the baths and into the hands of the newcomer, who waited for him in a lavishly-furnished sitting room. Gold-threaded curtains hung from the walls, and the lamps were shaded with chips of colored glass. A fig tree, its branches laden with ripening fruit, curled up a wall and undulated across the ceiling.

The newcomer was smoking a long, ivory pipe when Mero was pushed into the room. He set the pipe down in its golden cradle and leapt to his feet. His eyes were bright and green, and smoke curled from his mouth when he smiled.

"Ah," he said. "Better. Much better."

He circled Mero again, twitching his clothes into place and brushing the hair from his eyes. His feet were bare, and he moved like a dancer, making no noise on the plush carpet.

"Sanja Al-Sat will see you now," he said, still circling. "It is his pleasure that he will see you alone. You are to behave yourself. Remember it is thanks to his mercy that you were treated so well."

Mero said nothing. The claim that he had been treated well was laughable, yet he detected no irony in the newcomer's voice.

"There are six hundred men in this palace who live to serve Sanja's every desire," the man went on. "Upset him and you will wish you had never been born. Now follow me."

He led Mero to a heavy curtain at the far end of the room. From beyond came the unmistakable sounds of lovemaking, the ragged, rising breaths and falling moans of a woman mounting the peaks of pleasure. Despite himself, Mero's heat rose. The newcomer did not so much as blink. He pulled the curtain aside, letting out a blast of thick, musky air.

"Walk straight through to the end," he said. "Do not keep Sanja waiting."

13

It was like stepping through the hallways of a dream, one of the intense, prurient dreams of adolescence dredged up from the recesses of Mero's brain. Before him lay a maze of smoky rooms and mirrored alcoves. Lamps burned low, and curtains draped like jungle foliage. The floor was carpeted in animal skins, each pelt a fresh sensation under Mero's toes. The walls were covered with cavorting figures, a tangled forest of limbs without beginning or end.

Blue smoke hung in the air, tickling his nostrils every time he breathed in. The tingling soon spread up the back of his neck and circled his brow, making him feel like a giant poking his head into a bank of cloud. His heart hammered, and for a wild moment he considered crawling. The smoke smelled of tobacco and wine, ripening fruit, earthy musk. It filled Mero with shadowy memories of exotic places he had never seen, made him ache with nostalgia for a life he had never lived.

Voices rose and fell all around him. The maze must have been home to dozens of people. Some whispered, others moaned. Women laughed and men grunted. Sighs and squeals mingled in an endless susurrus of unseen carnality. Mero clenched his jaw, gripping futilely at the empty space where Sheathless normally hung.

A woman, tall and slender, slipped around a curtain to Mero's left. She was stark naked, a fine golden chain hanging between her pierced nipples. A man followed after her, his naked member half-erect, his body glistening with oil and rippling with muscle.

The woman started when she saw Mero, the chain between her breasts leaping. She dropped a short bow, then took her lover's hand and led him out of the room. The man didn't spare Mero a second glance—his eyes were elsewhere.

"Who is that?" The voice came from deeper in the maze. "Come here, please."

Mero ducked under the smoke, drew a deep breath, then straightened and strode in the direction of the voice. Doorways flickered past, each offering a fresh sight: a room full of men, some on their hands and knees, others standing, stroking, waiting their turn; a pair of women wrapped in ribbons that hung from the ceiling, like flies caught in a spider's trap; an enormous golden basin in which over a dozen men and women soaked, drinking wine and smoking from long ivory pipes. Mero lowered his head and kept his eyes on the passage ahead. At last he cast aside a final, heavy curtain, and stepped into the presence of Sanja Al-Sat.

His first impression was that of a brightly-colored ball. Sanja was a fat, fat man—not grossly fat, but roundly, happily so, his belly a firm swell like that of a pregnant woman, his cheeks rosy and plump. He was naked except for a rich red robe that spilled down his shoulders and arms and onto the great nest of cushions beneath.

Sanja was not the nest's only occupant. He was surrounded by slender men and curvaceous women in various states of nakedness. His bed was a confusion of oiled limbs and plump buttocks, of chains, jewels, and metal collars. A woman lay draped across his legs, her head nestled in his lap. Sanja stroked her hair with one hand and his own short-cropped beard with the other.

His eyes were beady, bright, and merry. He saw Mero and broke into a broad smile. Mero noticed with a jolt that two of his teeth were golden.

"There you are!" Sanja cried, wiggling his pudgy legs with excitement. "Come closer, closer—let me have a look at you." He beckoned with a hand engulfed in jeweled rings.

Mero did as he was told, all too aware that he was entirely within Sanja's power. He feared that Sanja would order him closer, and closer, and closer still, until he was asked to undress and join the ranks of the concubines, but the beckoning fell off when he was still five paces away.

Sanja leaned forward, slapping a hand down on his thigh, and for some time said nothing at all, only looked Mero over with an expression of great delight on his face. A woman bent over and nibbled his ear. He tickled her absently under the chin, never taking his eyes off Mero.

"Jaffar tells me you crossed the desert," he said at last.

"Which one is Jaffar?" Mero asked. "The one who never smiles, or the one who never stops smiling?"

Sanja's mouth and eyes widened into perfect rings; then his enormous belly began to jiggle with mirth. His laughter stirred his entourage into a renewed flurry of kisses and caresses.

"Yes, yes!" Sanja wiped a tear from his eye. "Jaffar is the one who never smiles. I should know, I've been trying for years. I've sent him women, men, even a dog once, a pretty bitch with nice soft fur. But all I get for my trouble is—" Sanja twisted his face into an exaggerated frown, then fell into another fit of laughter. "Ah, but enough about him. I want to talk about *you*. So, is it true? You walked the desert on your own bare feet?"

"Yes," Mero said.

"Show them to me." Sanja's laughter was gone. "Your feet. I want to see them."

It was a harmless enough request. Hopping to keep his balance, Mero grabbed one ankle and directed it at the fat man, flexing his toes to show off his red, calloused sole.

A few of Sanja's concubines squealed and covered their mouths. Sanja himself drew back as though Mero had offered him a snake. The red drained from his cheeks, and he burped and turned his head aside.

"Oh—oh!" Sanja waved a hand frantically in Mero's direction. "Away—put it away!"

Mero set his foot down, astonished at the reaction it had provoked. The newcomer hadn't overstated the delicacy of Sanja's constitution.

Sanja stroked the woman in his lap, running a hand from her hair down into the valley of her waist, then up along the swell of her hips. The act seemed to calm him. Each caress came slower than the last, and the glow returned to his cheeks. Still he struggled to look at Mero. His beady eyes flickered to his face, his feet, then away.

"How did you do it?" he asked at last. "I've never known a man to cross the desert without horse or camel."

"I had a horse. Bandits killed her."

"So you said." Sanja knitted his fingers under his chin. "But I've never known of bandits in the desert, either. There's nothing there, for anyone."

There was something there for Menahem, Mero thought. *A black rock, baking in the sun.*

"Have you lied to me, traveler?" Sanja's voice was honey-sweet.

"Only when the truth ran out," Mero said.

Sanja grinned. Leaning back in his throne of cushions, he snapped his fingers at a waiting attendant. The servant—a young man with soft, dewy skin—produced one of the long, ivory smoking pipes, ornately carved and capped with gold at both ends. He held it to Sanja's lips and lowered a taper into the bowl while his master puffed. Sanja wiggled happily as he smoked, a big red baby at an ivory teat. But his eyes watched Mero through the haze, and Mero reminded himself that whatever else he was, Sanja was the man who held the bazaar, and Mero's own life, in his palm.

Why is he wasting his time with me? Mero glanced at Sanja's entourage of lovers, ripe women and smooth-shaven men. *He clearly has better things to do. He wants something out of me—out of my story. What does he think I'm hiding from him?*

The answer hit him with a suddenness that made him rock on his feet. It was so obvious he couldn't believe he hadn't seen it before.

"So," Sanja said, "these bandits of yours—"

"You want to know if there's water hidden in the desert," Mero said. "You want to claim it for your own—use it to establish another settlement like this one."

Sanja froze, the pipe still to his lips. Smoke curled from the corners of his mouth. He waved his attendant away irritably, then leaned forward, resting his elbows in the small of the woman's back. Then he started to laugh.

"I knew you were clever," he said, wagging a finger at Mero. "I knew we'd have fun. Well! You've guessed my secret. I admit it! And why shouldn't I? That desert sits between me and the entire western half of the continent. I can go around it, but that is expensive. I can cross it, but that takes water—plenty of water."

"You have plenty of water," Mero pointed out. "You control the bazaar's well."

"I do," said Sanja, kneading the air with his fat fingers. "But there are over five thousand souls in this bazaar, and every one of them needs to drink. Water is what keeps them here. Even I can only draw so much."

Mero nodded. If it was Menahem's well Sanja was after, he was welcome to it. Perhaps some of the desert king's old followers could join Sanja's palace as cupbearers or concubines—though Mero doubted that. If a couple of calloused feet could make the merchant prince lose his lunch, Mero could only imagine what Sanja would think of Menahem's wretched band.

"I can tell you what I remember about the bandit's camp," Mero said. "It isn't much. I was half-dead when I found it, and more than half when I left. Still, your men should be able to find it. But," he added, seeing the undisguised greed on Sanja's face, "I will need a few things in return."

Sanja gurgled with pleasure, rocking side-to-side to settle his bottom in the cushions. He waved for his pipe, took a few puffs, then said, "Yes? And what are these few things you want in return?"

"My sword." The words leapt out of Mero's mouth faster than he would have liked. He hoped, without much conviction, that Sanja hadn't noticed. "And my clay whistle."

Sanja's face didn't change. "Yes? And what else?"

What else? "A good horse or camel. A second set of clothing. And enough food for ten days of travel."

Sanja raised a hand and smacked it down on the buttocks of the woman in his lap. She squealed in surprise, her toes curling, her olive skin already reddening where Sanja's palm had struck. Sanja let fly a stream of curses in his own language—though the words were unfamiliar, their intent was clear.

Mero was stunned. Sanja's face was ripening like a tomato on the vine. He gripped the woman's backside and squeezed. Her cries danced on the threshold between pleasure and pain.

"You insult me, traveler!" Spittle flew from Sanja's mouth. He jabbed an accusing finger at Mero. "What will you ask for next—a donkey and three bushels of grain? *YAAAGH!*" He balled his fists until they were as red and round as his face.

"My apologies!" Mero said quickly, though he wasn't entirely sure what he was apologizing for. "I meant no offence."

Sanja sat rigid, his arms and legs curled. It looked as though he was having a fit. Then the strangest thing happened. Sanja's concubines, men and women alike, coalesced around their master, stroking his arms, legs, and face. The woman he had spanked planted kisses on his stomach, lower and lower until her head was between his legs. A man with a figure like a marble statue stood at Sanja's shoulder; with gentle hands he pressed his master's cheek to the firm flesh above his groin.

Stimulated by his many admirers, Sanja Al-Sat slowly uncoiled. His shoulders drooped and his breath whooshed out. Reaching back, he cupped the genitals of the man who had held him and planted an audible kiss on the shaft of his penis. Then he rolled back, looking up at the ceiling as though utterly exhausted.

"All I have ever wanted," he said, "was beauty. To see it, to smell it, to hold and caress it. I have built my life around it. And yet no matter how I try…" He sniffled, and Mero realized he was crying.

Sanja wiped his eyes, then rocked forward, his concubines scattering to make room. He planted his feet and clasped his hands in front of him, pinning Mero under a cold, penetrating glare.

"Name your price, traveler. And this time, it had better be right."

Mero's heart pounded in his ears. What price could he name that wouldn't rouse Sanja's ire? It seemed his last had been too low rather than too high. Should he ask for gold? Jewels? Those were uninspired choices, and Mero wasn't convinced Sanja would like them any more than he had liked the first.

What, then? What did Mero need that he didn't already have?

Sanja's face hardened, all sense of playfulness gone. If Mero was going to name his price, he had better do it soon, or his chances of reaching the black mountains would be that much slimmer.

Just like that, the answer came to him.

"There is a place somewhere to the east of here," he said. "A range of mountains, only the mountains are tall and thin—like pillars of stone—and they're covered in lights, thousands of lights like stars in the night sky."

Silence reigned. At last Sanja said, "Yes?"

"I want to know everything you know about that place. Where it is and how to get there. Anything you've heard from your own men or from visitors to the bazaar. That is my price."

The intensity of Sanja's expression did not change, but its nature did. Where before had been wounded anger was now a sort of wry curiosity.

"And why do you want to know about this place?" Sanja asked.

Mero was too tired to lie. "I saw it in a dream."

Now Sanja smiled. "I have dreamed before, many times. But no dream could ever compel me to abandon my lovers and go wandering away. Did you dream about a big pile of gold hidden at the foot of the mountains?"

"No," said Mero. "Nothing like that."

"Then what?"

"It's where I dreamed I would die."

14

Mero stood at the threshold of the grasslands, watching the sun-bleached blades bend and sway under the wind. He held his new horse's reins in one hand and Sheathless in the other. Around his neck was the clay whistle, and on his back was a fresh linen shirt. The bazaar lay at his back about a mile down the road. He could still hear the dull roar of five thousand shouting, hawking, bargaining voices.

It had been ten days since his first meeting with Sanja Al-Sat. That meeting had ended in disappointment, for Mero if not for the merchant prince. After taking in Mero's descriptions of his dreams, Sanja had spread his palms and said,

"I'm afraid I cannot help you. I have heard many strange things in my time, but nothing of a place where the mountains twinkle like stars." He smiled a sad, humorless smile. "If you are that determined to die, traveler, you will need to seek someone else's advice."

That Mero intended to do, but Sanja would not consent to release him until his claims about water in the desert had been verified. Sanja had summoned Jaffar that very minute and commanded him to take a company of men into the desert to search for Menahem's valley. Jaffar had accepted the orders with his characteristic surliness, reserving his dirtiest look for Mero himself.

Mero was escorted out of Sanja's presence by the newcomer, the smiling, effeminate courtier whose name, Mero would eventually learn, was Malique. Malique did not lead Mero back to his old cell, but to a suite of rooms in the lower levels of the palace that, while no doubt stark by Sanja's standards, were spacious and richly furnished. The mattress was deeper than any Mero had ever slept on, and at night a warm breeze fluttered the gossamer curtains framing his window.

Mero, for all his newfound comforts, did not sleep well. He was not worried about what would happen if Jaffar was unable to find

Menahem's well. Rather, he was desperate to be on his way. More than once he considered leaping out of his window in the dead of night. But Sanja still had Sheathless locked away somewhere in his palace, not to mention hundreds of soldiers at his command.

No, it was better to wait, painful as that was. His lassitude weighed on him like a promise unkept; he tossed and turned as he tried to sleep, grinding his teeth to powder.

Jaffar returned to the palace eight days later, riding hard with his company behind him. His demeanor had not improved, but the news he bore spelled freedom for Mero and victory for Sanja Al-Sat.

"We found the well not two days' ride from here," he said, hefting a sloshing jug as proof. "It's good water—clear and deep." His eyes revealed what his words had not—that Menahem's well and Sanja's own likely owed their existence to the same force.

Hellhole, said the goddess.

As Sanja gurgled and cooed over the jug, Mero asked, "Were there people in the valley?"

Jaffar shot him a look even uglier than most.

"Corpses," he said.

That single word was all Mero ever heard about the fate of Menahem's kingdom. By that afternoon Jaffar was headed back into the desert, this time leading a convoy of sand-sledges guarded by men riding horse and camelback. The sledges carried timber and canvas, shovels and picks, workers and provisions—everything Sanja's men needed to establish the newest arm of his empire. Mero and Sanja watched them ride into the setting sun from a window of the palace's great hall. Sanja had taken to summoning Mero into his company several times a day, sometimes to pester him for tales of his travels and others for seemingly no reason at all.

As Sanja gloated over his success, Mero saw his chance to reiterate his request for freedom. Sanja, after all, had gotten all he wanted out of their relationship. Mero thought it about time the two of them parted ways—but Sanja, it seemed, did not feel the same.

"I have a proposition for you, traveler," he said.

"Yes?" Mero answered, wary.

Sanja tore his eyes from the departing convoy and looked up at Mero, who was a head taller than him. "Do not go into the East to die. Stay here instead. Join my palace and pledge your life to me. You clearly don't think much of it. Why not give it to someone who will put it to proper use?"

"And how would you use my life?"

Sanja grinned, a sparkle coming to his eyes. "By making you one of my wives, of course."

"I'm a man," Mero pointed out.

"A man can be a wife. All he needs do is take a husband. I like you, traveler. You move well. You're much too skinny, but that can be fixed. Drink enough peach milk and you'll soon have thighs like a woman."

"And if I didn't care to be one of your concubines?" Mero asked.

Sanja waved a hand at the convoy below. "Then you can be a soldier instead, and you and Jaffar can sit and scowl at each other while the rest of us are busy fucking."

A tempting offer. "I thank you deeply for your kindness. But I'm afraid I must refuse."

Sanja gave him a sharp look, one that hinted of the iron beneath the fat.

"Refuse?" he repeated, for an instant reminding Mero of the goddess. "You would turn down a life of comfort and wealth to seek your death in a distant land?"

"The choice isn't mine to make," Mero said.

"Stay here." Suddenly Sanja was pleading. "Be one of my wives, happy and plump. You can bathe my feet in oil, and I'll lick honey off your cock. We'll walk in the gardens and eat figs and sweetmeats until we're ready to burst. You can tell me stories of your travels, and I will dress you in my finest jewels. Our world will be here, this palace, these halls and alcoves, and you will never have to walk the desert on naked feet again. Doesn't that sound nice?"

It did sound nice—other than the requirement of sharing a bed with Sanja Al-Sat, and the fact that he would surely go insane if he were trapped in this palace any longer. Even if the goddess allowed him to rest, Sheathless never would. The hunger would always be there, gnawing, gnawing, and it would only be a matter of time until…

"I can't," Mero said. "My purpose compels me."

Sanja's lip quivered. Suddenly he turned away.

"Fine!" He spat the word like a hickory nut. "Go. Waste your beauty. I shall not mourn you, traveler. *Hai!*" Caught up in a storm of weeping, Sanja fled the hall with waddling steps, leaving Mero utterly bemused.

Soon after, Malique barged into Mero's room, flanked by two of Sanja's guard. One of them carried Sheathless, its blade rolled up in cloth, the cord of Mero's whistle wrapped around its hilt.

"You leave now," Malique said, as the guard threw Sheathless down on the bed. "A horse waits for you at the eastern gate. I have orders to chop off your head if you are not out of the city by sundown."

He said this with a healthy measure of smugness. By his sour looks and rude remarks over the previous eight days, it was clear he was none too pleased about Mero and Sanja's budding relationship. His jealousy, of course, had been misplaced, but Mero hadn't bothered to address it then and saw no reason to address it now. His eyes had followed the arc of Sheathless's fall, and now he stepped over to the bed and unwrapped it with trembling fingers.

Malique caught his wrist. "No naked blades in the palace."

Mero turned to look at him. Only he didn't see Malique; he saw a wineskin filled with gallons of blood, heart pumping precious liquid from lungs to limbs to organs and brain.

Malique stepped back, his handsome face turning purple-gray. He opened his mouth to speak, glanced at the men behind him, then shut it, turned, and left without a word.

At the gates of the bazaar, a stony-faced soldier handed Mero the reins of a horse, a lithe mare with a spotted coat on whose hips hung a pair of bulging saddlebags. Mero took the reins with a nod of his head and led the horse out of the city at a walk.

They reached the threshold of the grasslands, and Mero paused to consider the view. It was a dull, windy day, neither cold nor overly hot. Tarnished clouds scudded across a wan, milky sky, their vast shadows prowling the earth below. Hills rose and fell in swells of dun and blackish-gray, tufts of silvery grass flashing in the stark light. Here and there a lone tree pushed out of the ground, stunted and barkless, its bare skin smooth as poured metal, its dry leaves rattling in the wind.

Mero's path streamed out before him: a deep depression carving through the spongy earth, a furrow made by a giant's plough. Where the bedrock rose close to the surface, the path disappeared, and where the earth grew soft again the banks on either side rose nearly to the height of a man.

Nodding vaguely to himself, Mero swung into the saddle. The mare dutifully started down the path. She stepped lightly, and with a surety of foot that revealed the quality of her breeding. Despite Mero's refusal of his advances, Sanja had spared no expense.

Trusting the mare to her business, Mero turned his attention inward. Though he hadn't wanted to admit it at the time, his days in Sanja's palace had done him good. His burns, though still not fully healed, now brought stiffness more than pain. Regardless of what Sanja had said about him being too skinny, he had gained several pounds since his days in the desert. Sheathless was in his hand and the goddess's whistle was around his neck. His path was unmistakable, a scar cut clear across the landscape. The world was stark and empty, its edges sharp, giving an impression not of age, but of agelessness, of old bones hardened to stone by the weathering of time. It suited Mero fine.

Part III

15

Half a month later, Mero squatted in the lee of a hill, battered by hail-stones roaring down from a pitch-black sky.

The wind, howling unimpeded across the empty plains, uprooted trees, tore hummocks of earth free from the bedrock, and turned pellets of hail to slingstones. There was no defending against the barrage. The storm had been raging for hours and showed no signs of abating, the near-constant streaks of lightning revealing nothing but an endless ceiling of cloud.

Mero's horse was gone, and with her, the saddlebags that had held his supply of food. He would never discover exactly what had happened to her, but he suspected she had been stolen. That was something no one had told Mero about the grasslands: they were crawling with outlaws of every stripe.

Only a few hours into the first day of his ride, Mero had sighted a group of men approaching from the east. They rode hard—he could tell by the way the metal of their bridles flashed in the sun. On an instinct born from years on the road, Mero dismounted, turned his horse off the path, and walked her into the tall grass between two hills. The hard blades sliced at Mero's ankles while the horses thundered by on the hill's other side. Mero took his lunch in the shade, only regaining the road when it was once again empty in both directions.

The next day Mero had come across the blackened remains of a small village. It had been abandoned for some time. The wood and peat had all but rotted away, leaving only thigh-high rings of moss-covered stone open to the sky. A low wind moaned though the empty thresholds, the dirt floors carpeted in blowing grass. Mero rode on.

On the third day Mero smelled smoke on the wind. Tying up his horse, he dropped into a crouch and picked his way to the top of a nearby hill. A strand of grass slid across his cheek like a razor, drawing a line of blood that went unnoticed until he was back in the saddle. Hunkered among the blades, he scanned the horizon for the source of the smell. He found it in the form of three narrow columns to the south. The fires had been set by men—if it had been a grass fire, the smoke would have risen in a single, unbroken wall.

Returning to his horse, Mero led her off the path and into the underbrush. It was hard going, but it was better than being seen.

Of course—Mero reflected, as the hail hammered against his skull— all of his caution had ultimately come to nothing. Earlier that evening, he had tied the mare to a withered old tree so he could clamber down the banks of a nearby river and fill his waterskin. He couldn't have been gone for a quarter of an hour, yet by the time he returned his horse was gone. The thief must have been following Mero for some time, waiting for the perfect opportunity to make away with her. After realizing what had happened, he had tried to follow her trail of hoofprints and the occasional snapped-off blade of grass, but had hardly begun his search when the first of the hailstones fell.

It was then Mero knew he had been utterly outsmarted. The timing was too perfect to be a coincidence. The thief, clearly able to read patterns in the clouds to which he himself was blind, hadn't just chosen the perfect moment to steal his horse—they had chosen the perfect moment of the perfect day.

Mero's fingers were numb—not from cold, as the evening was eerily warm despite the storm—but from pain. He wanted to tuck them under his arms, but that would have left his head exposed to the battering hail. It was deafeningly loud, the rattling of a million icy teeth. The wind buffeted him first from one side, then the other. He felt as though his eardrums had burst, and the gusts were pressing directly against his brain. The sky was black, the earth an ocean of white. Reaching down, Mero scooped up a fistful of hail.

That gave him an idea. Stretching out with a groan, he shoveled hail onto his legs, burying them under the white pellets. He moved on to his hips and then to his chest, reclining against the side of the hill as he worked. He made a cage in front of his face with his left hand and scooped hail over his own head with his right, letting it roll down his shoulders and arms. He worked until all the earth within arm's reach was bare, and he was encased, entombed, in a cocoon of ice.

Mero tucked his right hand under the ice as best he could, then took a few calming breaths and surveyed his work. It was far from perfect. Hailstones still smacked against the knuckles of his left hand,

and some slipped through to strike his eyes or lips. But the rest of him was shielded from the worst of the hail, and his armor only grew thicker as more of it fell.

Would it be enough to keep him alive through the night? Would he die of exposure in his sleep, or wake in the morning to find himself buried alive? Mero didn't have the answers to those questions, and the more time passed, the less he could bring himself to care. His eyes fluttered shut. The roaring of the hail filled his brain, leaving no room for thought. He forgot whether he was awake or asleep, whether this was the present or the past. If he only made it through the night, he could find his horse in the morning. The two of them could ride into the east together, Mero and the unnamed mare, to the mountains that twinkled like so many wise and caring eyes…

16

Mero woke to a blinding light, white rimed with blue, that slipped between the fingers of his outstretched hand. He stared at it, not knowing what it was, not knowing where he was or what he was doing. His head throbbed. If water was the medium for thought, his brain was a frozen river oozing into motion during the first thaw of spring.

He tried making a fist with his left hand. It was stuck, glued to the white ceiling above him. When he yanked it free, he left some of his skin behind. He punched at the ice until it gave way, then forced his hand into the open air and picked at his shell from the outside. He tried to free his right arm, but it was stuck, buried under the ice and crushed under his own weight.

Mero felt as weak as a newborn. As he continued to pick and slap at his cocoon to little effect, the desperate nature of his situation grew apparent. The ice was melting under the sun, turning to water that soaked through Mero's clothes and leached the last of the warmth from his body. He shivered—deep, wobbling shakes that spoke of a profound cold—and his breath came in shallow gasps. He had survived the night by a hair's breadth. Now morning would be his death if he couldn't break free.

He tried smashing the cocoon with his fist, and couldn't. He tried lifting it off his chest, and couldn't. He tried moving his legs to give himself more leverage, and couldn't. The more he moved his free arm, the more loose snow landed on his face, blinding him and burning his bare skin.

No, he found himself thinking. *No, No! What a stupid way to die!*

Stupid, the goddess agreed.

There came a sound from beyond the ice. Mero froze, certain he had imagined it. But there it was again: the crunch of boots tromping through the snow.

"Help," Mero tried to scream, but it came out as a whisper. "Help. Help."

The crunching went on. Mero couldn't tell from which direction it came, or from how far. He waved his arm in the air, though it felt ready to come free of his shoulder.

"Help," he croaked, though there was no chance the owner of the boots would hear—Mero barely heard it himself. "Help. Please."

The crunching faded. Mero wanted to scream.

NO! Don't leave me here!

His flailing hand found a loose lump of hailstone. Mero seized it and flung it as far as he could.

The stone rattled along the frozen ground.

The crunching stopped.

Mero strained his ears, blind with panic.

Then:

"*Oh!*"

It was a woman's cry. Mero waved and waved, his shoulder a cloud of agony.

The footsteps returned. Their owner was running towards him. Something thudded down next to him, a shadow behind the ice.

"Who's there?" the woman cried. "Can you hear me? Can you speak?"

A hand slipped into his own, fingers intertwining with his. Mero squeezed. The woman gasped and wrenched her hand free.

"Wait there," she said. "I need to find something to break the ice."

"No!" Mero pointed at his own shoulder with his free hand. "I can—feel—it's coming free." He opened his hand and waggled his fingers. "Pull my arm."

He feared she would refuse, but a second later her fingers closed around his wrist. Mero braced himself for pain, but the agony as she started to pull was blinding. He went limp, his vision swimming.

The woman stopped pulling. Her shadow dropped close.

"Are you all right?" she said.

"Why did you stop?" Mero asked.

"You were screaming!"

I was? Mero shook himself. "It doesn't matter. You need to keep going even if I scream."

The woman gasped. "You're mad."

"Do it!"

She took hold of his wrist again. Mero twisted, coiling his right arm under him.

"*Now!*"

The woman heaved. Mero bellowed, straining the cords of his neck. Inch by inch the cocoon cracked open. Mero's arm burned as though thrust into a fire. He pushed off with the other, struggling to get his legs beneath him, every part of him screaming. The woman screamed, too, as though she were in labor.

All of a sudden he was free. He rocked forward, ice sloughing off his body. The woman kept pulling, dragging him to his feet. He was standing—standing in the open air, the world a blur of white scarred by black. Then, just as quickly, he keeled over and fell, unable to support his own weight, unsure even of which way was up.

A pair of warm arms caught him, but it wasn't enough. Mero was heavier, and the woman's footing was poor. She slipped off her feet and the two of them went sliding down the hillside together, caught in a slurry of half-melted ice. Each time she tried to catch her breath, Mero slid away with her, and each time Mero tried to stand, she dragged him down to earth. So they tumbled thirty feet or more, until at last the ground leveled out.

For a while they lay panting in the snow, she splayed on her back, Mero curled on his side. He was soaked through, and shivering horribly, exposed to the wind.

The woman rolled onto her belly and crawled over to him. She put the back of her hand to his cheek and wiped the matted hair from his eyes. Her face was dark and round, her nostrils wide. Mero guessed her age around forty or fifty.

"You're lucky to be alive," she said.

Mero tried to answer, but could only cough.

"You need to get out of those clothes," the woman said. "Can you walk?"

Mero nodded. "I'll try."

She looped an arm around his waist and helped him to his feet. He wobbled like a newborn fawn.

"Where do you come from?" Mero asked his rescuer.

The woman looked at him sidelong, her expression guarded.

"How far do we have to walk?" he clarified.

"I have a sledge," she said. "You can ride on that."

Mero scanned the horizon. The earth was sealed under a layer of ice, humped and uneven, the odd tree or snarl of grass pushing up through the white. He shivered.

"I'd rather walk. It will keep me warm."

"You should strip," the woman said. "Those clothes are doing you more harm than good."

Mero shot her a glance, surprised. The woman's expression revealed no hint of lust or shame, just a stolid practicality. Wordlessly he reached for the hem of his shirt and drew it up over his head. It was when the goddess's whistle knocked against his sternum that he realized what was missing.

"Wait," he said. "We need to go back for my sword."

The woman's brow wrinkled, but Mero was already mounting the hill, slipping and sliding on the treacherous ground. Reaching the remains of his cocoon, he hunkered down and picked at the ice. Sheathless glimmered under his fingers.

A shadow fell over him as he worked.

"You are *dying*," the woman said. "Leave it. Come back for it later, if it means so much to you."

"I can't," Mero snapped, tickling Sheathless's hilt. The tips of his fingers had started to bleed.

With a huff the woman lifted her leg, and Mero leaned out of the way as she brought her heavy boot down. The ice cracked under her weight. Mero tossed a hunk of it aside and grabbed hold of Sheathless. The blade, slick and cold, came free as though greased. Mero stuck its point in the ground and used it to stand.

"Then, can we go?" The woman wore a look of stern disapproval.

Mero nodded. "Lead the way."

She led him to the far side of the hill, where a sledge sat wedged against a clump of grass. It was little more than a plank on two wooden runners. The corpses of about a dozen small animals lay in a neat row down its length.

"What are these?" Mero held one of the creatures up by the tail. It had long hind legs and the gnawing teeth of a rodent.

"We call them *hapi*. They come out after a storm. Some of them are drowned, and others go lame or get their legs stuck in the ice. Now take off your pants and wrap this around you," the woman added, shrugging out of her heavy fur coat. "If you are lucky, you might live to see tomorrow."

Mero did so gratefully, piling his sodden clothes on the sledge while the woman untangled its rope from a tuft of grass. They set off northwards, into the valleys on the far side of the road. Mero, shivering violently, kept the fur coat tight around his neck with one hand and gripped Sheathless with the other. The sun came and went, one minute plunging them into dusky shadow and the next dazzling them with reflected light.

"Does weather on the plains always change so quickly?" Mero asked.

The woman nodded, her eyes on the ground ahead. "Winter today, summer tomorrow. It's the way things have always been."

"Not always," Mero said, before he could stop himself. "Scholars say the changing of the seasons used to be much more predictable."

The woman shot him a strange look, as though he'd said something rude. It cost her a stumble on the ice. For a minute they walked in silence.

"You haven't asked my name," Mero said then.

"You haven't asked mine," the woman rejoined.

The remark stopped Mero short, giving the woman time to outpace him. Catching her up, he walked alongside her for a few paces. Finally he said,

"Well?"

"Well what?"

"What is your name?"

She treated him to another withering look. "My name is Ruya. And yours?"

"Mero."

Ruya snorted and kept walking. "Let's hope I have a chance to use it. You look gray as death."

"I'll survive. How far do we have to go?"

Ruya stopped to stretch her back, looking up at the sky as she did. Wetting her lips, she said, "Three miles, maybe four."

"We'll see it soon, then," Mero said. "What sort of place is it?"

He asked this because of the way Ruya had licked her lips before answering his last question, and now he saw it again—her hesitation, her wariness, the shifting of her eyes.

"It is a place to live," she said. "We call it Palta."

"Are they welcoming of travelers there?"

Ruya didn't answer. She took up the sledge and pulled it along, keeping her back to Mero as she did. He caught up again and took her arm.

"Ruya, what is it you're not telling me?"

"Let *go!*" she snapped, yanking her arm back. "Is this how you treat the one who rescued you?"

Mero released his hold. Ruya staggered backwards, gripping the sledge for balance. For a moment silence reigned, cut only by the trickle of water underfoot.

"It's true that I owe you my life," Mero said. "But that doesn't mean I'll follow you blindly into a place of danger. These grasslands are teeming with bandits. Any village that stands must either be well-hidden or know something of war. Which is it?"

"It is neither." Ruya's eyes were in shadow. "But I will tell you this. When we reach Palta, you mustn't be seen. I will sneak you into the village. You can stay at my house, rest, and get warm. As soon as you are well again, you must leave. Do you understand?"

"Not at all," Mero said. "Why can't I be seen?"

"Walk. You'll freeze to death."

But Mero wouldn't budge. "Why can't I be seen?"

Ruya twisted the rope in her hands. She glanced left and right, as if there were anything within miles that might hear them. Finally she stepped close.

"If I tell you," she said, "do you promise to do as I say?"

"Would *you* make that promise to someone you had just met?"

"I saved your *life*," she hissed.

"Even so."

Her mouth fell open. "Fine! You want to know why? I'll tell you."

She moved even closer. Their brows nearly touched. Mero waited, but Ruya didn't seem able to speak. She swallowed once or twice, as though the words had stuck in her throat. Then, drawing a deep breath, she straightened. The transformation was remarkable; it was as though a decade had been shaved off of her life. Meeting Mero's eye, she said,

"Palta is not safe—for you or anyone else. There is a giant—a wicked giant named Gorgol who lives in the mountains near the village. He came out of the east years ago, from a land beyond the grasslands, and now he rules over us all."

Mero was stunned. Stories about giants were one thing, but Ruya had spoken as though every word were fact.

"A giant?" he said, drawing the word out. "Do you mean a gigas?"

Hellhole, said the goddess.

It was Ruya's turn to look surprised. But she shook her head. "Gigas are said to be tall as mountains. Gorgol is not so big. He is maybe as tall as three houses."

"You have seen this Gorgol with your own eyes?"

Ruya's jaw clenched. "I have seen him more times than I could ever want. He comes to us when the moon is full. His face haunts my dreams, and I can smell his putrid breath whenever the wind blows from the north."

"I see," Mero said. "And what does he do, when he visits your people?"

"I will not say. It is too horrible for words."

"Is he a maneater, this Gorgol?"

She shook her head. "Worse."

Mero weighed his options. He wasn't sure how much of Ruya's story he believed, and her refusal to go into detail made knowing the risks difficult. Death he had faced before, and would again if necessary. But this Gorgol—if he really did exist—might have some other way of threatening Mero's mission.

Or, perhaps, of aiding it.

He came out of the east, Ruya had said. *From a land beyond the grasslands.*

"How long do we have until Gorgol's next visit?" Mero asked her.

"Not long. Maybe five days."

"And would I be safe in your home, if he came while I was there?"

Her answer came a second late. "I am not sure. He has told us he can smell a man from miles away, but that might be a lie. He lies all the time. I think you will be safe as long as you keep out of sight."

Mero nodded. "All right. I'll come."

17

They walked in silence for half an hour. Mero offered to take a turn pulling the sledge, but Ruya refused. She told him to put Sheathless down among the bodies of the *hapi,* but he refused, though holding the long, curved blade made it harder to keep her coat shut over his chest.

Eventually Palta came into sight. It was a fair-sized settlement, some hundred homesteads piled against the southern face of a wide, shallow hill. The houses near the center of the village were stone, and those forming the outskirts were mostly wood and peat.

Ruya gathered up the bodies of the *hapi,* gesturing for Mero to stretch out on the sledge.

"Lie down," she said. "You cannot be seen."

Mero didn't care to be put in such a vulnerable position, but it was too late to argue. His limbs were stiff, and worryingly, he had stopped shivering entirely. Putting a hand down for balance, he fell into the sledge and let Ruya adjust the fur coat and tuck the *hapi* in around him. Once he was concealed, she took up the rope again and set off.

All Mero saw as he slid into Palta was a thin sliver of sky. Bemused, he watched it drift by, listening to the snicker of the wooden runners. The rocking of the sledge was pleasant. Mero couldn't remember the last time he had taken joy in such a simple thing.

Then Ruya's dark face eclipsed his sight, and she tugged at his arm, hissing, "Get up, *get up!* We're here."

He blinked stupidly as she grabbed his feet and set them on the ground. Mero stood reflexively only to collapse against a wall of rough stone, cutting his arm and cheek. Grabbing his head to keep him from hitting it against anything else, Ruya steered him through a low doorway and into the space beyond.

Something scratched at Mero's neck. He threw it off, only for the blot of shadow in the corner to loom over him and mutter,

"Stop that. You need to keep warm."

The scratchiness returned, worse than before. Mero tossed and turned, trying to escape it, closing his mouth so it wouldn't get in.

"Why don't you just kill him?" Mero asked. "There are plenty of you. Enough to kill one giant."

"We are too afraid of him." Ruya sat over him, wiping the sweat from his forehead with a soft white cloth. "You would be, too, if you had lived under his heel for years."

"I'll do it," Mero said, struck by a sudden inspiration. He groped at his bedside with his right hand. "Where is it?"

"Where is what?"

"Sheathless. I need it."

Even in his current state, Mero heard the tightness of Ruya's answer. "Don't be ridiculous. That is the last thing you need right now. Go to sleep."

Mero rolled over, shivering. "I need it," he murmured. "I need it."

His stomach was eating him from the inside out. He was collapsing, caving in. Even the air he tried to push out of his lungs was heavy as lead, sucking back down inside him and settling in his gut. He wheezed, clutching at the air above his bed. His blankets were in a bundle on the floor.

A hand covered his mouth. Mero's eyes rolled. He kicked his feet and slapped at the bedframe, his heart climbing up his throat.

"*Mero!*" Ruya hissed. "What's the matter?"

I'm being murdered. Even as he thought it, he realized that the hand over his mouth was none other than Ruya's. He looked at her in shock and betrayal, and saw the naked fear on her face.

"Please," she whispered, shaking. "You have to be quiet, or we'll both get caught."

As quickly as it had come, the fight left him. He fell limply back on the bed and was still.

"What does he do?" he asked Ruya, over and over again.

"Stop asking me that," she snapped. She was sewing by the light of a thin, crooked taper pinched in an iron holder. The half of her face in the light looked younger than before, the other half older.

But Mero couldn't stop asking. Ever since Ruya had told him of the giant, the question had expanded to occupy his entire brain: what could possibly be worse than death?

"I would tell you to visit the pens and see for yourself," she said brusquely, "but then you'd be caught, and all the work I've put into keeping you alive would be wasted."

Mero was already half-asleep. After much insistence, he had convinced Ruya to bring Sheathless inside and lay it down next to him in bed. He gripped the handle now, his other hand flat against the blade. The metal was warm as blood.

Mero walked down shaded avenues, a cold wind tugging at his shirt. The earth was black, the sky rent by flashes of silver. Sheathless was in his hand, bright and keen. A wall of piled stone ran along the path by Mero's right side. The stones were smooth, round and white. Shadows pooled in the creases between them, forming ranks of silent, snarling faces. Mero realized they were not stones, but skulls, and reached out to caress them as he passed by. They snapped at his fingers, but could not touch him. They were dead, after all, and he was still alive.

A lowing sound came from the field beyond the wall. Mero quickened his pace, slipping from shadow to shadow on silent feet. He vaulted the wall and sprinted out across the plain. The lowing grew loud and panicked. Mero raced toward the sound, leaping into the darkness.

There was an impact, a tussle against the hard ground, and then warm, warm, warm.

18

The next day Mero woke without shivers or sweats, indeed without so much as a headache. He swung out of bed, marveling at how easily the movement came. He wanted to show Ruya how much he had improved, but she was out. Mero was alone, the shutters drawn, the tiny house dark and still. It was only two rooms, a bedroom and a kitchen. The walls were stone and the floor was beaten earth. There was only one bed; Mero had no idea where Ruya had been sleeping while he was sick. A brick of peat burned in the oven, filling the house with a sour, earthy smell.

Mero remembered vaguely that Ruya had often left the house while he was recovering, stepping out in the morning and returning before the sun fell. When she came home after a day's work, she was sometimes cold and other times sweaty and hot, but always smelling of manure and turned earth. The scents were locked in Mero's memory even as the rest had slipped away.

He opened the shutters a crack. A yellow sun was breaching the horizon, and the hills beyond the village were blanketed in fog. The day was new, and it would likely be hours before Ruya returned. Mero was restless. He wanted to ask her how many days it had been, how long he had before Gorgol arrived. More than anything, he wanted to know whether the giant had already come and gone.

Sheathless winked in the morning light.

To take his mind off the nagging in his gut, Mero took to pacing the length of the house, walking into the kitchen then doing a circle of the bedroom. His body performed as well as he could have hoped, but his mind was still sluggish. After days in the dark, he wanted nothing more than to be out in the fresh, cold air. On a peg by the threshold hung a grass coat that would have covered him entirely, but though he eyed the door of Ruya's house more than once, he wasn't foolish enough to step outside and test his luck. He drank some water, put another brick on the fire, then fell into bed to pass the time, waking to a reddening sky. Still Ruya wasn't home.

It was fully dark by the time Ruya's boots crunched on the threshold. When she stepped inside, a billow of cold wind stung Mero's cheeks and breezed between his legs. She shivered in her heavy coat, her lips purple, her cheeks dark. Her eyes were red and puffy.

"You're back," was all he could think to say.

Ruya glanced his way, struggling to peel off her coat. She moved like a woman of eighty years.

"You should be in bed," she said.

"I'm much better. Why were you out so late?"

She took a moment answering, as if wondering whether Mero should know.

"Barkar got out of the pens," she said finally. "Someone must have left the gate open. We were out looking for him."

"You name your cattle?" Mero asked, surprised.

"He isn't *cattle*," Ruya snapped.

"What is he, then?"

She pressed her lips together and shook her head. Ripping off her coat, she collapsed into a chair and buried her face in her hands. Mero stood over her, not knowing what to do or say. The silence stretched on, pressing against Mero's eardrums. Ruya's shoulders shook. From behind her hands came the occasional dry sob.

"Ruya," Mero said finally, "how many days has it been?"

She looked up at him. "What?"

"How many days has it been since you brought me here? Has Gorgol come to the village yet?"

Her mouth moved silently, as if she had to repeat his words to understand them. "Gorgol has not come. But the moon is ripe. It could be any day now. Tomorrow, even."

Mero hunkered in front of her. "What will happen when he comes? Do you go out to meet him? Does he come right down into the village? What does he take from you each month? A tax—a tithe?"

Ruya's color rose. She leaned in until their faces were inches apart.

"He takes *a human soul*," she hissed. "One we choose, and offer to him. For payment, he calls it, payment for keeping us safe from the bandits. But I would rather—" her voice caught, then strengthened— "I would rather see Palta burned to the ground!"

Mero felt cold. He searched Ruya's face for a hint of a lie and found none.

"Who will it be this month?" he asked. Then, suddenly worried: "Not you?"

She shook her head. "It will be Mosin. He was a hard worker once, but his light went out when his sister died. Now he spends his days getting drunk behind the water shed. I heard the other men talking about him—how they were planning on giving him a bottle of wine and tying him up while he was asleep."

"How long has this been going on?"

"Longer than I have lived here. Many generations, I think. None of us are very old. We give the old to Gorgol."

"Where did he live before he arrived in Palta?" Mero pressed. "You said he came from a land beyond the grasslands. Has he ever spoken about other parts of the world?"

"I don't know. He has told us so many things."

"Like what?"

"That his mother was a mountain and his father was a fart!" Ruya shouted suddenly. "That he can jump to the moon and catch a cloud in his fist. That he can eat a mouthful of dirt and shit it out as gold. What do you care? It's all lies. He is a wretched, disgusting creature, and I wish he would choke on his lies and die a thousand deaths!"

Mero reached out to her, sensitive of the loudness of her voice. Ruya's neighbors were certain to find it strange to hear her shouting to herself in her home. But she slapped his hand away and stood over him.

"You are so healthy and strong," she said acidly. "And more curious than ever. I think you can leave, now. It's clear you have no more use for me."

"I can't leave yet," Mero said quietly.

"Why not?"

"I need to meet with Gorgol first."

19

Mero woke to a soft hand on his shoulder. He rolled over, squinting in the light that slanted through the shutters.

Ruya's face swam into view. Tears had carved dark tracks on her cheeks.

"Gorgol is coming today," she said. "Lias took Mosin away so he wouldn't hear. They will fetch him in an hour or so. With luck he will be asleep by then."

She stepped away without another word, leaning on the walls and furniture for support. Mero rose slowly, his eyes on the back of Ruya's head. Their argument the previous night had been vicious and uncompromising. She had called him mad, selfish, even a monster—yet this morning she spoke to him as though nothing had happened. Only sadness and dread remained, a miasma that infected the air inside the tiny house.

"What will you do?" he asked her knot of dark hair.

"I must be there. Gorgol demands we all bear witness to his evil. It makes his cock swell to frighten us."

"And me?" Mero said.

She wheeled around. "Stay. Here," she said, in the tones one took with a dog. "It's not too late for you to take Mosin's place. Strangers always go to Gorgol first, even sooner than drunkards do."

Mero nodded. "All right."

Ruya eyed him suspiciously, but said nothing else. She cooked a pot of porridge for breakfast, though had none herself, looking away as Mero ate. She took the empty pot to the rain barrel and washed it, then donned her coat and told Mero not to leave the house, no matter what he heard.

When she opened the door, Mero caught a glimpse of other figures walking down the street, for the first time since he had arrived in Palta. Then Ruya slipped outside and pulled the door shut behind her, once more leaving him alone.

He sat on the bed and took up Sheathless, laying the blade across his thighs. It was easy to forget how big the sword was. Its blade was almost as wide as his palm. He watched his reflection in the metal and counted the minutes until he reckoned half an hour had passed. Then he rose, crossed over to the threshold, and took the grass coat from its peg. It was bulky and coarse, made from heavy grassland blades woven into an animal's hide. Its shape was conelike; Mero felt like a haystack with it on. But it was tall enough to cover him from his head nearly to his feet, and spacious enough to hide Sheathless inside. Satisfied with his disguise, Mero opened the door a crack. The streets were deserted. He slipped outside.

It didn't take long for him to find the town square. There was a pull, a tension in the air that drew him down the ancient streets. Groups of women and men ran together like raindrops on the fan of a leaf, none of them speaking, all of them moving in the same direction. Mero followed at a safe distance, the taste of electricity on his tongue. The day was raw, the sky the color of an open wound.

The crowd filled the square and spilled into the streets nearby. Mero counted some four hundred souls, men, women, children, and infants. Their skin ranged in color from pale olive to ebony black. The men wore coats and the women heavy dresses. A few wore grass coats like Mero's own. No one seemed to be talking, yet a constant undercurrent of voices suffused the air.

All faces were turned to the north.

Mero took his place at the back of the crowd, half-hidden in the space between two houses. The street sloped downwards, offering him a good view of the square. His vision was a thin vertical strip between curtains of grass, but he didn't dare open his coat.

As one, the village waited. Men shuffled their feet and swatted at insects. Women held their children close. A baby started to cry and was quickly silenced. All the while, hundreds of eyes scanned the hills to the north.

Suddenly a young man broke from the crowd and ran across the square, neck pumping like that of a horse. Shouts followed after him, and he was soon intercepted and borne to the ground. Mero was confused. The man was too young to be the Mosin of whom Ruya had spoken. What reason did he have to run?

The sun climbed, bleeding orange into the sky. Mero sweated in his coat.

"*Mama!*" a child shouted.

A low groan passed through the crowd. The townsfolk bent like stalks of corn under the wind. More than one shrieked aloud. Near the front of the crowd a child started screaming, and wouldn't stop no matter how many times they were shushed.

Mero glanced at the ridge where the villagers' eyes were pointed. A freezing hand gripped his testicles, another closing around his throat. He stood paralyzed, gasping for air.

A head peeked over the hill. It was enormous; Mero could have stood inside the skull. It was vaguely human, though there was an apelike aspect to it. The mouth was too wide, the cheeks and jaw jutting out, the eyes sunken back below a heavy brow. And what eyes they were: a lurid, intoxicating purple, hungry and sucking like the view from the top of a cliff. The jelly was translucent, revealing every vessel and vein. The pupils snaked back into the skull like two fleshy tunnels.

The head shifted, and the giant's footfall rumbled through the earth as he emerged from behind the ridge. Gorgol was not as big as his head suggested he would be. Indeed, it was much larger in proportion to his body than a man's would be, fully spanning the width of his shoulders, melting into his arms and chest without so much as a suggestion of a neck. His limbs were long and stringy, tendons thick as mooring ropes writhing under his skin. His flesh was dark, red mixing with blue to make a mottled purple. He was much hairier than a man, adding to the impression of an enormous ape. His hair grew thickest around his groin, the base of his skull, and the backs of his elbows and knees.

Wordlessly Gorgol advanced on the square, the ground trembling with his every step, his globular eyes sweeping the crowd. His lips smacked and peeled back in a grin, revealing teeth like a row of tombstones.

"Fair day to you, kindred!" Gorgol cried, spreading his arms wide. "I've come to prevail upon your kindness once again. Yes, I'm afraid to say I've grown peckish. Though who can blame me—it's been most of a month since I ate."

The Paltans at the front of the crowd shrank from his voice, though they had nowhere to go, trapped as they were by those behind. Mero was wretchedly grateful to be standing at the back of the crowd. He didn't think he could move his legs if his life depended on it.

"Who shall it be?" Gorgol was saying. "I do hope you've chosen."

A man at the front of the crowd shouted something. Gorgol hunkered down, tilting his head to listen. His mouth moved constantly, as though he were working a piece of gristle from his teeth.

"Well, all right," he said peevishly. "But hurry up, now, don't keep me waiting. It's been a long walk down from the mountains, and a hungry one too. You know I practically starve myself for your sake. It could easily be two a month, or even ten! But I know that wouldn't be fair. It's this swollen heart of mine. I could never bring myself to cheat others. It will be the death of me someday, I'm certain of it."

A pair of men detached themselves from the crowd and ran off, undoubtedly to fetch the hapless Mosin. A terrified silence fell. Gorgol, squatting on his haunches, dug a finger into the hair of his collar and scratched. Flakes of dead skin fluttered to the ground. Children screamed.

"Poor weather, this month," Gorgol mused, still scratching. "The raiders are out in force, and more desperate than ever. I smell them, you see, from miles away, and when I do, down I come from the mountains to chase them off. Such wicked folk! They would slaughter the lot of you without a thought. Oh yes, and burn your crops and rape your women. They're not proper men at all, not if you ask me. More like beasts disguised as men. But enough about them. I wouldn't want to scare you."

His scratching complete, Gorgol examined the results of his handi-work. His nails were long and green, his fingers black. He tasted one and smacked his lips. Mero heard it clearly from his vantage point.

"Now, where are they?" Gorgol muttered. "If they take much longer, I might have to choose for myself." He grinned as those at the front of the crowd shrieked. "Ho ho ho! I'm only joking. I have patience enough to respect your choice, even if the ones you feed me aren't always to my liking. Yes, I could have better meals if I wished, but I let you pick as a favor to you. This way you can rid yourselves of the laggards in your midst. Really, you ought to thank me for taking Palta's chaff off your hands. A man is worth only as much as his contribution to society. Wouldn't you agree?"

No one answered, possibly because it wasn't clear who Gorgol was speaking to. He sniffed and scratched his armpit, yawning hugely.

There came a commotion a couple streets over. A group of men shouted to be let through, and the Paltans fell over each other in their hurry to obey. The crowd parted, and four men emerged, carrying a fifth between them. He was bound hand and foot, a wooden bit forced between his teeth. He was a big, heavy-set man, and was struggling fiercely. His face was red; he was trying to scream around his bit. The other four men cursed with the effort of holding him still.

Chills swept Mero as Mosin was half-carried, half-dragged towards the square. Gorgol's chatter fell off, the pink throats of his pupils fixed on the procession. His nostrils flared, the mottling under his flesh writhing.

"There you are," he purred. "Come up, come up. I haven't got all day."

Mosin screamed louder, spit dribbling around the bit and onto the ground. He was drunk—Mero could tell from the way he moved—but not nearly drunk enough.

The procession of men reached the square, the rift in the crowd closing behind them. Mosin struggled to the last, whipping his head back and forth as though trying to break his own neck. The men carrying him seemed little happier to approach the giant than Mosin himself, and the last few steps to Gorgol's feet took some time.

"Untie him, untie him." Gorgol breathed heavily, and wouldn't stop smacking his lips together.

The men bent to do as asked. Silence thrummed. Mero counted ten beats of his heart.

Then Mosin was free, and he scrambled to his feet and ran, head down, neck pumping, bare feet slapping on the stone.

Gorgol pounced.

Never would Mero have thought that such a large creature could move so quickly. Gorgol threw himself at Mosin's back, his long, hairy arms swinging out. The crowd shrieked, recoiling as a tide, a single organism driven by instinct. Gorgol pinned Mosin to the ground, pressing him down with both hands around his trunk, squatting over him like a child catching a toad by the riverbank. And like a toad, Mosin squirmed under his grip.

Gorgol, grinning his graveyard grin, stuck a nail in the waistband of Mosin's pants and tugged. It was a delicate gesture, dainty even, but Mosin's entire body was dragged along with it, scraping backwards on the cobbles. Mosin yelped, his palms flashing up in supplication, then slapping back down.

Gorgol gave another tug, harder than the first. "Come on, now," he muttered.

On the third tug Mosin's pants fell to tatters around his knees. As the giant pressed his face into the ground, Mero caught a wink from his bare backside. It was almost comically pale, at odds with the ruddiness of its owner's face, out of place and terribly exposed.

Holding Mosin fast with one hand, Gorgol raised the other to his face. He made a pinching motion, as if plucking a bird from the sky with his first finger and thumb. For a moment nothing happened. Then Gorgol's fingers started to shake, creating the strange illusion that his nails were growing. A second later Mero realized it was no illusion at all. The nails of Gorgol's finger and thumb slid from their sheaths with a dull rasping sound, growing and growing until they were as long as the fingers themselves.

Gorgol smiled with the satisfaction of a job well done, nibbling a bit of waste out from under one of the blades before turning his attention back to Mosin.

No, Mero thought, though even now he couldn't fathom what was about to happen. He only knew that Mosin's naked rump was winking in the air, and Gorgol was bending over him with a look of ferocious concentration on his face, the pink worms of his pupils opening wide like hungry mouths. Mero's bowels pressed against his perineum. His legs shook, and he leaned against the wall for support. He couldn't remember ever feeling this way while Sheathless was in his hand.

Gorgol crouched down, wielding his elongated fingernails as a surgeon might a pair of forceps. He lowered his hand down between Mosin's legs, then, eyes narrowed to a hairline crack, eased them forth.

If Mosin had been screaming before, it left no word for the noise he made now. It was the howl of an animal that knows its death has come and can do nothing to stop it, that is simply venting, expunging, squeezing out its last drop of energy in an effort to hasten the end, or at least shut out knowledge of it. Mero knew it well. It was the sound he himself had made when tied to Menahem's rock. Only Mero had had the goddess's whistle, while Mosin had nothing at all.

The tendons in Gorgol's arm writhed as the giant carried out his work. His eyes rolled up, and his tongue hung from the side of his mouth, a pink slug glistening in the sun. With each jerk of his arm, Mosin was pulled one way or another, bucking and heaving like a horse trying to throw its rider. Blood gushed between his legs. Streaming onto the cobbles below, it formed an expanding pool of red that drove the crowd yet further back.

Why doesn't somebody help him? Mero thought.

Mosin gibbered, froth gathering around the bit in his mouth. His arms and face shone with sweat. Still Gorgol bent over him, still Gorgol's long nails did their unspeakable work, still Gorgol's nostrils flared in anticipation.

Several children were by now screaming, the men and women of Palta shivering together in a single, huddled mass.

"There we are, it's nearly out," Gorgol growled.

A sickly taste swam around Mero's mouth. He spat it out hastily, though he would have been far from the first who had vomited. He couldn't look, couldn't look away, couldn't breathe, couldn't do anything.

Gorgol let out an excited gasp. Pressing Mosin flat to the ground, he withdrew his questing hand. It came free with a hideous sucking sound. More blood splashed onto the cobbles.

The giant drew up to his full height. Towering over the square, blotting out the rising sun, Gorgol brandished his prize. It was a tiny organ like a dark blue heart, round and wet, pinched between the giant's nails like a single grain of desert sand. The giant's eyes grew wide—wider—wider still, until they looked like they might burst from his skull. And he grinned, showing more—more—still more teeth, until his smile had become an infernal rictus, an abominable parody of joy. His mouth opened wide—out gusted the sickening stench of the winds of hell—and his tongue stuck out, a quivering, fleshy carpet.

Gorgol dropped the organ onto his tongue. He closed his eyes and then his jaw. And it just so happened that when he bit into his prize for the first time, Mero was watching the huddled shape of Mosin at his feet. The very instant the giant's teeth came down, a shudder passed through Mosin's body, and he collapsed like a puppet whose strings had been cut. There he lay prone in his puddle of blood, while Gorgol's teeth ground like millstones and the smacking of his lips echoed across the empty hills.

𝔇𝔒

Eventually a group of villagers came to take Mosin away. Mero knew the man must be dead, yet he moaned faintly as he was dragged from the square. Gorgol savored his meal for some time, rubbing his belly and swaying on his feet as though caught up in some pleasant memory. Blood dripped from the fingers of his right hand; the nails had returned to their normal size. At length he wandered to the far end of the square and sat down with a sigh. He scratched absently at the hair of his neck, burying his finger to the second knuckle.

"That's that, I suppose," he said. "My, but it's always over so quickly. Sometimes I can't help but feel I'm getting the short end of the bargain. Just one a month! Oh, but listen to me go on. Off with you, then. I'm sure you've plenty of work to do. I'll see you when the moon turns again. Try to make it a woman next time, won't you? I'm sick of all these hairy, wine-sopped men. *Fagh!*"

Mero only half-heard. Shock had stuffed his ears and nose and eyes with cotton, leaving the world dull and distant, the hard edges rounded off. So it was he didn't realize the Paltans had been given leave to disperse until the sea of bodies washed over him. Most of the villagers had their heads down and their arms around their loved ones, and a dozen or more had already passed him by without incident. But it was only a matter of time before someone slowed before this figure in the grass coat who hadn't yet turned from the square. After the first came a second, and then a third, and then a man who stopped in the middle of the road and peered into Mero's coat with suspicious eyes, and finally called in a strident voice, "Who are *you*?"

Mero saw only one path before him. He couldn't run, not with the crowd pressing in on all sides. Nor could he hope to bluff his way out, not in the village of Palta where every life was accounted for, its usefulness weighed against its neighbors.

With a surge of his shoulders, he threw off his grass coat and brandished Sheathless. His questioner shrank from the sight of the naked blade. Mero pushed past him and made for the square, cutting through the crowd with Sheathless as his prow. The Paltans melted out of his way, gasping and pointing. Mero didn't dare break his pace; the slightest stumble and the spell would be broken.

Gorgol soon took notice of the unquiet spreading through his audience. On the surface the giant's easygoing manner remained unchanged. He scratched under his arm and drove a finger up his nose. But his eyes—his eyes were like ruptured organs, exploding stars, and once they found Mero they never left him for an instant, though Gorgol turned his head and pretended to look away.

The wind changed, and Mero caught a blast of the giant's scent. It was sour, putrid, the stink of a diseased animal mingled with the reek of feces. He held his breath as he stepped around the pool of Mosin's blood. Gorgol curled his lips into an apelike smile.

"Now yours is a face I haven't seen before," he said. "You aren't from around here—or else someone has been keeping secrets. What is your name, traveler?"

"I am called Mero." It took all of his concentration to keep his voice steady. He gripped Sheathless, drawing strength from its weight.

"Mero," Gorgol said. Suddenly he lunged forward, reaching out with a blood-stained hand. Mero was paralyzed, the rank air displaced by the giant blowing down his throat, suffocating him. But Gorgol only pricked his finger on Sheathless's tip, causing the blade to hum.

"That's quite the blade you've got there, little Mero. Thinking of sticking me with it, are you?"

Mero's heart clanged. The contact, though brief, had given him a dose of the giant's strength. It was overwhelming. Images of Mosin swam in his mind's eye. Mosin, his buttocks pink in the sun. Mosin, laying sprawled in a pool of his own blood while Gorgol stood over him, savoring his meal. Sheathless's point quivered.

Stay calm! Mero admonished himself.

Calm, the goddess echoed gravely.

He lowered his sword. Gorgol's face grew sly.

"Changed your mind?"

"I've come to speak with you," Mero said.

Gorgol's grin widened, rows of graying teeth leering down.

"Is that so? Then by all means regale me. There's nothing like a good conversation to stimulate the digestion." Gorgol scratched himself, looking pensive. "How fortunate for you—and how unfortunate for poor Mosin—that you should appear the very instant my meal is concluded. You must have the devil's own luck, as they say, little Mero, eh? Ho ho ho!"

"I heard rumors of a giant in Palta," Mero said. "I've been watching the passes to the north, waiting for you to show yourself."

Gorgol swatted his words away. "Now, now—lies won't do you any good here. I can smell them, you know. Yes, a liar has a special smell all his own, and it's a stink I find quite untenable. So let's not waste our time fouling the air, you and I. Why don't you tell me why you're here?"

Mero hesitated, gauging his opponent. "I heard you are wise and well-traveled. There's a place I'm trying to find, far to the east of here."

"Oh?" said the giant.

So Mero told him about the range of mountains he had seen in his dreams, the sheer peaks and twinkling lights, the black lake smooth as glass. His memories of the vision were imperfect, blots of light and shadow scattered across his mind's eye. It was easy to believe he had imagined the whole thing, that the mountain range did not exist and had never existed. But Gorgol smiled as soon as he had finished his description.

"Oho," he said, plucking his bottom lip. "You were right to come to me. Of the creatures that walk this earth, I am perhaps the most worldly of all."

Hope flared bright in Mero's heart. "Then you know this place?"

"Of course I know it. But you've got the wrong idea—those aren't mountains you're talking about. The place you described is a city of the old world. Uron is its name."

Uron, Mero thought, enshrining the name deep in his mind. Then, working backwards from the name: *a city?*

That couldn't be right. Mero had seen remnants of the old world before. Nearly every traveler had—the ruins of old roads, cities, and waterways speckled throughout the world, reminders of previous ages of men come and gone. But Mero had never heard of an entire city preserved intact on the scale Gorgol was suggesting. And yet, the more he compared the idea to what he had seen in his visions, the more sense it made.

Not mountains, but towers. Not stars, but lights.

Uron. A city of the old world, far in the east. Could *this* be the place the goddess had shown him, time after time?

"What more can you tell me about this Uron?" Mero asked.

"It is a dismal place. Some call it cursed—a city of ghosts. It sits in the eye of a poison lake, and blood-sucking beasts are said to roam its streets." Gorgol spoke with undisguised delight.

"How far is it from here?"

Now Gorgol laughed, his vast belly heaving. "I could jog there in two days and a night. But you? You seem lively enough, but your legs are short. It would take longer—much longer, yes."

Mero steeled himself for his next question. "Can you show me the way?"

"And leave these poor folk unguarded?" Gorgol spread his arms, indicating the square full of people. The Paltans shuddered, as they did every time the giant moved. "No, I couldn't. It just wouldn't be fair. They depend on me for protection, you know. They're my responsibility."

This was beyond absurd, yet Gorgol spoke with such sincerity that for just a moment Mero wondered if he, at least, was convinced of the truth of his words. Then he looked into the giant's eyes, and realized two things: first, that Gorgol knew his lie for the nonsense it was, and second, that he didn't care in the slightest that Mero knew as well.

Mero's fear of Gorgol, kept at bay by their talk of Uron, bubbled to the surface. Some invisible force—the crowd at his back, or perhaps the wind itself—was drawing him closer and closer towards Gorgol's grinning face. He was struck by a sudden vision of being swept up into the giant's gullet, past his slablike teeth and into the pit of his stomach.

"There must be something you can do," he said. "I can pay—in labor, or in coin, if you give me time to raise some." *I can bring warm bodies to you*, he thought but didn't say.

Gorgol scratched his neck. "Payment, you say? My, my, my. Why should you be so eager to reach that wretched place? Going there could spell your death."

"I don't care," Mero said. "I have business there."

"Mm." Gorgol scratched and scratched, tilting his head back to hit the right spot. He gave every impression of being lost in thought, yet Mero caught him stealing glances his way.

At length, Gorgol said, "Well. If it's that important to you, I suppose we could work something out. But listen here. Whatever price we agree on cannot only benefit me, but also the poor Paltans, who will be deprived of their guardian's presence for as long as we are gone. By which I mean, there are not two, but three parties to consider here. Don't you agree?"

"Yes," Mero said.

Gorgol grinned. "I see you are a man of great intelligence, with a sense for what is fair and right in the world. In that case, here is what I propose. My agreement with the Paltans states that I am to have one meal each month in payment for my services. Given that I have just now eaten, we have until the moon turns again before my next meal. If we reach Uron in that time, I will consider the favor small enough that no payment is necessary. But if we do not—" and here he leaned forward, smiling, smiling—"*you* must take the place of my next dinner guest."

He leaned back. "Wouldn't you say that's a fair bargain? If you're swift enough, there's no cost to you at all—and if you aren't, the Paltans will have earned one month's reprieve. Rather generous terms, as I'm sure you'll agree."

Mero didn't agree, or couldn't. The pool of blood left by Mosin was still in his periphery. He swore the dark blotch was getting steadily larger. The charnel stench of Gorgol's meal hung about the square: feces and blood, fear and sweat.

This is your fate, if you don't reach Uron in time.

"How long will it take to reach the city?" he asked, knowing the answer before it came.

Gorgol's eyes positively twinkled. "Why, that's up to you, isn't it?"

And that was that. Mero was left with nowhere to go, nothing left to stall with, nothing to do but provide an answer to Gorgol's proposition. The giant knew the way to Uron, or at least claimed he did. More importantly, Mero was now known to the Paltans. What would they do to him if he refused Gorgol's offer? Would he go free? Of course not. Provided Gorgol didn't simply eat him here and now, they would rush him, bind him, and toss him in someone's cellar to await the next full moon. A month from now he would be in this very spot, only his arms and legs would be bound, a wooden bit forced between his teeth: fodder for the giant.

The more he turned it over in his mind, the more he realized he didn't have a choice at all.

"All right," he said. "I accept your offer. You will show me to the city of Uron. If we reach it before the moon turns, we will part ways amicably. If not—" his throat stuck—"you can extract your price from me."

Gorgol loomed over him, grinning. Mero could see the waste trapped in his teeth, the individual hairs sticking out from his nose. The giant reached out, and Mero shied away, but he was only offering his hand to shake. Mero took it, or rather held out his arm and let it be taken between Gorgol's first finger and thumb, the very same fingers with which he had violated Mosin. Gorgol held him delicately, and did not shake. Even so, his slightest movement threatened to tear Mero's arm from its socket.

Just as Mero started to think that Gorgol had no intention of releasing his hand, the giant did just that. He stood with a groan and sucked in a great breath. Blowing it out, he said,

"A good deal and well-struck! Then, let's be off."

Now? "I'll need some time to prepare for the road."

"Oh?" Gorgol's lips wriggled—he was struggling to hold back a grin. "Well, that's your choice. You're the pace-setter here. Only remember that the moon will change in twenty-eight days, however fast or slow we go."

Mero felt as though he'd swallowed a rock. Of course—the race had begun even before they had struck their deal. His time was already running out, precious seconds slipping between his fingers with every breath.

His heart raced. The terror growing in his stomach was made all the worse by its familiarity. It was an old fear, one Mero hadn't felt in a long, long time, but he recognized it at once. He would never forget it as long as he lived.

Sand falling through the glass.

He wanted to clutch his heart and scream, wanted to tear his hair out by the roots. His eyesight failed, black curtains drawing shut from the outside in. He gripped Sheathless, tried to draw power from its weight, but the monster remained. Sheathless couldn't save him, not from this.

I thought I had beaten you.

Beaten, said the goddess.

"Why, little Mero, you've gone rather pale." Gorgol's voice was all concern, but his pupils danced like flayed snakes. "I hope it isn't my breath. Ho ho ho!"

"We're leaving," Mero said. It came out as a bark. "Show me to Uron."

If Gorgol was taken aback, he didn't show it. He rose again, sniffing at the wind. "Of course. I'm eager as you to be off, you know. Follow me, little Mero. And as for you," he addressed the Paltans, "be good while I'm gone. Have lots of babies. I'll be back soon enough. You'll know me by the growling of my stomach. Ho ho ho!"

21

Mero left the village of Palta on foot, with no clothes but the ones on his back and no food but Ruya's half-digested oatmeal sloshing around in his stomach. It was very well he hadn't thrown it up — who knew when his next chance to eat would come?

The sun had worked its patient alchemy on the carpet of hail covering the grasslands. The hills were an ugly patchwork of white ice, black mud, and silvery grass, runnels of clear water flashing in the valleys between them. It was cold enough that Mero could see his breath. He bitterly regretted leaving Ruya's grass coat behind. How could he have been so foolish as to start a journey without the least bit of preparation?

Gorgol walked ahead of him, swinging his long arms back and forth, the earth groaning under his weight. It was perverse to see him strolling along on this bright, sunny day, naked as a babe, the long, wiry hairs of his groin and nape blowing in the wind. His buttocks were wrinkled, mottled red and blue like the rest of him. Every so often he reached back to dig a finger into the space between them. His pace was leisurely; whenever he inevitably left Mero behind, he would sit on a hummock and play with his toes or simply stand, swaying, and watch the clouds pass by overhead.

Once a bird with a long neck and slender gray body, possibly scared from its nest by Gorgol's passing, made the mistake of passing within arm's reach of the giant.

CLACK! Gorgol clapped his hands faster than Mero could blink. The resulting noise was so loud that his own ears pounded as if boxed. By the time he recovered, the giant was advancing on him, his hands clasped together. A blizzard of gray feathers fluttered around him.

"Got her!" Gorgol crowed. He opened his hands. A mangled carcass, the neck folded double on itself, fell spiraling at Mero's feet. A lifeless, beady eye stared up at him.

"There, see? I've caught you dinner. No, no need to thank me. I wouldn't hear of it. But hold on to her—food is hard to come by in these parts. Now let's press on, shall we?"

Mero wanted nothing to do with the murdered bird, but it was true he had nothing to eat. He picked up the carcass and hung it by its neck through the loop of his belt.

It was easy enough, that first day, for Mero to forget the predicament he was in. He matched Gorgol's pace as best he could, keeping his eyes to the east as though hoping to catch a glimpse of Uron on the horizon. He stole glances at his traveling companion whenever he dared, watching for any sign of a weakness. But as far as he could tell, Gorgol had none. He was simply a huge brute, stronger, faster, and possibly smarter than Mero himself. Whether or not his claims about his sense of smell were true mattered little. He was still more giant than one man could handle, even if that man had Sheathless as a weapon.

By the time the sun was red and setting, the hills of the grasslands had risen into a shallow range of mountains, lumpy and black like a bed of coals. The ground was dry, made of loose, shifting rock. There was not a hint of green to be seen anywhere.

"Why, look at that." Gorgol scratched his belly, looking back the way they'd come. "You'd hardly think we'd moved at all."

Mero glanced over his shoulder. Palta was a dark smear on the horizon, wisps of smoke rising from its many chimneys. It indeed looked much closer than he would have liked.

He turned back around. "Let's press on. We still have some light left."

Gorgol blew out his cheeks and smiled. "Whatever you say. Mind you don't twist an ankle."

They picked their way through the foothills, but it soon became clear that it was pointless to go any further. Ever since Gorgol had told him not to twist an ankle, Mero had grown silently fearful he would do just that, and his pace had slowed to a crawl. He found meagre shelter at the foot of a steep, rocky slope, and informed Gorgol he was turning in for the night.

"I think I'll carry on a bit," Gorgol said. "All this exercise is doing me good. Oh, don't worry about me. I can see quite well in the dark."

Mero was all too glad to see Gorgol's back, though he didn't for a second believe what he said about exercise. Huddled in the dark, he wondered what Gorgol was really doing with his time.

That brought him to the problem of the bird. He had had plenty to drink that day thanks to the abundant snowmelt, but his stomach was empty and growling. His strength wouldn't last if he couldn't find anything to eat, and Gorgol had dropped this meal into his lap. However, he had no way of making a fire. Even if he gathered blades of grass from the hills below, and even if they were dry enough to burn, he had nothing to light them with. The bird wouldn't last very long uncooked.

If he was going to eat it, he would have to eat it raw.

He sat contemplating his options, the darkness pressing against his eyeballs. In the end he decided against it. His chances of gaining anything of use from the meal were about as good as his chances of throwing it all up or shitting it all out. The last thing he needed in this race was to spend the next week of it with his intestines tied into knots. So he built himself a small windbreak out of loose stones and curled up with his hands pillowed beneath his head, shivering and miserable, drinking the spittle off his tongue and cursing the name of Gorgol the giant.

Mero woke to a soft, rhythmic breathing, not his own but deeper, louder. His eyes flew open and there was Gorgol, laying on his side not twenty paces off, his flabby belly hanging down, his head propped up on one elbow in a rakish pose. He breathed deeply, each breath washing over Mero in a hot wind, blowing the hair from his face and filling his nostrils with the stench of rotting meat. His eyes bored into Mero like worms.

"Ah, you're awake," he said, as Mero scrambled to his feet. "I thought you might sleep the day away."

"Where were you all night?" Mero asked.

Gorgol laughed heartily. "Just stretching my legs…seeing how much of the old country I remembered. It really doesn't change, you know. The old pass away, new generations take root, but it's the same old earth below." He pointed his nonexistent chin at the carcass hanging from Mero's waist. "What's the matter? You haven't eaten that bird I caught you."

"I have nothing to cook it with," Mero said.

Gorgol smacked his forehead. "Silly me! And now you've gone hungry all night. Well, no matter. Your luck is certain to change soon enough, mm?"

Mero's stomach growled. "Yes," he said. "Certain."

He struck camp—only there was nothing to strike—and they set off. Mero's legs tingled, and his vision darkened when he stood. He fetched a rock from the side of the path and stuck it in his mouth to suck on.

The morning was clammy and gray, a cold mist shortening Mero's horizons. From what he could tell, there wasn't much to see other than piles of rock. Gorgol strolled along, tackling the uneven path with infuriating ease, half-disappearing into the mist while Mero scampered along behind. By the end of the first hour Mero's heart was racing, and the ends of his fingers were numb. He hadn't had so much as a mouthful of water, and his throat was raw from cold.

All this, and only the second day, he thought.

They climbed at a steady rate, zigzagging to avoid the steeper peaks, their progress agonizingly slow. Mero reversed his grip on Sheathless and used it as a walking stick. The *TINK, TINK, TINK* of metal on stone formed a shrill counterpart to the crunch of Gorgol's footfalls.

"Aren't you worried it will break?" Gorgol asked.

"No," Mero said.

"Quite the weapon," the giant said. "Wherever did you get it?"

"I made it."

Gorgol's eyes lit up. "Is that so?"

His tone made it clear he wanted to know more, but Mero wasn't about to satisfy him. He kept grimly on, Sheathless's keen point biting into the rock below.

At long last the sun came out, burning away the worst of the mist. Mero's world unfolded like an opening flower. Palta was still in sight behind, though they had gained more height than Mero realized. They were well and truly into the mountains now. Ahead of them stretched a highland dotted with stunted trees, tufts of gray-yellow grass, and pools of water ranging in size from puddle to lake. Mero squatted next to one to see if he would finally have his drink. The water was standing, its smell brackish, its depths black as ink. Tiny insects gathered in clouds near the surface. Mero wished he were a dragonfly, or a fish.

There came a rush of air by Mero's cheek. Gorgol bore down on him, his enormous head terrifyingly close, his mouth open and grinning. He scrambled out of the way, grabbing for Sheathless—but Gorgol only flattened himself on his belly and dunked his face in the water, shattering the still surface. Insects darted every which way.

From the region of Gorgol's mouth came a sucking, slurping noise. The level of the pond fell visibly, exposing the blackened bottom halves of the stalks that grew in its shallows. Gorgol blew air from his nose, sucked in another breath, then took another enormous draught. He must have drunk a thousand gallons of water in a matter of seconds.

Gorgol reared up from the pond with a loud groan of satisfaction. His mane, sopping wet, was plastered against his skin, water streaming down his hairy chest. Strings of algae ringed his face in a slimy black halo.

"Oh!" he said, when he noticed Mero watching him. "Pardon me. You weren't planning on drinking from that, were you?"

"No," Mero said. "It would have made me sick."

Gorgol nodded sagely. "Yes, I reckon it would have. My goodness— first the bird and now this. However do you humans manage?"

22

ero threw the bird away a few hours later. Not because it had spoiled, but because an unwary footfall had sent him splashing into a brackish pool hidden by a ring of dry grass. Mero was soaked through, his nose and mouth overwhelmed by the smell of rot.

For a second or two he floundered in the darkness. Then, before he could drag himself to shore, a massive hand plunged into the water and scooped him up as though he were a leaf floating on the surface.

Coughing, he opened his eyes into Gorgol's grinning face.

"Careful, now!" the giant cried. "You'll catch your death, swimming in this cold."

Mero put a hand out for balance and his palm touched Gorgol's own. The giant's skin was warm and rough as leather, hanging loose on his frame. Mero's hand sank in to the wrist, pushing wrinkles and folds aside as it went. The sensation sent him into a blind panic, and he wriggled, froglike, until the giant was forced to put him down.

"What's the matter?" Gorgol said, in injured tones. "I was only trying to help."

Mero scrambled to his feet, watching Gorgol with wide eyes and pounding heart. Gorgol was smiling—always smiling—but made no attempt to touch him again.

"You'll want to watch your step," he said, before rearing to his full height and setting off.

Had Mero been alone, he would have stripped off his sodden clothes and dried himself with earth or grass. With Gorgol there, he didn't dare. So he shivered and dripped his way through the afternoon, falling further and further behind with every step. Gorgol snorted with impatience, his lips moving furiously as though trying to escape his face.

"*Really*, now," he said at last. "You can't ever expect to reach Uron at this rate."

"You'll have to forgive me," Mero said through gritted teeth. "I wasn't born a giant like you."

"Why don't you let me carry you for a spell?" Gorgol said. "That would be easier for the both of us, don't you think?"

"I'll walk on my own," Mero said. Gorgol let the matter drop.

They were still lost in the highlands by the time the sun set. Mountains penned them in on all sides. In the middle distance was nothing but scrub, pools of water, and the occasional boulder half-sunken into the muck. Mero could not feel his fingers or his toes, and his hunger had given way to a hollow ache that was somehow worse. He sat on a patch of dry earth and pulled off his shoes. They had been given to him in Sanja's palace and were not made for walking long distances. When he grabbed his foot to examine the sole, he found it covered in blisters, some filled with pus, others already burst. His groin itched, as did the undersides of his arms—no doubt he was developing a rash. His clothes were still wet, and he was shivering again. All of this he could have endured if he had been able to find water, but though there was plenty to be found, none of it was drinkable.

I won't last the night, he realized, with a sudden, inescapable clarity. The air was cold and getting colder. The night would have been hard enough to survive had Mero been watered and fed, and had dry bedclothes to wrap himself up in. As it was, he was certain to die of exposure sometime in the night.

There are worse ways to die, I suppose. But on the heels of that thought came another: what would he do when the silver fishhook buried itself in his soul and dragged it back to earth? Who would pay Sheathless's price to bring him back to full life? As far as he knew, there was no one around for miles but Gorgol and himself. What would happen if Mero tried to stick the giant with his sword? The thought of drinking Gorgol's blood was repellant. He imagined it burning in his veins like firewater, stripping away what little humanity he had left—turning him, perhaps, into something as evil as Gorgol himself. That, of course, was supposing he could manage the deed in the first place. Would Gorgol be so foolish as to let his guard down long enough to be stuck? Mero thought it unlikely. He was bound to be caught in the act. All it would take to disable him would be one flick of the giant's fingers. And then…

"Little Mero?"

He blinked stupidly, trying to focus his bleary eyes on the face above him.

"What?"

"I *said* you're not looking well. Are you quite sure there's nothing I can do to help?"

Gorgol hung over him like a cloud, blotting out the sky. Mero gripped Sheathless and said, "No, nothing. I just need some rest."

"All right, then. I hope you don't mind if I wander off again tonight."

"Again? Where are you going?"

"Would you rather I stay?" Gorgol grinned.

Mero's skin crawled. "Do as you please. Just be sure to be here in the morning. I want to set out as soon as it's light."

Gorgol pushed out his bottom lip. The flesh inside was glossy and pink. "Don't you worry about me, little Mero. I'll have you know I'm a man of my word. I'd worry more for myself if I were you. From the looks of you—" and he stood, creaking—"you're not going anywhere."

And he smiled, warmly, his head fetched to one side, and his expression said, *I've got you, you're mine.*

23

Mero hugged Sheathless and shivered as Gorgol's footsteps faded away. Darkness closed in. Already he could barely see the far end of the valley.

You need to think of something, now. But he couldn't think of anything beyond the pounding pain in his temples, the ache in his stomach, the stinging of his feet. *You could try lighting a fire,* he thought, but even if he could find the strength to stand and gather wood, and even if the wood was dry enough to light, he would still need to hand-drill it into life. He had done so before—could do it again—but in his enervated state, the thought of expending so much effort for a chance at warmth was unpalatable. Even if he got his fire started, what then? He had no pot to boil water with, no food to cook. He was utterly, hopelessly unprepared.

Why? He went back to the question time and time again. Why had he let himself be led into such a hopeless situation? Why had he put himself so entirely in Gorgol's power? Did he secretly yearn for failure? Or was it the opposite—had he really been so arrogant as to believe he could survive anything as long as he had Sheathless? If so, his time with Gorgol had certainly taught him the error of his ways.

Gorgol. The giant who could do something to men that was somehow worse than killing them outright. The giant who had filled the pens of Palta over generations of sacrifice. The giant who had not yet taken Mero though he certainly had the means—who was toying with him for some reason beyond Mero's comprehension.

It makes his cock swell to frighten us, Ruya had said. Perhaps she had been right. Perhaps the giant's real food was not the blue organs he plucked from men's assholes, but the fear he made them feel as he did so.

Mero realized vaguely that his chin had slumped against his chest. He no longer shivered; in fact he was pleasantly warm. And as though thought of her had summoned her to his mind, Ruya's voice trickled into his ear, hissing out of the wind: "*Mero! Mero!*"

A hand seized his shoulder and shook. Mero started awake, pawing for Sheathless.

"Who's there?" he croaked.

"It's me!" said Ruya's voice, and suddenly two white eyes swooped out of the darkness, the barest shine on her nose and chin showing where the rest of Ruya's face should be. She held Mero's shoulders, then his neck, then his cheeks. Her hands were engulfed in a pair of heavy mittens, and warmth radiated from her body.

"Look at you," she whispered. "You look half-dead—more than half. What have you done?"

"Ruya," Mero said. "It's you." He stared at her, uncomprehending. How was Ruya here?

"You're freezing," she said. "Here. Put this on."

There was a rustling noise, and something scratched Mero's cheek. Ruya huffed with effort. The scratching traveled across Mero's back, and a heavy weight settled on his shoulders. He realized it was a grass coat, likely the very one he'd stolen from Ruya's house.

"Ruya," he said, trying to get his thoughts in order. A sudden chill swept over him. "Gorgol," he croaked.

"He isn't here. I watched him wander off over the mountains. We'll hear him if he comes back. Here, drink."

She put a bottle to his lips, then tilted his head back until cool water trickled down his throat. He drank greedily, but Ruya pulled the bottle away after a half-dozen swallows.

"Not so fast. I only have so much, and we don't know how long it will need to last. Can you eat?"

Mero wanted to answer but could only nod.

"Then hold on a moment. And get *that* out of the way, would you?"

Though Mero could barely make out Ruya's shape in the gloom, it was clear from her tone that she was talking about Sheathless. The sword rested by his side, half-hidden in the grass. Mero didn't like to move it out of arm's reach, especially with Gorgol around, nor did he understand Ruya's distaste for the weapon. Perhaps if she had known what it was capable of—but Mero had never used it in her presence.

"I need it," he whispered.

"Why?"

"Protection." *Why else?*

The rummaging sound fell off. Mero got the distinct impression that Ruya had her hands on her hips.

"*I* don't feel protected when it's around," she said. "And you couldn't kill a *hapi* in your state, let alone a giant. Move it before I cut myself on it."

Mero ground his jaw and tossed Sheathless behind him. The blade winked in the dark.

"Thank you," Ruya said simply. "Here."

She took his wrist and placed something soft in his palm. She had pulled off her mittens; her hands were boiling hot. She sucked in her breath when their fingers touched.

"Your hands are like ice. Are you sure you can eat on your own?"

Mero nodded, the food already halfway to his mouth. It was some kind of flatbread wrapped around a few shreds of lean, gamey meat. It was cold, but the flatbread was spongy and the meat tasted of pepper and oil. Mero, knowing he could have wolfed the food down in two bites, forced himself to chew.

"We need a fire," Ruya said. "Water and food won't do you any good if you freeze to death in the night."

Mero swallowed. He thought he had chewed long enough, but the bite hurt going down. "Do you have a tinderbox?"

Ruya snorted. "Of course. Who sets off into the wilderness without a tinderbox?"

"We'll need wood." Mero made to stand, but Ruya pushed him back against the hummock.

"I'll go. You eat and get warm."

"Take Sheathless," Mero said, reaching behind him.

"What?" Ruya's voice came from over his head.

It took Mero a moment to realize she hadn't misheard him; she simply didn't know what Sheathless was. "My sword," he explained. "You can use it to cut wood."

"Oh." Ruya sniffed. "Thank you, but no. I have an axe."

"Sheathless is better," Mero pressed. "It's sharper than an axe, and the blade never dulls."

"I'll manage without it," Ruya snapped, and the next sound he heard was that of her heavy boots tromping away.

Mero waited in the sudden silence, watching his breath silver then fade. Somehow Ruya had been keeping the cold away, and with her gone it was free to close back in. He pulled the grass coat tighter with one hand and fed himself another bite of food with the other. The coat crackled as it moved. The outside was soaked but the inside was warm and dry. It was so conical and rigid that it rested on the ground like a tent, keeping most of its considerable weight off his shoulders.

He fed himself his third and final bite of food. A tiny leg bone was lodged in the meat. Mero cracked it with his teeth and chewed it down to powder. He wondered if it had been one of the *hapi* that had ridden in the sledge with him.

The night was quiet, the air cold. Every so often Mero heard Ruya tramping about or whacking at a branch with her axe. Having nothing to do, he retrieved Sheathless and used it to carve a fire pit into the side of the hill, shoring up one end with clods of earth taken from the other. It was unimpressive and largely pointless, since the wind was low, but he hated the thought of sitting around while Ruya did all the work.

The clouds were breaking by the time Ruya returned, the night growing brighter by inches. Her face floated above an armload of wood, mostly small white branches taken from the trees nearby. They looked grotesque, like intestines or calloused fingers. Ruya's sledge, piled high with provisions, rested at the foot of the hill on which Mero sat. He marveled that she had dragged it all this way.

"I dug a pit," Mero said, gesturing at his handiwork. Ruya nodded tiredly and dumped the wood beside it, the blade of her axe flashing on her belt.

"We'll need more," she said, already turning down the hill.

"I'll go," Mero said.

"No, you won't." Ruya waved a hand at the sledge. "The tinder box is in the pouch at the front. See if you can get something started."

Mero rose on shaking legs, dragging the grass coat with him over to the sledge. There were five or six bundles of provisions, tightly packed and lashed down with cord. Mero picked at the first knot and the package fell open, spilling its contents onto the bed of the sledge. Cursing silently, he set the tinderbox aside and tried to stuff the remaining items back where they had come—but even though there was one less of them than before, he couldn't figure out how to get them all fitting right. He abandoned his work when his fingers grew cold and his knees started to hurt, telling himself that it wouldn't do the supplies any harm to sit out for an hour or two. He rose and returned to the firepit.

The wood Ruya had harvested was freshly cut and dense with water, but the limbs were small and covered with tiny protruding twigs—more like brambles than branches. They would generate good airflow and likely burn quickly. Mero shaved a few down to filings with Sheathless, then built a small fire, opened Ruya's tinderbox, and drew out the striker and a handful of coarse gray fiber. He stuffed a wad of it under the filings and dropped a few sparks onto it with the striker. By the time Ruya returned with more wood, the first flames had taken hold.

Ruya dropped her second armload on top of the first, then rounded the pit and sat next to Mero, helping him shield the fire from the wind. It whistled and popped, flickering low, a weak soul straining to stay alive. It leapt to another branch, crawled up its length, then wheezed and died out.

Mero sighed. "I'll make more filings."

He whittled kindling while Ruya adjusted the fire and fetched another wad of tinder. This time the fire gobbled up a few leaves, turning their twigs to candle-ends. A few of the larger branches caught and Mero knew they had won. He sat back, satisfied, already taking great comfort in the light and heat the fire gave off. It grew large enough that Ruya dropped another branch onto it. Then, only a minute later, it faltered. By the time Mero realized the fire might go out, it had. The flames vanished in a puff of sour smoke, gone as quickly as they had come.

Mero cursed. He felt robbed. How could a fire simply decide to go out, after so much effort and forethought had gone into its creation?

He reached for Sheathless, but Ruya clucked her tongue and said, "Stop that. It just needs a little air."

"It's *out*," Mero said, but Ruya was already rocking forward, her stomach pressing against her knees. She put her cheek to the cold earth and blew. The embers brightened, and a puff of ash was expelled from the far side, but no flames appeared.

"You're wasting your time," Mero said, as Ruya drew another breath. It irritated him to see her crouched in the wet grass. He was tempted to grab her shoulder and pull her away.

She blew again, and again the fire didn't light. Now he actually did reach for her—but the next time she blew, a bright new flame sprung up out of nowhere, a tiny orange pennant dancing on its own wind. Ruya grunted with satisfaction and sat back. Mero bit his tongue, feeling foolish.

This time the fire stayed lit, and soon Ruya grabbed her axe and set out for a third time. Mero's annoyance was quickly burned away by the heat. He aired out his shirt and pants, and they drank more of Ruya's water. The fire crackled merrily, and Mero and Ruya crowded around it, sharing in its warmth and in each other's.

"Do you have any pots?" Mero asked. "We could boil some pond-water. Then we wouldn't have to be so careful with what you brought."

"I hate boiling water," Ruya announced. "It always gives me the shits."

"It works," Mero assured her. "You just have to do it long enough."

Ruya huffed but rose and went over to her sledge. A moment later, she cried out,

"Who made this mess?"

"It's hardly a mess," Mero said. "I was looking for the tinderbox."

"You're not to touch my things again until you've learned to put them back where they belong. Look at this." She went on in a language Mero didn't know, then returned and dropped a small, thinly-hammered pot in his lap.

"There," she said. "*You* can fill it up, and *you* can be the first to drink from it once it's done. I'm not spending the rest of my night squatting in a bush."

The wood burned quickly, as Mero had thought it would. Ruya made another trip and Mero made two of his own. He felt infinitely better, in body and soul, than he had earlier that night, when he had contemplated the overwhelming likelihood of his own death. Already those dark hours seemed nothing more than a bad dream.

For all the time they had spent together, Mero and Ruya hadn't spoken much. There was a marble in Mero's throat that kept him from talking. It was only once the fire had faded to flaky ash that he found his voice and said, loud in the silence,

"You saved my life."

"Again," Ruya said.

"What?" Mero was thinking of how alien his voice had sounded — loud and childish.

"That's the second time I've saved your life. Have you forgotten already?"

Oh. Tension hummed, and for an instant Mero was back in the dark dream he had had in Palta — of the wall of skulls that chattered under his touch. Then he said, "No, of course I haven't. Thank you for saving me. Twice."

She snorted and pulled her coat tighter. "You don't have to thank me for that. You might as well thank every man you meet on the road for not slitting your throat."

"Ruya," he said then, "why are you here?"

She looked at him. Her hair was tied back, but a few wiry strands — some black, some gray — framed the sides of her face. "I wondered how long it would take you to ask. Or even if you would."

"Then, what's the answer?"

"Isn't it obvious? I'm coming with you."

It *was* obvious, but it was also so foolish Mero didn't know where to begin. "Ruya, you can't. You don't know the first thing about where I'm going."

"I don't care. Anywhere is better than Palta."

"I'm traveling *with Gorgol*," Mero reminded her. "Do you really think he'll let you come along?"

"I don't plan on asking his permission," she snapped. "I'll follow along behind, like I've done these past two days."

Of course Ruya had been trailing them—what else could explain her presence?—but Mero was still amazed she had done so without being discovered. "How?"

She laughed bitterly. "It's easy. I just follow the smell. I used to track *hapi* across the hills. This is nothing."

"He'll find you out sooner or later."

"Then I'll take my knife and slit my own throat before he can get his hands on me. I don't care. I've wasted too many years already." She pulled her coat tighter again, rocking a little. The fire threw her face into sharp relief, bright ridges and pools of deep shadow.

Mero's hand went to the whistle around his neck. Yes, he had blown it more than once, and each time the goddess had answered. But he had Sheathless to drag him back. Did Ruya not understand how fragile she was?

"You only have one life," he said slowly. "Wouldn't it be better to live it out someplace safe?"

"Why?" Ruya said. "So I can live to be an old maid, withered and bent, and die wasting away in my bed—or in front of all my kinsmen, with Gorgol's fingers up my ass?"

The heat of Ruya's words was startling. Mero stared into the fire, mulling over his thoughts. Ruya calmed somewhat, stirring the coals with a bent stick. Then she said,

"Why do you want so badly to go to Uron?"

What am I supposed to tell her? "I saw it in a dream."

But that didn't work on Ruya any more than it had on Sanja Al-Sat. "That's not a reason."

"It wasn't an ordinary dream. More like a vision."

She looked skeptical. "You don't strike me as the kind of man who puts much stock in visions."

"I never used to be," Mero said.

No, you never used to be, said a voice in his head. *You never used to believe in visions or gods or heaven or hell. Nothing you couldn't touch with your own two hands. Nothing you couldn't weigh or measure, or take apart and put back together. But she showed you the error of your ways, didn't she?*

She did, Mero thought.

She did, the goddess echoed, smug.

"Anyway, it doesn't matter what kind of man I am," he said, standing up. "I *need* to go to Uron. The choice isn't mine to make."

"Of course it is," Ruya said, watching him pace back and forth. "Our choices are always our own—even when we're choosing between evils. If you think you don't have a choice, that's just a lie you're telling yourself."

He turned on her. "How do you know that? How do *you* know what's going on inside *my* head?"

She looked up at him, remarkably calm. "I suppose I don't."

Mero felt as though he'd charged a locked door only for Ruya to open it at the last second. He stared at her for a moment, then kept pacing.

"It may not exist," she said then. "Or it may be west of here instead of east. I told you Gorgol is a liar. You must have noticed yourself."

"I know it's—" Mero gestured vaguely eastward—"*that* way. I can feel it. As for the rest… I suppose I'll just have to wait and see."

"He won't let you go," Ruya said softly. "He never lets anyone go, once he's caught them. He'll wait until you're begging—he loves to see us beg. Then he'll have you on your knees and do to you what he did to poor Mosin."

Mero's sphincter clenched involuntarily. "He hasn't caught me yet. I'll find a way to escape him."

She heaved a weary sigh. "I hope you're right."

"You'll have to leave before dawn breaks," Mero told her.

"I know that," Ruya said, a little testily.

He pulled off the grass coat and handed it to her. "You'll need to take this, too." She looked at him in confusion, so he added, "We can't leave any signs that you were here. I'll bury the fire pit and play up my weakness. But you need to take away everything you brought here."

"Oh. Of course." She took the coat, eyeing him sidelong. "But what about you? You'll freeze."

"I survived last night, and I'll survive this one, thanks to you."

Reluctantly she ducked inside the coat. "I'll come again tomorrow night, as long as that big brute leaves you alone."

"Thank you," Mero said simply. "Sleep well."

"And you." Ruya seemed hesitant to leave him, but she slipped the axe through her belt, tossed her stick into the fire, and tramped back to her sledge, packing it up and lashing it down as she had before. She gathered up the rope, slung it over her shoulder, and dragged it off into the night.

24

"Oh, look, look!" Gorgol cried.

Mero grit his teeth, scaling the rocky slope with his palms on his knees. He hadn't needed to fake weakness for long. The night had been cold, and Gorgol had pressed him hard all morning, jubilantly bounding from outcrop to outcrop while Mero struggled along behind. They had quit the watery tablelands only to lose themselves in a maze of stony peaks, where boulders of every size littered the ground, interspersed by narrow, naked spires. Now they were climbing again, though judging from the way Gorgol stood outlined against the sky, that at least would soon be over.

Mero crested the ridge on Gorgol's upwind side—he had had enough of the giant's stink for one day—only to be assaulted by a smell so unbearably sharp that he swiped at his nose, thinking an insect had flown into it. Tears sprang into the corners of his eyes and needles stabbed at his forehead. It was the sinus-burning smell of mustard mingled with a dull, pungent odor Mero couldn't place.

"Ahhh!" Gorgol drew an enormous breath, his belly swelling like a frog's throat. "Smells even worse than I do, eh? Ho ho ho!"

They were looking out over a flaky, pockmarked land. The only living things Mero saw other than Gorgol and himself were a few growths of tubular, wormlike grass clustered around the odd pillar or shelf of rock. A greenish haze hung in the air, nearly imperceptible up close, but thickening into a dark brown fog at the horizon.

"Of course, it gets worse the closer you are to the ground," Gorgol said amiably. "At my height it's not so bad. In fact there's a bit of a breeze." And he closed his eyes, letting the wind play across his whiskers. "You're welcome to ride on my shoulder if it gets to be too much for you."

Mero didn't trust himself to answer. He was thinking of what a day of walking through the stinking fog might do to his lungs and eyes, wondering if Ruya would follow them into this hellish place or if she would have the good sense to give up.

"I'll walk," he said, sticking Sheathless into the ground.

Gorgol bunched his eyebrows together. "I'm only trying to help, you know."

"Then lead the way and let's get this over with."

"Oh, we won't be over with this for a while yet. These plains stretch for miles. Yes, we'll be sleeping here tonight."

Mero's skin crawled, and he hesitated when Gorgol started down the path. But what choice did he have? Even if he skirted these plains to the north or south, he couldn't escape Gorgol, or the wager he had struck.

He held his breath and stepped into the fog.

It was worse than Mero had expected. The smell wasn't so bad inside the fog, but only because it was replaced by pain. Each breath burned Mero's throat and lungs as it went down, then burned like vomit as it came up. He spat convulsively, but nothing could get the acid off his tongue. His eyes streamed, burning as though sweat had gotten into them. He narrowed them to slits and breathed through his shirt. It helped, but only a little. He couldn't even hold his breath, as then he felt the air corroding him from the inside out.

Gorgol, of course, was utterly unaffected. He waddled across the plain with his vast belly lurching from side to side, leaving a trail of swirling fog in his wake. As the distance between them grew, the fog nibbled at his silhouette, until he was little more than a huge, wobbling shadow.

They walked for an hour that felt like five. Mero stumbled along, coughing into his palm, keeping his eyes shut whenever he could, opening them to reorient himself when he sensed he was veering off-course. Had it not been for the fog, the walk would have been easy: the earth underfoot was firm, flat, hard-packed sand, the uniform mundanity broken only by the odd spray of scattered pebbles or spire of rock. Then there were the clumps of tubular vegetation, pushing up like barnacles from the odd finger-wide fissure in the earth. Mero pulled one out of the ground as he walked by. It came out easily; the root ball was small, like that of a cactus. The flesh was pale, waxy, and hard. Mero's instincts told him it was no good to eat, likely indigestible even if cooked. He wondered if these strange plants thrived in the fog or merely endured it. He had certainly never seen anything like them. They grew outwards from the fissures but never more than a few feet high, as though an invisible ceiling kept them from reaching any higher.

An idea struck him. Tossing the plant aside, he sank to his knees, then stretched out onto his belly, bringing his face close to the ground. He emptied his lungs, then breathed in.

Sweet!

No, not sweet—the breath still itched going down, and left a tobacco taste on Mero's tongue. But compared to the air four feet above, merely bitter was a marked improvement.

Mero's heart soared. *I can sleep here.* Until now, the thought of spending a night in this fog had filled him with dread. But that still left the problem of travel. He couldn't follow Gorgol without standing to walk—could he?

Rising to his hands and knees, Mero tried crawling along the ground. Even this small difference in height made the air taste worse. The going was slow, and he scraped his palms and knees on the sandy ground. Still, it was better than breathing poison.

"What's this? You're not planning on crawling all the way to Uron, are you?"

Mero jumped, rocking back on his heels. Gorgol loomed over him, a mantle of fog wrapped around his neck.

"I was just tired," Mero said. He didn't want Gorgol to know he had figured out the secret of the fog, though of course there was a chance he already knew. The giant's face never gave away anything. It was always the same joyless smile, the same leering eyes.

"I'm not surprised," Gorgol said. "The air here is quite toxic. I believe it's a leftover from one of the ages of man. Some poison they put in the earth—either by accident or on purpose, who can tell with men?—that keeps anything from thriving here." He fetched his head to one side and added, "if you want to escape this place with your life, I suggest you walk on two feet."

That made Mero want to crawl more than ever, but perhaps that was what Gorgol wanted. He stood, and his throat immediately started to burn. He wanted to scream, or weep, or both, but Gorgol's esophagus eyes were trained on him. He clapped a palm over his mouth.

"Lead on, then."

25

By the time they were ready to stop for the night, blood was streaming from Mero's nose, and he couldn't swallow without sending a lance of pain down his throat. He collapsed next to a pile of rock and sucked in mouthfuls of the sweet air near the ground. Gorgol watched with an expression of amused pity on his face.

"I think I shall leave you again tonight," he said. "I've a hankering for sweeter air. It's just a skip and hop for me, you know—I can be out of this fog and back in a matter of minutes. If only you'd consent to ride on my back! But a man has his pride, I suppose. Well, farewell! Don't go wandering off. This place is home to all sorts of dangers: sinkholes and boiling lakes and pits that could swallow a man whole." And with that he lumbered off, stepping neatly over Mero, who couldn't help but notice something strange: nothing hung between Gorgol's legs but a dense crop of hair.

Mero was too exhausted to care much about what Gorgol said, or about his lack of genitalia. He focused on drawing deep, cooling breaths, using Sheathless to carve himself a small trench that, with luck, would serve as a pool for cleaner air. This had been one of the longest days of his life, and he would have wept with relief had his eyes not already been red and streaming.

As the worst of the pain receded, however, new problems bubbled to the surface. Mero's lips were cracked, his throat raw and dry, his stomach once again hollow. He had seen no water and no signs of life all day other than the indigestible plants. His only hope was Ruya, following along somewhere behind. But what were the chances she had made it all this way? Mero had barely made it himself, and he was a man used to long days of travel, with no heavy sledge to pull along. The more he thought about it, the more he grew convinced that Ruya wasn't coming. He looked back the way they had come, but saw nothing. The fog was red in the failing light. Beyond it everything was black.

Finished with his trench, Mero walked a few paces from the pile of rubble and stuck Sheathless in the ground point-first, the flat of its blade facing west. With any luck it would catch the light of the setting sun and signal his position to Ruya. It was all he could do. He crawled back to his hole—the earth was pleasantly cool—and fell into a fitful sleep.

*M*ero! Mero!
His eyes snapped open. Joy and disbelief warred for dominion. She was there—Ruya had found him. Her eyes were red and puffy, her forehead beaded with sweat. She had wrapped a heavy scarf around her mouth and nose, and was panting heavily.

"Mero!" she said again, shaking him.

"I'm awake," he murmured, bemused. "Your voice, I—I thought you were the goddess."

The visible strip of Ruya's face scrunched in confusion. "What? What goddess? Have you lost your mind?"

"No—no, I'm fine." Mero patted the ground next to him. "Lay down. The air—it's clearer closer to the ground."

Ruya rifled through her packs. "I can't lay down just yet. There's work to do." She handed him a rough, homespun shirt. "Tie that in front of your face."

Mero did as bidden, knotting the sleeves behind his head, massing the rest of the cloth over his mouth and nose. He crawled over to Ruya and looked over her shoulder.

"There's some meat left," she said, dropping a couple of flatbreads into his hands. "And here—drink."

Setting the flatbreads down in his lap, Mero accepted the bottle and drank gratefully. The water was lukewarm and ached going down. He fought the urge to swill it around his mouth and spit it out.

"Thank you," he said. "At this rate you'll be saving my life once for every night I spend out here."

"Isn't that what we do?" Ruya said, busy at her work.

"Hm?"

"Isn't that what we do?" she repeated. "Save each other, day by day?"

Mero was perplexed. "*Who* does?"

She waved a hand. "Men. Women. People."

"In my experience, people are more liable to cheat and kill one another than anything else."

"Then you have lived a pitiable life," Ruya said, "and it's no wonder you're the way you are."

Mero was more confused than ever. "What way is that?"

She threw down her hands and shot him a red-rimmed look. "Mero," she said, "my throat is burning, my legs are aching, and my arms feel ready to fall off. Can it wait until we've eaten supper?"

"Of course," he said, feeling foolish.

Their meal was the same as that of the night before. Mero no longer crunched the tiny bones between his teeth, as the thought of swallowing them made him shiver. They shared a few sips of water, doing everything in a half-recline, as close to the earth as possible. Then there was nothing else to do but stretch out and rest.

Mero was troubled. He was walking the razor's edge. Each day with Gorgol brought fresh tribulations, and he was utterly dependent on Ruya to stay alive. What if, despite everything, he perished out here where there was nothing to draw life from?

Not nothing, said a voice in his head. He was keenly aware of Ruya's rattling breath by his shoulder.

It won't happen, he thought firmly, shutting the door on that line of thought.

"Mero?" said Ruya.

"Yes?"

"Who is the goddess?"

He shifted uncomfortably. "It's nothing. Forget I said it."

She propped herself up on one shoulder. "So that's how it is? You won't speak to me, even though I'm the only one around to listen— even though both of us might be dead tomorrow?"

He covered his face with his arm, shielding himself from her accusatory eyes. "You already think I'm a madman. Isn't that enough?"

"Tell me."

"She's a voice I hear in my head. She's the one telling me to go to Uron."

Ruya was quiet for some time. Then she said, "How do you know she's a goddess?"

"I don't. That's just what I call her."

"What does she sound like?"

He shrugged, still covering his eyes.

"Don't do that," Ruya said, annoyed. "You said you hear her so she must sound like something."

"She sounds like me." Mero's heart was quickening, but he couldn't seem to stop talking.

Ruya's brow furrowed. "How can she sound like you if she's a woman?"

Mero swallowed, searching for the right words. "She sounds like—she sounds like how I would sound if I were a woman."

Ruya said nothing. She laid back down and stared at the sky.

"Satisfied?" Mero said.

"How long has she been speaking to you?"

"A long time. Years." He almost went further, but the words stuck in his throat, and Ruya had already moved on.

"Does she tell you anything else—anything other than to go to Uron?"

"She never actually *told* me that. Not in words, at least. She sends me visions of the city when I'm dreaming." Mero took the arm from his eyes and tucked it under his head. "When she speaks, it's only ever to echo my own words. It's like she can't say anything I haven't already said."

Already said, the goddess agreed.

Ruya breathed heavily through her nose, hands knitted over a rising and falling chest. She seemed to be asleep. Mero should have been relieved, but for some reason his heart ached. He considered nudging her awake.

Then she said, "Thank you."

He blinked. "For what?"

"For talking." She rolled her head towards him. "It helps take my mind off the pain."

They lay side-by-side for half an hour more. At one point Ruya started coughing and wouldn't stop. She coughed until she had nearly risen into a sitting position, crunching in on herself. Tears trickled down her cheeks, and she slapped her chest with her palm. Mero listened in vexation. He wished he could take Sheathless and carve the fog out of her, cut away her raw windpipe, her spasming lungs. But keen as Sheathless was, it was no surgeon's scalpel. So he lay in the darkness and listened to her hack and wheeze, wishing she would either stop, or fall asleep, or succumb to her illness and die.

26

They settled into an uncomfortable rhythm. Each morning Mero awoke to the sight of Gorgol's apelike face and swinging belly, to the smell of rotting death that emanated from his every pore. The giant was always watching him, from the crest of a nearby hill or reclining twenty paces away or even directly above his head. He would greet Mero jovially, always finding a way to remind him of some unpleasantness they had encountered the day before or hint at some danger they would face in the days to come. His smile never budged, though as the days went on Mero noticed a tightness to it, as though it were going stale. Mero thought he knew why: Gorgol hadn't expected him to last this long.

They would start walking as soon as Mero rose, and would often walk straight until sunset, with only the briefest of pauses for Mero to catch his breath or drink from whatever source of water they managed to find. These were few and far between: the further east they traveled, the emptier the world became.

When evening fell, Mero would collapse into a trembling heap, and Gorgol would make up some reason to leave him for the night. Why the giant did this remained a mystery, but Mero could hardly complain. With Gorgol gone, Ruya was free to catch him up and share her food, drink, and warmth.

Mero didn't understand Ruya any more than he did Gorgol. Now that she was free of Palta, she had no reason to come to Uron. Surely she would be better off keeping her food to herself, and striking out into the wilderness alone? Mero resisted the temptation to ask her, in case she decided he was right. He was keenly aware that her nightly visits were the only thing keeping him alive and sane. The second Gorgol's footsteps faded, Mero would turn back along the way they'd come, straining his eyes and ears for a glimpse of Ruya and her sledge.

Sometimes she walked with its cord slung over one shoulder and sometimes she folded her hands behind her back, shuffling along with her back stooped. Sometimes it was minutes before she caught up and sometimes it was hours, but catch up she always did, and she and Mero would sit side by side and rest, talking over the buzzing undercurrent of fear and desperation that dominated their daylight hours.

"I'm always asking about you," she said to him one night. "Now it's time for you to ask about me."

"Hm?" Mero said. His eyes were closed, as there was nothing to see. The night was black, and he couldn't remember what their surroundings looked like. For all he knew, nothing existed but Ruya and himself.

"Every night I ask you questions, and half the time I don't get any answers. If you don't like talking about yourself, why don't you ask about me?"

"What should I ask?" Mero said, confused.

She snorted. "What do you want to know?"

It had never occurred to Mero that there might be things about Ruya he didn't know. "Where did you live before Palta?" he asked.

"With my husband," Ruya said promptly. "He had a cottage on the outskirts of a village called Ganjur, far to the northwest."

"You had a husband?" Mero asked, startled.

She treated him to one of the looks he had come to recognize and dread. "I've had two. Salik was the first. Rustam was the second."

It took Mero a moment to digest this information. "Then, the cottage..."

"Was Rustam's."

"He was a farmer?"

Ruya nodded. "He grew barley and bladegrass. But my favorite were the fig trees. He had three of them—they were old and fat, they came with the land. You have no idea how many figs we got, just from those three trees!"

"Did you have any children?"

Her enthusiasm drained away, as though the wind had snatched it from her face. "Not with him."

"Then with Salik?"

She pulled her knee to her chest. "Three," she said.

At first Mero thought she had somehow gotten back to the fig trees. Then he realized what she was saying. "You had three children?"

"Two boys and a girl." Ruya's voice was thin.

Mero didn't want to ask the next question, but it was already slipping out of his mouth with the inevitability of an ocean tide. "What happened to them?"

Ruya, still hugging her knee, rocked gently back and forth. "Asse is still alive. He came with me to Rustam's farm, but the two of them never got along. He was too old to take another father—he was more of a man than a boy by then—and Rustam never made much of a father in any case. He left me to seek his fortune when Rustam died."

"How long ago was that?"

She gave a little laugh and brushed the hair from her face. "I'm not sure. Eighteen, twenty years, perhaps."

"Then how do you know he's still alive?"

Again that look, that mixture of pity and scorn. "I would know if he had died. I would feel it in my heart."

Mero decided not to challenge that. "What about the others?"

She drew a deep breath that rattled on its way out. "Nazli was adopted when she was still a girl. She was pretty and bright, and soon enough one of the rich ladies from the next city came by and asked me if I would sell her."

"You sold your daughter?" Mero blurted, shocked.

Ruya was still rocking. She had gone very stiff; Mero felt it in the touch of her shoulders every time she leaned back. "I didn't want to. I told her no. I didn't like how pale she was—she wore a long, purple robe, and when I saw her riding up the path I thought she might be the specter of death come to take my children away. And I was right. Only—we were very hungry, the four of us—this was after Salik died— and she offered me four golden *dariks*, enough to buy barley for all of us for a year or more. Little Ratna—he was the youngest—he was very weak, even as a baby. I'll never forget the way his bones poked out. His skin was so tight I thought it would tear like rice paper. So when the purple lady came, I thought—if I couldn't save all of them, I could at least save him, with the money from giving Nazli away."

"But if the lady wanted to adopt her, surely she must have meant to give Nazli a good life."

Ruya shook her head. "I don't know. I never saw her again. She cried at first, but I told her of all the wonderful things she would see in the city, and soon she got excited. She promised she would write me a letter once she learned how. But the years passed and Ratna passed and no letter ever came. So I left Asse with the house and paid my way onto a merchant caravan headed for the city. I asked everyone I met but no one knew who the purple lady was. Finally I found a manor in the rich part of town that I thought might be hers. I banged on the gates but they wouldn't let me in. I tried to tell them who I was but they called me a crazy woman and told me to leave and never come back unless I wanted to be whipped. I stayed in the city as long as I could, but I ran out of money and had to come home."

The rocking stopped. Ruya sniffled quietly, head hanging between her shoulders. Mero looked out into the night and discovered that the world had gained some definition during their conversation. Gray earth unfolded beneath a dark blue sky. Now he remembered where they were: down in the bowl of a dried-up lake that served as a passage through the mountains.

"You must think me a wicked mother," Ruya said.

Mero didn't know what separated the wicked mothers from the saintly ones. His memories of his own mother were mere shapes in the sand, all but lost.

"I think you were a good mother faced with a terrible decision," he said. "Death came for your children and you saw a way to forestall it. It can't be wrong to choose life over death."

"But what kind of life?" Ruya pressed. "What if the purple lady was horrible to her? What if she was married off to a cruel man? Wouldn't it have been better to stay with us, her mother, her family?"

Mero had no answers to those questions, so he said nothing. Insects chattered, and the wind rasped across the barren earth. Ruya buried her face in her hands and began to weep.

27

The plains beyond the ancient lakebed were red and featureless. A gray smudge covered the horizon to the south. Gorgol claimed it was an old forest, but advised they skirt it, as passing through would take longer than going around.

"And time isn't something you can afford to waste," he said cheerily. Dropping his voice, he added, "My stomach's been growling these past few days. You'd better hurry if you don't want to join Mosin in here." He gripped his belly with both hands and shook it, the blubbery flesh sloshing audibly as it jiggled.

Mero didn't answer. He felt sick to his stomach. Not because of the threat—though that was frightening enough in its own right—but because of a creeping suspicion that had stolen over him as he watched Gorgol's display. He hadn't seen the giant eat anything in the time they had been together, yet his belly was always full, the mottled skin stretched tight.

As the giant played with his paunch, a thought had taken root in Mero's mind. It was pure conjecture, yet it filled him with overwhelming dread.

They're still in there. All of them—all of the people Gorgol has eaten. They don't get digested. They never disappear.

He doesn't kill people. He hoards them.

"Is something the matter, little Mero?" Gorgol purred. "Those *were* the terms we agreed upon when we made our wager. Sulking about it now won't do you any good."

Mero's heart hammered. He wanted to dart out of Gorgol's reach, to disappear into the forest like a deer.

"I wasn't sulking," he said. "Just thinking."

"Oh? And what were you thinking about?"

He forced himself to meet Gorgol's eye. "That we should be walking, not talking."

Gorgol grinned. "Ho ho ho. Just as tenacious as ever, I see. Good, good. I admire that in a man. You would have made a fine giant—if only you'd been born one!"

"Enough," Mero said. The thought of being like Gorgol was repellant. "Let's go."

He tried to push Gorgol's words from his mind, but that night he saw the moon for the first time in days. It had changed already, and a thin sliver showed of its right side. The month was more than half over, and Mero had no idea how far they had to go—assuming that Gorgol was leading him to Uron in the first place. He sensed the city was drawing closer, but there was no telling whether this route would actually take them there. There could be any number of impassable obstacles in the way: a range of mountains, an arm of the sea, another stretch of infected, poisonous earth, this one strong enough to kill.

He resolved to broach the subject with Ruya, but as it happened she beat him to it.

"What are you planning on doing about Gorgol?" she asked him bluntly, pulling up with her sledge. She pointed behind her with a mittened hand, indicating the thin fingernail that hung on the horizon. "If you're hoping to make your escape, now is the time to do it."

"Not yet," Mero said reflexively. "We have almost half a month to go."

"Why wait?"

"Because he's still leading me to Uron. I want him to bring me as close as possible before I leave him."

"You say that as though he will give you the chance. Why push your luck? If you see your moment, take it."

"I'll think about it," Mero said, knowing it wouldn't happen.

Ruya watched him from the corner of her eye. "Why are you being so stubborn?"

"I'm not stubborn just because I won't do things your way."

"Do you want to him to catch you? Do you want his fingers up your ass?"

"No, I—" Mero wiped a hand down his face, cleaning it as one might a slate. "Of course I don't want that. I'm just taking advantage of him while I can. I need—"

"Yes, yes," Ruya snapped. "You need to go to Uron. So you've said. But you won't be going anywhere if that—that *thing* gets its hands on you."

Silence fell. Mero opened and closed his left hand, gripping Sheathless with his right. He was tired and cold, his head pounding. He couldn't remember the last time he had been comfortable. His stomach growled loudly. He felt the air moving through his intestines.

"Can we eat?" he said.

Wordlessly Ruya opened her pack and started preparing dinner. They had run out of *hapi* meat several days ago, and their nightly meals now consisted of flatbread, goat cheese, and a dry bean paste that needed to be mixed with water to be palatable.

"I'm running out of food," Ruya said as she handed Mero his portion. "I thought there would be animals to snare, but there's nothing. It's as though the earth itself is dead."

The news that they would soon be starving couldn't unseat the image of Gorgol's heaving belly. Mero could still see every vein, every fold of skin where the great gut hung down over the giant's pelvis.

"What does he take?" he said aloud.

"Hm?" Ruya said.

He stared at her, food untouched. "What does he take, Ruya? I keep thinking about it but I don't understand. I've studied human anatomy—I've performed autopsies. There's no organ there. There just isn't. There's nothing for him to steal. So *what does he take?*"

He closed his teeth over his tongue, startled by the force of his words. Ruya watched him for a long time, chewing thoughtfully. She had a very expressive forehead. Her eyebrows bunched down, then popped up again as she chewed, three horizontal wrinkles spanning her temples.

She swallowed, sniffed once or twice, then said, "I've already told you what he takes. He takes your soul."

Mero scoffed. "There's no—"

She talked over him. "You asked me what he took and I told you. If you're too stubborn to believe me, that's your fault."

"But Ruya—"

"Don't 'but Ruya' me. I know what I know. You've only seen one soul get taken. I've seen dozens, hundreds. You never went to the pens. You never saw the way they acted, after Gorgol got to them."

Mero thought of the wall of skulls. His grip on Sheathless tightened. *Don't say anything. She doesn't know.* "Why? How do they act?"

She faced him squarely, her eyes blazing. "They act like cattle. Like drooling idiots. They're never the same, even if they live fifty years more. There's a candle inside each of us and Gorgol blows it out. Without it you're nothing, you're worse than dead. If that isn't a soul, I don't know what is."

Mero took a bite of food to avoid answering. He considered telling

Ruya about his theory—that the small blue organs were still inside Gorgol's stomach—but decided against it.

"I'll find a way to escape him," he said instead. "I don't plan on losing my—whatever it is—to him."

"No one ever does," Ruya said. "That's what keeps us in Palta."

28

Mero blinked and the night was over. Ruya was gone, Gorgol in her place. The giant hovered over him, his face mere feet from Mero's own, his fetor stifling. Mero sat up and scrambled backwards, grabbing Sheathless as he did. The giant's eyes followed him, pink veins throbbing in the translucent jelly.

"What?" Mero asked roughly.

Gorgol's nostrils flared. The hairs sticking out of his nose were as long as Mero's fingers. He smacked his lips together and said,

"Good morning. Did you sleep well?"

"Until now," Mero said. "What do you want?"

Gorgol was squatting as though preparing to move his bowels. Mero had scrambled off to his left, and he had turned his head to follow, so that it was now bent almost completely sideways. It gave him a perversely youthful look, as though he were a child watching a column of marching ants.

"Oh, nothing in particular," he said breezily. "I was merely curious."

"Is that so? What about?"

"You," Gorgol said, and he stretched out, crashing down on his side and cupping his chin in his hand. "I haven't seen you eat a bite since we set off, but you've still got a fair bit of meat on you. By rights you should be skinny as a stick by now."

"I've always been skinny," Mero said, keeping his tone flat and uninterested.

"No doubt. But you keep remarkably well for such a skinny man. You ought to be half dead—or dead all the way—yet here you are, little worse for the wear."

"I'm sorry to disappoint you."

Gorgol laughed raucously, blasting Mero with his foul breath. "You misunderstand me. I'm happy to see you well—yes, very glad. It's only the mystery that's been nagging at me. Could it be you're sneaking off at night to find food? But I wasn't aware anything in these parts was fit for a man to eat. But look—there I go again! Please, don't pay me any mind." And he stood, chunks of earth tumbling from his body. It might have been Mero's imagination, but the giant's hair was even wilder than before, his hands and feet longer, the mottling of his skin more pronounced.

"What business of it is mine how you eat and hunt and stay alive?" he said, half to Mero and half to the sky. "None at all, that's my answer. My business is Uron, and getting you there—yes, I haven't forgotten! We're getting close now. But first we'll have to skirt that awful wood."

"I'd like to go through it," Mero said, "not around."

"Hm?" Gorgol looked genuinely surprised. "But that will add days to your walk, little Mero."

"It doesn't matter," Mero said, though he knew it mattered very much. "I'm sick of all this emptiness. I want firewood, and shelter."

Gorgol scratched his chin, perturbed. It was clear he was suspicious, though of what he couldn't decide. "Well—all right. It's your choice, after all. But don't think I'll forget our wager."

"I don't expect you to," Mero said.

By that afternoon they were under the canopy. The forest was brittle and dry, the trees leafless, the packed ground bare and hard as rock. Mero watched Gorgol carefully as the afternoon progressed. What he saw did not fill him with confidence. The giant cut a wide swath through the forest, snapping entire trees under his weight as easily as Mero snapped the branches near his head. He seemed in poor spirits, muttering and grumbling to himself as he shoved his way through. That was of little use to Mero; more important was the fact that he could not rely on the trees to slow Gorgol down in any significant way. Perhaps if the forest had been greener, the trees healthier. As it was, they may as well have been rushes.

You'll figure something out, Mero told himself. *You'll find another chance.*

Another chance, the goddess said.

Traveling through the forest did have its advantages. The meal Mero and Ruya shared that night was the first hot one they had eaten in weeks, and though the dry old wood stank like marsh gas as it burned, the flickering light it cast pushed back against the encroaching night.

"Why are we headed south?" Ruya asked. "I thought Uron was east of here."

"Southeast now," Mero said, gesturing in the direction of the draw. "Anyway, I wanted to travel through the forest—to see how Gorgol dealt with the trees."

"And?"

He shook his head and stared into the fire. His plan hadn't been a particularly good one, but its failure would have been easier to swallow if he had had any others in reserve.

Ruya sighed through her nose. She was a stocky woman and often sighed heavily, especially while she worked. Her nose, wide and flat, was as expressive as her brow; her nostrils had a way of flaring open wide.

"I can set my snares tonight and see if there's anything to catch in these woods," she said.

"I thought you might. Thank you, Ruya."

She gave him a strange look, different from the long-suffering one to which he was normally treated. It made Mero uncomfortable. He almost would have preferred her scorn.

"Your husbands," he said, to change the subject. "Salik and…"

"Rustam," she said charitably.

He nodded. "What were… Why did you marry them?"

She sniffed and prodded the fire. "Why does any woman marry?"

Mero wondered that himself. He understood why men married women, or at least pursued them, but had never been able to comprehend why a woman would marry a man. "You loved them?"

Ruya made a noise between a laugh and a snort. "Salik I loved. I was young and foolish then. He was a small man, no taller than me, but his eyes danced when he was happy, and his hair…!" A smile lit her face. "It was so thick and black. He used to sprinkle it with oil so it would shine in the sun. His moustache, too. It was short and tidy, and it hitched up on one side when he smiled. I liked to make him smile. I wanted to be a good wife, one who made her husband smile often. I was always surrounded by bitter women who wanted nothing to do with their husbands but make their lives miserable. I thought marriage would be so easy—all I had to do was keep my husband smiling and all would be well."

"What happened?"

"He smiled—for a time," Ruya said. "But there are only so many things a woman can do when she is poor and her husband is poor and there are children to feed and food is scarce and there is no money to be had anywhere. It wasn't long before he stopped smiling, for me or for anyone else. After that he became cruel. Everything made him angry. I suffered the worst from his anger, but the children suffered too. They learned to avoid him. Even Ratna knew not to cough when he was around."

"How did he die?" Mero asked, remembering that Ruya had been alone with her children when Nazli was bought.

"He went out drinking and didn't come back. I wasn't worried—he often did that. But a few days later one of the women in town came by and told me his body had been found in the street. He had been robbed and beaten to death. I thought he might have owed money to some of the men in town, but I never found out if that was why they killed him."

"I'm sorry," Mero said, wondering how pathetic a life could be, wondering how Ruya still had the strength to live.

She shrugged. "It was a long time ago. They brought the body to me, wrapped in a sheet, dragging it behind a donkey. When I unwrapped it, the first thing I saw was his hair, shining in the sun." She gestured at her own temple. "His skull was smashed in—his brains were showing—but on the other side of his head, just inches away—perfect." Her voice had grown thick.

"Rustam?" Mero said, wanting to steer her away from her grief.

Ruya wiped a tear from her eye. "That was never love, for either of us. We were both too old to believe in such things. He was twenty years my elder, and after three children I wasn't as beautiful as I once was. Yes, I was beautiful once, if you can believe that!"

"Of course," Mero said, but she had already moved on.

"I married him because I thought it would be good for Asse. I thought he could inherit the farm when Rustam died. But then he left me and I ended up tending the land alone. I sold it soon after—a storm was building in Ganjur and I didn't care for my chances, me a widow of forty years with plenty of land and no one to protect it. So I sold it for a fraction of its worth, the barley and the bladegrass and the fig trees I had loved so much. I took a whole packful of figs before I left. I didn't know where I was going. I thought I might just wander the mountains until I ran out of figs and starved or got eaten by a wolf. That's when I found Palta."

Mero said nothing. Ruya shifted her weight from one hip to the other, wincing at the stiffness. "I was afraid they would rob me or rape me. I expected them to chase me away. But they let me in, gave me an empty house to sleep in, practically begged me to stay. As luck would have it, it had only been a few days since Gorgol had eaten. I think if I had arrived as you arrived—just a day or two before he came—they would have fed me to him right away. But I made myself useful and so they chose someone else. And then again, and again. Fifteen years later and it just kept happening. There was always someone weaker, someone older, someone who didn't work as hard. But I'm older now, and I'm getting tired. I could tell I didn't have long."

The fire popped as Ruya's story wound to a close. Mero didn't know how to react. He felt that Ruya had stuffed a bundle into his hands—pieces of a shattered vase, or a tangle of knotted rope—and he knew it was precious to her but to him it was nonsense, it meant nothing. He didn't know how to use it but knew he couldn't throw it away. He wondered how he was supposed to act, having been given such a painful and pointless gift.

"Well?" Ruya said, an edge to her voice.

He swallowed and said, "You've certainly faced your share of hardship."

She snorted. "Who's to say what's my share? I've suffered far less than some. This world holds no shortage of grief. But that just makes the beautiful things in life all the more precious."

Mero wondered what parts of his life Ruya would consider beautiful.

"What about you?" Ruya asked. "Were you ever married?"

"No."

"I'm not surprised. You're married to that sword of yours."

His cheeks burned. Instinctively he clutched Sheathless tighter. "I'm not married to it. I'm just… responsible for it."

"That sounds like marriage to me." Ruya stretched her legs towards the fire. They were shorter, though thicker and stronger, than Mero's own. "You told Gorgol you made it."

Mero sensed the question hiding behind her words. "Yes. Though it would be more accurate to say I invented it."

"Invented? What does that mean?"

"It means I discovered something no other man had discovered before." There was pride in his answer, and Ruya heard it.

"And? What did you discover?"

He almost told her. He came within inches—the answer built in the back of his throat like a gobbet of phlegm. But he swallowed it at the last minute and said instead,

"The goddess."

Ruya was silent for a long time. It was clear his answer had confused her. He stared into the fire, his heart pounding as it always did when he talked about Sheathless. *Why don't I stop answering her questions?*

Why do I keep letting her do this?

Do this, the goddess said.

"So what does that mean?" Ruya asked at last. "Does she live inside the sword, this goddess of yours?"

"No," Mero said. The thought was ludicrous. "No, she—I think making the sword attracted her. Drew her attention."

Ruya's silence sucked at his words, begging to be filled, a siphon where truth begat truth.

"She's punishing me." Mero wrung his hands to stop them from shaking. "She's punishing me for making it. I—it was wrong. But now it's here, and it's too late to take it back. The blade—I can't break it. It can't be snapped or melted down. It can't even be scratched. And it—" he drew a shuddering breath. He was shaking all over, his sight swimming. The fire was an orange blob. "It gets hungry. I have to—to use it. Every so often. If I don't—it's like a fishhook in my heart. I don't dare deny it. I don't know what will happen if I do. That's why I have to go to Uron. I think—if it's a city from the old world, they might have technology that—I think the goddess is showing me where I can go to break the curse."

Curse, the goddess said.

He couldn't see Ruya anymore. Like the fire, she had melted into a formless blotch of color. Mero was unsure if he was sitting or standing, awake or asleep, alive or dead. The earth was escaping him, leaving him floating in space. Then Ruya wrapped her strong arms around his shoulders, pinning his own arms to his sides, and she bore him to the ground and held him fast while his mind flapped like a pennant in the wind.

His own breath rushed in his ears. His heart pounded in his head, obliterating all thought. The world had collapsed down to a single point, a distant star he could not feel or touch. Ruya's arms were like an iron shackle, warm and hard. Her own heartbeat slammed against his back, like a palm slapping a choking man.

At last Mero's breathing calmed. His eyes focused; he lay on his side, the fire dancing in front of him, Ruya behind him, her chest pressed against his back, her legs pressed against his legs, her breath hot on the back of his neck. He was trapped—trapped by the fact that Ruya was his only tether to this world, that he would go spinning into space as soon as she let go. He couldn't bear to be held by her, but nor could he bear to be alone.

"Please," he said, "don't let go."

"I won't," she said.

She didn't.

29

The next day it snowed.

Carpeted in white, the dead forest was almost pretty, but to Mero this meant a day of teeth-chattering cold. Though he and Ruya could keep warm at night, they had still not solved the problem of how to clothe him during the day without arousing Gorgol's suspicion. So Mero was still dressed in the flimsy shirt he had worn when he left Sanja's palace, and the only way he could keep reasonably warm was to press himself all day, walking hard and long until sweat broke on his brow. But this solution brought its own challenges. Mero was living on one meal a day, and a small one at that. By afternoon he was irritable, dizzy and parched. By evening he was nearing collapse. It was only the thought of seeing Ruya again, of sharing a meal and sitting by the fire, that kept him alive during those desperate, interminable days.

Gorgol was behaving strangely. One minute he would be jollier than ever, practically skipping along as he knocked trees aside. The next he would sink into brooding churlishness, shooting baleful, lingering looks at Mero when he thought he wasn't watching.

He's hungry, said the dark part of Mero's mind. *He's sizing you up. You'd better think of a way to escape him, and fast.*

But though Mero kept his eyes and ears open, and turned the problem over and over in his exhausted mind, he saw no way out of his predicament other than blowing the goddess's whistle, and feared that would make his problem worse instead of better. If he allowed himself to die and returned a worm on Sheathless's hook, and if Gorgol caught him in that state—what then? Would he remain a drooling simpleton until the end of time, not living, not dying, unable to restore himself and unable to end it all for good? The thought was darkly terrifying, and he backed away from it as one would from the edge of a pit.

"How long until we reach Uron?" he asked Gorgol once, not caring what the giant thought of the question.

Gorgol grinned, showing his millstone teeth. "That depends."

"On what?"

"Whether the weather holds or breaks. Whether we're able to cut through the mountains or forced to go around them."

"More mountains?" Mero said, dismayed by the news.

The grin widened. "Oh yes. We'll cut east tomorrow or later today. Then it's across the plains, around the lake, and through the mountains on the far side. I make it five days, maybe six."

Mero resisted the urge to search the sky for the moon. It had swelled visibly the past couple nights, the better part of its face revealed. Even so, his distress must have shown: Gorgol chuckled, his belly sloshing.

"Yes, you're cutting it rather close, I'd say. But if you keep up your pace"—his eyes twinkled—"who knows?"

More than once, Mero considered charging Gorgol and hacking him to pieces. He imagined slashing the giant's calcaneal tendon, which was thick as his wrist and tight as a bowstring. He felt the ground shake as Gorgol collapsed to one knee, saw himself dance under the giant's flailing arms and slit his belly from hip to hip. A torrent of blue organs would spill out, lost souls released at last, and Gorgol would wail and try to gather them up but Mero would hack off his fingers and gouge out his eyes and leave him bleeding in the snow.

It was a comforting vision, and when Gorgol's back was turned he allowed himself to believe it would come true. But then Gorgol would pin him under those hateful purple eyes with the undulating, umbilical pupils, and Mero would remember the giant sucking the pond dry with a single draw, his clapping the gray bird out of the air faster than Mero could blink. And the vision would die, and Mero would feel more helpless than ever before.

A small creature was strapped to Ruya's sledge when she caught him up that evening. It was about the size of a fox and there were three gray rings around its tail. Mero hardly believed their luck. He built a fire while Ruya drew out a knife and butchered her catch.

"Do you know what it is?" Mero asked her, pointing at the carcass with his chin. The creature had dark eyes and a stubby snout, also dark, as though it had been nosing around in coal dust.

Ruya shook her head. "Do you?"

"No. I've never been this far east."

"Nor I. It feels like we're at the end of the world."

Mero knew what she meant. The animal Ruya skinned was the largest living thing he had seen in weeks other than Gorgol, Ruya, and himself. The silence surrounding them was so profound it rang in Mero's ears. At times the emptiness of the world outside invaded his own thoughts, eating away at his memories, rendering him as barren on the inside as out.

"Well?" Ruya said. She had opened the animal's belly and was pulling out its guts. Her arms were red to the elbows.

"Well what?" Mero returned.

"What do you think?" She leaned in. "*Gorgol*. Do you have a plan yet?"

Mero bristled. "No."

"Time is running out."

"I know that!" Mero caught Ruya's expression and fought his anger down. "No," he said more softly. "I don't know what I'm going to do. Anything I can think of involves either killing him or tricking him, and I'm not sure I can do either."

Ruya sniffed and wiped her nose with her arm. Taking up her knife, she hacked off the animal's legs. "How far is it to Uron?"

"I don't know. Gorgol told me we're close but he could be lying."

"Of course he's lying. But what about your goddess? What does she say?"

"I told you, it doesn't work like that. She can't tell me anything I don't already know."

"You can't feel how close we are?"

"We're getting closer," Mero said. "I know that much is true. But anything more than that…"

Ruya nodded. "So we can't reach Uron in time and we can't outrun him and we can't kill him. So we have to trick him somehow."

Mero pressed his hands together and pushed them against the bridge of his nose. He had come to a similar conclusion himself, but it brought little comfort. Trickery required cunning, leverage, knowledge of one's opponent, but though they had been traveling together for nearly a month, Mero still knew vanishingly little about his adversary.

"We should just run away in the night," Ruya said. "We can hide somewhere in the forest and wait until he gives up and goes home."

"You told me he could smell a man from miles away," Mero said.

"What I *told* you was that he was probably lying."

"Bet your life?" Mero said.

Ruya pushed out her lip, the three uniform ridges appearing on her forehead. "It's been nearly a month and he hasn't smelled me."

"Unless he *has* smelled you, and he's been stringing us along this whole time. He's getting suspicious of me. He knows I should be dead by now."

Ruya impaled one of the creature's hind legs on the end of a stick and gave it to Mero to hang over the fire. "Then what's he waiting for? If all he wanted was our souls, he could have had them weeks ago. Why go to all this trouble?"

"Maybe he just likes seeing us squirm," Mero said, though he thought, *Ruya's right. There's more to this than meets the eye. Nothing Gorgol does makes any sense. Why gamble for my soul when he has hundreds waiting back in Palta? Why bother leading me to Uron instead of just getting me lost? Why leave me every night and give me a chance to run away?*

Mero's head ached. He was so tired he couldn't keep his eyes more than half open, and the smell of the meat cooking on the end of his stick was equal parts enticing and nauseating. He wanted to collapse against the earth and sleep away the night and maybe the following day, too—or better yet, blow the whistle around his neck and retreat to the goddess's kingdom, the place where everything was not.

"*Mero!*"

He jerked awake to discover that his stick had dipped into the fire, and the haunch of meat was being devoured by the flames. Cursing, he pulled it free and blew on it until it went out.

"I'm sorry," he said to Ruya. "And after all the trouble you went to capture it."

She shrugged. "What's done is done. But don't you dare throw that out. There's good meat on it still."

He nodded and lowered it towards the fire, this time watching it carefully.

"I still say we find some way to hide from him," Ruya said. "If we get far enough away and cover ourselves with mud and earth he won't be able to smell us out."

Mero stared at the piece of meat on the end of his stick. His mouth watered, though he couldn't tell if it was from hunger or from a desire to vomit.

"Well?" Ruya pressed.

"I don't know," Mero snapped. "I don't know what he can and can't smell. Neither of us do. You say he won't smell us but that's just a guess. You don't *know*."

"So what?" Ruya snapped back. "As if any man ever *knows* what's going to happen to him tomorrow, tonight, even five seconds from now. We all walk this life with one eye closed. If we didn't, what would be the point of living?"

"What?" said Mero, stunned by the idea that anyone could consider knowing little to be preferable to knowing much.

"What? What? What?" Ruya mimicked, her nostrils flaring. "Do you understand anything? Do you *care* about anything? Sometimes when I look at you I wonder how you are still alive. Would you even bother to feed yourself if I didn't come by? You're like a dead thing wearing the skin of something alive. Half the time you don't even seem to know where you are. You're confused by things a baby could understand. What happened to you? Where has your spirit gone, and why did it leave the rest of you behind?"

Mero stared at Ruya, her heaving chest, her wild eyes, her hands still drenched in blood. He had no idea how to react. The things she had said did not hurt him because he did not believe them. He was as alive as the next man—he should know that better than anyone. He pressed a palm to his chest, and sure enough, there was his heartbeat. Sheathless was quieted, for now. He was whole.

The fire popped in the silence.

"If you're afraid of Gorgol," Mero said at last, "you don't need to keep following us. This was my bargain—it's my burden to bear. If he catches me it's no one's fault but my own. You can stop caring for me, and save all your food for yourself. Your chances will be better that way."

Ruya stared at him, shaking, her lips pulled back in a horrified grimace. Tears glistened in the corners of her eyes, and she wiped them away, smearing blood on her cheeks.

"It's all right," Mero soothed, thinking he understood why she cried. "Don't worry about me. Worry about yourself. This fate isn't yours—it's mine."

Her chin trembled, the ridges on her forehead darkly pronounced. She shook her head, in small motions then in larger ones. She bit her lip and wiped her cheeks again and now her eyes were angry.

"Fine," she said. "Fine! I'll go. And good riddance! You're right—I don't need to worry about Gorgol stealing your soul. Do you know why?"

"Why?"

"Because you have none!"

She slammed her knife into the dirt, leaving it quivering next to the half-butchered carcass. Wiping her bloody hands on her coat, she stomped over to her sledge and stuffed her belongings pell-mell into the mouth of the topmost sack. Slinging the rope over her shoulder, she bent her weight against the heavy load and started dragging it back the way she'd come.

"Wait!" said Mero. "What about your coat?" He was wearing the cone-shaped grass coat, as he always did on cold nights.

"Keep it!" Ruya bellowed.

In seconds she had melted into the darkness. Mero was left alone with the coat and the fire and the knife and the carcass of the ring-tailed animal, its haunch still smoldering on the end of his stick.

Mero sat awake for some time, wondering what had happened. He was in a daze, the details of his argument with Ruya slipping away like quicksilver whenever he tried to focus on them. At length he realized the haunch of meat had cooked through and was getting dry, so he withdrew it from the fire, let it cool, then pulled it apart with his fingers and ate it. The taste of meat ignited his appetite, and soon he carved off more pieces of the animal and roasted them. He used Sheathless for all of his butchering, even the fine work, though Ruya's knife was still stuck in the ground where she had left it. The meat was dark and gamey, with a sour, peppery taste.

His meal complete, Mero fed the remains to the fire, then built a new fire a hundred paces away from the first, in case the smell of his meal attracted unwanted attention in the night. He sat by the second fire for a while, watching it burn out, telling himself he should fetch more wood even as the last of the flames gave way to embers and then to smoke and then to darkness, darkness.

30

"Here we are," Gorgol said expansively, gesturing out over the lake in a wide, sweeping motion. He was joyous today, ebullient even, a bounce to his every step as though his tendons had been keyed one turn tighter than normal. His belly was a great offensive ball rounder than the moon; he looked like a woman eight months pregnant. Blood danced under his skin and his eyes were like amethysts.

He squatted down to Mero's level and pointed. "See those mountains on the far shore? Uron lies just beyond them. You may win our wager yet."

Mero saw the mountains, a thin smear of gray. He looked at the expanse of still water that lay between him and them. He looked north up the shore, then south down it. The lake was a perfect mirror that reflected the sky, empty and vast.

"It's too big," he said. "We'll never get around it in time."

Gorgol looked delighted, and why shouldn't he? Everything had gone his way. "Well, that may be. But don't tell me you're giving up now—are you?"

Mero stared, eyes burning.

Gorgol widened his squat, hunkering closer, his bare feet knifing into the ground, displacing huge mounds of earth. "Tell you what," he said, in a conspiratorial whisper that echoed across the plains. "Since you've been such a good sport about all this, I'm willing to let you cheat a little."

Mero said, "How?"

The giant smiled. "If you wish it—and if you can promise not to lose your grip and get yourself lost down there where I can't reach you—I can ferry you across the lake."

"Why would you do that?" Mero asked, instantly suspicious.

"Why, it's just like I've said. I admire your pluck, and I want to give you a fighting chance. Wagers are no fun if there's no chance of losing. Oh, take me up on my offer, won't you? What have you got to lose?"

Mero didn't know what he had to lose, and that was what worried him. This wasn't the first time Gorgol had offered to carry him. Again the burning question: *why?*

"How will we ford the lake?" he heard himself ask. "Will you swim?"

"I'll walk along the bottom, and come up for air now and then. I can hold my breath for hours, you know. But I'll make sure to surface often enough so you don't drown."

He can't be trying to kill me, Mero thought. *He wants my ball, and he always takes them from his victims live.* Every time he thought of the little blue organs, he heard Ruya calling them "souls"—but he himself never thought of them that way.

"All right," he said. "You can carry me across. But I'll need to hold on to Sheathless with one hand."

"That's fine, that's fine," Gorgol said. "As long as you promise not to slit my throat with it. I'm taking a chance here, too, you know. I'm not entirely sure I trust you, the way you look at me sometimes. Just remember that if you kill me while we're out on the lake, you'll be certain to drown as well."

Mero blinked in the light of that sudden, dazzling thought. *Could he kill Gorgol out on the lake, while the giant was distracted and Mero rode mere inches from his neck?* It was true he would drown after the deed was done, but he had the silver fishhook to drag him to shore.

He could do it. This was his chance.

Careful, careful. Don't let it show.

"You can trust me," he said.

Gorgol reached down, palm facing the sky. His fingers uncurled, each the width of a young tree. The same fingers that had stolen Mosin's ball, and they burned with an infernal heat.

"Come along, I won't bite." Gorgol wore his best smile, his slablike teeth on display.

Mero stepped between the thumb and forefinger even as his instincts screamed at him to run. He put a foot on the pad of the palm and pulled himself up. Gorgol's flesh was stringy, his skin elastic. Mero's feet wobbled and he lost his balance. The fingers curled up, forming a cage with him inside.

"Careful," Gorgol said, in tones of great amusement. He rose to his feet, the ground under Mero's fleshy prison falling away. A story, two stories, three stories up, and the air was cooler, the wind higher. Mero wished he had had some way to keep Ruya's grass coat, for of course he had been forced to leave it behind when morning came.

Gently Gorgol brought Mero to his ear. He had almost no shoulders to speak of; his broad head melted easily into his torso, a great shaggy mound of flesh and hair like a hill covered in pale, wiry grass. He deposited Mero on a tiny shelf of bone that stuck out beyond his ear. Mero, gripping Sheathless with one hand, had to bury his left arm into Gorgol's mane for purchase. The hair was greasy and matted with filth, its smell that of a hog house. Wrinkling his nose, Mero wormed his fingers deeper, wrapping the hair around and around his wrist.

"Ouch!" Gorgol said. "No tugging, please."

Mero didn't apologize. He was too focused on keeping his balance. If he fell now, he would break every bone in his body.

"Ready?" Gorgol's throat vibrated through Mero's hand.

"Yes."

The bony platform swayed, and the wind intensified. They were moving. The sensation of flesh and bone shifting beneath him triggered in Mero the same unease he sometimes felt when riding horseback—the knowledge that he was beholden to a living creature outside his control. He kept his eyes on the shimmering lake, watching it draw rapidly closer.

"Hoh, that's cold!" Gorgol bellowed, his shins carving great channels in the water. "I can feel my grapes shriveling on the vine."

The ground rose up to meet them as Gorgol sank further into the lake—knees, thighs, waist. Mero would have been content to remain that way, out of the water yet close enough to drop safely into it. But the giant kept on, pushing against the water's resistance, leaving twin whirlpools in his wake. Steam rose from the ring around his belly where the surface met his flesh.

They were about a quarter of the way across the lake. The water had risen to Gorgol's chest and soaked the ends of his beard. Mero had been splashed once or twice and was shivering, his knuckles white. His right hand was a vise; he was terrified of dropping Sheathless.

"We're going under!" Gorgol cried. "Take a deep breath and don't let it go!"

The lake had swallowed Gorgol to his neck, Mero to his thighs. The force of the current was incredible. Mero sank into a sitting position, reversing his grip on Sheathless and thrusting his right hand into Gorgol's mane alongside the left. A second later, the giant took another step, and Mero was plunged underwater.

It was cold, so cold. It wanted to suck the breath from Mero's lungs, but he clamped his mouth shut and forced the air deep into his chest. Water rushed through his hair and clothes. His ears sang from the pressure. The lakebed was a landscape of rolling, sandy hills, utterly bare. There were no fish, no fronds, no shells, no hunks of blackened, half-rotten wood. Just water and sand, a desert described in muted shades of blue.

Gorgol trailed a cloud of filth as he walked along the lakebed. His mane streamed out behind him in a tangled mass, wild, powerful, and perverse. Clouds of bubbles escaped towards the surface.

Bubbles. Breath. Mero's own breath strained against his ribcage, pushing at the backs of his teeth. He glanced upward and his panic spiked. The surface was a distant, shimmering veil. How had they sunken so far so quickly?

An involuntary moan escaped him. A large bubble slipped between his lips and floated away. His heart roared. He untangled his arm from Gorgol's mane and beat on the side of the giant's head. His brain was on fire; he was almost blind with panic. He tugged at Gorgol's ear, not caring if this angered him.

Slowly Gorgol's head came around. His apelike features were curled in a victorious snarl. Threads of spittle swayed on his lips.

As he stared into the twin esophagi of Gorgol's pupils, Mero heard the giant's voice as clearly as if they were on land.

Hungry for air, are we? Isn't that a pity. I can hold my breath for hours, you know.

Perhaps we'll just stay down here a little longer.

No, Mero thought. *No, please.*

No? Don't you know it's too late to be saying "no" to me? Don't you know that it's always been too late? Foolish creature. You want to know why I struck that bargain with you, why I let you follow me around all month like a lost child? It was to teach you your place, to show you that there is nowhere you can go, nothing you can do, no one you can be to escape me! You're mine, all of you—you and the Paltans and that little bitch Ruya, too. I'll have you all for supper, your blue organs, your soul-candles, your delicious dama!

His hair unfolded in a crazed halo, and water rushed up Mero's nose: Gorgol had dropped into a crouch. He flexed his mighty thighs, dug his feet into the ground, and kicked off in a tremendous underwater jump. They rocketed upwards, fast as a breaching whale. Mero was flattened against Gorgol's shoulder, pinned down by the force of the current.

They exploded into sunlight, a geyser of froth and particles suspended in air. Mero's ribs creaked as his diaphragm expanded and his screaming lungs snapped open. A soaring instant of joy and relief was cut short when he swallowed about half a gallon of water and spit it back up, hacking and coughing.

"*Down we go-oo!*" Gorgol roared.

NO! Mero wanted to scream, but he couldn't afford to waste his precious breath.

They plunged back into the water, Gorgol falling feetfirst, Mero clinging to his beard. Mero's ears popped and water boiled up his nose, but between Gorgol and Sheathless he couldn't shift a hand to plug it. They sank towards the lakebed, the water getting colder with every second.

How much do you wish you were like me, Mero? Gorgol asked him in the silence and the darkness. *Look at how easy it all is for me. Look how I can bend the world to my will. Don't you wish you had been born a giant? Then you wouldn't even need that little toy of yours to keep you alive. But it must come in handy sometimes, being able to masquerade as a human.*

I am human, Mero thought desperately.

Oh, I don't think so. Perhaps once, but not anymore. Ruya was right about you. Even so, I'm willing to bet you still have a dama *to steal. Let's find out together, shall we? Ho ho ho!*

They struck the lakebed. A cloud of dust erupted all around them, grit settling in the crooks of Mero's eyes, the waistband of his pants. The sensation in his chest was so intense it was beyond pain. He was collapsing into a single dense point somewhere around his sternum. That part of him was boiling hot. The rest was icy cold.

Gorgol kicked off again. Mero's head swung down and smacked against the giant's shoulder. His teeth scythed down on his bottom lip and his mouth filled with blood.

The water brightened. Bubbles poured from their bodies like the trail of a comet. They breached the surface again, and Mero drew another desperate breath, gaping like a fish.

"Almost there!" Gorgol said cheerfully.

"*STOP!*" Mero screamed.

Gorgol either didn't hear him or didn't care. He sank into the water, dragging Mero down with him, taking up his lecture as soon as they were below the surface.

You see, little Mero, you humans are like dogs: you're only strong when you band together. You knew that once, and together you held the earth in the palm of your hand. You built each other up, great roads and cities and civilizations — much like this Uron you're so desperate to reach. But somewhere along the line you forgot the secret to your own greatness. You had stood on each other's shoulders so long you became convinced you were giants yourselves. And a giant doesn't need anything to survive but himself. But men are not giants, no matter how high you build. As individuals, even the greatest among you is frightfully weak. The worst thing that can happen to a man is to find himself alone, yet you do it to yourselves willingly—just like you did with poor Ruya.

It's enough to make me laugh.

Ho, ho, ho.

Did you think that little sword of yours would be enough to keep me at bay?

Ho, ho, ho.

Foolish, foolish Mero. That toy only works against other humans. And a giant is not a human, nor is a human a giant, no matter how much you might wish it otherwise.

Ho, ho, ho.

They struck bottom. Mero was incoherent, fading in and out of consciousness. Sensation came to him in fits and spurts, a twinge of pain here, a sweep of cold there. Some of Gorgol's hairs were wrapped around his neck, choking him. But what he felt most was a gray, tingling emptiness.

Rushing, frothing speed, then sunlight slipped under his fluttering eyelids. He heard the scrape of feet dragging in the sand. Then red darkness closed around him, and he was thrown onto his back. He raised Sheathless but it was swatted out of his hand. The next time he tried to move his arm, it wouldn't obey him.

Gorgol's face swam into view, blotting out the sky, blotting out everything. He was as vast as the universe, as inescapable as death.

"Don't worry, now," Gorgol said soothingly. "You won't feel a thing."

Mero screamed and screamed, but there was nowhere he could go, nothing he could do, no one he could be other than himself.

Part IV

31

The beach was cold and waterlogged, the sand dark where it met the lake. A solitary bird waddled by the shoreline, honking softly to itself.

Mero felt a presence by his shoulder, behind him, just out of sight.

"He didn't find anything," it said. "I kept it safe, don't worry."

Mero's eyes were vacant, open to the sky. Light poured into them, sending signals to his brain—blue, gray, light blue, white—but the colors were meaningless, words whispered from too far away in a language he didn't understand.

"You will be able to complete your mission," the presence went on, "but I need a favor in return."

What favor?

"I can't tell you," said the goddess. "I can't tell you anything you don't already know."

Mero asked her, *why did you let this happen to me?*

"I let everything happen. I don't ask you to understand. I don't ask you to do anything—except this once."

What do I need to do?

"You don't get to know. We all walk through life with one eye closed."

Ruya?

He rolled onto his side, and his lower half exploded with pain. He gasped and fell back, but that only made the pain worse. His pelvis had shattered into a thousand bony razors that shredded his flesh every time he moved.

"Stop," said a voice. A gentle hand touched his shoulder. "Don't move. Just don't move."

His eyes were open, pointed at the sky. White, gray, mustard yellow. The pain had receded to a dull throb that flared with every movement. And he was moving—he could hear the rasp and trickle of earth sliding past his ear.

"Uhn," he said. He tried to move his arms but his left shoulder was on fire and he couldn't tell where his right arm was, or even if it was still there. A choking sound bubbled up from his throat.

"Gorg—Gorg—"

"He's gone," Ruya said. She stroked his hair, his cheeks, his hair again, rapid motions like she was soothing a crying dog. "He's long gone. He got what he wanted and he'll leave you alone forever, now. You'll never see him again. You're still here and that's all that matters."

Mero's lip quivered. Ruya swooped down and planted a kiss on his forehead. It burned, lingering long after she drew away.

"It will all be better soon, you'll see. Every day it will get better. That's how you escape a giant, Mero. You escape into tomorrow."

Tomorrow:

He had sweated and groaned through the morning, though Ruya was the one pulling the sledge. She stopped for a rest and wiped both of their faces with the same dry cloth, breathing heavily through her nose as she worked. Mero focused on the three smooth ridges of her forehead.

"I was angry with you," she said, "but I couldn't leave you. I found the coat you left behind and saw Gorgol's footprints headed for the lake. By the time I found you he was gone. I thought he had killed you, but you were still breathing."

Still breathing, said the goddess. Mero felt surreptitiously at his chest, slipping a hand over his heart. It was quiet.

"I don't know where we're going," Ruya went on, worried. "I turned south when we reached the mountains because I didn't think I'd be able to pull you over them. The sky down here is very strange, and sometimes I hear noises on the wind, like the earth is moving around. There's nothing to eat." She smiled sadly, snatching a drop of water from Mero's cheek. "We're alive for now, but I don't know how much longer we'll be able to last. We may starve after all."

"Ruya," Mero said, "where is Sheathless?"

Her face soured. "I found it in the sand." She hesitated a moment, then added in a rush, "I tried to break it. It was lying there winking at me and I just hated it and wanted it to break. So I pushed two rocks together and tried to snap it between them. But it just bent like a bow and I imagined it slipping free and slicing me open somehow. I swear I heard it snarling at me, and I wondered if it had sent me that vision as a warning. So I stopped trying to break it and brought it with me. I wish I hadn't."

"Ruya," Mero grasped at her, finding her wrist and holding it tight. "Ruya, you have to run, as far away from me as you can."

"I'm not leaving you again."

"It's not safe. I can't—I won't be able to control myself."

Her frown deepened into a scowl. "Is that how it is? Are we just chickens in a pen, you and me and Gorgol? He pecked you, so you'll peck me? Are you no better than a giant?"

"I'm no giant," Mero whispered. "I know that now."

"Then I am safe with you," Ruya declared.

32

Days later he could stand but not sit. Ruya wanted him to ride in the sledge but he insisted on walking. At first, every step was agony. The bones of his pelvis rasped together, and to set his foot down was to push a long, thin needle of pain up through his leg and into his stomach. His entire waist from his navel to his knees was one enormous bruise, red, purple, and yellow-green. But despite the pain—perhaps even because of it—the act of walking on his own two legs brought a fierce sense of accomplishment, as though these timid, halting steps were his first. Ruya watched him carefully, holding out a hand whenever he needed it, insisting he rest if his nausea got too strong. In this manner they proceeded south, across endless expanses of sand and rock, the sky a sickly, lemon yellow.

"There it is," Ruya said, letting the sledge's rope go slack. "That sound, like the earth is moving. What is that?"

It was distant and low, a groaning like a galley at sea, more felt than heard.

"I think I know," Mero said, though he hardly believed it.

"What do you think you know?"

He shook his head. "Just watch where you step."

The rumbling of the earth followed them all day and into the night. It shuddered up from below when they stretched out to sleep.

Nighttime was a source of constant agony for Mero. It brought relief from the pain of walking, but the cost was hours of rock or hard earth pushing against his pelvis, jabbing at his bruises no matter which way he lay. It was warmer here—that was a mercy, as Mero could sleep on top of the grass coat instead of under it. His clothes were all Ruya's, too small for him. She had left his own on the beach after seeing the state they were in.

The first night they were together, Ruya tried handing him a flat-bread covered in bean paste. He waved it away, saying,

"I don't need it."

Ruya was too confused to be angry. "What are you talking about? You haven't eaten since you woke, you must be starving."

"Not for that," Mero said.

The silence that followed teemed with unspoken words. The flatbread flopped sadly off the ends of Ruya's fingers. Slowly she withdrew it.

He expected her to question him, to ask him why he wasn't hungry, to wonder why he still had his wits about him. But she didn't, possibly because she, like he, sensed that to ask these questions and to hear the answers would spell the end of their relationship. So the silence between them stretched on, a gulf slowly widening though they sat shoulder-to-shoulder in the dark.

Mero could still not think directly about what had happened between him and Gorgol on the beach. He could think around it, could look at it from a distance, but when he tried to focus the lens of his thoughts he met resistance, as though a gentle hand was steering him away, saying, *not yet, not yet.*

At night he dreamed of purple eyes in the darkness, and woke whimpering, drenched in sweat. Invariably he would wake Ruya, and she would rise, bleary-eyed, and sit by his side, stroking his face until he calmed down.

Sometimes the nightmares struck even during the day. Mero would be walking along, wincing, each step a third of its regular length, and suddenly a feeling of panic would sweep over him like a rising tide. Within seconds he would be helpless and shaking, dark curtains drawing shut across his sight. He would suck in breath after shallowing breath, but there was no air inside his lungs or out.

"Mero, Mero," Ruya would say, stroking his face and arms. "Look at me. Look at my eyes. Look at the ground. Look at the sky."

Once, Mero simply stopped.

They had been plodding along, Mero with Sheathless, Ruya with her sledge, across featureless plains underneath an equally featureless sky. The earth was the color of iron and the sky was yellow from horizon to horizon, hazy and thick with half-formed cloud. It was neither hot nor cold.

Mero stopped between one step and the next, looking at the ground. Ruya got twenty paces ahead of him before realizing she had left him behind. She sighed, cracked her back, then dropped the sledge's rope and doubled back.

"Mero?" she said. "Are you all right?"

He didn't answer.

"Are you tired? Would you like to rest?"

"No," Mero said.

She watched him for some time, her hands on her hips. Where before she had been plump, now the bones of her shoulders and hips stuck out from her frame. Even her cheeks and neck were thinner, her dark skin stretched tight. The wrinkles on her forehead were more pronounced than ever as she looked at him with pity.

"Mero," she said, "if you need to rest, rest. It doesn't make you any less of a man."

"I don't need to rest," Mero said, though that was a lie; he wanted to fall asleep and never wake up.

"Maybe your legs don't," Ruya said, "but your heart does."

"What's the point?" Mero meant it as a genuine question, and when Ruya didn't answer he looked into her eyes and said, "Ruya, what's the point of anything? What's the point of life? Of death? Why do we continue to live? Why am I here with you? Why are you here with me? What does it all come to—what does it mean? When creatures like Gorgol—"

It was the first time he had spoken the giant's name since the day on the beach, and it winded him like a blow to the stomach. He staggered and nearly fell. He realized he was crying and swiped his tears away.

Ruya folded her arms and drew a deep breath through her nose. Breathing it out, she said, "I don't know the answers to any of the questions you asked. I'm only a foolish woman who's had her heart broken more times than she can count. I've lost two husbands and three children and still think I'm fit to be a mother. I don't know why I'm here and not someone else. I don't know why Gorgol is allowed to walk this earth without God's wrath striking him down. But I do know this. Life is a bird. We leave our mother's wombs and take flight, and sometime later—forty years or a hundred or one or none—we fall back down to earth. Much of life is outside our control, and it hurts—how it hurts. But it's all we have. It's a vessel that holds everything inside: our hopes, our fears, our loves and our losses. And when we die, it breaks, and everything spills out, and we have nothing left forever, until the end of time." She looked away, over the empty plains. "I don't think life has a reason. I don't think anything does."

"Ruya," Mero said, "I will live forever if I don't reach Uron."

She looked at him, hard.

"Sheathless is the key to eternal life," he said. "I discovered it myself, forged it myself. It was my lifelong obsession, ever since I realized I would die someday if I didn't find some sort of cure. I'm older than I look. I don't know how old I am—I've forgotten—I'm not sure how much I've forgotten but I think I've been alive for over two hundred years."

Ruya's mouth came open, her expression crystallizing into one of horror, anger, disbelief.

"It works on the same principle as the gigas," Mero said. "I studied them—I funded an expedition to the lost continent so I could see them up close. It steals energy from other living creatures—from other humans. When I kill with Sheathless, I take the life force of my victim into myself. It makes me stronger. But Sheathless has a mind of its own. It gets hungry. It demands a kill every so often, even when I'm perfectly healthy." He breathed deep and said, "I've lost track of how many lives I've taken. Based on how long I think I've been alive, I reckon it's at least a thousand people."

Ruya fell heavily to the ground, landing on her rump. Mero's own tailbone twinged in sympathy. She looked at him, at Sheathless, at the sky, but found nothing to say. Then she gasped.

"It was *you!*" she cried. "*You're* the one who killed Barkar!"

"Yes," Mero said. "You thought you had saved my life when you pulled me from the ice. But I was already dead—or perhaps I died on the way to the village. Either way, I had no choice."

"*You had a choice!*" she shrieked. "*You could have—you could—*"

"I'm not asking for you to forgive me," Mero said, "only to understand. Everything I do is because of Sheathless. Everything I am is what Sheathless made of me. I'm the same as Gorgol, a parasite that exists to drain the life from those around me. The only difference between us is that he's stronger."

Ruya's shoulders shook, and she buried her face in her hands. Mero was taken aback. He had expected her to be furious with him, possibly to scream or even try to kill him. He hadn't expected tears. He reached out to her, waiting to see her reaction. But she neither saw nor heard his approach, and he decided not to touch her after all.

Finally the sobbing stopped, and Ruya took her hands from her face. She didn't look at him, but at the palms in her lap, as if wondering whose they were. She was still for a long time. Mero's hips throbbed.

"Ruya?" he said softly.

"Why are you telling me this now?" Her voice was froglike.

"I don't know," Mero said. "I thought you might be able to tell me."

Ruya snorted. "My mother once told me it wasn't a woman's job to fix a broken man. I asked her, what about Father?" She laughed shortly. It was a stretched, woeful sound. "I'll never forget the look on her face when I said that. I thought she might beat me, but she only laughed and said I knew everything I needed to know about being a woman." She turned her shining eyes on him. "What do you think of that?"

He shook his head. "I don't know. I don't know anything anymore."

"You know plenty of things. Just none of the things that matter."

"How did you do it?" Mero asked her. "How did you become so wise?"

"I've had children, and I've lost them. Once you've held your lastborn to your breast and felt him go from hot to cool to cold in your arms, nothing else can puzzle you."

"Do you hate me?" Mero asked then.

"Right now? Right now, yes, I do hate you. I hate you for what you are and for what you did to Barkar, and to all the poor souls who crossed your path. But I think your goddess has made you suffer in equal measure to the suffering you have caused. And in the end..." She trailed off.

"In the end what?" Mero pressed.

She shrugged, spreading her hands as if to say, *it's gone*. "In the end I can't be bothered. I'm too old to hate anymore. It never does any good. I'll leave the hating to the young and foolish, those who still think you can make the world a better place by chopping away the parts of it you don't like."

"You're not so old," Mero said, wanting to compliment her.

She gave him that look that made him feel like a child. "I'm closer to death than I am to life. My peak is behind me—but that suits me fine. When your back aches as much as mine does, you don't mind walking downhill."

The earth rumbled into the silence that followed. Chips of stone shuddered and leapt at Mero's feet, making a noise like so many chattering teeth.

"Now what *is* that?" Ruya said.

"I think it's a gigas," Mero replied.

33

Again Mero offered to pull the sledge and again Ruya refused. He was secretly relieved. A deep, throbbing ache had settled into his hips, and the muscles of his thighs and buttocks were seizing up. He thought of the baths at Sanja's palace, of the scalding pools wreathed in plumes of fragrant steam, and wished he could strip himself bare and sink into the water until it swallowed him whole.

"I thought the gigas were nothing but stories." Ruya spoke to the ground, bent nearly double against the sledge's rope.

"Not at all," Mero said. "They're very real."

"You said you studied them."

"On the lost continent, yes."

"I've never heard of that, either."

"It's across the western sea. You need a special boat to reach it—one that can handle the storms—and months' worth of provisions."

"What was it like?"

"It's a wasteland." Mero looked at the yellowing sky. "The gigas have picked it clean. No one knows who created them or why, but the sight of men or anything built by men drives them into a frenzy. According to some texts, the lost continent was once home to the greatest civilization of men the world has ever seen. If that's the case, it might explain why the gigas have destroyed it so thoroughly." He scratched the back of his hand. "The earth there looks like a leper's skin. There are no animals, and all of the plants are poison."

"That sounds like the place Gorgol took us," Ruya said.

The same thought had occurred to Mero. "Before I came here, I visited a bazaar on the threshold of the desert. There was an old hellhole there filled with water—they were using it as the town's well. And there was another, deeper in the desert." He scratched his hand again and gave voice to his hypothesis: "It could be the goddess has had me following this gigas' tracks the entire time."

"Hellhole?" Ruya said. "What is that?"

Mero thought of the well at Sanja's bazaar, of the cool, dark waters running deeper than the eye could see. "It's what gigas leave behind when they feed."

A ridge of mountains rose in the distance and they turned towards it without speaking, eager for shelter from the wind. Their pace had slowed considerably, Mero weakened by his injuries and Ruya's seemingly bottomless well of energy running dry. The mountains loomed over them like the spine of some ancient and terrible creature, all but buried by the sand.

The rumbling grew worse that night, earth and sky shaking as though the very foundation of the firmament was crumbling. The wind rose until it stripped the land bare, scooping it up in massive clouds and sending it crashing back to earth in a fusillade of sand and rock. The din was incredible. Mero and Ruya, for fear of being buried alive, climbed as high up the mountain's shoulder as they could manage, then squeezed behind an exposed knife of rock for shelter. They huddled in each other's arms, hiding behind their coats as the storm pelted them with chips of rock.

Dark clouds boiled in the distance. Every so often Mero caught a flash of red among the black. The shaking earth struck his bruised hips and the pain grew and grew until it was all-encompassing. He wished he could stand and stretch, or fall asleep, or perish and be rid of the pain. But the storm didn't abate, and sleep didn't come, and he was trapped in that nightmare world until he thought he would lose his mind.

A trumpeting noise slammed against Mero's already-battered eardrums, startling him awake. Despite everything, he had fallen into a fitful doze. Ruya was curled under his arm, not moving.

The sky was red from horizon to horizon.

The trumpeting came again, impossibly loud, the bellowing of an elephant god. Mero clapped his hands to his ears, but Ruya barely stirred. Her lips moved, but he couldn't hear a word she said. In the crimson light, it looked as though her face was covered in blood.

"WE HAVE TO GET OUT OF HERE!" Mero screamed.

She blinked, uncomprehending. An eel of fear wriggled in Mero's gut. Ruya's skin was stretched tight, her hair curled and graying. He hadn't noticed just how gaunt she had become.

"GET UP!" he bellowed. *"WE'LL DIE IF WE DON'T MOVE!"*

He tried to help her stand but could barely move himself. His waist was a column of stone. He pushed Ruya onto her stomach and she groaned, coughing. Stabbing Sheathless into the earth, he managed to pull himself to his feet. He almost bent to help Ruya before realizing she would pull him down long before he pulled her up. He settled for shielding her from the wind with his body, shouting at her all the while.

"WAKE UP! THERE'S A GIGAS OUT THERE —"

The sky-rending bellow came again, and the shaking under their feet intensified. At last Ruya snapped out of her daze. She stumbled to her feet, looking around as though she couldn't remember how she had gotten here.

"Aza?" she cried. *"Aza, is that you?"*

Mero took her by the cheeks and screamed in her face. *"RUYA! IT'S ME, MERO! WE HAVE TO GO, NOW!"*

There was a sound like the spine of the earth cracking. A shower of rock and earth slid past them. A stone the size of a man's fist kicked up from the landslide and struck Ruya squarely on the cheek. She screamed, spinning halfway around.

Mero wasted no more time on words. He seized Ruya's hand and ran, headed for the foot of the mountain.

"MY SLEDGE!" Ruya screamed.

Mero ignored her. The earth heaved, a fissure opening along the mountain's base. A cascade of rock spilled into it, red falling to black. Mero pulled Ruya along the fissure's length, dancing on top of the shifting stone, not daring to rest even for an instant—that was all it would take for them to be swept under and crushed.

They reached the end of the fissure and Mero dragged them across its path, away from the mountain and out onto the open plain. The earth here was firmer, and they made it twenty paces before an earth-shaking concussion knocked both of them from their feet. The impact was accompanied by a booming vortex of wind, a slipstream powerful enough to suck them back towards the mountain.

Mero landed hard on his back, his right leg folded under him at an unnatural angle. Red flowers bloomed in front of his eyes. A muffled sound filled his ears and a warm lassitude spread over him like a blanket.

Then he was back, rolling onto his stomach, crawling to Ruya. She was curled on her side, cradling her head in her arms. She jumped when Mero touched her, revealing a face wreathed in terror.

"Is it the end of the world?" she cried.

Mero only motioned for her to stand, hating that he didn't have the strength to pull her up himself. He grabbed her hand to lead her away, but it slipped limply from his own, forcing him to turn back and see what had distracted her.

The mountain had come alive.

It was impossible to see the true shape of the gigas among the expanding cloud of dust and debris, just as it was impossible to see that of the gigas that had attacked it. The mountain gigas—the one whose back Mero and Ruya had scaled—was reptilian in shape, with a sinuous body and thick, lashing tail. It had over a dozen pairs of legs and undulated across the ground with eellike grace.

The other gigas looked nothing like it. Its torso was a weighty column like the trunk of the tree of life, at the top of which was balanced a wide, flat disc. Hundreds of long, tubelike arms hung from the disc, whipping rapidly in complex patterns. Red lightning arced between them, bright enough to brand flaming scars on the backs of Mero's eyes.

"LOOK AWAY!" he shouted at Ruya.

She swayed on her feet a few paces away, arms at her sides, head hanging at an angle, illuminated in silhouette by the red lightning of the tower gigas. Cursing, Mero limped over to her and grabbed her hand again. She let him pull her for a step or two, but her arm was dead weight, the fingers limp, sausage in its casing.

"WHAT'S THE MATTER WITH YOU?" Mero bellowed. *"HURRY!"*

Tears streamed from her eyes, her hair swept back from her face. *"Mero,"* she wailed. *"I can't. I can't."*

He didn't know what she thought she couldn't do, just that they would be killed if they didn't get out of the way. The only thing a gigas hated more than humans was another gigas. These two would keep fighting until one or both were dead, and gigas were almost impossible to kill. Their battle might last for months.

The mountain gigas wrapped itself around the tower gigas and spewed a green substance from its mouth, something that crawled up and down its opponent's sides in living tendrils like tree roots. The tower gigas responded with an ear-splitting klaxon, the disc on its head sprouting a fresh array of segmented arms. They formed a wiry sphere, spinning rapidly.

The wind rose, and Mero tasted iron. A bolt of red lightning arced from the sphere, grounding itself with a crash. It was followed by another, and more after that. Soon bolts rained down in incredible numbers, some burrowing into the mountain gigas, others leaving sizzling craters in the earth. A wave of intense heat billowed over the plain, hot enough to burn.

That, at least, was enough to pull Ruya out of her daze. She screamed, and the next time Mero took her hand, she almost fell over him in her haste to escape the hideous lightning. She ran and Mero limped in a direct line away from the gigas, chased by wave after wave of blistering heat. All the while the earth shook and the terrible sounds of the gigas' battle assaulted their ears: the shriek of metal on stone, the sizzle and crunch of electricity, the gigas' eerie, inhuman cries.

They ran and ran, their clothes smoking, Mero's hip a white-hot furnace. They snatched glances over their shoulders, but the gigas never seemed any further away. The cloud of dust the gigas kicked up caught them up and engulfed them. Mero pulled his shirt over his mouth and nose, closing his eyes to slits.

"*RUYA!*" he bellowed. She had been nearly within arm's reach, but suddenly he couldn't see her.

"*Mero?*"

Her voice came from up ahead. He stumbled towards it until they almost ran into each other. Ruya screamed.

"It's me!" he said. "Ruya, it's me."

She clutched her heart, her mouth drawn down in a horrified grimace. She coughed, and Mero grabbed a fistful of her shirt and pulled it up over her face.

"*Where are they?*" she shouted.

Mero planted his left foot and lurched around in a circle, but the dust was so thick he might as well have been blind. He pushed an arm into the cloud and it disappeared up to the shoulder. He still heard the bellowing of the gigas, but the noise was so intense it seemed to come from every direction at once.

"*This way!*" he shouted, though it was more a guess than anything. Ruya followed with shuffling steps.

They plodded through the swirling darkness. Mero sweated profusely from the pain in his pelvis, and his face was caked in dirt. Behind them the gigas' battle raged on. The mountain gigas had a broad range of vocalizations. Sometimes it roared like a large predator and sometimes its voice took on a singing, flutelike quality. The noises the tower gigas made were not like those of any living animal. They were flat, mechanical sounds, bells and sirens and a low, ominous hum that made Mero's teeth ache whenever it vibrated up from the earth.

"They're killing each other," Ruya wailed.

"Better each other than us," Mero said.

"I can't listen." Ruya was hysterical. "It's horrible."

"Then keep walking."

So they did, for a period of time that had no meaning in the endless cloud of dust. Mero's shoulder ached from holding Ruya's hand, but he didn't dare let her go lest they lose each other for good. He couldn't tell if they were walking in the right direction. Light flashed on the horizon to their left, jarring him into uncertainty. Surely they hadn't turned a circle? He tried adjusting their course, but now it sounded like the gigas were directly ahead of them. He staggered to a stop, stuck in indecision.

"Which way do we go?" he asked Ruya.

"I don't know," she said sullenly. The dust had turned her gray from head to toe. No doubt Mero looked the same.

He spun around again, trying and failing to orient himself. His throat was raw and stinging. He longed to collapse and sleep, even here on the hard desert ground. His legs trembled. It would be so easy to just let them buckle.

He rubbed the dust from his eyes, slapped himself a few times, then picked a direction at random and started to walk. "This way."

Eventually he realized he no longer heard the gigas. Their battle had been impossibly loud, the percussive blows and claps of lightning agony on the ears—yet Mero was so tired he hadn't even noticed those sounds fade to an eerie silence. Dust still hung in an oppressive cloud, and the air was musty and stale.

"Mero?" Ruya asked tentatively. "Where are we going?"

He kept his head down. "I don't know."

They shuffled along, a pair of clay statues. Sheathless weighed heavily in Mero's hand. The sword pulled him onwards and down, even as Ruya pulled him back.

His focus flagged. His sight became a smear. He brought his hand to his face and was shocked to find it empty. Despite his best efforts, he had let Ruya go.

"*Ruya?*" he called into the emptiness. "*RUYA?*"

He thought he heard her calling him, as if from a great distance. He squinted into the dust. Was that a dark shape, huddled against the ground? He stumbled towards it, the earth pitching and swaying like the deck of a ship.

"*RUYA!*" His voice cracked, and the next time he tried to scream it came out as a whisper.

There *was* a shape close to the ground, about ten paces away. Ruya must have fallen, but the fact that she hadn't cried out worried him. Her form was utterly still.

She's dead. The thought was loose before he could hold it back, and he staggered into a run, his mind on fire.

"No," he said aloud. "Don't be dead, you can't be dead, you can't—"

He realized many things at once.

The first was that the dark shape on the ground had been much closer than he realized.

The second was that Ruya *was* calling him—only her voice was behind him and far away.

The third was that the dark shape he had been running towards was not Ruya, but the mouth of a hellhole.

The fourth was that he was falling.

His arms scraped the sides of the hellhole once or twice, but otherwise he dropped smoothly and silently into the bowels of the earth. It was strangely peaceful. There was no light, just the constant rush of wind from below.

Then nothing.

34

ubbles escaped his clothes, crawling over his skin in their bid to reach the surface. It was cold, so cold, but a fire burned in his lungs. He didn't need to breathe, but his body still thought it was drowning.

As his awareness seeped back, instinct took over. He kicked off in the direction of the bubbles, scooping water with his hands. His palms scraped against an underwater wall, hard and flat, and he crawled up it, panic rising higher and higher in his throat. The world was black. He had no idea how far he had sunken while dazed.

Suddenly there was a lack of resistance above his head and he broke out of the water with a gasp. He sucked air greedily, pedaling his feet, and slicked the water from his face. He blinked several times, even holding a finger near his lashes to feel them flutter, but still couldn't see anything. Fear gripped him.

Have I gone blind?

Carefully he struck out, feeling his way through the water. It wasn't frigid, but the cold of spring water yet to be warmed by the sun. Mercifully, his swim was short. An inclined surface rose up under his feet, a ramp dipping into the water. He crawled onto land on his hands and knees. There he collapsed and lay curled for an indeterminate time.

It was still utterly black when he came to, the darkness pressing against his eyes and ears. The surface under him was hard but smooth, too smooth even for rock. Mero supposed it was metal. When he coughed, the sound reverberated all around him. A tunnel made of metal, then, strange as that was.

Realizing he wasn't holding Sheathless, Mero flew into a momentary panic, feeling around for something he knew wouldn't be there. As he crawled up the metal ramp, the fishhook dug into his chest, pulling him back towards the water. He realized the sword was far below him, at the bottom of the pool from which he had emerged.

He moaned aloud. The thought of diving into that water was appalling, but that of leaving Sheathless behind was even worse. The fishhook would only grow hotter, crueler, more insistent, drawing him implacably back to this place. Such was the hold Sheathless had over him. He would crawl through hell itself to retrieve it.

Suddenly he found himself hating the sword—truly and utterly hating it, wishing not only to destroy it, but to make it suffer as he had suffered. How many years had he wasted in the thrall of that cursed blade, sacrificing strangers, friends, and loved ones on the altar of its insatiable appetite? And for what—this miserable half-life filled with pain and regret?

In that moment, Mero hated Sheathless more than he hated Gorgol the giant.

You were right, Ruya, he thought, though even then he wasn't sure what he meant. *You were right about everything*.

He started to take off his shoes, then realized he might not find them again if he set them down. That meant there was nothing to do but wade into the chilly water, feeling the way forward with his hands and feet. The ramp descended steadily into the pool, then fell off abruptly about five feet below the surface. Mero held his breath, ducked under the water, and prodded around with his foot, but felt nothing beyond it. He sensed that Sheathless was quite a ways below—perhaps twenty feet, perhaps more. It was a dive Mero never would have attempted alive, even if he could have seen the bottom.

He stood shivering for a moment, marshalling his courage, then drew a huge breath and plunged straight down, kicking furiously. The temperature plummeted as he descended. His lungs once again burned—with every stroke that brought him deeper into the pool, the screaming of his animal senses grew harder to ignore. He opened his eyes, but there was nothing to see, not even his own arms; he might have been swimming in ink. Sheathless was still further below. He let the silver fishhook guide him, his lungs on fire, his shoulders on fire, his muscles seizing up in the cold. Suddenly he collided with a hard stone floor and his spirits soared. He skated his fingers over the smooth surface, groping for Sheathless like a blind man for his cane. And there it was—a hard metal edge biting into his finger. He closed his fist around the blade, not caring when it cut his skin to the bone, and kicked off from the bottom with both legs. He soared upwards, racing his bubbles, then breached the surface in another flurry of coughing and spitting.

Mero waited until he was at the top of the ramp to release his grip on Sheathless, and even then it was only to take the hilt with his other hand. Pulling his palm free of the blade was like pulling an axe from a chopping block—there was a sickening moment of resistance, and Mero imagined a gash in his palm like a thin red mouth.

He sat in the dark for some time, gathering his strength, then rose to explore his surroundings.

It *was* a tunnel made of metal, about ten paces wide, with a ceiling low enough to brush his fingers against. Metal pipes snaked along the walls. Mero rapped one with Sheathless's pommel and the resulting knell reverberated down the corridor. Mero instantly regretted what he had done. The ringing of the pipe was unnaturally loud and lingered far too long. When it finally faded, it left a hollow, expectant silence in its wake.

He started down the corridor, tracing his fingers along the leftmost wall to keep himself from getting lost. A moment later, he froze in place, cold adrenalin trickling down his spine.

Something was in the tunnel with him.

He strained his ears, not breathing, not moving, but heard nothing else. He couldn't tell if the noise had come from ahead or behind. The cold walls threw sound back and forth between them.

Eventually he convinced himself he hadn't heard anything at all. He took a tentative step forward, then another.

Soon he realized what had happened. It was his own footsteps he had heard. They echoed down the length of the tunnel, doubling and redoubling, then reached his ears again seconds after he had made them. It was enough to sound like someone was following him, but he was only following himself.

Drunk with relief, Mero quickened his pace. It was easy going. The tunnel ran perfectly straight, its floor perfectly flat. His wet shoes slapped loudly against the metal.

Emptiness yawned where the tunnel wall had been a second ago.

Catching himself, Mero groped backwards until he found a hard corner where the tunnel angled sharply to the left. Or perhaps it branched—blind as he was, Mero couldn't tell if there was anything ahead. He considered taking his hand off the wall to check, but judged it too risky—in this utter darkness, one wrong move could get him lost.

Lost, said the goddess.

Of course—he reflected bitterly, shivering there in the dark—he was already lost, about as lost as it was possible to be. He had no idea how far he had fallen, no clue what kind of place this was. It was clear it had been excavated by man—man being the only animal that worked in right angles—but when or by whom or for what purpose Mero could not guess.

If it was made by humans, there will be a way to the surface, he reassured himself. *Man doesn't live underground.*

Thought of the surface reminded him of Ruya. He remembered how weak she had been on their final night, how vulnerable and afraid. They had had to abandon her sledge when the mountain gigas awoke, which meant she had no food, no water, and no hunting tools. She had no chance of returning to Palta, and no chance of reaching Uron without Mero's guidance. She was doomed to die out there on the plains—if she wasn't dead already.

In his mind's eye Mero saw her wandering alone across the wasteland, her face gaunt, her hands trembling, her steps growing more and more unsure as hunger and fatigue overtook her. He saw her collapse face-first in the dirt, a woman wizened before her time, a woman who had lost two husbands and three children and suffered four lifetimes' worth of agony, fated never to reach her promised land. There would be no one to mourn or bury her. Her corpse would be picked apart by animals or simply left to rot in the sun. Her organs would bloat and then rupture, one by one. Her skin would blacken and peel away. In the end even her bones would crumble to dust, and Ruya's assimilation into the greater universe would be complete.

No, Mero thought, pushing the terrible image away—partly because he cared for Ruya, and partly because in it he saw reflected the truth of his own death. *No, it won't happen.*

But, of course, it *would* happen—to Ruya, to him, to everything he had ever known.

Everything, the goddess said.

I have to get out of here, Mero thought wildly.

Gripping Sheathless, he turned down the tunnel to his left. Soon he broke into a trot. His own footsteps followed after him, the sound strangely mocking. *I'm right behind you*, they seemed to say. *The faster you run, the faster I'll catch you up.*

Mero's breath came short in his throat. Another tunnel opened on the left and he plunged down it, slipping as he rounded the corner. The air was wet and clammy. His skin was alternately cold and hot.

The tunnel veered right, and Mero followed it. Water covered the ground. The ceiling dropped, the walls pressing in. Mero waved Sheathless in front of him, trusting it to cut away any obstacles he might encounter.

Then he tripped over an exposed pipe, swinging down face-first and smashing his nose against the floor. Sheathless went skittering into the darkness.

"*NO!*" Mero tried to shout, but he was winded and his nose was flattened against his face, and the word came out as a croak. He got on his hands and knees and crawled in the direction he had heard Sheathless fall. His fingers soon tickled the hilt, but the tunnel into which the sword had fallen sloped downwards, and his touch sent it sliding down the ramp and out of reach.

"*NO!*" Mero croaked again, and reached into the tunnel—only this tunnel was not just smooth, but slick with algae, and his palms gave way under him and his chin smacked down and he lost his balance and tumbled headfirst into the shaft.

35

Mero slid for four breathless seconds, palms scraping against the floor, clumps of slime accumulating in the spaces between his fingers. The shaft abruptly ended, and he fell onto a hard, flat surface. His chin struck the ground and his teeth snapped shut with a painful *CLACK*. Groaning, he pushed himself up and looked around.

There was nothing to see. This chamber, like all the rest, was in pitch darkness. Mero sensed it was vaster than the others had been, a vault instead of a tunnel. The floor was not metal, but uneven brick, slick and cool with moisture.

Sheathless was ahead. Guided by the tugging of the fishhook, Mero scrambled towards it, desperate to close his fingers around the hilt. He knelt on the floor and swept his arms from side to side, inching forward each time his pass failed to turn anything up. In that manner he progressed deeper into the chamber until at last his thumb fetched up against something hard. Pouncing on the blade, he scooped it up and cradled it close, warm relief sweeping over him.

It was only once he stood that he realized his mistake. He had been so eager to go after Sheathless that he had taken his hand off the wall, and now had no idea where he was. He moved forward tentatively, his footfalls making a soft *plik, plik* on the wet floor.

He made it a half-dozen steps then stopped, straining his ears. The feeling that he was not alone in the chamber crept up on him again. He started off more slowly than before, counting his footsteps.

Plik. Plik.

Adrenalin turned his spine to ice. The hairs on his arms and the back of his neck stood up.

There's something out there. He had no proof, but felt the truth of it in the marrow of his bones.

"Who's there?" he cried out. His voice was shrill. He waited, weaving

Sheathless through the air, but no answer came. He took two more faltering steps.

Plik. Plik.

Plik.

Mero spun viciously, swinging Sheathless in a wide arc. The blade hummed as it cut into the darkness, but it met no resistance. Mero tried to wet his lips, but his tongue was dry. In fact all of him was dry; after all, he was nothing but a corpse animated by Sheathless's curse. He breathed in short, rapid gasps, though he had no reason to breathe at all.

"WHO'S THERE?" he shouted again, swinging Sheathless about at random, fencing with shadows, trying to conquer a foe he could neither see nor understand. "*SHOW YOURSELF!*"

Plik. Plik. Plik.

Mero was rigid with terror, every nerve on fire. He couldn't tell where the footsteps came from, couldn't tell if they were his or something else's. His imagination populated the darkness with innumerable, faceless horrors. He wanted to run, but there was nowhere to run to. All he could do was stand and wait.

A hand slipped into his own.

36

Mero jumped as though electrified, yanking his hand free. He spun on his heel and delivered a wicked slash with Sheathless. The tip of the blade nicked something soft. There was a *whump*, as of a body hitting the ground.

Before Mero knew it, he had bolted like a hare and was blindly fleeing the sound, fleeing the soft warmth of the hand that had so suddenly taken his own. He still felt its touch on his palm, and was struck by the urge to pin his hand against the ground and bring Sheathless down on his wrist. But there was no time—he had to get as far away from the hand's owner as possible.

He smacked into a wall and scrambled along it, hoping there was a way out, that he wasn't trapped here forever with that *thing*. He found a threshold and dove through it, slipping and almost losing his balance, then pedaling his feet and building up fresh speed.

Soon after, his toe struck something hard and he fell forwards. He reached out to brace himself and his hands cut into hard shelves of metal, high off the floor. The impact made a loud *CLANG* that ascended as it traveled away from him. He realized he stood at the foot of a metal staircase.

Plik. Plik. The sounds trickled down his neck like drops of cold water.

He scrambled up the stairs, which rattled and coughed under his weight. He took them two at a time, not caring when he slipped and bashed his shins on the steps. A sickly yellow light shone at the top of the stairwell, the first he had seen since he fell into this place. He redoubled his pace, desperate to escape this world of the unseen.

The door at the top of the stairwell was closed. The light above it was a rectangle of yellow glass, caged in thin metal wires. The door was heavy metal, and instead of a latch or bar, a large wheel was set into its center. Mero felt around the edges of the door, then gripped the wheel and tried to turn it first one way, then the other. But the wheel wouldn't budge, even when he tucked it under his armpit and leaned his entire weight on it.

The light overhead flickered, and Mero caught movement in the corner of his eye. He glanced down the staircase. Swooping terror filled him.

A figure stood at the bottom of the stairwell. It looked like a human child, a girl wearing a lank, filthy dress. Her limbs were blue and pale. Her feet were bare, and she was bald—the light from the doorway reflected off a skull as shiny and smooth as an egg. But what struck Mero like a blow to the sternum, leaving him breathless and weak, was her face.

She had none.

Her chin was turned up as if to look at him, but she had no eyes to see him with. Pale skin stretched from her forehead to her cheeks, unblemished by brows or lids or lashes. Where her nose should have been was only the faintest of ridges. Her jaw was fused shut, as though her lips had been sewn together and grafted over with smooth, featureless skin. The shells of her ears were visible, though Mero had no doubt that if he were to peer into one he would find that it ended before it passed her jaw, sealed with a neat plug of skin like the rest of her features.

The faceless girl took a tentative step towards the staircase.

Plik.

Mero whirled around and bashed at the door with Sheathless's pommel—the wheel, the hinges, even the heavy metal sheet itself. Discordant echoes filled the hallway. He buried Sheathless into the seam and tried to pry the door open. Chips of rust rained down on him, but the door didn't budge.

He spared a glance down the stairs. The faceless girl was halfway up, climbing slowly in the manner of a child, getting both feet onto the same step before reaching for the next one.

Mero hacked at the door. Metal screamed, and sparks rained down. He was running out of time. He stabbed and cut, wedged Sheathless into every crack, scrabbled at the door until his fingertips were stripped raw, but he couldn't pass through.

He turned again and she was there, with him at the top of the stairs, almost within arm's reach. Blue veins spidered down her face where her eyes should have been. The skin over her mouth was stretched tight as a drum. Her dress had once been lovely, white on the bottom, red on top, cinched around her waist with a length of ribbon. Now it was slick with grime and the red was the dark brown of old blood. She reached out to him, her arm so white it glowed.

Mero's legs failed him. He collapsed onto his rump and wedged himself in the corner by the door, slashing at her outstretched hand.

"*STAY BACK!*" he screamed. "*GET AWAY FROM ME!*"

The faceless girl hesitated, then reached out again.

"*NO!*" Mero slashed madly, Sheathless skating off the walls and floor. He pushed away with his feet and free hand, squeezing himself further into the corner though he knew there was nowhere to run. "*NO! NO!* No…"

He sobbed, his strength leaving him. He was so terrified of what might happen when the faceless girl touched him that he dropped Sheathless and curled into a ball, making himself as small as possible, wishing that he could disappear, wishing that he had never been born.

The faceless girl froze with her hand inches from his face, her fingers half uncurled, her palm turned up in silent supplication. She didn't move. Her chest didn't rise or fall—indeed, how could it, lacking as she did a nose or mouth? Her dress, however, fluttered slightly, and a chill breeze touched the back of Mero's neck.

"What are you?" he whispered. "What do you want?"

The girl reached out further, her dress rustling. Mero couldn't tear his eyes away from her missing face. He searched it over again and again, looking for something, anything, to hold on to, but its stark smoothness denied him purchase.

"Will you hurt me?" he asked, his voice like a candle going out.

Will you hurt me? the goddess answered.

It was then Mero noticed the dark crescent on the girl's upper arm. A drop of blood coalesced in the corner of the wound and slipped down her elbow. He remembered lashing out with Sheathless in the dark, the soft resistance of flesh, the *whump* of a body hitting the ground.

Slowly, still pressing against the wall, Mero rose to his feet. The faceless girl took a hasty step back. Mero grabbed Sheathless off the floor, the blade singing as it scraped the metal stair. The faceless girl flinched, bringing both hands to her chest. Mero froze, watching his adversary carefully.

The moment stretched on, neither Mero nor the faceless girl willing to make the next move. She seemed harmless, pitiable even, yet she evoked in Mero a fear so visceral he thought he might lose his mind if he remained in her presence much longer.

Where is her face? he wondered, again and again. *Was it stolen, or did she never have one to begin with?*

"Are you lost?" he asked, for something to say.

Are you lost? the goddess said.

"I'll help you find a way out," Mero said.

I'll help you find a way out, the goddess replied.

The faceless girl fetched her head to one side, as though listening to their conversation. Then she turned, put her hand on the wall for balance, and descended the first three stairs.

She's leaving, Mero thought, with supreme relief—but the next moment she turned to look at him again, her skin yellow in the light of the door.

Mero's mouth was dry. How could a creature with no eyes have such an arresting gaze?

"You want me to come with you?" he asked.

You want me to come with you? the goddess answered.

Mero didn't want to go. He would rather wear his fingers to the bone clawing at the unyielding door than go where the faceless girl would take him. But the goddess's word was final.

He fell in behind his guide and allowed her to lead him into the darkness.

37

By the time they reached the bottom of the stair, the faceless girl was little more than a gray smudge. When she passed into the chamber beyond—the chamber where they had first met—she was swallowed entirely, along with Mero himself.

Mero's brief respite from the oppressive darkness only made it harder to return to. He heard the patter of the faceless girl's feet ahead of him, but soon lost any idea of where they were; she had brought him to the center of the chamber, where there were no walls to hold on to.

"Where are you?" he called out, and instantly regretted it—not because it was a waste of breath, but because it invited the possibility that the faceless girl might respond.

Footsteps—a little flurry of them, as though she was scuttling around in the darkness—then suddenly she took his hand again, warm little fingers slipping around his thumb. He cried out and wrenched his hand away—then regretted that, too, fearful he had angered her.

He felt her freeze somewhere close by. Breathing rapidly, he thrust out his hand, offering it to the darkness.

"I'm sorry," he said. "I didn't mean it. You just frightened me." That was no lie, and as she stepped closer, it took all of his self-control not to withdraw his hand.

No, I can't, he kept thinking. *I can't touch her, I just can't, anything but that, please, I can't...*

She took his hand again, her touch feather-light. She tugged gently, and Mero stumbled after her.

Mero's emotions bubbled as the faceless girl led him through the tunnels. Shock, confusion, foreboding, puzzlement—and over all, fear like a metal rasp scraping across his nerves. He told himself a hundred times that he would pull his hand away, that wandering alone in the dark was preferable to following this creature that, for all he knew, was a demon come to guide his soul to hell. He had expected her touch to be cold and clammy, but instead it was so hot it burned.

He made no attempt to keep track of their route, though the impressions he gleaned of their environment changed subtly over time. First they were walking on metal, then stone. First the chamber was vast and high-ceilinged, then narrow and long, then still long and low but now very wide as well. The temperature rose and fell by degrees, dropping to a wintery chill, then heating and drying to a suffocating stuffiness.

Sounds emerged in the distance—the *pluk-pluk-pluk* of dripping water, the *clank* and *groan* of some vast machinery. But most disquieting were the scuffling, slithering sounds of flesh against stone. When he heard these noises, Mero would freeze and widen his eyes, raising Sheathless to strike at whatever might lunge out of the darkness. The faceless girl would slow her pace obediently so they could listen; then, after a moment, she would start tugging again, more and more insistently until Mero was forced to relent.

After an eternity of stumbling through the underground, they reached another staircase. The steps were made of braided wire and a smooth metal handrail ran along one side. The wall to which the handrail was bolted was a cage made of the same braided wire. Beyond it, a dozen pipes of varying sizes snaked up the stairs and down the length of the passage beyond.

Mero absorbed all of these details before absorbing the fact that he could see. A thin strip of yellow, no wider than his thumb, ran along the far wall near the ceiling. It glowed with the same sickly light as that above the door. It must have been some sort of chemical light, as it was far too steady to be fire.

The faceless girl, already two steps up the staircase, turned to see what was the matter. Mero's breath caught in his throat, the cold wind gripping him again. He feared her as he had feared little else in the course of his long life, her blank, expressionless features a canvas on which his own nightmares imprinted themselves. He nurtured the irrational, yet unshakeable conviction that she *did* have a face, and that the next time she turned she would be wearing it again.

Blood trickled from the wound on her arm. She gave him a gentle tug, but with the light had returned Mero's confidence, and he let his hand slip free from hers.

"Thank you," he said. "I can walk for myself now."

The faceless girl froze in the act of reaching out to him again. Her shoulders fell, and she hung her head, gathering her hands in front of her. Mero realized he had made her upset, and pitied her—but not enough to offer her his hand.

Still hanging her head, the faceless girl climbed the stairwell, slowly, like a condemned man on his way to the gallows.

38

They were never in darkness after that. After passing through the hallway with the pipes, they entered a gloomy shaft girt with a metal staircase that spiraled up and up. The walls dripped with moisture, and pipes looped down like hanging vines. The shaft was square, and at each corner was a landing featuring a metal door and one of the sickly yellow lights. The doors were all identical, except some had red signs painted on them at eye level and others had numerals stamped into their jambs. Mero could read neither, nor even recognize the language in which they were written. He was tempted to test the doors, but the faceless girl passed them without hesitation.

Finally they arrived at a door like all the others. The faceless girl stood by it, hands folded expectantly. Mero reached past her and tried the latch. The door opened, and she slipped through.

Past the door was a huge chamber with a low ceiling, made even lower by a multitude of hanging pipes. The walls were daubed in stripes of paint—red, green, and yellow—and there were a half-dozen doors on either side. A metal fan taller than Mero was embedded in the far wall. It spun rapidly, filling the room with a deep hum. The air was sterile and dry. The ceiling was held up by a series of columns so wide that Mero wouldn't have been able to get his arms around them had they been twice as long. They were perfectly round and uniformly gray. Mero brushed one with his fingers as they stepped past; its surface was unnaturally smooth. This must have been the material some scholars called poured stone and others called cement.

Touching the pillar stirred in Mero a spark of scholarly curiosity. Which of the fallen civilizations of man had created this place? What was its purpose? The pipes suggested some sort of sewage system, but there were no settlements around for miles.

Was it possible that one of these pipes led all the way to Uron?

A small hand grabbed his sleeve and tugged. Mero jumped, his fear of the faceless girl rekindled. She tugged insistently, the way a child might to get her mother's attention. An unfamiliar urgency charged her summons, and she wouldn't stop glancing at the ranks of doors along the far wall.

Then Mero heard it, the same as before: the dry slithering of flesh on stone.

The faceless girl darted away, headed for the corner of the chamber. She stopped at the last door but one and gestured earnestly. Mero tried the latch and found the door locked.

"It's no good," he told the faceless girl. "We can't get through."

She watched him with that expressionless gaze, shifting her weight from foot to foot. Then she dashed off again, this time for the first door on the same side. Mero followed obediently and tried the latch. It was locked. The faceless girl stamped her feet and ran to one of the middle doors. Her dress crackled—it was stiff with mud—and one of the straps slipped off her shoulder, exposing a pale strip of collarbone.

By the time Mero reached the third door, the slithering had intensified. He couldn't tell whether it belonged to a multitude of smaller creatures or a single, enormous one.

The third door was locked. Mero's fingers had hardly brushed the latch when the faceless girl ran off. He wedged Sheathless into the gap around the door and tried to pry it open, but it wouldn't budge, and the girl came to tug on his arm again, clearly convinced he was wasting his time.

The slithering grew louder, and now it was accompanied by another sound, familiar and innocuous yet terrifyingly out of place in this underground labyrinth: a chorus of voices talking over one another in waves, rising and falling.

In the end they tried every door on the near side, and every last one was locked. The faceless girl paced back and forth, swinging her arms in a silent tantrum. Her panic was catching. Mero squeezed his temples, trying to think clearly.

"Can we go back?" he asked her. "Is there another way out?"

The faceless girl swung her head around.

Mero crossed to the opposite end of the room. "What about these doors?"

Instantly she stopped pacing and ran after him. This time she didn't settle for tugging his sleeve—she wrapped both arms around him and wouldn't let go. Mero's flesh rippled at her touch.

"All right, all right. But if we can't go forwards, and we can't go back, then—"

The door nearest him exploded off its hinges. Shrieking, it skimmed along the ground, leaving a comet's tail of sparks in its wake. The slithering, muttering sound rose to a crescendo as the mass heaped against the door spilled into the chamber.

It looked like an enormous slug made of human flesh, an amalgam of random parts—arms, legs, eyes, spines, tendons and teeth—that moved with a listless, reflexive intelligence. Feet dug their heels into the ground and dragged the body forwards. Hands opened and closed spasmodically, grasping blindly at whatever they could reach. Eyes of every color and size rolled in their sockets.

The muttering Mero had heard came from the creature's multitude of mouths. They were human mouths, some still decorated with noses, each speaking a constant, random stream of syllables.

"Ga, ga, ga," said one.

"Ba da," said another. "Ba da. Ba da."

The mass heaved further into the chamber, expanding and contracting in waves, reaching towards them every time it stretched out.

Mero cursed and scooped the faceless girl into his arms. He ran for the door by which they had entered the room, thinking that lost progress was a small price to pay for escape. But the faceless girl wriggled out of his grip and darted in the opposite direction, towards the huge fan at the back of the room.

"NO!" Mero shouted over the creature's babbling. "*This way! Come to me!*"

Come to me! the goddess cried.

Mero was frozen in indecision. If he abandoned the faceless girl, she would certainly be caught, and his chances of escaping this place alone were next to none. On the other hand, he had still not decided whether he could trust her. It was possible she was just as dangerous as this creature, albeit in a different way.

Whatever he intended to do, he had better do it quickly. The chamber was rapidly filling with the monster's bulk. Soon he wouldn't be able to reach the other side of the room whether he wanted to or not.

One of the creature's eyes alighted on Mero. A nearby mouth cracked open, and a woman's voice spilled out.

"*Huuuuuuuugh*," she wailed, plaintive and forlorn, the last gasp of the dying.

Mero made up his mind. He rounded the monster, giving it a wide berth. A crooked arm lunged at him, fingers grasping. He cut savagely with Sheathless and the hand came free with a dry *thup*. Mero didn't wait to see where it landed.

The faceless girl had hooked her fingers into the grille protecting the fan and was yanking desperately, filling the room with the rattle of metal. Mero pushed her out of the way, reversed his grip on Sheathless, braced the pommel with his other hand and jabbed the blade into one of the square gaps between the wires. The gap widened and distorted. Mero brought Sheathless back and thrust it forward again. This time one of the wires snapped, and the blade shrieked as it sank halfway into the grille.

Mero glanced over his shoulder. The amalgam issued through the door like a lump of feces through a sphincter, arms and legs pushing indiscriminately against floor, columns, and ceiling pipes. The muttering of the mouths grew insistent, a mob working itself into a panic.

Mero sawed at the grille, widening his cut into a lopsided smile. The metal, old and brittle, was no match for Sheathless's keen edge. Once his cut was two feet across, he dug his fingers into the metal and pulled upwards, creating a half-moon opening. The faceless girl wasted no time in scrambling through. The sharp metal dug into her dress and skin, opening wide tears in the first and streaming red gashes in the other. Her waist caught when she was halfway through and she kicked her feet in the air. Mero grabbed her soles and pushed, and she tumbled into the shaft.

The creature was no more than ten feet away. Though most of its eyes swiveled in their sockets, several were focused on Mero. Its hands scurried along the floor like mice, searching for holds.

"*Uaaaah! Uaaaah!*" cried a man's mouth.

"*Oh no, oh no, oh no,*" cried a woman's.

Mero turned back to his hole and realized with grim dismay that while it had been wide enough for the faceless girl, it wasn't wide enough for him. With a strength born of panic he attacked the hole again, chopping at it the way a lumberjack would chop at a tree. On his third cut, Sheathless sheared through fully a foot of metal. Mero pulled the hole open, tossed Sheathless through, then climbed through himself.

The sharp edges sliced at his arms, his cheeks, his belly, but he barely felt the cuts and they did not bleed. Soon he was through and staggering to his feet, the booming of the fan a constant pressure on his ears. It was recessed no more than seven feet from the grille, trapping Mero and the faceless girl in a pen with barely room enough to stand. Before them lay whirling blades, behind them the flimsy grate that separated them from the amalgam.

The faceless girl wrung her hands, turning her chin up at Mero in a mute appeal for help. Three parallel cuts marked her forehead where she had pushed it through the grille, and more crisscrossed her bare arms. Still, none were as deep as the one Sheathless had opened on her upper arm.

Mero considered the fan. It was about half a foot taller than him, filling the entire shaft. By moving his eyes quickly from side to side, he could make out three skinny blades chasing each other around its hub. A trio of metal braces divided its circular face into thirds.

What he didn't understand was *what* made the fan spin. It couldn't be a mill, buried as it was far underground—so it must have been intended to pull air in from outside. But Mero couldn't see any mechanism, any source of power making it turn. It was a mystery of the old world, a mystery that stood between them and freedom.

"AU! AUUU! AYAUUUGH!"

The faceless girl grabbed his shirt and flattened herself against his stomach. The amalgam had reached the grille and was probing at it with hands and feet, nudging itself into the hole Mero had made. The metal lacerated the creature's flesh, exposing nets of tendons and bumps and ridges of cartilage. Mero sank Sheathless into the creature's flesh once, twice, thrice, puncturing an eyeball and opening large gashes in its skin. The amalgam withdrew, seizing up like a slug that had been poked with a stick. Then it ventured forwards again.

Mero turned back to the fan. It was their only way out; they had to find some way past the spinning blades. He prodded them with Sheathless, and they slapped it away with a clatter of metal that made the faceless girl wince. He marked the direction of rotation with his finger, then took Sheathless's hilt in both hands and aimed its point at the space immediately to the left of the topmost brace.

He thrust. The fan's blades repelled Sheathless and it went scything to one side. The faceless girl cowered against the wall.

Mero leveled Sheathless and thrust again. There was a sharp, violent moment. Sheathless slipped past the blades of the fan, only to be crushed between them and the metal brace. The impact almost jolted the sword out of his grip. The fan screeched to a halt, and sparks flew from its casing. Deep in the walls came a strange whining noise that carried an unmistakable air of tension, of water rising behind the walls of the dam.

The three blades had jammed in near-perfect alignment with the three metal braces. The bottom third of the shaft was open.

"GO!" Mero shouted, Sheathless quivering in his hands. The faceless

girl fell to her hands and knees and squeezed past the straining blade. Mero carefully took his hands off Sheathless. It did not move. He fell to his belly and crawled after her.

They were through, and a seemingly endless shaft stretched before them, as round and straight as the hole left by a bore drill. But there was a problem. Sheathless was still wedged in the fan, and the amalgam was forcing its way through the grate, using sheer weight to widen the hole Mero had left. Fingers reflexively gripped the metal wires and pulled them in all directions. The grille whined, bowing in and out. The amalgam might not be fast—but it was strong.

Mero grabbed Sheathless's blade and tried to pull it through to his side. But the pressure on the blade was immense, and he could only gain ground by yanking hard, an action which would soon shred his muscles and tendons to the point that his hands would be useless.

Reaching around the blade of the fan, he slapped Sheathless's hilt towards the ceiling. The fan blades didn't extend all the way to the edges of the shaft. The extra space might give him the room he needed to pull it through.

"*BA-BA!*" bellowed one of the amalgam's mouths. "*BA-BA! BA-BA!*"

There was a *CRACK* like that of lightning striking the earth, and the grille snapped into halves. The amalgam carried the top half away, crushing the other beneath it as it forced its way into the shaft. It was covered in wounds that streamed blood, pus, and digestive fluid. The sharp odor of offal billowed into the tunnel.

Sheathless was now pointed at the floor, all of it through but the hilt. Mero jiggled and slapped the sword from both sides but couldn't get it unstuck. He turned to the faceless girl, who hung back shifting her weight as though uncertain whether to stay or run.

"*Help me!*" he shouted. "*HURRY!*"

She came forward and took Sheathless's blade in both hands. Mero dug his fingers into the space between the fan and the metal brace and pried the two apart until he thought his shoulders would catch fire. The fan shrieked and more sparks fell. He gained an inch, then two. The faceless girl seesawed Sheathless's blade, trying to get the hilt through.

"*UWAAAAAH!*" the amalgam screamed.

The hilt came through. The faceless girl tottered backwards, throwing her arms over her head as Sheathless clattered down beside her. At that moment, a hand reached through the gap in the blades and closed firmly around Mero's ankle.

The amalgam yanked, and Mero fell onto his back, knocking his skull on the ground. The fan whirred to life, and something bumped hard against Mero's leg. Pain sparked, faded, then flared into agony.

Mero lifted his chin, looking down the length of his body. His left foot was missing. The fan had sheared it off. The impact had knocked off his shoe; one of the amalgam's arms picked it up and waved it around.

His severed foot was disappearing inside the amalgam, tendrils of flesh wrapping around his toes, prodding into the bloodless stump where it had met his ankle. The creature still reached at him through the fan, though it recoiled whenever the spinning blades took off a chunk of flesh.

A hand touched Mero's shoulder. He flinched, but it was only the faceless girl. He stumbled to his feet and limped down the shaft after her, using Sheathless as a crutch.

Half a mile later, the shaft had yet to end, and the echoes of the creature's many voices still chased them along. Mero shook badly, from the pain and from the memory of his foot being folded into the amalgam. He had seen many hideous things in his time, but one detail about that sight was burned in his mind, and, he thought, would remain so until the day he died.

Just before his shoeless foot had disappeared under the many folds of flesh, the toes had started to wiggle.

39

Eventually the voices faded.

Other tunnels connected with their own, always at exacting right angles, always of the same gray stone. The faceless girl kept on straight, not even bothering to look down the other tunnels—and she *could* look, Mero was sure of it: though she had no eyes she clearly was not blind—and he hopped after her, trailing the stump of his severed leg, the *tink-tink-tink* of Sheathless's tip against the ground the only sound other than his own ragged breathing.

The hem of the faceless girl's dress swished as she walked. Mero focused on that, on keeping his balance on the sloping floor, on not letting Sheathless slip and falling on it by accident.

Light grew in the distance, dim at first, soon so bright that Mero had to open his eyes only in short bursts. Though painful, it filled him with an overwhelming sense of relief. The light was yellow and warm, flowing into the shaft like a liquid. It could only have been sunlight.

The tunnel stretched for another half-mile or so, then opened to the sky. Its mouth was a golden disk, a coin shining up from the bottom of a well. Hope kindled in Mero's chest. The faceless girl ran ahead of him, the ribbon on her dress flapping like a tail. The coin grew into a discus, a brass gong, then, at long last, a doorway.

The mouth of the tunnel was blocked by a barred door secured with a length of rusty chain. It was still too bright to see much of the world beyond it, but there were hints of a hillside peppered with dark green grass sloping down and away.

Mero fell to his knees to give himself room to swing, then brought Sheathless up over his head. The faceless girl, who had been pressing her forehead to the bars, scampered out of the way. Mero brought Sheathless down in a bold overhead cut. There was a *SNAP*, an explosion of rust, and the chain slithered to the ground. Mero put his palm to the bars and pushed. The door swung open, squealing, until the old hinges gave way with another loud *SNAP*. The door fell from the opening and rolled down the hill, turning end-over-end three times before toppling over and coming to rest in the grass.

Balancing on his remaining foot, Mero jammed Sheathless's point into the ground and stood. Like a man emerging from the tomb, he limped through the doorway and into the sunlight.

40

The first thing Mero noticed was the sweetness of the air.

He had often heard the word *fresh* used to describe air, as though it were a fruit that grew moldy when left too long on the vine. But until that day on the hilltop, he had never truly understood what it meant for air to be *fresh*. The air in the underground labyrinth had been still, stale, and clammy, as lifeless as the sediment at the bottom of a pond. This air tasted as though it had been freshly minted in some great forge among the clouds. It was *new* air, *young* air, as guileless and virginal as the first snow of winter. Mero was almost ashamed to breathe it, to abduct it into unclean lungs that didn't even have a use for it.

The sun hung directly ahead, a hand's breadth from the horizon—the blinding light they had experienced had been that of the rising sun shining into the tunnel's mouth. Battalions of cloud marched across a cobalt sky, slicing the sun's rays into golden beams that spanned the vault of heaven.

The vastness of the sky made Mero feel tiny by comparison. He imagined his place and that of the sky reversed: he hung from the underside of a tiny stone marble hurtling through the firmament, with nothing below him but the clouds, the sun, and the sky—a thin blue skin that soon yielded to emptiness black and eternal. He was aware, then, that the sweet air filling his lungs was no less ephemeral than he, and that both would soon return to the nothingness from whence they had come.

It was not the first time Mero had entertained such thoughts. But instead of sparking fear in him, a warmth spread from his chest down to the tips of his extremities—even into his missing foot, whose presence he still felt—and up into his cranium, where it filled his head with a pleasant buzzing sensation, as that of a swarm of bees.

He could have stood there for half an hour, and he did, balancing effortlessly on his single foot. He didn't even notice when his hands came open and Sheathless tumbled to the ground.

At last the sun was hidden behind a bank of cloud, and reality reasserted itself. Mero retrieved Sheathless, then leaned on it and scanned the horizon. The earth rippled in a series of hills dotted with dark green grass, the bare patches between the tufts a dull, reddish gray. The hills behind them grew into a small mountain range. Those on their left flattened into a vast plain, while those directly ahead were interspersed with a series of shimmering lakes.

In his current state, Mero had no more need for water than a fish had for air. Still, it was an opportunity to clean himself, to wash off the grime of the underground labyrinth. He looked around for the faceless girl and found her sitting a short ways away. Her knees were drawn up to her chest and she pulled at random stalks of grass, letting them tumble between her fingers and be taken by the wind.

"You there," Mero said, not sure what to call her. "Come here."

Obediently she stood and brushed off her dress, then tottered over to him with her hands clasped behind her back. A thrill of fear trickled down the back of Mero's neck, and for a moment he regretted calling her over. She was even more grotesque in sunlight than she had in darkness, the light throwing her freakish features into sharp relief. She was so pale as to be almost blue, the veins and arteries under her skin standing out against the whiteness. Her skull was shiny and smooth, too big for her body. The patch of skin stretching from her brow to her cheekbones was darker than the rest, having no bones behind it to lighten it. Mero was struck with the sudden urge to brandish Sheathless and cut twin slits into that skin. Perhaps there *were* eyes concealed behind that fleshy curtain, and a mouth, too. All it would take would be a couple of cuts...

He shook himself and offered her his hand. "Would you like to come down to the lake? You can wash off, and—" he stopped himself from saying *have a drink of water.*

She hesitated, rocking back and forth, but finally took his hand and followed him down to the lakeshore. Mero set Sheathless down and hopped into the chilly water, clothes and all. It was an incredible relief to be off his feet at last. He pulled himself through the water with strong, even strokes, dirt and grime falling off him in clouds. He ducked his head and scrubbed his hair, then pulled off his shirt, gathered it into a wad of cloth, and used it to scrub his arms, face, and chest. That was about the best he could do. There were bloodless cuts all over his body, the worst being the two deep gashes in his palms where he had handled Sheathless's blade. When he flexed his fingers, they opened in silent, supplicating mouths. But at the very least, he was clean. He hopped ashore streaming water, feeling better than he had in a long while.

The faceless girl watched him as he bathed, sitting on a rock by the shore dangling her feet in the water. She was filthy all over, her dress covered in grime, the cuts she had received from Sheathless and the metal grille oozing dark red blood.

Mero paused in the process of hopping past her. "What's the matter? Don't you want to swim?"

She looked at the ground.

"You don't know how to swim?" he guessed.

She hunched her shoulders and turned away.

"It would do you good," Mero said, though he asked himself why he was going to the trouble. "You don't need to know how to swim as long as you stick to the shallows."

No response.

"Why don't I come with you?" Mero said. "You can ride on my back. I won't let anything happen to you."

The faceless girl tried not to show interest, but she was starting to glance his way. He hopped over to her and sank to his knees, offering her his bare back.

"Put your arms around my neck," he said, tapping his shoulder. "I'll walk you in, a little at a time."

Gingerly she uncurled and reached for him, wrapping her arms around his shoulders and her legs around his waist. She weighed almost nothing. Mero stood with hardly a wobble.

"Ready?" he said.

He hopped into the shallows. The faceless girl trembled as the hems of her dress touched the surface, and once she was deep enough to float, she tightened her grip on Mero until she was nearly strangling him.

"Let go," he said, tapping her hands and her crossed ankles. "Don't worry, I'll hold you."

It took some coaxing, but he finally got her to loosen her grip. He offered her his hands and she pressed down on them with her own, holding herself near the surface. She kicked convulsively in the manner of a child, tilting her head back to keep her nonexistent face from touching the water. Mero glided backwards, hopping easily along the bottom of the lake, dragging her in small circles while she kicked and kicked.

As he watched her struggle to stay afloat, Mero felt a ripple of fear and disgust. What was this frail, pathetic creature? How dare she affront him with her otherness, her dependency, her porcelain fragility? In the darkness of the underground labyrinth, he had feared her. Now, under the light of the sun, he pitied her—and for that hated her more than before.

As quickly as it had come, the moment passed. Mero was left with an uneasy feeling in his gut. Why did the faceless girl stir such feelings in him? In the past, he had often been assailed by emotions he did not understand. His usual strategy for dealing with them had been to ignore them. By the time he forged Sheathless, his emotions had almost entirely disappeared. Yet every so often they flared to life, like embers of a forest fire concealed under the earth.

Perhaps that was why Mero had so disliked Ruya's company at the start. She had often stirred that feeling in him, with her admonishments and pitying looks. She had made him feel ashamed for not feeling more. But why should she care whether he felt anything or not? Surely what passed inside his own mind had no effect on her?

In a rush he realized he hadn't thought about Ruya since falling down the hellhole. With the faceless girl still holding his hands, he twisted one way and then the other, scanning the horizon as though he might see her trudging along, dragging her sledge behind her, coming to meet him and make camp and share her warmth and food as she had done time after time. But of course she was nowhere to be seen. Mero and the faceless girl were alone, and Ruya was most likely dead.

The faceless girl's kicking intensified, bubbles of foam leaping in the sunlight. She kicked her way into Mero's arms and hugged him around the chest. She was cold and shivering. Mero's skin crawled at her touch.

"You're finished?" he said, fighting the impulse to push her away. "You want to come out?"

She tightened her grip, flattening her cheek against his sternum. Mero turned in place with a wave of his arms and half-swam, half-hopped back to shore. The faceless girl's dress was sodden and she was much heavier than before. Mero had to sink to his knees and ask her several times to let him go so he could stand. Finally she did, scampering back to the rock on the shore. She was much cleaner for her bath; Mero thought he saw flowers printed on her dress.

"I'm sorry I can't make a fire," he said. "We'll sit in the sun a while to dry off, how's that?"

She said nothing.

It was a brisk day, though it grew warmer by degrees as the sun rose in the sky and the clouds blew off to the north. Soon Mero was merely damp, and he began to feel restless again. His two driving hungers, neither of them his own, warred for supremacy. The goddess chanted *east, east,* in her gentle but irresistible voice.

The song Sheathless sang was far more sinister. Mero closed his mind to it, knowing it was only a matter of time before he would be compelled to obey.

Beside him, the faceless girl shivered and shivered.

41

They set out around mid-afternoon. They had warmed and dried, and Mero had dressed the worst of the faceless girl's wounds, patching them with strips taken from his own shirt. He saw no reason to delay further. Reaching Uron with only one foot would not be easy; he might as well get started. He pulled on his clothes and picked up Sheathless, which attracted the faceless girl's attention.

"It's about time I set off," he said, by way of explanation.

The faceless girl watched him with reproach.

Mero wetted his lips, or tried to. "I'm going to a dangerous place. A faraway place. You don't want to come with me."

She looked at him impassively.

"It's a city of the old world, called Uron. It's supposed to be cursed."

No reaction.

He tried to speak but the words stuck. He cleared his throat and tried again.

"I'm going there to die," he said.

The faceless girl's dress fluttered in the wind. Otherwise she was attentive and still.

"You don't want to come with me," he said again, with some roughness. "There's nothing I can give you. I'm at the end of my life. There must be somewhere else you can go."

The faceless girl stood and brushed herself off. There *were* little flowers dotting her skirt. She walked over to Mero and gently slipped her hand into his.

He drew a deep breath and blew it back out. "All right. We'll go together."

42

For three days and nights they walked without eating, sleeping or stopping.

Mero hopped along using Sheathless as a crutch, while the faceless girl either skipped ahead or lagged behind, squatting to peer at a beetle or pull up a few strands of grass. At first when she did this Mero would call after her, saying "come along" or "hurry up" because he still had no name for her. But he soon learned that if he simply walked ahead, she would always catch him up sooner or later. She seemed to know exactly where he was at all times, even when they were walking in the dark or pushing through a copse of trees. Accidentally leaving her behind would not be a problem—though doing so on purpose might.

The landscape was hilly and green. When Mero stood still and listened, he would hear the far-off cry of a bird or a rustle in the under-growth, sounds he had scarce heard since taking up with Gorgol the giant. The bird calls were unfamiliar to him, as were the shapes of the leaves on the trees. They were deep into the eastern continent, past the edge of the world. Even the smells were exotic. When the sun shone brightly, the air grew redolent with an astringent, sappy fragrance that Mero eventually traced to the bark of a certain tree. He couldn't decide whether he liked the smell or not. An afternoon of smelling it made him nauseous, but he soon found himself missing it when none of the offending trees were around.

One of the reasons Mero never stopped to sleep was that neither he nor the faceless girl ever needed to. The other reason was the faceless girl herself. Mero was still afraid of her. Though she seemed utterly harmless, the sight of her filled him with an irrational, creeping dread that was all the worse for being inexplicable. If walking alongside her in daylight was difficult, the thought of bedding down next to her at night was unbearable. He couldn't stop thinking about her missing face—where it had gone, and what she might look like, what she might do, if it were to return.

The more Mero thought about the faceless girl, the more unnerved he became. A strange notion began to take hold of him: that the faceless girl hated and feared him as much as he hated and feared her. He grew convinced that she blamed him for her missing face, that she thought him responsible for its loss.

He felt her eyes on the back of his neck, though she had none. More than once he caught her watching him, and she looked away guiltily when he did. He started watching her in turn, observing her movements, the way she scrambled up hills he could climb easily with his one leg, the way her dress rode up when she squatted in the grass. He thought of the wounds she had sustained, of the cut on her arm he had both caused and tended, and said to himself,

She might not be alive, but she has blood. And if she has blood…

His fingers tightened around Sheathless's hilt.

She started to avoid him. It was as though his eyes were spinning metal fans that blew her away when he trained them on her. The more closely he watched her, the further she slipped away, putting bushes and trees between them, preferring to scramble through the undergrowth than follow along in the trail he blazed. That made him irrationally angry. *He* was the one who had saved her from the amalgam. *He* was the reason she was walking free under the sun instead of rotting away in the underground labyrinth. The least he could expect was a measure of gratitude—instead, she was behaving as though he were some kind of beast.

"What's the matter?" he asked her once, when she opted to climb a small ridge rather than take the same path as him. "Are you that afraid of me? Or is it just the way I smell?" He laughed roughly. "I'm dead, you know. We corpses are liable to smell from time to time."

She paused mid-climb to look at him. And though she had no face, her expression spoke plainly of fear, reproach—and heartbreak.

That only made Mero angrier than ever. "Three days ago you were clinging to my back. Now you've decided you don't care for my company? What's changed? I'll tell you—only that I've caught on to your little game. You think I haven't noticed you watching me—sizing me up like I was a side of beef?" He jabbed an accusatory finger at her, wobbling on his one leg. "Well, let me tell you something. I've survived the lost continent and I've survived the gigas. I've survived Menahem, Sanja Al-Sat, and Gorgol the giant. I've survived all that and more, and do you know what else? I'll outlast them, too! All of them!" He was shouting now, globs of spittle forming at the corners of his dry mouth. "I'm immortal! I'll never die! I'll be here when the earth is nothing but a hunk of rock hurtling through space. I'll be here when the last of the stars winks out and the sky goes dark for the final time. I'll be here until time itself comes to an end! So whatever you're planning, give it up! *You won't have me, understand? Not now, not EVER! DO YOU HEAR ME?*"

The faceless girl scrambled up the ridge, loose stones kicking down on Mero's shoulders and chest. With a cry of anger he rushed after her, thrusting Sheathless into the side of the hill to pull himself up, digging the stump of his severed leg into the ground for leverage.

"*WHERE DO YOU THINK YOU'RE GOING?*" he roared. "*YOU CAN'T RUN FROM ME!*"

You can't run from me, the goddess said.

The faceless girl slipped, the sole of her foot flashing like a fish. Mero grabbed at her ankle, but she pulled her leg up just in time. Snarling, he tried to find a hold to hang from while he repositioned Sheathless. The faceless girl kept climbing. Small rocks rained down on Mero's head, and dirt slid into his open mouth, making him cough and spit.

That bitch is trying to bury me alive!

He found his hold and pulled Sheathless from the hillside with a ring of metal, plunging it back in three feet further up. He kicked with his legs, worming his way upwards with his chin scraping against the rock.

The faceless girl reached the top of the hill. She stumbled to her feet, brushed off the front of her dress, then darted away, disappearing from sight. Mero bellowed in frustration and redoubled his efforts, grinding his stump into the ground, clawing upwards with both hands to find his next hold. He soon crested the hill and rose to his feet, panting heavily, already seeking out his prey. There, in the bushes: a flash of red and white. He leapt after her, no longer hopping, but limping on his injured leg, pulling aside branches with his empty hand.

"*COME—BACK—HERE!*"

He had lost sight of her in the thicket, but still heard the patter of her feet. He crouched low, trying to glimpse her through the greenery. He caught movement in the corner of his eye and lunged after it, hacking at the undergrowth with Sheathless.

"*YOU'LL PAY!*" he screamed, slashing left and right. "*YOU'LL PAY FOR WHAT YOU DID!*"

There she was, directly ahead, the tail of her dress streaming out behind her. Mero fixated on that and bounded after her. He no longer felt any pain, and ran as well as he had when both his feet had still belonged to him.

He made a grab for the ribbon; it came free in his hands. He tossed it aside and ran on. The faceless girl was nimble, but utterly without guile. Instead of ducking sideways into the bushes, she ran straight on, though she couldn't hope to match Mero's speed. Once he was close enough to feel the wind of her passage, he gathered his legs under him and pounced like a wildcat. His palms struck her shoulder blades. She fell, and Mero fell with her.

The faceless girl scrambled along the ground, trying to crawl out from under him. One of her heels kicked back and struck him squarely in the nose. It startled him more than hurt, only slowing him for an instant. She tried to gain her feet, but Mero caught her ankle and she fell again, scraping her forehead and palms in the dirt. Mero dragged himself up over her as she twisted and kicked. She ended up on her back, Mero straddling her chest with his knees pinning her arms to her sides. He bent over her, his hair falling in lank curtains, his breath rattling in his own ear as though a wild beast had mounted him from behind. The faceless girl arched her back, digging her shoulders into the earth, trying to buck him off, but Mero didn't so much as take notice.

He took Sheathless in a reverse grip and raised it high over his head, the tip quivering inches from the faceless girl's heart.

"How does it feel?" Mero whispered. His breath was cold around his teeth. "How does it feel to be so helpless? To know what's coming and not be able to do anything to stop it? Answer me, damn you! *ANSWER ME!*"

The faceless girl shook her head, her skull rolling left and right. Sheathless's point danced crazily in the air.

"I'll kill you," Mero growled, low and vicious. "I'm the one with power now. I'm the one in control. See this sword? I could snuff you out like a candle. It will be better for the both of us. I'll live my life and *you*—you'll go back to wherever she sent you from." He arched his back, preparing to thrust down and pin her to the earth like a butterfly in a specimen box.

The faceless girl no longer struggled. She appealed to him with a stare empty of expression—expression, but not emotion. Indeed, when Mero looked down Sheathless's length and into the blank canvas of her face, he saw pleading, fear, betrayal, disbelief and, deeper than any of the others, the embrace of the inevitable. It was that acceptance which had enabled her to stop fighting—the understanding that however she might have wanted this story to end, it was Mero who held the pen, a pen which dangled a hand's breadth from her sternum.

Mero's lip quivered. Sheathless swayed like the clapper of a bell.

His arms burned, but he couldn't seem to move them. And that was no surprise, for while his body was here, pinning the faceless girl under his weight, his mind was traveling, into the west and into the past.

Gorgol swatted Sheathless aside, contemptuously, as though it were a fly. It skittered across the sand, and with it went Mero's last illusion of control.

"Don't worry, now," Gorgol said soothingly. "You won't feel a thing."

That had been a lie, like everything else Gorgol had ever told him. But none of what had come after could ever match the horror of that first crystalline moment, that moment where Mero experienced true helplessness for the first time. He had faced pain, hardship, humiliation and death, but never had he experienced this stripping away of his most fundamental right—his agency, his free will as a human being.

Gorgol hadn't needed to reach for Mero's soul. He could have bent down and planted a kiss on his forehead and the violation would have been just as complete. And once opened, that door could never again be closed.

Even if he lived to outlast the stars, he would always remember that day on the beach.

Mero rocked back as though punched in the chest. His right foot offered resistance, but the stump of his left offered none. He keeled over sideways, Sheathless clattering to the ground. The faceless girl scrabbled out from under him.

Mero rolled onto his hands and knees. The crown of his head came down to touch the earth. His face twisted into an ugly grimace, and he started to sob. He beat the earth with his fist, harder and harder until the pain consumed his entire hand and he couldn't tell if the bones were broken or even if it was still attached. The cords of his neck stood out—he ground his teeth together so hard he thought they might shatter. Then his mouth cracked open and an agonized scream billowed out. It sounded like the howl of a wild animal, nothing at all like his own voice. When the scream was spent, he fell forwards and pressed his face into the dirt, knitting his hands behind his head, raking his fingers through his hair.

Time lost all meaning.

Eventually the tension flowed out of his body. He stopped pulling his hair and melted down into the earth. His breathing slowed until he couldn't tell if he was breathing anymore. He felt spent, emptied, kneaded and pounded into an inert lump.

A hand touched his shoulder. The sensation was distant, ripples on a lake as seen from its floor. Mero surfaced with difficulty, waking up from the outside in: his fingers and toes, his arms and legs, his core, and finally his head. His vision was bleary, as though he'd slept for hours, but sunlight rained down from directly overhead.

It was the faceless girl that had touched him. And she was still touching him now, with her whole palm and all five fingers, standing close enough to him that he could have hooked out an arm and snared both her legs. Her trust sent Mero into disarray. Though it was impossible he had dreamed the entire incident, it seemed equally impossible that the faceless girl had forgiven him.

He rose to his knees, then rocked back onto his seat, coming down harder than he had intended thanks to his missing foot. A puff of breath escaped his mouth. He stared at the faceless girl in foggy incredulity.

"Ruya?"

She shook her head and stuck out her hand. He took it and rose to his feet. She started to skip off through the bushes, but Mero limped back the way they had come and bent down with a grunt. He came up holding a dark red eel, the ribbon he had torn from the faceless girl's dress.

He motioned for her to come and she came. He knelt and wrapped the ribbon around her waist, tying it behind her back in a neat, symmetrical bow that wouldn't come undone.

"I know it means nothing, coming from me," he said, "but I'm sorry."

No response. The faceless girl darted off as soon as he had tugged the bow tight. Mero figured that was about what he deserved.

He started down the path, but this time it was the faceless girl who lagged. She stood over Sheathless; it lay among the tall grass, a snake with silver scales. The sight of it filled Mero with revulsion.

"Can't we leave it?" he begged. "I don't want it anymore."

She shook her head insistently and pointed at her feet. Mero sighed and limped over. Touching Sheathless's hilt made him feel dirty, as though he were picking up a piece of dung. He wanted to wrap it up, stash it away, hide it from the world and from himself, but of course he couldn't.

Now they were ready, and they set off together into the east—the girl with no face, the sword with no sheath, and the man who stood between them.

Part V

43

Days later, with the setting sun at their backs and the sky aflame in roaring hues of orange and red, they found Uron.

At first Mero could not or would not believe the evidence of his eyes. He froze in place, afraid to move his eyes lest the mirage slip away between saccades. Uron was distant, little more than a blue comb on the horizon.

When Mero blinked and blinked again and the image failed to dissipate, he slowly began to accept that the city was real. He had seen Uron so many times in his dreams—the empty streets, the towers he had once mistaken for pillars of rock—but had never been certain it existed in actuality.

The faceless girl took his hand, as she often did. Mero's answering smile was toothy: he was drying out, and his gums were receding. The silver fishhook twisted constantly in his gut, like an angry weasel. Sheathless wanted him to *KILL, KILL*, but he was finding its voice easier and easier to ignore.

"There it is," he said. "We're almost at the end. *I'm* almost at the end."

The faceless girl rocked on the balls of her feet.

Mero decided to make camp for the night, though he had no reason to. He was beyond food, beyond sleep, beyond desire, yet he spent the better part of an hour gathering wood and shaving tinder and crafting a fire plow so they could sit around a small fire and watch the sunset. The blazing sky purpled to a deep, calming hue, and the first of the stars came out. Crickets chirred in the underbrush and light-bugs danced over the surface of a nearby lake. The faceless girl sat with her feet outstretched, warming her soles by the fire. Mero wished he could have found her a pair of shoes, but she didn't seem to mind walking barefoot.

He leaned back, breathing in the smoky smell of the fire, listening to it mutter and spark. The smoke trailed up and up before dissipating into the boundless sky. Mero wondered how it might feel to be borne upwards within that black column, to dance among the tiny particles of carbon and tar. A feeling of weightlessness stole over him; he wouldn't have been surprised to discover he was hovering a few inches off the ground. Everything seemed both close and far, intimate and grand. He could have reached out and burned his fingers on one of the twinkling stars.

There was a shuffling sound as the faceless girl rose to her feet. She crossed over to where Mero lay and stretched out in the grass next to him. Rolling onto her side, she rested a hand on his stomach and her head on his heart. She was warm, hot, from the heat of the fire. Mero still feared her—he would never stop fearing her—but he put his arm around her and held her close, while the day drained away and night swept in.

The next day, they found a road.

At first, Mero assumed it was made of cement, the same material that had formed the pillars in the underground labyrinth. But this road was black as volcanic stone, its surface pitted and scarred. Once it must have wound smoothly across the countryside, but now it was in pieces, its surface broken into chunks of rubble. The faceless girl plucked one of these fragments from the roadside and handed it to Mero for inspection. The black stone glittered as he turned it over. Half its face was covered in a stripe of bright red paint.

"This should lead us right into the city," he said, letting the stone roll off his fingers. "Provided the rest of it hasn't been buried."

His throat tickled as he spoke, and he coughed into his fist. The air had grown sour over the past few days, and the greenery he had become accustomed to seeing since escaping the underground labyrinth had all but disappeared. The sky was uniformly gray, and it rained often, in short, fitful bursts. Normally Mero would have welcomed the rain, but this rain left a greasy sheen on his skin and burned when it got into his eyes. Whatever transpired in Uron must have polluted the earth and sky for miles around. He only expected it to get worse as they approached the city.

The road was the first remnant of the old world they encountered, but it was far from the last. As the day wore on they encountered more and more signs of the settlements sitting at the fringes of the city, or perhaps the outskirts of the city itself. First was a stack of shiny black pipes, overspilling the gutter at the side of the road. Each of the pipes was easily a hundred feet long and large enough for the faceless girl to crawl through. Then there was a marching column of dozens of identical metal constructs like giants made of scaffolding, each complete with four hooked arms. Some were still standing, while others had collapsed into rusty piles. Wires snaked between the giants, heaped in massive tangles and snares—hundreds, no, thousands of miles of wire it must have been.

Soon after that, Mero found the jug.

It was a bright, creamy white, the color of milk, with a bright red cap, which was the reason it caught Mero's eye. It sat wedged between a pair of bushes growing by the roadside, looking at first glance like a nesting goose. Mero hopped over to it and bent to pick it up. He expected it to be heavy—it was the size of his head—but it was light as paper. It was cylindrical in shape, with a handle just large enough to slip two fingers through. It had clearly been cast from a mold, as an imperfect seam bisected its middle. The side of the jug was caved in, as though someone had stomped on it.

Mero rapped the jug with a fingernail. It made a dull, thudding noise. He tossed it to the ground and it bounced several times, none the worse for the mistreatment. Mero's curiosity mounted. Whatever that jug was made of could be cast like metal and molded like glass, yet weighed almost nothing and would not shatter or rust. But what struck him more than the jug's strangeness was its mundanity. It was a jug, a vessel for liquid. Perhaps it had once held milk, or water, or cooking oil. It had belonged to one of the men or women of Uron. Perhaps it had rested on a shelf, or in a cabinet. It had been filled and emptied hundreds, perhaps thousands of times, being passed from generation to generation. And now it was here, lost and forgotten. An empty vessel, one that had far outlived its contents.

The faceless girl watched him solemnly. He beckoned her on and they left the jug behind.

Lakes dotted the countryside, the road curving smoothly between them. The lakes were cloudy and black. Garbage was everywhere. Stacks of scrap metal, heaps of rubble and stone, and mountains of objects made of that strange, pliable material. Jugs, boxes, tables, chairs, bags, barrels, cans, cups—it was as though a great storm had swept through every household in Uron, snatching up their worldly possessions and depositing them miles from the city.

Mero's sense of awe increased steadily as the towers in the distance grew larger. It was no wonder he had once mistaken them for mountains: they were staggeringly, mind-bendingly tall. It seemed impossible that they could exist, and Mero watched them assiduously, expecting a sudden gust of wind to snap them all like twigs.

The road banked to the right. It crossed over a small gulley, effortlessly leaping across a series of stone supports and setting down on the far side. As Mero and the faceless girl crested the bridge, a huge body of water unfolded before them: a lake of black, shimmering water so vast that it touched the horizon to the northeast. To the north was a scattering of islands and, far in the distance, a smudge of blue coast.

To the east, Uron.

The city sat on a peninsula jutting far out over the lake. Its placement felt unnatural, as though the water had risen around it, or else the entire city had been built on floats. It looked like a giant's graveyard, the towers dark and brooding. In Mero's dreams, the windows in the buildings had been lit, giving it the appearance of a night sky. But Uron in daylight was dull, dead. A pall of fog hung over it like a mantle, clouds snared among the rooftops. The wind gusted, raising gooseflesh on the surface of the lake and wafting its smell to Mero's nose. It was brackish and sour. Mero started coughing again, and this time he couldn't stop.

44

As twilight descended on the world of garbage, Mero began to suspect they were being watched. Every so often his ears twitched with a whisper of movement—the clink of a glass bottle, the sigh of fabric stirring in the breeze—or he would catch a shadowy flicker in the corner of his eye. He needed Sheathless to walk, so he couldn't hold it at the ready, but he tightened his grip on its hilt and held the faceless girl close.

The road had disappeared, swallowed under layers of filth. They picked their way between hills of rubble and twisted metal, listening to the mournful wind. Rain spattered down, and Mero's cough worsened. He tried to suppress his urge to breathe, but failed—his brain thought he was dying, even though he was already dead. So he kept sucking air past the raw patch behind his Adam's apple, feeding oxygen to a bloodstream that no longer flowed.

Mounds of rubbish rose all around them, looming, misshapen silhouettes. Mero watched them carefully, but couldn't catch sight of whatever pursued them. The faceless girl squeezed his hand and pressed her cheek against his hip.

The mound nearest them collapsed into a landslide. Dozens of metal cans tumbled down the side of the pile, rattling loudly in the cool air. Mero brandished Sheathless and dragged the faceless girl behind him.

"*Who's there?*" he demanded.

Three seconds of ear-ringing silence. One of the fallen cans rolled slowly towards Mero's feet.

"*SHOW YOURSELF!*" he bellowed.

The twilight erupted with moving shapes.

It was so sudden and silent that Mero thought his eyes were playing tricks. What he had thought were inanimate piles of garbage suddenly skittered along the ground like giant beetles, closing in on them in swift, darting movements. A clump of old fabrics swooped towards them while smears of darkness moved in Mero's peripherals. There were at least half a dozen of them, each as large as a man. Mero waved Sheathless to and fro, trying to threaten multiple figures at once.

The foremost pile grew a hand and raked it across its head, peeling back a flap of dun-colored flesh. Light glinted off a pair of huge, glassy eyes.

Mero watched in paralyzed fascination as another hand appeared. The creature grabbed its own eyes and pulled them out of their sockets, then tugged at the mask covering its chin. A pale, round face caught the moonlight. It was a woman—a human woman. She stared at Mero with blazing eyes. As he watched, she slowly and deliberately clamped a hand over her mouth.

The wind howled, pushing the metal can along. The sound of its rolling was that of water trickling into a pool.

Another sound grew in the distance. It was fast and rhythmic, the steady *whup-whup-whup-whup* of air being displaced. It pressed on Mero's eardrums, reminding him of the spinning fan that had sliced off his foot. A groan rose from one of the other piles. They, like the woman before him, had frozen in place.

The whirring sound grew louder. The woman's eyes darted towards the shadows, as though she were considering flight. Mero grew very afraid. He watched the woman's face for clues, but she seemed trapped in a dilemma herself.

Slowly, quietly, the woman inched towards Mero. An urgent whisper emanated from one of the other piles. The woman hissed something back. A sheen of sweat covered her face.

WHUP-WHUP-WHUP-WHUP—

The woman ran at Mero, ducking past Sheathless and seizing his wrist. A hiss erupted behind her, but she was already dragging Mero into the shadows. The faceless girl stumbled after them, losing her grip on Mero's waist. Another one of the piles animated itself, sweeping close and snatching her from Mero's side. She disappeared under their filthy mantle. Mero stumbled, nearly falling on top of the woman that had grabbed him. She looped an arm through his own and dragged him off the path, throwing her cloak over them both. They huddled in the shadow of an enormous pile of scrap metal, their noses inches apart, her breath hot on his cheeks. Mero opened his mouth and the woman slapped a hand over it.

All this happened in the breathless space between one moment and the next. In that time the whirring had grown shockingly loud, seeming to come from every direction at once. Mero could see nothing inside the woman's cloak. The knowledge that danger was out there, present but unseen, was maddening. He wanted to throw the woman off and claw his way out from under the fabric. But these folk knew something about the whirring noise that he did not, and frightened as he was, he knew his best chances of survival lay in doing as they did.

The sound continued, drilling deep into Mero's skull. He pictured swarms of insects buzzing through the heaps of trash, carpeting the ground, alighting on the woman's cloak. Just once through a gap in the fabric did he see a flash of something small and bright, like a silver bird. His throat seized up and he scratched it with the back of his tongue, struggling not to cough. He felt the woman's breath on his face but could not read her expression in the dark. Her hand was still on his mouth, warm against his cold, dead skin.

At long last the sound began to fade. In the space of a minute it was gone, leaving blissful silence in its wake. The woman, however, didn't move, only shifted her head imperceptibly, listening. It was another minute before she relaxed, throwing off her cloak and pushing herself off Mero.

Mero stood cautiously. Minutes spent under the woman's cloak had not helped his eyesight; the earth below the setting sun was a smear of gray on black. Something thudded into his side and he jumped, but it was only the faceless girl hugging his waist. He transferred Sheathless to his other hand and stroked the top of her head.

Figures coalesced around them. They were human—Mero knew that now—though they moved low to the ground, each weighed down by a heavy covering that disguised them as a pile of garbage. The camouflage was excellent, clearly the result of meticulous attention to detail. Each of the junk-people wore a pair of colored lenses over their eyes and a mask over their mouth and nose, such that hardly a strip of bare flesh showed. The woman who had rescued Mero had already replaced her own, looking once more like a giant brown insect.

One of the figures spoke, a man with red lenses and a red mask. His voice was muffled and he spoke rapidly. Mero didn't understand a word.

"I'm sorry," he said. "I don't understand you."

"Na?" said red-mask. Chatter broke out among his companions, multiple voices rising and falling together. They were unarmed except for red-mask, who carried a length of pipe which he tapped constantly against his leg. He spoke again, gesturing at Mero's missing leg with his pipe. His comment drew noises of assent from his companions.

The woman in the brown hood put a question to Mero. He knew it was a question because it turned up at the end, but the words themselves were nonsense to him. They sounded like a string of random syllables: "Ko-ra-da-mo-mi-ra-ne?"

"I mean you no harm," Mero said. "My companion and I aren't here to cause trouble. We're trying to reach Uron."

The word *Uron* drew a gasp from the brown-hooded girl and a hop of surprise from red-mask. One of the figures at the back of the group—a tall, broad-shouldered man in a green mask—turned and looked over his shoulder in the direction of the city.

"Uron?" the woman repeated. Her accent was so strong the word was barely recognizable: "*Uluron?*"

Mero felt a thrill of excitement. "Yes, Uron. I have important business there. I've traveled halfway across the world to reach it."

A discussion broke out among the junklanders. It started low, but soon grew heated. From their voices Mero determined that there was one other woman among them, a slight girl with a dark blue mask, the one who had snatched the faceless girl from him. The six of them spoke rapidly, with great intensity, constantly interrupting and talking over one another. Red-mask tapped his pipe against his thigh and the woman in the brown hood gestured with gloved hands. Mero watched and wondered who these strange people were, how they had come to live in Uron's shadow.

Suddenly the junklanders surged towards him, examining him from every angle. He held the faceless girl close and stood rigid, aware that the slightest mistake could turn them hostile. Red-mask crouched to peer at the faceless girl and yelped when she turned his way, jumping in the air like a startled cat. Mero's chest tightened, and he gripped Sheathless, fully expecting violence. But though red-mask pointed and cried out and the other junklanders pressed in to look at her, none of them were horrified by what they saw, merely surprised and curious. Mero hardly believed it. Anywhere else on earth, the faceless girl would have been driven out as a demon, and he alongside her.

The discussion resumed, more urgent than ever. Night was falling, and the figures of the junklanders flitted in and out of sight like ghosts. They spoke in rapid, hissing whispers, hopping up and down and smacking each other on the arms to drive their points home. Red-mask kept glancing at the faceless girl, touching his own face to reassure himself it was still there.

Finally the woman in the brown hood approached Mero. He acknowledged her with a nod, slicking the wet from his eyes—it was raining again, stinging droplets spattering down from the dark sky. The woman in the brown hood clapped her hands together, then held them out towards Mero, palms up. Her eyes narrowed behind her colored lenses. Mero thought she was smiling.

"I don't understand," he said.

She rolled her eyes and reached out, taking his wrist. Green-mask—the tall man at the back of the group—grunted and folded his arms in a clear gesture of disapproval. Mero tried not to look at him, focusing his attention on the hooded woman.

"You want me to come with you?" He gestured at the faceless girl. "Can she come, too?"

The hooded woman nodded, tugging at his wrist. He fell into pace behind her, the faceless girl following along in his shadow.

45

They gave him a strip of cloth to tie around his mouth and nose. It was different from the masks they wore, which seemed expressly made for the purpose of breathing Uron's atmosphere, but it helped stifle the tickle in Mero's throat. Then, to his surprise, green-mask—the only junklander who acted hostile towards him—pulled the colored lenses from his eyes and gave them to Mero to wear. Mero knew better than to refuse his charity. He pulled the strap over his own head and adjusted the lenses over his eyes. To his surprise, the tinted glass actually made it easier to see in the dark, the edges of the rubbish piles standing out sharply against the grimy backdrop. He thanked green-mask several times, who grunted in acknowledgment.

They set off deeper into the world of trash, forming a marching column with red-mask in the lead and green-mask taking up the rear. The woman in the brown hood stayed near Mero and the faceless girl in the middle of the pack. The junklanders moved with the effortless confidence of those who had committed their route to memory, seeming to know which obstacles to skirt and which to scale, down to the placement of every footfall. Red-mask was the only one that didn't stick to the prescribed path. He played among the twisted piles, prodding at things with his pipe, picking up pieces of rubbish and turning them over in his hands, invariably tossing them aside when they proved uninteresting.

Mero walked using Sheathless as a crutch, keeping one arm around the faceless girl's shoulder. When the junklanders noticed him struggling to match their pace, red-mask swooped down from the mound he had been climbing and presented his back to Mero, squatting and slapping his shoulders—a clear invitation to hop on and ride the rest of the way. Mero refused with as much grace as he could. The others tittered at red-mask, shoving him around and slapping him on the back. Mero couldn't tell if they were amused, annoyed, or offended on his behalf. Regardless, red-mask soon wandered off, and the incident was quickly forgotten.

The junklanders questioned Mero as they walked, and he tried questioning them in turn, even though they all knew it was a pointless exercise. The urge to communicate was simply too strong—it seemed they all shared the hope that the barrier of language might crumble if they asked enough questions of each other. But none of them knew a single word of Mero's language, and Mero likewise could not understand anything the junklanders said. Though he was familiar with several languages, theirs didn't seem to share roots with any of them, so he could only listen to everything they told him in polite perplexity. It was supremely frustrating. Mero burned with questions: who were these people, and how did they survive in this country where so little grew? How many of them were there? Where were they taking him? Why hadn't they driven him away at the sight of the faceless girl? And of course—what did they know about Uron?

Their path met the shore of the black lake, then curved southwards. It was a relief to be out of the forest of garbage, though the rain here was more intense. Mero was thankful for green-mask's lenses. They formed a seal around his eye sockets, keeping the stinging water out.

Large segments of the coast were buttressed with enormous quantities of poured stone. Even so, the road was washed out in places, huge chunks of black rock crumbling into the water. Mero wondered how long ago the men of the old world had imposed their will on the shore, and how long it had taken the lake to reclaim it. Uron lay across the water on their left. Several times Mero caught the others glancing at it, just as he himself did. Even when he wasn't looking at it, the city pressed against his awareness like a spider crouched in the corner of a room.

A shadow grew on the horizon. It might have been another city, smaller than Uron, facing its counterpart across the lake—or it might simply have been an enormous garbage heap, larger than the rest. At the sight of it, the hooded woman squeezed Mero's shoulder and pointed excitedly. Their party turned inland. It seemed this second city was their destination.

Once more they walked between mountains of junk. The ancient piles did not stink, but they carried a stale, musty smell that was somehow worse. Rot, at least, indicated life. This was the smell of something completely inert, wholly outside the cycle of life and death. Many of the doctors Mero had studied with in his past had been miasmists, believing that certain smells could pollute the lungs and cause illness. Mero had not ascribed to the theory himself, but if there was any smell in the world that could make one fall sick, it was that of the trash heaps of Uron.

They came to a heap much like the rest—a pile of metal, stone, and the mystery material of Uron, as tall as twenty men. Lodged in its side was some kind of vault, a smooth white rectangle with a heavy metal handle. Red-mask strode up to the vault and rapped on the door with his pipe, three short bursts of two: *TANG-TANG, TANG-TANG, TANG-TANG.* The sound echoed down into the earth.

There was a heavy *CLUNK* from the other side of the door. Red-mask pulled the handle and heaved, and the door squealed open. He ducked his head through, nattering away in the breathless language of the junklanders. To Mero's astonishment, an answering voice drifted up from inside.

It can't be, he thought. There was only one possible explanation for what was happening, but he still couldn't believe it.

The exchange between red-mask and the mysterious speaker grew heated, as every junklander conversation seemed to do. The other members of Mero's party gathered around the vault door, and he limped forward, trying to see inside. The brown-hooded woman joined in the conversation, weaving patterns in the air with her hands.

Green-mask pushed Mero towards the door, his face impassive, his eyes red and streaming. The other junklanders parted to let him and the faceless girl through. He peered inside the vault and discovered a crooked passage disappearing into the earth. It was shored up with beams and metal pipes and illuminated with strips of glowing light just like the ones in the underground labyrinth. A man crouched in the tunnel's entrance. His face was swarthy but clean, his clothing plain. His eyes flicked to Mero and then to the faceless girl, and he sucked air through his teeth. He fired a question at red-mask and then at Mero himself.

"She's mine," Mero said, holding the faceless girl close. "I know she looks strange, but she's harmless. I promise."

A few more words were exchanged, then the man smiled gamely and gestured them inside. Red-mask ducked past him, clapping him on the shoulder. Three other members of their group went next, the blue-masked girl and two other boys who had barely spoken throughout their journey, one in a black mask and one in a yellow one. The brown-hooded woman went next. She pulled off her lenses and mask, then turned and smiled over her shoulder at Mero. Her face was round and unblemished. She was young, Mero realized, more of a girl than a woman, her prettiness only accentuated by the ugliness of their surroundings. She beckoned Mero forth, then disappeared down the passage.

The faceless girl hesitated in the threshold. Mero wondered if she was thinking of the labyrinth where he had found her.

"Go on," he said, giving her a nudge. "I'll be right behind you."

She, too, looked over her shoulder, as if reassuring herself he was still there. Far from the spike of fear Mero was accustomed to feeling, warmth spread across his face and down his limbs.

She went inside, and Mero followed.

46

The tunnel was narrow and cramped—perfect for the faceless girl, but Mero was forced to duck. Glowing yellow strips embedded in the walls at regular intervals created patches of light and darkness. It was musty and dry, yet the air tasted cleaner than it had outside. Mero's companions pulled off their lenses and masks, and Mero followed suit.

The junklanders chattered constantly as they descended, pushing and shoving, red-mask barking laughter that struck like a physical presence in the confines of the tunnel. The light of the glow-strips was dim, and Mero only saw his companions in fits and spurts—a pair of shoulders or a flapping cloak, the occasional flash of a pale face.

The tunnel had obviously been excavated by hand. It descended haphazardly, widening and narrowing, its nature and composition changing every twenty paces. At one point the soft noise of their footfalls changed to a loud *CLUNG-CLUNG-CLUNG* as they stepped onto metal grating set into the floor. They passed an alcove lit by the steady glow of a chemical lantern. It was stuffed with boxes and containers, and a pipe ran through it at head-height, appearing out of the tunnel wall then disappearing into it again a few feet later. A man sat on the pile of boxes, seemingly attending to the pipe. The junklanders hailed him loudly and he grunted in response, turning to watch Mero as he passed by. The man had a swarthy face, a drooping mustache, and a patchwork of greasy black hair. As the lantern glow illuminated his features, Mero saw that the right half of his face was covered in boils, his right eye fused shut.

The tunnel widened, and the girl in the brown hood—though she no longer wore her hood—turned and pulled the faceless girl into the space beyond. Mero followed, seeing lights up ahead. What he saw struck him speechless.

It was a city.

The area before them was a courtyard of sorts, an irregular chamber the size of a large house excavated out of the hard-packed earth. Embedded in the walls were several enormous containers of corrugated metal serving either as private residences or hallways connecting to other areas of the warren. The chamber was lit with light-strips and chemical lamps, and was absolutely crammed with people. There were at least three dozen of them in this chamber alone, talking, lazing, stacking boxes, sorting through heaps of scrap metal, coiling lengths of wire. Children climbed shrieking among the piles of supplies. Wires hung from the ceiling and pipes snaked along the walls, scraps of drying laundry hanging from each. A large metal fan, not unlike that which had severed Mero's foot, hummed softly from a hole in the ceiling.

The air was full to bursting with junklander voices, and the volume rose noticeably as Mero and his companions entered the chamber. Men and women pointed and cried out, and a crowd soon coalesced around the party.

Mero gripped the faceless girl's shoulder, unsure of the kind of welcome they were about to receive. The chamber crackled with energy. There was life here, overflowing life, a chaos of densely-packed emotion. He struggled to meet the faces that turned towards him, unsure of where to direct his attention.

Excitement rose to a fever pitch as the junklanders realized there were strangers among the returning party. Mero's companions formed a half-circle around him, fielding a barrage of questions. The brown-hooded girl looped her arm through his and yelled to be heard over the noise. Even so, she could not hope to match red-mask's volume. He hopped up and down, gesticulating wildly, his eyes bulging as he recounted what must have been a greatly exaggerated version of their story. He had a sly, angular face with prominent cheekbones, and his build was thin but wiry. A pretty young woman had extricated herself from the crowd and wormed her way under his arm. Every so often, she reached up to stroke the line of his jaw, and he interrupted his story long enough to kiss her noisily while his onlookers jeered and slapped him on the shoulder.

The girl in the brown hood tapped Mero's arm, then nattered off a sentence, gesturing at the press of people around them. Mero saw a sea of faces, curious, dubious, excited, scared, and heard the conciliatory tone in her voice. He nodded, though he didn't know what he was agreeing to. She smiled and gestured at Sheathless with her palm, waggling her fingers gently.

Mero understood. He reversed his grip on the sword and presented the hilt to her. Leaning in close, he said, "Be careful with it. The blade is very sharp."

She smiled thankfully and took it with exaggerated care. A rough blanket was produced, and she wrapped Sheathless up in it, hiding the glittering sword from sight.

Emboldened by Sheathless's disappearance, the junklanders surged towards Mero. They examined him and the faceless girl from every angle, touching his arms, his shoulders, even his cheek, peering into his eyes and tugging on the ends of his clothing and hair. As they observed him, he observed them. They were small in stature—Mero was not a tall man, but he was the tallest in the courtyard other than green-mask. A few of the junklanders were as young as the hooded girl and most were older, though few were old enough to have any white in their hair. Their skin ranged in color from a pale cream to a dark swarthiness, and many of them shared the hooded girl's roundness of face. Their features did not align with those of any of the tribes with which Mero was familiar.

As his eyes jumped from face to face, he soon understood why the faceless girl's appearance had not caused the uproar he expected. Physical deformities were common among the junklanders. The best of them had skin that was scarred and pockmarked with the remembrances of old sores. Most of them had worse than that. Boils and goiters were the most common, along with chunks of missing hair. Some, like the man they had seen in the tunnel, had one or both eyes fused partially shut. One woman had no nose, only a stretched upper lip and two narrow holes halfway up her face; a man at the opposite end of the crowd had a mouth that looked as though it had blown outwards from inside, his lips peeled back to expose browning gums, his teeth pointed outward instead of down.

Mero thought of the cough he had acquired since approaching the city, and of the way his eyes streamed whenever it rained. Was this the cost of living in Uron's shadow? If so, why did the junklanders remain? From their appearance Mero would have expected these folk to be miserable, but they seemed none the worse for their mutations.

Questions were put to him, endless questions, to which he responded over and over again with variants of "I'm sorry," "I don't understand," "I don't know." The junklanders marveled at his height and wholeness, though they pointed and nodded knowingly at his missing foot. They gave him a length of pipe to use as a cane, then grabbed hold of him and dragged him deeper into the warren.

47

Accompanied now by no fewer than twenty people, Mero was escorted through the junklander city. He was astonished. This was no simple hiding place—this was a hive, a complex of earthen chambers and metal tunnels in which every scrap of space was put to use. They climbed a flight of metal stairs and passed through a narrow threshold, entering a steam-filled chamber dominated by a huge basin in which men and women washed their dirty clothes. Another threshold, and here was a pair of children harassing their mother, who was trying to cook. The metal floor rattled with every step, the ceiling shaking with those of the neighbors upstairs.

Now the hooded girl pinched her lips and they ducked under a canvas curtain. Mero sucked in a breath. It was a sleeping room. No fewer than forty people of every sex and age were spread out on the floor, some under blankets, others clothed, still wearing their shoes. The members of Mero's entourage stepped between them as if this were the most natural thing in the world, and the sleepers did not so much as stir.

On and on it went, private rooms, workrooms and communal spaces stacked one on top of the other in an endless confusion of chambers, hallways, and staircases. There was no cohesion in the style of construction or the materials used, just junk stacked on junk stacked on junk, held together with cables or cords or old bags tied in knots. Pipes undulated along the ceiling and floor, threatening to trip the unwary. Tubs of supplies lined every wall. It was gloomy and claustrophobic, yet none of the junklanders seemed to mind it in the least.

They descended a flight of metal stairs that bent and creaked under their weight, then emerged into a large, L-shaped chamber. The air was muggy and smelled of sulfur. Just as in the initial courtyard, the walls were formed of corrugated metal, huge storage boxes stacked in such a way that this chamber could exist in the space between them. Several layers of matting concealed the earthen floor.

From wall to wall the room was filled with chairs and stools and tables, the vast majority of which were occupied. Mero estimated that two hundred people were crammed into this space—men, women, children, and elders. It was deafeningly loud. Half of the room's occupants were busy eating, spooning broth out of hard blue bowls that clinked and clacked, while the other half laughed, shouted, and shoved one another about.

In the din of the dining hall, even the entrance of Mero's party went unnoticed. Red-mask had started bouncing on the balls of his feet as soon as the smell of cooking wafted over them. Now he tapped the hooded girl on the arm and darted off. The hooded girl stepped onto the corner of an occupied chair—the man eating looked around briefly, then returned to his food—then cupped a hand to her mouth and shouted something at Mero's entourage. Laughter rippled through them, and one man shouted back. The hooded girl answered, her voice angry but her face smiling. Slowly the crowd dispersed.

The hooded girl hopped down from her chair, using the diner's head as a hand-rest—again he turned, shrugged, and turned back—then offered one hand to Mero and the other to the faceless girl. Tugging them along like a pair of carts behind a horse, she plunged into the crowd, headed for an unoccupied corner at the far end of the hall. She steered Mero towards a beam against which he could rest his back, then put a hand on either shoulder and said,

"Battu."

It could only have meant 'stay'. Mero nodded. "I will."

She flashed him a smile and trotted off. Mero watched the bobbing curtain of her hair for as long as possible, but soon lost her in the haze.

Mero settled his shoulders against the beam, fighting to regain his composure. Of all the strange things he had learned about the junklanders, it was their very existence he still struggled to accept. How had they survived this long living off of Uron's refuse? Even from what little of the city he had seen, it was clear there were more people living here than in any of the settlements he had visited in the past hundred years.

Humans could not live in large cities anymore. The earth was simply not productive enough. Fertile soil was difficult to find, and crop disease was rampant. Large settlements inevitably attracted the attention of raiders, but even those that didn't tended to collapse under their own weight once they reached a certain size. People were distrustful, and preferred independence to reliance on others. A strong ruler like Sanja Al-Sat might succeed in uniting a region for a time, but even at their best, these societies were only one bad harvest or one botched succession away from collapse. Mero had seen it, lived it, time after time.

What made the junklanders so special?

He watched the crowd, wishing desperately that the hooded girl would return. A flood of people flowed past Mero's resting spot — diners with brimming bowls looking for a place to settle down to their meal, those with empty ones headed in the opposite direction.

A commotion near the middle of the chamber drew his attention. Someone had dropped a stack of bowls, the *CRASH* of falling ceramic accompanied by jeers and shouting. A hassled woman appeared on the scene. She was small and slight, of middling age, and a baby sat on her arm. She glanced around, and her eyes fell on Mero. Without a word, she strode over and offered the baby to him.

"Oh, no," Mero said. "No, I can't—"

The woman wasn't listening. She pushed the baby against Mero's chest then showed him how to hold it, moving his arms as though he were a wax doll. The baby, sitting upright, chewed its fingers and watched the process with calm, dark eyes. Once it was secured to the woman's satisfaction, she cupped Mero's cheek and pushed off into the crowd.

Mero was horrified. He stared at the baby and the baby stared back, unperturbed. It was about a year old. Like many junklanders, it had a round face and a short crop of jet-black hair. Its eyes were wide and liquid, and it was dressed in a homespun shirt and tattered pair of trousers.

Taking the fingers from its mouth, the baby prodded Mero's face, pinched his lip, tugged his nose — a miniature doctor examining his patient. The work was completed in studious silence. Mero shifted his weight uncomfortably, overcome with images of losing the child, of dropping it, of disaster striking before its mother returned. He had scarcely held a child in all his life and had no idea what to do with it. He held still as best he could, enduring the baby's exploration of his features.

Now he had two people to watch for in the crowd: the hooded girl, and the baby's mother. He couldn't believe anyone could be so trusting as to give their baby to a complete stranger. Perhaps the old woman hadn't wanted the child, and had seen a convenient excuse to be rid of him. Whatever the reason, Mero trusted the hooded girl would be able to help.

The baby fussed, making a "*keh, keh*" noise in his throat. Panic washed over Mero in an icy sheet.

"What's the matter?" he said, rocking his arm. "Are you choking?"

"*Keh,*" said the boy. Mero thumped him on the back, scanning the crowd desperately for someone who could help. But before he could think of hopping from his resting place, the boy pitched forward and coughed a stream of vomit onto Mero's shirt.

Mero stared at the baby. The baby stared back, a glob of yellow on his chin.

Warmth spread across Mero's chest as the vomit soaked through his clothes. He expected to be disgusted, but all he felt was that spreading warmth.

"*Cup,*" the baby coughed. Mero gathered up a corner of his shirt and used it to wipe the baby's face. The boy squirmed for a moment, then allowed himself to be cleaned.

"Better?" Mero said.

An older man approached Mero. He was short and paunchy, with a wide, ruddy face and prominent ears. The top of his head and the left side of his face were dominated by a scarlet rash. Smiling broadly, he gestured at the baby.

"He's yours?" Mero said. The man looked about the right age to be that woman's husband.

The man nodded, smiled, beckoned at the baby.

Mero hesitated, then realized that the baby had twisted around and was reaching for the paunchy man. With deep relief he handed the baby over to his father, who boosted him up in the crook of his arm. He thanked Mero profusely—then his eyes fell on the vomit drying on Mero's shirt. A look of comical dismay crossed his face.

"*Oh!*" he said, pinching the fabric between his fingers. He babbled what sounded like an effusive, protracted apology.

"It's all right," Mero said. "It's no problem, really."

The man gripped his shoulder, then held up a finger and disappeared into the crowd. The baby stared at Mero over his father's shoulder.

Mero looked down at his shirt. The boy had painted a white-yellow streak from the neckline most of the way to the hem. Mero still couldn't smell the vomit over the hot, muggy air of the dining hall.

"*Ay!*"

Mero looked up. It was red-mask, his female companion, and a few others. Red-mask hooked his arm around Mero's shoulders, then turned and chattered to his friends, obviously proving to them that the one-footed man he had encountered outside had not been a figment of his imagination. He prodded Mero's chest, unknowingly sinking his finger into the cooling vomit.

Red mask's bluster quickly turned to dismay. He stared at his finger, then at Mero's shirt, then at Mero, his eyes begging for an explanation.

"A baby threw up on me," Mero said.

"*Na?*"

"A baby," Mero said, miming cradling a baby in his arms. "Threw up. Vomited." He made a throwing gesture from his mouth.

The reaction among red-mask's group was tremendous. Red-mask wailed and clutched his wrist as though the vomit was an infectious disease crawling up his arm. His friends fell into gales of laughter that earned them nasty looks from nearby diners. Red-mask wielded his finger like a weapon, wiggling it in his lady friend's face, making her shriek and duck behind the others for protection. He went after the rest of his friends, driving them back until at last one of them bumped into a diner carrying a steaming bowl of soup. Soup slopped on the floor, the diner shouted, and the laughter redoubled until Mero's ears rang.

A bark cut through the noise and a short woman—the same woman who had lent Mero her baby—pushed her way onto the scene, a towel slung over her shoulder and a wet rag in her hand. The hooded girl followed in her wake, a bowl in each hand and a look of quiet amusement on her face. She caught Mero's eye and grinned.

The woman used the rag to slap liberally at red-mask and his friends, chiding them for causing a commotion. Red-mask cringed under the blows, crying out with each slap as though being flogged. The woman gave him one more smack for good measure, then crossed over to Mero, touched his neck, and wiped him down. Mero protested, but of course the woman ignored him. Suddenly she grabbed the hem of his shirt to pull it off.

"*Hey!*" Mero exclaimed. He tried to stop her, but she slapped his hands away, scolding him. Soon she had tugged his shirt over his head and wadded it into a ball. She only paused in her work when she saw the condition of Mero's chest.

Like the rest of him, it was wreathed in scars.

The worst of all was the puncture wound where the goddess had clawed her way to his heart. That scar was the size of a fist, a crater punched into his sternum. But there were others, too, many others big and small, crisscrossing his stomach and arms. Old wounds closed by Sheathless's influence—and some opened by Sheathless itself. A crooked channel ran down the inside of Mero's left wrist. He had tried bleeding himself to death once, and had succeeded, though this adventure had only resulted in another innocent life being swapped for Mero's own. There was a puncture wound in his stomach and burn marks all over his chest, from when he had been shot off his horse and taken prisoner by soldiers from a faraway land.

Each of these scars marked one of Mero's failures—a lapse in judgement, a loss of hope, or a simple bout of bad luck. Sheathless had erased these failures, had balanced the ledger time after time. But the scars had remained, each a reminder that while Sheathless might have made Mero immortal, no force on earth could make him infallible.

Mero caught the hooded girl's eye and was jolted by the familiar expression on her face, a mingling of pity and love.

The older woman patted Mero's arm, speaking in a soothing voice. She pulled the towel from her shoulder, and it was revealed to be a plain green shirt, much too big for him. He reached out his arms and she pulled it over his head. The fabric was coarse and dry, the simple ruggedness of the garment strangely comforting.

"Thank you," Mero said. He touched the woman's cheek, as he had seen many of the junklanders do. The transformation this simple gesture sparked in the older woman was remarkable. Her face flushed and she smiled prettily, cupping his hand with her own to prolong the touch. She bustled off, and the hooded girl stepped forward, offering him one of her bowls.

48

They found a cluster of empty seats in the middle of a crowded table and sat, surrounded by the sounds of scraping spoons and smacking lips, the faceless girl hiding in Mero's shadow.

It was a simple vegetable soup the junklanders ate, the broth thin and unsalted, the ingredients all foreign to Mero. There were mushrooms and tubers and leafy greens, all unceremoniously chopped into large, square bites. Mero stared with trepidation at the bowl the hooded girl had given him. He had been dreading this moment ever since they entered the dining hall.

He did not need to eat in his condition. He was still capable of chewing and swallowing food—indeed, his body welcomed it the same way it welcomed breath—but after what Gorgol had done to him, he doubted his digestive tract still worked. Even if it had, he didn't want to waste any of the junklanders' food.

He appealed to the hooded girl, who fetched her head to one side and said, "*Na?*"

Suddenly Mero was ashamed. How was he supposed to refuse this food without causing offence? How was he supposed to explain to the smiling girl in front of him that he could not eat because he was not alive, that the sword she had taken from him was the only tether binding him to the earth? He cast around for something to say, and his eyes landed on the faceless girl. He touched his fingers to his own mouth, then reached down and laid his palm on the top of her head. She looked up, aware that she was the subject of discussion.

"I'm like her," Mero told the hooded girl. "No mouth."

The hooded girl blinked once or twice, clearly confused. She took the bowl from in front of Mero and set it aside, watching for his reaction. He nodded, and she smiled, pleased she had understood. She gestured apologetically at her own bowl and Mero said,

"I don't mind. Please, eat."

And that was that.

The hooded girl stole several glances at Mero as she ate. He knew this because he did the same to her. She was pretty—so pretty it was puzzling. How could such a winsome girl flourish in such an ugly place? From what Mero knew of the world, it was not in a woman's best interests to be remarkably beautiful, not unless she had a powerful patron to care for her. It was almost frightening, the way the hooded girl wore her beauty and youth in plain sight. She acted as though she hadn't a care in the world, smiling and laughing as easily as the rest of the junklanders. Was she protected by some force Mero had yet to recognize—or had she merely been lucky so far?

They were soon joined by red-mask and blue-mask—the small, dark girl who had been a member of the original party. Red-mask ate with gusto, his elbows firmly planted on the table and his shoulders hunched around his meal. He indicated Mero's new shirt, and the hooded girl made an inquisitive comment. Red-mask acted out the tale of the baby and the vomit, his mummery so exaggerated that even Mero could follow along. By the end, the hooded girl was crying with laughter—and the more she laughed, the louder red-mask became, and the more attention their table drew. Soon a new crowd gathered; word about Mero had spread, and junklanders of all ages came to stare at him and the faceless girl. One woman even asked him to pull up his shirt so she could see the scars on his chest. They asked him a million questions, but he could only shake his head and shrug. The hooded girl tried to shoo them away, but the junklanders were persistent. Finally there came a commotion at the back of the crowd and a man stepped through carrying a huge bundle of paper. To raucous cheers he dropped the bundle on the table in front of Mero and slapped an oddly-shaped pen—another remnant of Uron, no doubt—into Mero's hand.

Mero considered the vast stretch of canvas before him. The table gave an audible creak as his audience leaned in to watch.

Where to start? he thought.

He drew himself. He drew Sheathless. And he drew the goddess.

49

The junklanders kept him sketching well into the night. Doubtless they would have kept him sketching forever, if the hooded girl hadn't noticed him massaging his wrist and put an end to the exercise.

By that time, the bundle of parchment had become a tapestry, sheet after sheet covered front and back with Mero's illustrations. Ink stained the edge of his hand from the tip of his finger down to his wrist. His eyes were strained, his buttocks sore, and his wrist aching, but he didn't want to stop. He hadn't practiced illustration in years—his days of cataloguing flora and fauna and natural phenomena were far behind him. Now he was cataloguing the events of his own life, from his earliest remaining memories through all his long, lonely years of wandering.

He was far from lonely now. People crowded in from every angle, gasping, pointing, nudging each other as the narrative unfolded. The faceless girl sat at Mero's left shoulder, the hooded girl at his right. He felt their heat on his skin, and that of all the junklanders as they watched him draw, and though he generated no heat of his own, warmth grew in his heart. His pace quickened and he spilled more and more ink, feeling lighter and lighter with every stroke.

Of the time before Sheathless, almost all of his memories had faded. He had often wondered whether this was yet another aspect of Sheathless's curse, or merely an effect of his unnaturally long life. He couldn't even remember the faces of his parents—yet for some reason, he had never forgotten the steps outside his childhood home. They had been chiseled out of white stone, and when the sun shone down on them, they had been so bright they were almost blinding. His mother had always kept those steps sparkling clean. He would often come home to find a rivulet of soapy water running down the street, the front steps wet and brown, his mother either in the process of cleaning them or having just finished doing so.

The last time Mero had seen those steps, the stone had been weathered and cracked, weeds pushing up between the slabs. He had spied a beetle trundling along the once-pristine stone, and crushed it underfoot in a fit of disgust. But that only sprayed the beetle's guts out from under his shoe, guts that glistened in the sun just as the steps themselves once had.

That had been the day he killed the scholar.

Mero hesitated, wondering how the junklanders would react to this development. But the hooded girl stroked his arm, and he touched pen to canvas and drew himself running his oldest friend through the heart. His hand shook, but he couldn't cry—he had no tears left. Hands came from nowhere to touch his shoulders, back, and face. He nodded thanks and took up the pen again.

He drew Menahem's desert and the black stone, and the eagle that had pulled out his heart. That drew excited gasps from the crowd, and he was obliged to lift his shirt again. He drew the bazaar and Sanja Al-Sat, smoking his pipe and surrounded by concubines. He drew the grasslands and the village of Palta. Again his hand shook. But—*damn him anyway*, Mero thought, *he can't hurt me anymore*—and he drew Gorgol the giant towering over the villagers, capturing the veiny tubes of his eyes.

Next he drew Ruya. He paused on her face. He wished he could have spoken to her one final time, thanked her for all of the lessons she had taught him and apologized for those he had been foolish enough to miss. But that was in the past now. She was just a face on his canvas, and there was still so much more to tell.

He drew their journey through the empty lands and his final confrontation with Gorgol. He was still unclear on what had happened that day on the beach. All he knew was that he had been saved by the grace of the goddess. Clearly she still had more use for him, or else she wouldn't have intervened.

Next was the underground labyrinth and his meeting with the faceless girl. The junklanders recognized her at once, of course. They pointed and cried out, and she cringed against Mero's arm, unused to all the attention. He drew the amalgam and the severing of his foot, which likewise drew a strong reaction.

Finally he was out of the labyrinth and closing in on the present. The only detail he left out of the entire story was his attack on the faceless girl. He told himself it was because she was sitting right next to him, and he didn't want to upset her—but the simple reality was that he was ashamed. He was more ashamed of those few minutes than he was of anything else he had ever done, and the worst part was that he still did not understand what had caused him to act that way. His feelings towards the faceless girl were complicated, certainly. He loved her and feared her, and these emotions seemed not to compete with one another but to multiply, so that the more he wanted to push her away the more he was compelled to hold her close.

He did not want to know what would have happened if his will had failed and he had pinned her to the earth with Sheathless. The thought was so distressing that he turned away from it the moment it entered his mind.

Someone jostled him and he realized he had stopped drawing. This was the moment the hooded girl saw him knuckling the tendons of his forearm and called for an end to the undertaking. But Mero touched her shoulder and bent to the canvas one more time, filling in drawings of her and her companions, placing them together with him and the faceless girl under a giant mound of junk. Then, leaping a few inches over the canvas, he drew Uron—Uron with its dark spires, Uron of the black lake. He tapped the city once, twice, thrice with his pen, then laid it down with a *clack*.

The conclusion of Mero's story prompted tremendous cheers from the junklanders. As the loose sheets were gathered up and carefully rolled into a single scroll, men, women, and children poured forth to touch Mero's arms, to take his hand, to feel his scars, and to ogle at his missing foot.

It was an incredible celebration for such a simple thing. All Mero had done was tell them who he was, yet the junklanders applauded his story as though it were that of a great hero instead of a coward and murderer.

Who is it that doesn't understand? he thought. *Them, or me?*

50

The hooded girl attempted to shout the crowd down, but her voice wasn't strong enough. In the end it was red-mask who climbed onto Mero's table, stood with his legs wide and his arms akimbo, and screamed at everyone to go to bed. His shout was challenged several times and he jabbed his finger into the audience, calling out the offenders by name until finally the energy went out of the crowd. The junklanders disappeared up the stairs and through the doors on either end of the dining hall, though a few stragglers still stopped by to take Mero's hand or offer him a few incomprehensible words of support.

Finally they were left more or less alone. Mero inhaled deeply, flexing the muscles of his shoulders and back. As he came out of his stretch, he noticed the hooded girl watching him with a strange look on her face. She turned her chair to face him head-on. The movement had a ritualistic feel to it, and Mero was compelled to do the same. Smiling, the hooded girl reached out and touched three fingers to his chest, just below the collarbone.

"Hachi," she said firmly, pressing harder as she said it, as though stitching the word to Mero's chest.

She waited for his reaction, but he had none to give. He glanced at red-mask and blue-mask, who watched in anticipatory silence.

"I'm sorry," Mero said at last. "I don't understand."

The hooded girl laughed and poked him with three fingers again. "*Hachi*," she said, pushing hard. Then she took his hand, uncurled his first three fingers, and touched them to her own chest, nodding encouragingly when he continued to hesitate. Mero was just about to tell her he still didn't understand when the pieces came together in his mind.

She just named me, he realized. *And now she wants me to name her*. But that was backwards—wasn't it?

The hooded girl watched him, waiting to hear his name for her. Dozens of possibilities occurred to him. He could name her for someone he had known, or for one of the women in his history books. He could name her for a flower—certainly she was pretty enough. But none of those felt right.

When the hooded girl had named him, she had looked him full in the face. He did the same to her and said, "Lia."

He wasn't sure where the name came from. Possibly it had been a real name, sometime in the distant past. All he knew was that it was simple and short and sweet, a pleasure to speak, and when he had looked at her it was the name that had come.

Lia's face glowed. She squeezed Mero's hand.

"Lee-ah," she said, testing the pronunciation.

"That's right," Mero said. "I hope you like it."

Red-mask whooped, making them jump. He slammed his palms on the table and squinted at Mero, leaning over until his belly was nearly parallel with the floor. He reached out, jabbed Mero once with three fingers, and shouted, "*Kanwo!*"

Mero was stupefied. Lia had just given him a name, and now red-mask was giving him another? Was 'Hachi' only Lia's name for him? Was he to acquire another for every relationship he forged in this city?

He had no choice but to return the gesture, looking red-mask in the face. As before, the name came easily, without thought. "Baki," he said.

"*Ooh!*" Baki's face erupted in a gratified smile. Blue-mask patted him on the back before leaning forward herself. The smile she wore as she looked Mero over was a mysterious one. She was so short that she had to put a knee up on the table to touch his chest.

"Fafan," she named him.

Hachi, Kanwo, and Fafan, Mero thought. He gave her the name Una, and for now at least the naming was done. Mero was bemused. He had six new names to remember, three of them his own. He felt them in his chest where the junklanders had touched. It was a familiar pressure, like a heartbeat.

51

Una waved them goodnight soon after. Mero and the faceless girl were left with Lia and Baki, who led them up a winding path through the cramped tunnels of the junk city. Silence pervaded; Mero figured it was late at night. They climbed a narrow staircase whose steps, embedded in a sloping earthen floor, came up to Mero's thigh. Mero had to lean his weight on Baki to hop up the steps while Una carried the faceless girl.

At the top of the stairs, Lia held a rapid-fire discussion with Baki, who thumped his chest and disappeared down a side passage. Mero and the others carried on, through storage rooms, workrooms, rooms humming with machinery. Lia tapped Mero's shoulder and ran her fingers through a scrap of cloth hanging from an overhead pipe. It was bright red, and at the other end of the tunnel she touched another cloth of a different color. From then on, Mero tried to memorize the colors of the banners they passed: red, blue, yellow, orange.

They came to a long, narrow staircase spanning the gap between two huge rows of storage boxes, stacked at least a dozen high and stretching into the middle distance. At the top of the staircase the boxes formed a narrow hallway made entirely of corrugated metal. It was quiet and dark. After only ten feet, the hallway split left and right.

The left side of the hallway was lined with sliding doors. Lia pointed at the first, holding up a single finger. In this manner she counted seven doors. The eighth door she leaned against, pushing the heavy panel to one side before motioning for Mero to enter.

Beyond the door was a room no larger than a jail cell. Clearly the inside of one of the storage boxes, it was made entirely of metal—metal floor, metal walls, metal ceiling. There was no furniture, though a panel had been riveted to the far wall. Lia crossed over to it and showed him how to swing it open on its hinges.

Moonlight flooded into the room.

Mero's mouth fell open. He hadn't realized how high up they had come. They weren't underground anymore—they had climbed up inside one of the massive stacks of boxes surrounding the city. The window was made of the strange, flexible material of Uron, and the view it offered was foggy, as though the panel had been greased. All the same it let in a fat beam of light from the swollen moon, a light that took on an aching, unearthly quality when compared to the wan chemical lights of the underground city.

"Beautiful," Mero murmured, only realizing he had said it out loud when Lia looked his way. She smiled briefly, then tapped him on the shoulder and rattled off a sentence in the junklander language. She made a strange gesture—forming a ring with her thumb and second finger and placing it in front of her eye as though peering through a telescope—then quickly and pointedly swung the shutter closed.

Fear fluttered in Mero's belly. "I'm sorry, I don't understand. Eyes? Someone is watching?"

Lia frowned, clearly thinking of a way to get her point across. She made a fist and bobbed it in front of her face, making a rhythmic 'whop-whop-whop' sound.

Now Mero understood. She was warning him of the same creatures they had encountered when they first met: the buzzing silver birds that had sparked such fear among Lia's party.

"I'll be careful," Mero assured her, nodding. She shot him a gratified smile.

A pipe ran along one side of the room where the wall met the floor. Lia crouched next to it and beckoned Mero closer. Even from a foot away, he felt the warmth radiating off it.

"Incredible," he said. "How do you do it? Do you heat water and pump it through the pipes?"

Lia smiled, knowing he didn't expect an answer.

At that moment, Baki returned, another junklander following in his wake. It was green-mask, the tall, broad-shouldered man who had lent Mero his lenses. He carried a stack of wooden skids, while Baki tottered under a huge sack knotted at the top. Lia pulled Mero out of the room and the two men stepped in. Green-mask dropped his pile of skids in the corner and arranged them into three stacks of three, forming a long, narrow frame. Baki dumped his sack on the skids and pulled the knot. A pile of wrinkled blankets and crumpled clothing spilled out. In less than a minute they had created a rudimentary bed, complete with a pillow made from an old shirt stuffed with other articles of clothing.

Green-mask stepped out and returned with a simple wooden box, little more than a cube two feet on the side. He plopped the cube in the corner and filled it with the remaining laundry from Baki's pile: shirts, socks, and a threadbare blanket.

This—so Lia and green-mask communicated in pantomime—was Mero's room. If he grew too cold in the night, he could move his bed closer to the heating pipe. All the clothes in the box were his. If he wanted to use the box as table, he simply had to turn it upside down.

Their explanation finished, they watched Mero's face, waiting for his reaction. He stepped past them and peered out the window. Most of his view was of towering piles of junk, but a sliver of the black lake was also visible. Sparks of moonlight shimmered on its surface like diamonds scattered on a velvet cloth.

He turned to Lia, Baki, and green-mask.

"Why?" he said. "Why are you giving me this room? Why did you give me food? Why did you let me into your city, and why did you let me stay once I told you about the things I had done? What about the scholar, Menahem, and Barkar? How could you possibly think yourselves safe when I'm around? You know what I am and what I do. You know it's only a matter of time before I take another life. So why not run me out of town while you have the chance?"

Green-mask grunted and folded his arms. Baki bugged out his eyes, appealing to the others for direction. Lia just smiled and shook her head. She pointed at Mero's bed and made a pillow with her hands. She pointed at herself and then out the window: *Sleep now. I'll come and get you in the morning*.

Mero sighed. He hung his head, then raised it again.

"Thank you, Lia. Thank you, Baki."

He hesitated when he came to green-mask. The man stepped forward and touched Mero's chest. "Arochi."

Mero returned the gesture. "Boz."

Boz grunted with the air of someone who had completed an unpleasant task. He did not seem particularly fond of Mero, yet that hadn't stopped him from helping with the rest.

"Thank you, Boz," Mero said.

Boz nodded and ducked out of the room. Baki whooped and punched Mero on the arm. Lia touched Mero's cheek, then knelt and embraced the faceless girl. She pulled Mero's door half-closed as she left.

52

Mero sank down on his bed, hands clasped between his knees. He closed his eyes, trying to make sense of the images dancing behind his eyelids. The faceless girl sat next to him, almost but not quite touching, hands folded demurely in her lap.

They sat side-by-side for some time. Snatches of distant conversation drifted up through the floor. Every so often the heating pipe gurgled and clanked. It was chilly, but not cold. Spatters of rain struck the window, painting streaks across the opposite wall.

Uron waited somewhere in the distance, its presence a shadow over Mero's heart. He had dreamt about the city for so long. Now that he was finally on its doorstep, his emotions were knotted and confused. He couldn't be happy to have come to the end of his journey, yet the dread bubbling in his stomach made him feel light instead of heavy. His head was full of ice that numbed the bitterness of his memories.

In the darkness, everything felt unreal.

He glanced at the faceless girl. The sight of her sent a horrible chill down his spine. What had he been thinking, letting the others leave him alone with her? He was convinced her blank skull would soon split open, revealing a black, gaping mouth—a mouth lined with teeth pointing inwards, like the gullet of a shark. Once she got hold of him, there would be no escape.

But she only touched him on the arm, the way the junklanders often did. The touch was warm.

"What do you think of this place?" Mero asked her. "Do you like it here?"

No answer.

Eventually he decided he had best get some rest. His body did not crave sleep, but his mind did. He stretched out on the narrow cot and the faceless girl stretched out next to him, filling in the spaces of his body with her own. He put his arm around her and held her close. Her little heartbeat thudded against his chest.

What are you? he wondered, not for the first time.

What are you? the goddess answered.

53

"*Where are we going?*"

Mero had to shout to make himself heard. It didn't do him any good—Lia just laughed and beckoned him on.

They had joined a small flood of junklanders descending into the city proper from the sleeping chambers above. The crowd was several hundred strong, which meant the tight tunnels of the junk city were packed from end to end. Men and women chattered and laughed as they shuffled forward at a snail's pace. Mero and Lia bobbed through the crowd, corks borne on a human tide.

Eventually they pushed through a doorway and emerged into a huge chamber constructed entirely of poured stone. Stacks of supplies lined the far walls, but the space was so vast that most of it stood empty. It reminded Mero immediately of the underground labyrinth, and he surmised that this chamber almost certainly predated the heaps of junk under which it lay. The crowd expanded to fill the space, friends and families breaking off and claiming small corners of the chamber as their own.

Baki, swimming through the crowd, drew up beside Mero and slapped him on the shoulder. Mero wobbled but didn't fall. He was still using the length of pipe the junklanders had given him as a cane. They had returned Sheathless to him earlier that morning, but he'd left it in his room. He'd expected the pain of leaving it behind to be overwhelming, but somehow the sword's hold on him had weakened. It only hurt when he thought about it, as he was now—but the junk city was such a busy place that another thought would soon uproot it.

Soon the chamber teemed with people from corner to corner. They stood at arm's length of each other, all facing the same direction. Now a wrinkled, smiling man stepped onto a low platform erected against the wall. He waved at the crowd and many of the junklanders waved back. A few of them shouted something, and the old man made a remark that sent a ripple of laughter shivering out. Folding his hands behind his back, he leaned out and peered into the crowd. Baki cried out and waved his hands over his head, gesticulating wildly at Mero.

Several hundred heads turned. Mero would have flushed if there had been any blood in his body. The old man squinted in his direction, then made a distinct "Ah!" sound and spoke again. He stood on one foot, hopping to keep his balance, and the junklanders erupted with laughter. Baki, bawling, hugged Mero from the side, and Lia rubbed his back—*please don't be angry, it's only a joke*. Mero, however, was too puzzled to be offended. Had all this been for the sake of a little comedy?

The old man, still standing on one foot, let his head fall forward and shook the tension from his body. Instantly the crowd fell silent. Mero looked left and right and realized that this was because all the junklanders, Lia and Baki included, were following the old man's example, hanging their heads and shaking out their limbs.

Another call brought Mero's attention back to the platform. The old man raised his knee and wove his arms through the air, slowly as though underwater. His stance shifted, and he kicked his foot back, reaching forward to maintain his balance. The junklanders followed, the sea of heads sinking towards the ground, hundreds of palms flashing up.

Understanding flooded in. It was a mass exercise—performed on one foot so Mero could follow along. Though he would not usually have exercised in such a manner, he did not want to insult the junklanders' way of life. He sank into the same lunge as the people around him, and a few encouraging whispers flitted in his direction. The old man called out another pose and Mero shifted into it, emulating the slow, deliberate movements.

The exercise lasted half an hour. The old man took them through stretches, bends, and twists, sinking to his buttocks, then onto his back, then guiding the crowd back to their feet. Mero was shocked and more than a little embarrassed by his performance. Even those junklanders ravaged by physical deformities moved with a grace and control he could not match. The exercises called for muscles Mero had not engaged in months, and they creaked like wagon wheels rusty with disuse.

At last the old man—who had not set his foot down for the entirety of the exercise—raised his hands over his head and delivered a stirring cry. The junklanders responded to deafening effect, and the man waved and stepped off the platform. Mero sank to the ground, panting with exertion.

Baki plopped down next to him, blowing out his cheeks. Mero was gratified to see the sheen of sweat on his face. Lia leaned on his head, fanning herself. She stank; all three of them did.

"You do this every morning?" Mero asked.

Baki grinned and picked at the front of his shirt, turning it into a bellows.

They returned to the dining hall for a meal of cooked grain and cold vegetables, then Lia and Baki dragged Mero to yet another part of the city. The air here was humid and warm, a steady stream of people both coming and going.

They stopped at the end of a T-shaped hallway and Lia turned left, waving to Mero and Baki as though meaning to leave them. Baki made to follow her and Lia made a scandalized noise, shoving him hard in the chest. Baki laughed—he was always laughing, his face as red as the mask he wore—but made no attempt to follow her again. The look Lia shot the two of them as she disappeared down the hallway was vaguely naughty, and Mero soon learned why.

Baki clapped him on the back and directed him down the hallway to the right. The air grew warmer and still more humid, and water pooled on the floor. They entered a room filled with shoes and shirts and other articles of clothing, piled in the corners and hung from nails hammered into the walls. Baki immediately began to strip. For a second Mero was alarmed—then understanding dawned.

Baths, he thought.

Soon Baki was completely naked. He wadded up his clothes and tossed them carelessly atop the others. He was lean and muscular, his skin not quite as dark as Ruya's had been. He rapped Mero's arm with his knuckles, clearly indicating that Mero should strip as well. Mero leaned his cane against the wall, then pulled off his shirt and trousers, folding them with a little more care than Baki had shown and placing them on top of a nearby pile.

They stepped into the next room. This one was large and rectangular and utterly featureless, except for half a dozen rows of pipe that ran along the ceiling. The room was crowded with men and boys, at least three dozen of them, each as naked as the last. A few pairs of eyes flitted their way and one or two of them lingered on Mero. But the pervading air in the muggy chamber was one of boredom. One chubby man sat on the floor with his back to the wall and his chin on his chest. His eyes were closed and he snored rhythmically.

What now? Mero wanted to ask, though he didn't care to break the silence. Baki wandered into the room, looking for a clear space to stand. Finding one, he gestured at Mero, then pointed upwards. They stood under one of the pipes, directly beneath some kind of valve that looked like a small metal flower. Mero had never seen piping like this, but guessed its function easily enough. He was impressed by the junklanders' ingenuity. This technology must have been salvaged from Uron—but how had they gotten it to work?

The more pressing question was, how long were they supposed to stand naked under this pipe waiting for the water to come?

Baki made a hammock with his hands and leaned his head into it, resting on nothing, whistling tunelessly under his breath. A neighbor— another slight young man—rapped him on the arm and asked him a question, and Baki responded in a drawling voice. It was warm and quiet in the chamber, almost womblike. Mero understood why the chubby man had fallen asleep.

CLANG! The noise reverberated through the room. It sounded as though someone had struck the overhead pipes with a hammer. The buzzing set Mero's teeth on edge.

Immediately the chamber came to life. Men beckoned their sons to stand under the pipes, and the chubby man snorted awake and lurched to his feet. Baki slapped Mero's arm and pointed at the metal flower. Mero nodded his understanding.

CLANG! The noise came again, vibrating from one end of the chamber to the other. Metal groaned, and the pipes overhead flexed. A gurgling sound built in the walls. Mero kept his eyes on the metal flower, which turned out to be a mistake.

There was a loud *HISS*, and every flower spat water at once. Shrieks filled the chamber. A jet of water struck Mero right in the face, and he staggered, bumping into another bather and nearly sprawling on the floor. Baki laughed uproariously even as he hogged water, rubbing his scalp and face and armpits at a breakneck pace. Mero joined him under the spray, letting the water wash over him, but Baki clapped his hands and stamped his foot, shouting something that must have meant, *"faster, faster!"* He was already rubbing his legs and crotch, his manhood slapping around in circles as he scrubbed furiously. Mero followed his example, but there was another challenge besides keeping his balance: the pressure and temperature of the water changed constantly. The flower hissed like an angry cat, spitting out water that was one moment warm, the next freezing cold, and the next so unbearably hot that Mero thought it would leave him skinless. There were yelps and shouts throughout the chamber as these changes were felt by the other bathers, but no one was willing to give up his spot under the pipes for even a second.

Then, as suddenly as it had started, it was over. The pipes fell silent and the spray turned to a spiritless dripping. The chamber filled with moans and complaints, and a few men slapped the pipes overhead, demanding another round from the invisible master of the bath. But no more water was forthcoming, and the bathers soon shuffled out.

An incredible amount of grime had sloughed off Mero's body as he showered, but despite Baki's warnings, he hadn't been quick enough: he still did not feel entirely clean. He would have liked another minute under the jet, or several, but resolved to enjoy what he had been given. He was cleaner today than he had been yesterday, and tomorrow he would be cleaner still.

54

Mero awoke to a knock on his door.

The faceless girl sat bolt upright. Mero woke blearily by comparison, propping his window open to let in the sun. The knock came again, and the faceless girl stiffened.

"It's all right," Mero soothed. "There's no one in this city that's going to hurt you. You should know that by now."

She watched him suspiciously as he hopped to the door and pulled it open. Lia was outside, along with Boz, Una, and an older man Mero didn't recognize. The man smiled and greeted Mero, who returned the gesture, puzzled. Lia touched their shoulders and beckoned them down the hall.

As they stepped out of Mero's room, Una caught sight of the faceless girl and cried out to her, holding her arms wide. Eagerness winning out over shyness, the faceless girl jumped out of bed and went to her. Una lifted her into her arms, chattering at her and stroking her back.

Try as he might, Mero did not understand. *I can love her because she's mine. But how can Una love something like that?*

Out in the hall, the older man proffered what looked like an old boot. Mero took it without thinking, thanking the old man on reflex. The others leaned in, watching for his reaction.

Mero turned the gift over in his hands. It *was* a boot, hand-woven out of thick plion fibers—*plion* was the junklanders' name for the mystery material of Uron—with a sturdy heel of the same material. Straps as thick as two fingers climbed from the ankle, some long enough to be fastened above the knee. Mero peeled back the boot's tongue. It was stuffed full of rags.

The stranger, catching Mero's expression, grinned and pointed at his own foot. An identical boot was strapped to his right leg, fastened tightly around his calf and thigh. Visible under the folds of his pants were a few protuberances of bubbled, waxy skin: this man was a victim of the same deformations that seemed to strike all junklanders in their old age.

Plucking the boot from Mero's hands, the stranger hunkered down and set the heavy sole on the floor, laying out the straps so they wouldn't tangle. Lia offered her arm for balance, and with her help Mero guided the stump of his leg into the boot's mouth. The stranger set about tightening the straps, one around Mero's shin, two more under and over his knee.

The stranger stood, brushing off his hands. Gingerly, Mero leaned his weight on his prosthetic foot. There was too much give, the stump of his ankle crushing down the padding inside the boot. He felt he would teeter over sideways. But as he limped up and down the hallway, his confidence grew. By the time he had taken fifty paces he no longer needed his cane to walk. Lia cheered and clapped her hands as Mero walked by. Una used the faceless girl's hand to wave at him. Mero was overwhelmed. Giddiness swept over him every time the boot *thudded* down on the metal floor, growing stronger and stronger until he could hardly see or think. He went to shake the stranger's hand but the old man slipped past his arm and pulled him into an embrace.

"Thank you," Mero said. "Thank you. Thank you."

The stranger touched his chest and named him 'Warru', a name that caused Una and Boz some amusement. Mero, in turn, named him 'Toko', and he responded with a broad smile and a short bow.

"How can I pay you?" Mero asked then. "What do I owe you?"

Toko stared in polite confusion. Mero pantomimed giving him something and Toko leaned away, holding up both hands: *I don't want any*. Mero was distressed, but Lia touched his arm reassuringly. His work complete, Toko gave Lia a kiss on the cheek and the rest of them a hearty wave, then disappeared down the hall, his own limp almost imperceptible.

Mero tested his balance again, adjusting the tightness of the straps. He caught Lia watching him with open delight, Boz with aloof acceptance.

"How did you learn to live this way?" Mero asked. "What have you figured out that no one else has?"

Lia smiled and offered him her hand.

55

They showed him the place where all of their food was produced.

Mero figured they had postponed this trip until his prosthetic foot was ready. It was a long walk to a new section of the city, a walk that took them through dark, cramped tunnels, up twisting flights of stairs. People were everywhere, working, sleeping, playing games with small metal chips. The only thing Mero didn't see them do was eat: that activity was confined to the dining hall. He wondered if this was motivated by a desire to keep vermin out of the city.

The tunnel swung sharply upwards, turning into a vertical shaft. Lia pointed towards the distant ceiling, then put her foot on a metal ladder set against the wall and climbed. Una and the faceless girl followed her. Hinges squealed, and a square of sunlight appeared at the top of the shaft. Boz tapped his shoulder and indicated the ladder with his chin, clearly wanting Mero to go first.

Mero struggled with the ladder. His prosthetic fit well, but it was hard to tell when his boot had struck something solid, and setting the arch down on the rung meant resting his weight on nothing—he had to inch his boot forward and stand on the heel instead.

The light grew as he approached the top of the ladder. Lia took his hand and helped him climb out of the shaft. A blast of hot, humid air struck his face. He blinked in the dazzling light.

They stood in the corner of an enormous structure like a glass house, supported by beams of wood and metal and hemmed in by piles of junk. The ceiling, forty feet above them, was made of panels and sheets of transparent plion that let in a good deal of sunlight—more than Mero had seen in days.

The house was crammed with plants of every kind: herbs, flowers, fruit-bearing trees, crawlers and vines, tubers and grains. This was no farmer's field—this was a wild cacophony of growth, plants cavorting together, twisting around one another, resting on each other's shoulders in their bid to gather sunlight. The trees massed near the center of the chamber—where the roof was highest—looked mature enough to be a hundred years old. The tree closest Mero groaned under the weight of hundreds of yellow, pear-like fruit, which he recognized from the dining hall.

The air was sweet with the smell of growth, so full of moisture that dew gathered on Mero's skin with every step. He imagined the water seeping into his pores, rejuvenating him—filling out his sallow cheeks and swelling his collapsed chest, ironing out all the wrinkles and scars he had accumulated throughout his journey.

It was quiet in the chamber, sound muffled by moisture and heat, and for a moment Mero stood and enjoyed the simple pleasure of existing in such a peaceful place. He opened his eyes to discover that Lia and the others had wandered off, leaving him to his silence. He was almost offended, until he realized they had done exactly what he would have preferred them to do.

Mero, Lia, Boz and Una were not alone in the indoor forest. Caretakers walked among the plants, fussing over the junklanders' crop. An elderly woman squatted in a patch of tubers, pulling them from the earth and depositing them into a plion tub. On the other side of the path, a slender, middle-aged man planted trellises into the ground, unwinding clinging vines from a nearby tree and draping them over the wooden scaffolding. In the back a pair of women examined the leaves of a large, fruit-bearing plant, holding a rapid-fire discussion under their breath. Each of these waved at Una as they passed by; it seemed she was a regular here. Mero drew his share of stares as well, and one of the gardeners, a stout woman with curly hair, waddled over to touch his face and examine his prosthetic. She asked a question of him, smiling, and he said, "Yes, it's wonderful. I owe Toko a great deal." She couldn't have understood him, but her smile brightened and she clapped him on the arm with a gloved hand before returning to her work.

All the while the plants worked their subtle magic on Mero. His lungs filled more with every breath, and the stiffness in his hips—which had never fully faded since that day on the beach—began to ease. And not for the first time since coming to the junk city, Mero wondered whether he could ever bear to leave.

56

"*Kanwo! KAN-WOOOO!*"

"*NA?*" Mero called out without turning his head. He was performing repairs to the roof of the indoor forest, balancing on a rickety piece of scaffolding with his arms stretched over his head. One of the plion panes forming the roof had cracked, and was letting out moisture and heat. Mero had removed the old pane and was just sliding a fresh one into position when Baki came bounding down the walkway, waving his arms energetically. Baki was a master of poor timing; Mero had never seen his equal.

"*Koro wakera hatta nan jun ditano jen bo KA-AA!*" Baki shouted, hands cupped around his mouth.

Mero frowned. His grasp of the junklanders' language was rudimentary, and Baki was a fast talker. But he understood 'jun'—'old woman' or 'grandmother', 'wakera'—'west', and 'koro', a sentence modifier that meant 'happening', 'change', or 'news'. Those three words burned in his mind like fire, and he found himself thinking, *No, it's impossible.*

"*Na jun wakera?*" he asked. *An old woman from the west? Tell me more.*

"*Na?*" Came a plaintive voice from below. It was Karo, the elderly gardener who had been building trellises the first day Mero visited the indoor forest. He had been observing Mero's progress from the ground, shielding his eyes with his hands, and was no doubt wondering why Mero was letting all the heat drain out the roof.

"*Jun doji ika ya! Nan MUUU-ROOO!*" Baki shouted, loud enough for Karo, and likely the rest of the city, to hear.

'Muro' meant 'sick'. Mero knew this because the word was so similar to his own name—it had been the cause of some confusion and humor when he had revealed his old name to Lia.

A sick old woman from the west.

"I'm sorry," Mero called down to Karo, all knowledge of the junklanders' language forced out of his mind by a wave of roaring emotion.

"I'm sorry, I have to go. A sick old woman from the west. It can't be her, but it has to be. I'm sorry, I'll be back later to help with the roof. I have to go."

57

Baki picked up on Mero's sense of urgency as they moved through the city. Though Mero would never be able to travel as quickly as he once had, he had become quite comfortable with his prosthetic foot. Keeping his eyes on the space between Baki's shoulder blades, he followed his companion towards the city center.

They reached a T-shaped hallway and Baki turned right, away from the group sleeping rooms and towards the infirmary. Mero's unbeating heart climbed into his throat.

The infirmary was warm, the walls waterproof and thickly insulated. A group of junklanders lingered outside a curtained room, craning their necks to see inside. Baki turned sideways and cut through the crowd, pushing against shoulders to propel himself forward. Mero only had to wait for the onlookers to step aside. He was known all over the city now as the westerner with the prosthetic leg, in whose shadow followed the girl with no face. His oddity alone had earned him a measure of respect, or perhaps it was simple fear. Not even the junklanders were immune to some of man's baser emotions.

Baki waited for Mero to catch him up, then pinched his lips and pulled the curtain aside. The room beyond it was no larger than Mero's own: it had space for a bed, a bedpan, a single chair, and an old wooden box serving as a table. The bed was piled high with blankets, rags, and coats. It looked like an enormous nest in which incubated a single, dark brown egg, and that egg was the bald head of Ruya of Palta.

Mero leaned against the threshold for support. The room's other occupant was an elderly nurse, about an age with Ruya herself. She held Ruya's hand and watched the slow rise and fall of her breath, her blankets a sleeping mountain heaving under frost and thaw. The nurse glanced at Baki and a look of disapproval crossed her face. Then she saw Mero, and the disapproval changed to surprise.

Wordlessly, Mero stepped to the bedside. The clump of his prosthetic leg sounded like a fist pounding on a coffin lid. The nurse shuffled out of his way and he picked up Ruya's hand where she had left it. It was thin as a stick, the skin like paper. Every knuckle, tendon and vein stood out. Ruya had been a stout, sturdy woman. She had wasted away to nearly nothing.

His eyes traveled to her face. Here the story was no different. Almost all of her hair had fallen out; what little wisps remained were white as spiderwebs. Her eyes were deeply sunken, her lids clinging so tightly to the surface of her eyeballs that the mounds of her pupils were visible through the skin. They were not moving.

Her mouth was a thin gash, the lips dry and cracked. Her jaw was slack, the skin of her throat loose and manifold. Her pulse fluttered in her neck.

"When did she get here?" Mero asked. "And how?"

He waited for the nurse's answer, but none came. He realized he had forgotten to use the junklanders' language. "Na tei?" he said. *How is this the case?*

The nurse answered low, appealing to Baki for help. Baki, in a mixture of junklander, pantomime, and Mero's own language, contrived to explain that she had stumbled across a scavenging party about an hour ago. She had come out of the west, just as Mero had done, carrying nothing but her clothes. She had been weak and feverish, collapsing into the scavengers' arms moments after they found her. They had carried her into the city on a stretcher.

"Koro iya?" Mero asked the nurse. *Will she live?*

He learned all he needed to know from the look on her face. Keeping his hold on Ruya's hand, he pulled the chair close to her bedside and sat down heavily. He brushed his fingers against her cheek, then rested his palm on her shoulder. He couldn't tell if her skin was cold or hot. He hadn't told anyone, not even Lia, that his sense of touch was fading. He could stand under the showers now and never flinch though the other bathers yelped and screamed. He figured it had to do with his nerve endings breaking down.

He leaned in closer.

"Ruya," he whispered. "It's me, Mero. We both found our way to the same city. Ruya, you would love it here. There are children—so many children—they climb all over you and ask you questions you don't have the answers to. Or rather, I don't, but I reckon you would. And I have a child now, too. She frightens me but she's beautiful. There are green crops and the people always smile and laugh. There are no giants here, not even man-sized ones. I lost my foot but they gave me another one. Ruya, it's everything you ever wanted. If you can just be strong and wake up, you'll get to see it for yourself."

He squeezed her hand. Her chest rose and fell. Her breath did not rattle, but it sounded raw. Mero eyed the basin on the table next to him.

"Fwei?" he asked the nurse. He still struggled with the junklander word for 'water'—sometimes it sounded like 'shwei' and sometimes 'fei' and sometimes 'huei'.

The nurse shook her head, her expression telling him that the question had been foolish: of course you couldn't get a senseless woman to drink. Mero swallowed, his own mouth dry, and turned back to Ruya. But he could think of nothing else to say, nothing else that could persuade her to wake and join him in life. So he sat holding her hand until Baki had left and the nurse had left and he sensed that night had fallen. Eventually the curtain drew back and Lia stepped in, looking shockingly beautiful in the dim light. She slipped her arms around Mero's neck and pressed her face against his cheek. He barely felt her touch.

"Joi?" she asked, in a low murmur. *Friend?*

"Joishi," Mero answered. *Good friend. Family.*

She sighed into his neck and squeezed him more tightly. Ruya's breath reached them faintly from the bed, a hot, dry sound.

"Frese," Lia said. *You're cold.*

"It's because I'm dead," Mero replied.

She pulled away, searching his face for meaning. Eventually she said one word, "Zanu."

The junklander language was highly contextual. The primary meaning of 'Zanu' was 'future'. In this context, it meant 'not yet'.

"But it's true," Mero said, cold misery seeping into his gut. "Ruya, too."

"Zanu," Lia said again.

Mero hung his head. "I can't, Lia. I can't be happy all the time. It's too much work. I feel like I'm climbing a ladder into the sky. I get so scared."

Lia stroked his shoulders. She said something in junklander that he could not translate, but he caught the words for 'happy' and 'sad' and 'friends' and 'mealtime'. He ached to understand her. Here were the two women who seemed to know everything Mero did not, yet one was dying and the other's words meant nothing to him.

Where are you? Mero asked the goddess. *Why can't you ever teach me things in a way I'll understand?*

The curtain drew back a second time, and Mero sucked in his breath. The faceless girl stood in the threshold. Una was not with her. She was alone, with no one else to hide behind. Her weight was spread evenly between her two feet, and her arms were at her sides. She wore the same ribboned dress as ever before. The red top looked black in the dim light of the sickroom.

Mero held his hand out to her.

"Come here," he said. "This is the woman I've been telling you about."

The faceless girl stepped into the room, ignoring Mero's hand. Lia shrank away instinctively. The faceless girl passed them both by and stood at Ruya's bedside. Standing on the tips of her toes, she brushed a single strand of hair from the old woman's cheek.

Ruya's eyelids fluttered.

Lia gasped and Mero leapt to his feet, his chair clattering. The faceless girl stroked Ruya's temple, and she groaned, a low, drawn-out sound like wind through an old barn. She coughed, the mountain of blankets trembling, and her head lolled to one side.

Her eyes came open. They were sharp and focused. She contemplated the faceless girl, then smacked her lips and said, "Oh, it's you."

"Ruya," Mero said.

He didn't recognize his own voice, but Ruya did. Her eyes locked with his own. They were exactly as Mero remembered them.

"You're here, too," she said. "How nice. Did you find your city?"

"I can see it from my room," Mero said.

"Will you go?" she asked him.

He swallowed. His teeth clacked. "Yes, I'll go."

Ruya closed her eyes, drawing a slow, deep breath. The blankets swelled. She let it back out, and her eyes opened again. This time they fell on Lia, looking lost and frightened in the corner.

"You made the same mistake as me," she said. "Only it isn't a mistake. It never is. You know that, don't you?"

Lia glanced at Mero, but he couldn't help her. After a moment she nodded imperceptibly. Ruya coughed. A single tear slipped down her cheek and into her pillow.

"Sweet girl," she sighed. "Oh, to be young and beautiful." She shot Mero a sly sidelong look. "What's the matter with you? I'm the one who's dying."

"You're not dying," Mero said at once, but Ruya drowned him out in a storm of coughing.

"Don't treat me like that. I may not know death as well as you, but I know it well enough. There's a black wind blowing under my door, and it will scoop me up and carry me away, soon as the last of my roots have withered."

"Have some water," Mero said, grabbing the basin and holding it under Ruya's chin.

She protested at first, but Lia helped her sit up, and she managed to suck a few gulps past her dried lips. In the end she drank too quickly and started coughing again. Her head slammed against her pillow, and she covered her mouth with a fist. Each cough made Mero's own throat clench in sympathy.

"Is there anything you need?" he said. "Just say the word. I can bring you broth, blankets—"

But Ruya shook her head. Her eyes found the faceless girl again. "Where did you find that one?" she asked, pointing with a clawlike hand.

"Down a hellhole," Mero said.

"Then she's a demon?"

"That's just a myth. Hellholes are just regular holes, only very deep. Each gigas comes equipped with a sort of proboscis called a hellspike. They drive it into the ground to feed off the earth's energy. Each hellhole is an old gigas feeding site."

Ruya shot him another sly look. "Then it was only chance, you meeting her down there?"

"I don't think any part of this journey has been chance," Mero said.

Ruya laughed. It soon became another cough. Mero reached for the basin but Ruya waved a hand irritably.

"Why doesn't she have a face?"

"I don't know. I can't figure it out." Mero cleared his throat, words pressing against his teeth. In a rush he added, "She doesn't have anything. No—orifices of any kind. The junklander women told me, after they took her in for a bath."

Ruya sighed. "How sad."

"I'm not so sure," Mero said. "At least she's safe. After what happened with Gorgol—"

Ruya's hand shot out and clamped around Mero's wrist. He cried out—her strength was surprising.

"Listen to me," she hissed. "Sewing up your womanhood because you're afraid of rape is like plucking out your eyes because you're afraid to cry. It's like chopping off your legs so you never fall down. Every part of you can cause you pain. That's no reason to cut it away. Keep cutting and you'll have nothing left. Keep cutting and you might as well be dead."

Mero felt he was being electrified. The current ran from Ruya's hand up his wrist and all the way to his brain, their locked eyes completing the circuit. He tried to pull his arm away but he either couldn't or wouldn't muster the strength to break Ruya's grip.

The faceless girl appeared by Mero's side. She put her palm on Ruya's forehead and pushed her back against the pillow. The old woman went limp, her hand sliding from Mero's wrist. There were deep impressions in his skin where her fingers had gripped.

Ruya's eyes closed and her breathing returned to normal. Mero massaged his wrist, thinking about what she had said.

"There's some basis in science for it," he told Lia. "By definition a living being has to be able to absorb resources from its surroundings and process them into waste. Anything that doesn't take from its environment and give back to that environment can't be said to be alive."

He checked her face, expecting to see support, a smile. But she looked frightened and confused. She reached out to him, then thought better of it and shrank back. That tiny gesture, that single moment of drawing away, came down between them like a guillotine blade. Mero was still there, and Lia was still there, but now something else divided them. Transparent but hard as steel, like a sheet of plion. And a bitter bile climbed Mero's throat.

"What's the difference?" he asked her, more roughly than he had intended. "What's the difference between what I do and what everything else does? Am I really so evil?"

Lia shook her head, backing away. She pressed her lips together, holding back sobs.

"You loved me," Mero accused her. "You thought you could patch me up, like a leaky bucket. But look at me—look at all the holes. Too many for you. Too many for anyone."

He had pulled up his shirt, revealing the scars crisscrossing his body, the greatest of them the deep cleft in his ribs. At the sight of them Lia did start to cry, clapping a hand over her mouth and nose.

Mero stood. Lia backed away from him, covering her mouth with one hand and searching for the edge of the curtain with the other. Mero took one clomping step forward. Then the curtain pulled back for a third time, and Boz stood in the threshold, fists bunched at his sides. His eyes swept the room and settled on Mero. As Lia shrieked for him to stop, he took two bold forward strides and punched Mero hard in the face.

Stars exploded in Mero's brain, his nose crawling up into his skull. He staggered backwards, and his prosthetic foot came down sideways. His leg crumpled under his weight and he fell heavily into the wooden chair. One of its three legs snapped off, and it all came tumbling down. Mero wound up in a crumpled heap on the floor, his ears ringing, his bottom lip embedded in his teeth.

Shame overwhelmed him. Hanging his head, he drew the curtains of his mind, unable to cope with what he had done. Dimly he was aware of Lia trying to approach him and Boz dragging her out of the room by the arm.

Silence fell.

Soft footsteps tickled Mero's ears. It was the faceless girl, standing in the triangle of his outstretched legs, facing him as one would their reflection in a mirror. Mero pulled his legs back and curled into a ball in the corner. It was not unlike the first time they had met.

"Leave me alone," he said. "Go bother someone else."

No answer.

"You're wasting your time," he said. "I'm beyond help."

No answer.

"Or maybe you just enjoy torturing me," he said, unfolding. "Is that what all this has been about? Revenge? Then go on—hurt me again and again. I'm your plaything. I can never die, remember? So you can keep on killing me as many times as you want. But here's a word of advice, from one killer to another. It doesn't work. You get less and less every time. You don't fill up—you just get hungrier and hungrier, until nothing satisfies you anymore."

The faceless girl regarded him stoically.

"What?" Mero snapped. "What is it, damn you? I've done everything you asked. Why me—why not Menahem, or Sanja, or Gorgol? Aren't we all beasts of the earth? Equal in our struggle?"

Nothing.

Mero opened his mouth to shout at her, balled his fists to strike. But he was tired—tired of falling and losing his way, and though his cheeks and head burned with rage, his heart knew it would come to no good.

His fists unclenched. His jaw went slack. He collapsed against the wall and wept.

58

He stayed that night in Ruya's sickroom, squatting in the corner, reaching out every so often to take her hand and feel her pulse. It was regular but weak, at times so faint Mero couldn't feel it at all.

The faceless girl stayed by his side. Mero watched her run her fingers through Ruya's hair, his eyes tracing the lines of the dark blue veins that climbed her temples.

"I don't think she has much longer," he said. His own voice in the silence startled him. He pressed his tongue into his lip where his teeth had cut in. "Could you—do what you did earlier? Wake her up, so I can talk to her?"

The faceless girl turned her head in his direction.

"Please," Mero said.

She turned back and stroked Ruya's cheek, once, slowly, the way a mother who did not want to wake her child might. And Ruya's eyes fluttered open, for the last time.

Groaning, Mero rose to his feet and clasped her hand.

"Ruya," he said. Her eyes rolled towards the sound, but no sign of recognition appeared on her face.

Mero whetted his lips, or tried to. Now that she was awake, he couldn't think of anything to say. Seconds slipped by, sand falling through the glass, yet in this critical moment everything seemed like too much and not enough.

What did you say to a dying woman? Words—so many words to choose from.

I'm glad I met you, even though it meant meeting Gorgol.
I hope you see your children again.
I'm sorry I wasn't a better friend to you.
Thank you for everything you taught me.
I'll miss you.

I don't think I know how to love, but if I did, I would have loved you.
Don't go.

He leaned down and kissed Ruya's forehead, then held her in his arms and pressed his cold, dry cheek to hers. Her heart pattered against his ribs. Slowly, one of her arms rose out from under the blanket and slid around his neck.

Ruya's breath caught. It sounded like a hiccough. Her body jerked, and Mero stroked the top of her head. She was still for a few breaths. Then she coughed again, a feeble sound that barely escaped her lips. She tried to breathe in, but it stuck in her throat. She jerked again.

Gently Mero detangled himself from her, laying her hand atop her chest. She spasmed again, her head rolling to one side. Mero folded his hands and watched, the faceless girl at his hip. For half a minute more Ruya was still. Then one final shudder took her, and her last breath slipped between her lips. It had the sound of a long, tired sigh. Her chest flattened, the mound of blankets sinking down.

The pipes gurgled. In the distance someone was laughing.

Reaching under the blankets, Mero took Ruya's other hand and laid it over the first. He wanted to do more, but there was nothing else to do. Her eyes were already closed. She did not look peaceful, only slack, every muscle of her face devoid of tension.

What now? Mero thought. The words echoed in his empty mind. The faceless girl slipped her hand into his and they stood vigil over the corpse together.

59

Mero dumped his bedding in the laundry and returned his pallets to the storage room down the hall. He had tucked Sheathless in the space between his bed and the wall, covering it with blankets so he didn't have to see it glimmer when he entered his room. He hadn't touched the blade in weeks. Now he took it up again, and was shocked to discover how heavy it was. Ever since he had forged it, Sheathless had felt like an essential part of him, an appendage he couldn't live without. Now it merely felt absurd. The blade was oversized and unwieldy, its balance poor, its luster distracting and ostentatious. But he knew he would need it before the end, just as he knew Ruya's death had been a sign this end had come.

The faceless girl watched him from the corner of the room. She jumped when the door slid open, shrieking, but it was only Lia, looking gray and forlorn and more beautiful than ever.

Mero set Sheathless's point down with a *thunk*. "Lia," he said.

Her eyes went from him to the sword to the faceless girl and back. "Uluron?" she said.

He nodded.

60

They made their farewells in the dining hall, it being the single largest space in the city other than the exercise chamber. The crowd was huge, the noise deafening. Junklanders Mero hadn't even named came to see him off, touching his arms and face and wishing him well. A few of them tried to give him food, which he refused as politely as possible.

A few familiar faces appeared. Toko, the creator of Mero's prosthetic, came by to check on his work, making one final adjustment to the straps around Mero's knee. Mero clasped his shoulders and thanked him for his work.

"*Kanwo! KAN-WOOO!*" Baki bounded through the crowd, pushing others aside in his haste. He looked panicked, as though he thought Mero might slip away any second. He drew close, red-faced and panting, and Mero was unsurprised to see tears standing in his eyes. The junklanders thought nothing of loud, conspicuous displays of emotion, and Baki was like a pot always ready to bubble over. He drew Mero into a rough embrace, sobbing noisily.

Una and Boz arrived a short while later. While Una tickled the faceless girl, Mero and Boz faced each other from a few paces away.

It was Mero who broke the silence. "Thank you for punching me."

Boz cocked an eyebrow. Mero thrust a fist at his own face, pitching his chin backwards. "Iya." In this context, 'iya' meant *it is right*.

Boz snorted, but he rapped Mero on the arm and handed him a bundle of black cloth. It was a set of colored lenses, dark gray, and a scavenger's mask, made to be worn over the nose and mouth.

The junklanders prized their masks. They were made of a special material effective against Uron's pollution. Mero had never figured out what the material was, but he had gathered that the junklanders could not make it themselves. Once they were out of masks, they wouldn't be able to send out scavenging parties—and once they could no longer do that, the city was finished. Boz had just given him a piece of his people's future.

"Thank you," Mero said again. "I'll treasure it."

As Mero and Boz talked, Una presented the faceless girl with a gift of her own: a hood of transparent plion that would protect her from Uron's toxic rain. The faceless girl did not seem to like changing her clothes, but she allowed Una to pull the hood over her head and adjust it around her shoulders. Una kissed her on the forehead and she shuffled her feet shyly.

It was time to go. Lia crooked a finger at Mero, who in turn beckoned to the faceless girl. Obediently she came to his side and took his hand. Lia hollered at the crowd to make way, and slowly but surely they pushed through. As they were about to duck into one of the tunnels leading out of the chamber, Mero turned and swept his eyes over the assembled junklanders. Faces familiar and unfamiliar stared back at him. The youths were bright-eyed, the elders bent, blind, and deformed. Wretched and poor, living off the dregs of the civilization that had come before them — but smiling, all smiling, smiling even as they wept.

"I love you," Mero said. "I love you all. I've been all over the world and I don't know if there's a future for humanity anywhere. But if there is it's here."

He turned and followed Lia down the passage.

Part VI

61

Lia led him northwards through the city, past the laundry and mechanical rooms, then down an unfamiliar tunnel. They didn't speak. The tunnel was much like the one through which they had entered the city, small and cramped, all packed earth. Mero didn't know how many entrances and exits the junk city had, only that there were many, each as carefully hidden as the last.

The passage terminated at a small alcove. A heavy metal door was set into the wall. A shadow stirred in the gloom, and with a jolt Mero realized a man sat there, a man dressed in an oily black coat. He was bald and middle-aged and bore no signs of deformity.

He rose and inclined his head to Lia, talking in a soft, dry voice. His hands were gloved. He kept them folded as he spoke, looking over Mero and the faceless girl with a critical eye. Mero was unnerved, but the faceless girl, usually shy of strangers, was not.

The black-coated man now addressed Mero, his voice measured and slow. Of all the words he used, Mero only recognized one: 'Uluron'.

"Yes," Mero said. "Please."

The stranger nodded. Sliding a hand into a pocket of his coat, he produced a black scavenging mask and a pair of colored lenses. They were dark gray, the same as the pair Boz had given Mero. The stranger looked pointedly at Mero and Lia, his meaning clear. They donned their lenses and masks in the mouth of the tunnel, and the stranger pulled on a wide-brimmed hat. He flipped a latch, spun the metal wheel set into the door, then pushed his weight against it. The door opened a crack. Wan sunlight trickled in, and Mero heard the *slup-slup* of waves breaking on the shore. The stranger stood stock-still for a few seconds, listening, then swung the door open halfway and slipped outside, the brim of his hat brushing the threshold. Another handful of seconds passed, then the stranger appeared in the doorway and beckoned them through.

The sight that awaited Mero on the other side of the door filled him with an overwhelming sense of familiarity: it was a scene plucked directly from one of his visions. They stood no more than a hundred paces from the shore of the black lake. The coastline was hard-packed earth, dusty brown, filled with shards of metal, glass, and plion. Beyond it the black lake stretched smooth and faultless all the way to the horizon, punctuated only by the city of Uron. It lay directly ahead, framed between water and sky. Mero had never been closer.

From this vantage it was apparent that the entire city had been constructed on an artificial island, an irregular geometric shape made entirely of poured stone. The city's shoreline—if it could be called that—was a smooth, featureless gray slope. But any invader hoping to enter the city by water would not find it such a simple thing: at the top of the slope was a cement retaining wall, easily fifty feet high. Buildings rose from every inch of land right up to this wall, in places even overspilling it. Uron was a root-bound plant, a city grown too big for its borders.

No lights were on in the city. The air was hazy and full of rain. A northerly wind blew, and Mero smelled chemicals though his mask— though judging from Lia's expression, the nerves in his nose must have been deadening, as well.

The stranger beckoned them onward, picking his way down to the shore. As they emerged from the mountains of garbage stacked on either side of the tunnel entrance, a bridge of poured stone appeared on their right. It was suspended several stories off the ground by a double column of supporting pillars, massive gray trunks marching into the distance, rooted somewhere under the surface of the black lake. The bridge was wide enough for a hundred people to walk abreast and ran in a straight line all the way to Uron.

"What about the bridge?" Mero asked the stranger's back.

The stranger turned, and Mero repeated his question, pointing. The stranger looked at the bridge, looked back at him, then slowly and deliberately shook his head. He said a few words in junklander, then formed a ring with his thumb and second finger and peered through it. It was the same symbol Lia had made when showing him his room. Seeing it repeated by this black-clad figure filled Mero with foreboding.

The bridge is watched.

He posed no further questions of the stranger. They reached the lake soon after, and Mero peered into the water. It was fully opaque, its surface swirling with oil. He picked a chip of rubble from the shoreline and dropped it into the lake. The water shimmered in a rainbow of colors, the chip disappearing under the surface with a soft *plup*.

The stranger hitched up his coat and waded into the water, circling a small island of garbage three feet from the shore. Most of it was a filthy plion tarpaulin colored a dark, lifeless green. The stranger peeled the tarpaulin back, the stiff material crackling sharply. As he rolled the plion in on itself, a dull black shape was revealed, and Mero realized it was a boat.

Mero had never seen a metal boat before. This one was constructed of thinly-hammered plates riveted together in seams that ran half the length of the hull. It was no more than ten feet long and was narrower across than the span of Mero's arms. Its stern was squared-off and two metal benches spanned its width. It was painted black inside and out.

The boatman hauled his vessel halfway onto the shore, the hull groaning as it scraped along the ground. He shared a few words with Lia, then stood by with his arms folded, waiting patiently.

Lia took Mero's hand.

"Frese," she said. Though her expression was unreadable behind her mask, Mero could tell she was near tears.

"It's all right." He squeezed her hand between his own. "I'm not afraid anymore. I just have a little further to go. Then it will all be over."

She pulled him into an embrace, then knelt and held out her arms. The faceless girl came to her, even wrapping her arms around Lia's middle. Then Lia stood and backed away, back towards the entrance to the junk city. Mero waved to her once, then turned and joined the boatman on the shore.

62

The boatman held his vessel steady as Mero and the faceless girl climbed inside. The faceless girl was nervous. Mero couldn't get her to sit on a bench, so she ended up sitting on the bottom, between his legs. Sheathless he laid along the boat's length. Silver against black, it looked like a crack opened in the night sky.

The boatman waited patiently for them to settle, keeping a watchful eye on the coast. As soon as the boat stopped rocking, he dug his boots into the earth and heaved, pushing off and leaping aboard in one smooth motion. His coat flapped open as he leapt, giving him the appearance of an enormous raven. The faceless girl shuddered against Mero's legs.

Taking up his position at the stern, the boatman hefted a long, black paddle and dipped it into the water. There was a slight tugging sensation as the boat began to move.

The trip across the lake was eerie and silent. The boatman rowed with exquisite care, never once knocking his paddle against the boat's hull, dipping it in and out of the water in slow, fluid movements. He stood upright, the brim of his hat never wobbling. It was so quiet the creak of his heavy gloves could be heard.

Mero and the faceless girl sat facing the boatman, which meant Uron was at their backs. The faceless girl had no interest in the city, but every so often Mero twisted around to watch it crawl closer. Dark spires loomed in the haze. They did not seem threatening, merely there. It was as if the city were saying it did not care whether Mero came or went, confident that nothing he could do would make the slightest bit of difference. Mero, of course, was still ignorant of his purpose after all this time. He knew the goddess wanted him here, and figured she would reveal the reason once it was time. Mero wanted to be afraid, had expected himself to be. But the black lake was oddly serene, the gentle pull of the boat calming.

All would be what it would be.

The boatman kept them in the shadow of the great bridge as they approached the city. It soared overhead, gray, dull, and implacable, its vast stone legs stained black where they met the water. It terminated at some kind of gate leading into the city, but Mero could see little more than that. Uron was now close enough to fill the sky, its tallest spires dropping down across Mero's sight like the bars of a cell. The boatman steered them towards the shore underneath the bridge, the ramp of poured stone that climbed out of the lake before rising into a retaining wall.

Suddenly they were there, and the boatman turned his vessel sideways, pulling up to shore. He sculled gently to keep the boat in place, waiting for his charges to disembark. Mero, who had been lulled into a daze by the gentle rocking, surfaced from his reverie and squeezed the faceless girl's shoulders.

"We're here," he said, more to hear his own voice than anything else. It sounded muffled, as though he were wrapped in an invisible cocoon. The boatman acknowledged his statement with the slightest nod of his head.

Mero stood on stiff legs, picking up Sheathless and driving its point into the hard gray stone. He swung his prosthetic over the side, then kicked off with his good leg, landing with a stagger on the sloped surface. The faceless girl gripped the lip of the boat as if reminding Mero not to leave her behind. He lifted her onto the shore with a minimum of effort—as always, she was light as a bird.

"Thank you," Mero said to the boatman.

The boatman touched the brim of his hat. His face was hidden behind his mask, but Mero imagined him smiling with the satisfaction of a job well done. Mero took the faceless girl's hand and they climbed the shore together. The boatman watched them for a moment, then dipped his oar and steered his vessel into the mist.

63

Mero and the faceless girl rested in the shadow of the great bridge. The stone ramp on which they stood wrapped around the city in both directions. The retaining wall, a featureless mass of gray stone, lie directly ahead. Above it rose Uron's spires, watchful and domineering.

Mero looked left and right. Both directions offered the same view: black lake, gray wall, and the sloping ramp in between.

"It doesn't really matter which way we go, does it?" he asked the faceless girl.

She hung her head and didn't answer. Their trip over the lake seemed to have shaken her. She shivered slightly, her plion hood crackling. Mero limped over to her, scooped her into his arms, and set off along the shore.

The faceless girl only grew more listless as they walked. At first she crunched herself tight in Mero's arms as though she had a stomachache. Then her arms began to dangle, her ankles knocking into each other with a faint *click* of bone that struck in the off-beat between Mero's footfalls. He shook her, urging her to stay awake, and she did for a time—but eventually she reverted to her ragdoll-like state, her head swinging dangerously on her skinny neck. Finally Mero knelt, setting her down with her back against the retaining wall and her feet pointed towards the lake. He squatted next to her and searched the empty skin where her face should have been, wondering what to do next.

"What's the matter?" he probed. "Are you tired?"

She shook her head, her chin brushing her chest. She lifted an arm with agonizing lethargy, curling her fingers into a point. She pointed up—up—over and behind her head.

"The city?" Mero said. "Uron's doing this to you?"

The faceless girl nodded.

"That's no good," Mero said to himself. Anger flared as he considered this new development. "You should have told me. Did you know this was going to happen?"

The faceless girl didn't respond. Her head rolled to one side, her hands resting palms-up on the ground. She looked like an old discarded doll. Mero grabbed her shoulder and shook her, wishing he had given her a name.

"Listen to me," he growled. "You can't give up yet. We're almost there. Once I've gotten inside the city and done whatever I came here to do, we can—we can—"

We can what?

He squeezed her hand, touched her shoulders and face, but she wouldn't respond. In a flash of inspiration he took the goddess's whistle from his neck and looped it around the faceless girl's own. She lifted her head slightly when it thudded against her chest. She took the whistle in her hand and examined it.

"Just hold on to that," Mero told her, "and I'll be back for you. All right? Just stay right here and I'll be back before you've had a chance to miss me."

He stuck Sheathless into the ground and used it to stand, the faceless girl watching with the whistle cupped in her palm. She looked more inhuman than ever, her skin pale and lifeless, the veins of her skull standing out. But Mero's fear of her had utterly evaporated, and it nearly broke his heart to leave her behind. She was so small, so vulnerable, in her bare feet and flowery dress, clutching the goddess's talisman to her breast. Mero bent down and touched his forehead to hers, then patted her shoulder and limped away.

"Don't move," he said. "Just stay right there. I'll be back. I promise."

64

He walked for half an hour with the retaining wall on his right and the black lake on his left. The ramp of poured stone comprising Uron's shoreline was about twenty feet wide, the grade steep enough to make walking awkward.

For the initial stretch the shore progressed in a perfectly straight line, and the faceless girl's gaze pressed against Mero's shoulders. Then his path angled sharply to the right, and the line of sight between them was severed. Mero didn't look back before turning the corner. He could imagine the sight of the faceless girl well enough. The faster he finished his business in the city, the faster he could return to her.

Of course, the question of how he would get into the city still remained. Mero kept an eye out for chinks in Uron's defenses, but there was little to see. The retaining wall rose unblemished to his right, featureless, gray, impregnable. But Mero didn't allow himself to despair.

All living things take of their environment, and all living things produce waste. A city is full of living things and thus is bound by the same rules. Uron must have orifices. It must have places where it consumes and excretes.

Those thoughts kept him walking for another hour, as the shoreline cut left and right and left again, always at sharp, sudden angles. The sky turned a dark, rusty orange, and the sun touched its twin living under the lake's surface.

One by one, the lights in the city switched on.

Mero turned a corner and his attention was caught by an ellipse of darkness that consumed a portion of the retaining wall ahead. He quickened his pace, and the ellipse widened until it became a circle. It was the terminus of an enormous pipe, a metal mouth at least eight feet in diameter. Its lip was perfectly flush with the retaining wall, its bottom edge a foot off the ground. A huge black stain spread outward down the shore beneath the pipe, but nothing flowed out of it at present.

Mero gripped Sheathless and approached the pipe cautiously, circling away from the wall so he could peer inside from a safe distance. What he saw astonished him.

The pipe was filled with treasure.

In the slanting light of the setting sun, the pipe's contents were a molten river, blazing red-gold. It was a dragon's hoard of treasures of every kind: cups, plates, coins, panels, chests, and statuettes, not only of gold, but of silver, bronze, precious gems, and other materials Mero did not recognize. There were fine silks and patterned rugs, and strange devices made of metal and glass. It seemed all the treasures of Uron had been flushed down this effluence pipe when the city was abandoned. The hoard filled the lower half of the pipe with only a narrow path down the center. The sun revealed that it extended at least two dozen yards inward.

Mero crept closer, watching the hoard for signs of movement. The sheer number of baubles and the intricacy of their design confounded the eye and the mind alike. Mero was not interested in wealth for wealth's sake, but his scientific curiosity was aroused. There were answers in this trove, no doubt—information to be gleaned about the people of Uron and possibly their demise.

Seeing no sign of the hoard's owner, he stepped into the pipe and crept along the narrow path between the piles of treasure. Gold, silver, metal and glass twinkled at him from every angle. Sheathless glowed as if in response, the curved blade humming contentedly in the sun.

"That's quite the treasure you've got there. I'd be happy to trade you for it."

It was a man's voice and it came from the direction of Mero's armpit. He spun and raised Sheathless, searching frantically for the speaker. At first he saw only edges and facets of glowing gold. Then his gaze fell upon a statue of a man—or perhaps a god—sitting cross-legged on the floor. He was made entirely of gold. His boots were gold, his cuirass was gold, his gauntlets were gold, and he wore a golden crown upon his head. His faces were masks of gold, and he had not one but three. The first, facing forward, was calm and contemplative; the second, facing left, snarled as if in fury; and the third, facing right, wore a pitiful expression that might have been envy or unrequited lust. The idol sat snugly among its providence, blending in with the piles of treasure surrounding it. It was no wonder Mero had failed to spot it.

The idol's face turned up to meet him. The dozens of rings and baubles dangling from its headdress twinkled and clinked.

"What do you say? Leave that trinket with me and I'll let you walk away with another one of my treasures. I've all sorts of priceless things here, wonders you won't see anywhere else in the world."

Mero was still recovering from the shock of seeing the idol move. In the time it took him to lower Sheathless and bring order to his scrambled thoughts, the statue leaned forward and said,

"If you're not interested, I'm sure there's something else you could offer me. Come now, life is short. Make a trade."

Mero found his tongue. "I'm sorry to disappoint you, but Sheathless isn't for sale. And I have nothing else to offer you."

"Oh, we all have something to offer," the idol cooed. He held up a finger as though an idea had just occurred to him. "There's something I'd like to show you. If you're not interested, you're free to walk away. But I think you're going to like this very much."

He presented his hand with a flourish, his fingers opening like the petals of a flower. Balanced on his palm was a ring of black glass. Its surface had a deep luster, as though it had been lacquered over many times. It was pretty enough, but Mero was unmoved.

"A ring?" he said.

"An *artifact*," the idol corrected. He took the ring in three fingers and gestured at Mero, obviously intending to slide it on as though they were being wedded. When Mero gave no indication of offering the stranger his hand, the idol, without missing a beat, slipped the ring onto his own finger and stroked it once. The ring's uniform surface sprang to life, bright blue lights describing a honeycomb pattern against the black backdrop. Mero leaned forwards, amazed, as the idol stroked the ring again and the pattern of lights changed. He squeezed the ring a certain way, and a fan of light shot out the top, resolving into a perfect rectangle like a pane of glass floating in air. Images were projected onto the glass, and they moved as though this were a window into another world, a world the size of Mero's palm. In this world lived people of breathless beauty and grace—men with strong jaws and smoldering eyes and slender women in glittering dresses.

The idol swiped a finger in the air, and the images changed. Now the window looked down on a pristine beach of white sand, flanked on one side by a row of swaying, fruit-laden trees, and on the other by a shimmering ocean of brightest blue. It was a scene of such exquisite beauty that an involuntary moan climbed Mero's throat. He wanted to squeeze through the tiny window and emerge onto the snowy beach, feel the sun on his skin and wash the filth of Uron from his soul. He reached out to touch the image, but the idol had already swiped on to the next.

Now the window showed food—tables groaning under racks of ribs and roast chickens, shellfish doused in butter and lemon and vegetables tossed with spices and herbs. Loaves of freshly-baked bread were cracked open by disembodied hands, steam gushing from their fluffy insides. Mushrooms were speared on narrow forks and dunked into fountains of melted cheese. Fruits were sliced open, their blushing insides presented to Mero as though the curators of the feast were aware of the window's presence. Mero's cheeks prickled, and his stomach growled, but already this illusion was being swept away.

Suddenly the window was filled with monsters.

They looked like men, but they were hairless and red-eyed, their clothing caked in mud and blood. They howled silently at Mero, raking the air with their nails, lurching towards him in a growing stampede. Mero gasped and drew away, but the idol said,

"Look! You can kill them!"

He tapped on the monsters with his finger. With each tap the window flashed white, and the chosen creature exploded in a fountain of blood. Tapping away merrily, the idol blew off heads, blasted open ribcages, and severed arms and legs, reducing the monsters to piles of twitching gore. Still more spilled in from out of sight, and still the idol kept tapping away, killing and killing, until—

"Stop it!" Mero shouted. "What in hell do you think you're doing?"

"It isn't real!" the idol said, delighted. "It's only a game."

Mero was stunned. "It's not real?"

"Of course not!" The idol cried. "Nothing the ring shows you is real."

"Then what's the point of it?"

"The point is to enjoy yourself. Live someone else's life for a while. With this device, you can be anything—go anywhere—with just a few swipes of your hand. Lovely, isn't it?"

"I've already lived more than my share of lives," Mero said flatly. "I don't need any more."

The idol was flummoxed. He stared at Mero while monsters the size of his thumb shambled and raged on the other side of the window.

"No more?" he murmured. "But you can always use more."

Mero had heard enough. "Will this pipe lead me into the city?"

"Oh *no*," said the idol at once. "You don't want to go in there. The city is haunted, you know."

"Then it *does* lead inside?"

"Yes, but it's dangerous—more dangerous than you can possibly imagine. Just thinking about it makes my knees go weak."

"Why?" Mero said.

The idol shook his head, medallions jingling. "There's a monster. A horrible monster. It drove me out, you know—would have killed me if I hadn't escaped. It kills everything it can't enslave, and its eyes are everywhere. Don't go—stay here where it's safe and there are pretty things to look at. I don't mind you keeping my company. Find a place to sit and settle down."

Mero looked around, taking in the dingy, excrement-stained walls of the tunnel and the heaps of treasure which clogged its lower half—treasures like the black ring and its bottomless supply of visions.

"There's nothing pretty in this tunnel," he told the idol. "It's all worthless junk. And I would rather be killed by the monster in Uron than spend the rest of my life here with you."

He swept down the tunnel without another word, leaving the golden man sitting among his glittering piles. If he had bothered to look back, he would have seen the idol bring the black ring to his face, awaken it with a stroke, and swipe feverishly between visions, his shadow pinned to the wall behind him.

65

The tunnel ran straight for at least a mile, growing darker by inches as Mero penetrated deeper into the city. It was an easy walk. The tunnel was tall enough for Mero to stand upright, and the debris accumulated along the bottom formed a hard, earthy floor. The walls were stained with every kind of filth and the air was rank and stifling. Mero knew his senses were dulling by the fact that the smell was merely irritating instead of incapacitating.

What do you call it when something that's already dead starts to die? he wondered.

The tunnel reminded him of the underground labyrinth. He wished the faceless girl could have joined him on this final journey. The first time she had crept up to him in the darkness and taken his hand, he had been terrified. Now he gladly would have given any of the idol's treasures to feel the heat of her palm against his.

The tunnel split, one fork running slightly left and the other slightly right. Of course, in actuality the tunnel was not splitting but converging, two sources of effluence joining together to empty into the lake. Mero saw no difference between the paths. On a whim he took the leftmost one.

It was now entirely dark. Mero crept forward, brushing his fingers along the wall. His uneven footfalls, coupled with the rhythmic *tink, tink* of Sheathless striking the ground, echoed down the tunnel ahead.

How deep under the city am I? Mero wondered.

The tunnel split again, and again Mero took the leftmost path. The bore of the tunnel decreased with this split, and he now had to crouch slightly or let the top of his head brush the ceiling. Deprived of sight, he strained his ears into the dark, but heard nothing but the sounds he himself made.

The tunnel split again, this time into four, two stacked on two. The new tunnels were little more than two feet on the side—large enough to crawl into, but not large enough to turn around in. Mero determined all this by touch, just as he determined that the lower holes were impassable: too much debris had accumulated in the bottom of the pipes.

He stood at the junction for some time, tracing the mouth of the upper left pipe with his hand, gauging its size and considering his options. He had no reason to believe the tunnel would widen further up. Indeed it was likely to split yet again. If he crawled into this tunnel and met a dead end, he would need to crawl backwards the entire way he had come—if he didn't get stuck and perish down here in the suffocating dark.

What were his choices? Turn back and attempt another tunnel only to be faced with the same problem again? Leave this pipe entirely and find another way into the city?

No. The goddess did not intend for him to turn back, not until this was over. If he had done something wrong, she would have found some way to inform him.

Tossing Sheathless into the top-left tunnel, Mero stuck his hands in the narrow pipe and leapt inside. Hinging on his stomach, he pulled himself forward until he could drag his legs up under him. At first he didn't mind the small size of the tunnel—then his back bumped against the ceiling and he realized how truly limited his movement was. All he could do was crawl forward on his hands and knees. He couldn't crouch, let alone stand. A ripple of claustrophobia stirred in his gut. He bit it down and started to crawl.

66

Mero's ears rang. His breath came from behind him, as though he were breathing over his own shoulder. His knees were tender and sore, begging for relief, but none was coming. His nose itched, but his hands were filthy and he didn't want to scratch it. He settled for mashing his face into his shoulder.

He didn't know how long he had been crawling. It couldn't have been more than half an hour, but it felt like ten times that. The tunnel had to end eventually; the question was how. Every time he slid Sheathless forward, he feared the blade would strike against a blockage and his worst fears would be confirmed.

Time melted under the monotony of his movements: right hand and left knee, left hand and right knee. Pain, and pain. A sliver of progress, possibly accompanied by a painful scrape of his back if his focus wavered and he rounded his spine. To rest he stretched out long against the floor of the tunnel, twice rolling on to his back to give his knees and palms a much-needed reprieve. But starting up again after these interludes became harder and harder, and at last Mero didn't trust himself to rest at all. He closed his eyes and let his body take over. Right hand and left knee, left hand and right knee. Pain, and pain. A sliver of progress.

He pushed out his right hand and instead of stone it met air. His eyes snapped open, but it was too late. His stomach swooped horribly as he fell headfirst into the darkness.

Before he even had a chance to cry out, his palm struck something hard and his arm crumpled beneath him. His right shoulder came down and a spear of pain lanced into his chest. Sheathless clattered to the floor.

Mero lay curled on his side like a rabbit in shock, waiting for the pain and confusion to subside. It didn't take long; the fall had been startling but short. Though his right wrist twinged in protest, he was able to push himself to his hands and knees and crawl over to Sheathless. At first his eyes were open to a wall of black, but the second his fingers brushed Sheathless's hilt, there came a sound like grains popping in a kettle, and lights flickered on overhead. They were dim yellow strips just like the ones in the junk city, and they illuminated a hallway of dark green brick. A trench four feet deep ran by Mero's arm, a walkway parallel to his own on the far side.

A red-runged ladder climbed the wall to Mero's left, no more than ten paces away. It disappeared into a round shaft drilled into the ceiling. Mero was tempted to take it, but the hallway split up ahead, and he was curious to see where else these tunnels led. He limped past the ladder, scanning every shadow for signs of movement. There were none.

The hallway split in a cross shape, a dark green tunnel identical to Mero's own intersecting it at a right angle. He pressed himself against the wall and peered around the corner. Empty hallways stretched in both directions. Light or no light, it would be a simple thing to become utterly lost down here. Mero waited at the intersection for half a minute, but heard and saw nothing.

He limped back to the red-runged ladder and peered up the shaft. There was no light at the top, but what would be the purpose of a ladder leading nowhere? He put his hands on the rungs and started to climb.

67

By the time Mero reached the top of the ladder, he was blind again. He reached for the next rung and his knuckles smarted against a hard metal ceiling. He probed the edges of the shaft, looking for a latch or handle, and found none. He hooked an arm through the rungs and hung there in the darkness, considering his next move. He could climb down the ladder and try his luck with another one of the green hallways, but that presented the same problem as the pipes had half an hour before. He didn't have time for second-guessing or retracing his steps. The goddess was at his back, urging him on to the end of his journey.

Besides, these tunnels were clearly intended to be traversed—why else would they be lit? And if this ladder was for leaving the tunnels, why close it in a way that couldn't be opened from underneath?

Armed with that logic, Mero put his shoulder to the metal ceiling and heaved. To his surprise, it moved, and rather easily too—it shifted half a foot from the opening, letting in a crescent-shaped beam of light.

The noise of the metal cover scraping against the ground was cacophonously loud. It vibrated in Mero's skull and echoed far overhead, hinting at a vast, open space. He froze instinctively, straining his ears for an answering sound: if anything occupied the space above the shaft, he had just alerted it to his presence.

He waited a full minute, but deep and total silence had once again descended. Easing his fingers into the space he had created, he pulled the metal cover further back. He moved as slowly as he could manage, but even the slightest shift in the metal plate caused a reverberation that echoed six or seven times before fading. Mero grit his teeth and drew the plate aside until the crescent of light had fully waxed above him, then quickly retreated down the ladder until he was in darkness again. He waited several minutes this time, expecting at any moment to be set upon by the monster promised by the golden idol.

But no monster came, and at last Mero was satisfied that he was alone. He ascended the ladder and peered out. His eyes widened, partly to drink in the dim light and partly out of simple awe.

He was still underground, but this tunnel was nothing like the one he had just left behind. To begin with, it was several hundred times the size, and was made of poured stone instead of brick. The area to Mero's left appeared to be some kind of underground highway, a long, wide tunnel through which swooped several enormous beams of metal. The area to his right was nothing less than a miniature city of glass and poured stone, complete with tiered walls, staircases, and box-like dwellings arranged in stacks ten or twenty units high. There were lights on in some of them, and glowing signs that hovered in the air like the window created by the idol's black ring. Mero recognized the language of Uron from the garbage the junklanders had dealt in, but they could not read the mysterious letters and neither could he.

Mero had long since concluded that the lights of Uron had minds of their own. Some turned themselves on and off at a whim, while others followed a set schedule, no doubt one established hundreds, possibly thousands of years ago. It boggled the mind to behold these lights, lights of every color and design, and know that they had shone upon this empty cavern for dozens of generations of men.

These lights had long outlasted the people for whom they had been made. Were they destined to outlast the stars themselves?

Mero pulled himself out of the shaft, sitting on the stony ground. He pulled off his mask and breathed deeply, testing the quality of the air. It was fusty and dry, but clean. He pulled off his colored lenses, too, massaging his temples and cheeks.

With new eyes he contemplated the underground city. He had no doubt it was abandoned. There were no caches of food, no piles of waste— no sights, sounds, or smells of human life.

The dwellings carved into the walls were stacked all the way to the roof of the cavern, and Mero was confident they continued upward to the surface and possibly beyond. For all he knew, he already stood inside one of Uron's black spires—buildings of that height would require deep foundations.

He headed for the city, no longer using Sheathless as a walking pole but brandishing it in a forward grip. He knew the goddess intended him to use it against something in this city. The question was *what*.

Light washed over Mero's face as he stepped between the first of the stone houses. While some of them had no windows at all, others featured entire walls of glass. These windows shone with lights of yellow, blue, green, pink, and red, offering views into businesses and living spaces in varying states of disarray. The first was some sort of public house or dining hall whose walls were lined with glittering devices of gold and silver. Inside, every piece of furniture was smashed. Broken glass littered the floor, and several of the devices bore dents and gashes or had been ripped free from the walls and thrown to the ground. The next was a tailor's, or so Mero guessed from the brightly-dressed mannequins standing in the window. Their bodies were human, but their heads were those of various animals—a swan, a lion, a deer, a fox. The clothing they wore was garish and scandalously erotic. The deer-headed woman wore a short red dress that struggled to cover the curve of her buttocks, and showed a strip of flesh four fingers wide all the way up her sides. The interior of this store was pristine, as though frozen in time. None of the mannequins had been disturbed, and not a speck of dust had settled on their shoulders.

Mero limped on, resisting the urge to peer into every window. In the past he would have stopped to study every storefront, every scrap of clothing, cataloguing and categorizing the artifacts left behind by Uron's residents, hypothesizing about their technology, their culture, their way of life. But his appetite for science had dulled ever since he had created Sheathless, and besides, part of him knew that whatever he might learn from studying the people of Uron was not worth learning. His time—if he had had any to spare—would have been better spent living among the junklanders and learning how to live as they lived. The junk city, after all, had succeeded where Uron had failed.

He reached the cavern wall, where a massive device like a tube of glass ran from his floor all the way up into the cavern's ceiling. He couldn't tell if it was a pipe, a lift, or something else entirely. He circled it, looking for a way in, and found a pair of panels that appeared to be doors. But the panels had no handles, nor any other obvious way to open them. He tried wedging them open with Sheathless but could not get them to budge.

Defeated, Mero turned from the shaft and searched for another way up. He found it in the form of a vertiginous staircase that switchbacked up the cavern wall. They were not one continuous stair, but a series of flights that landed at every floor of the underground city, forcing travelers to walk past every storefront on their way to the surface. Mero followed the trail with his eyes, dismayed at how much walking it represented.

If only I hadn't lost my foot, he thought, and put his prosthetic on the first stair of many.

The stairs were made of poured stone, like everything else in the underground city, and were caged in railings of metal piping, painted blue. A narrow strip of blue paint marked the lip of each stair, and grooves had been etched into the surface of each to make gripping easier. Still, it was a long, arduous climb, Mero's uneven footfalls echoing hollowly in his ears.

TUNK tunk TUNK tunk TUNK tunk TUNK... then *shff, shff, shff* as he rounded the landing, the stairs turning back the way they had come... then *tunk TUNK tunk TUNK tunk TUNK tunk...*

The first flight terminated at a business Mero couldn't identify — possibly a bakery or confectioner's. Its door was guarded by a bizarre statue of a round, man-sized creature with boggled eyes and a wide, buck-toothed grin. It was dressed in a white-and-red-striped apron and was frozen in the act of pouring syrup on itself. Mero rapped on its body with his knuckles. It was made of plion and, unlike the golden idol, was certainly not alive. Even so, Mero felt its eyes on the back of his head as he turned to find the next stair.

68

ventually the stairs entered a tunnel with white, foggy walls that emitted a gentle glow of light. They had widened considerably throughout Mero's climb and were now as wide as the main thoroughfare of a city, clearly intended to accommodate a heavy traffic of people heading to and from the underground.

The light emitted by the walls was soft but eerie. Sound was muted, and Mero kept seeing vague, shadowy shapes moving behind the plion panes. He checked over his shoulder for signs of movement, but he was utterly alone.

If he had expected the stairs to lead him outside, he was mistaken. Instead they opened onto yet another cavernous indoor space, this one all curving angles and swooping walkways. Directly ahead was a vast empty floor of multicolored marble. It was spotted with shards of glass and grains of clear sand. Mero looked up: an enormous chandelier hung over the atrium like a fallen star, twinkling coquettishly in the dusky light. As he watched, a pendeloque detached itself from the glittering mass, fell for a breathless moment, then shattered against the floor with a loud *POP*, spraying glass in every direction.

Mero crossed the empty chamber, giving the chandelier a wide berth. Several sets of doors lined the far wall. Each door was a single panel of transparent glass, and through them Mero glimpsed a darkened street. Excitement swelled in his breast; it felt like a lifetime since he had seen the sky. But sure enough, these doors had no handles, and would not yield to a push nor to Sheathless being wedged into the jambs. Mero's excitement curdled to frustration. The street outside taunted him as he leaned his weight into Sheathless, trying to pry the doors apart. He was exhausted from his climb and the oppressive silence of Uron was getting on his nerves.

He cursed under his breath and drew Sheathless back through the seam. Reversing his grip, he smashed at the door with Sheathless's pommel. A spiderweb crack appeared on the glass, centered around his fist.

Everything went red.

Mero blinked, dumbfounded. It was as though the world had been drenched in blood. Sheathless was red. His hands were red. The marble swirls on the floor had turned to a river of gore.

An ear-splitting klaxon descended on Mero like a crashing wave. Next to the battle cry of a gigas, it was the loudest sound he had ever heard. There was a sharp rattling noise and metal blinds sliced down over the glass doors, trapping Mero inside the atrium with the bloody light and shrieking siren. It was as though the city itself had realized an intruder was scurrying around inside of it, and had taken measures to capture him.

Mero flew into a panic, running wild with speculation about just what the booming siren was meant to summon. He dashed back across the atrium, heedless of the shards of scattered glass, and climbed the first staircase he found. It terminated in a long hallway lined with identical doors. He slammed his shoulder into the first and it opened. The room beyond was some kind of office filled with strange devices and airy furniture, but there was no way out. Mero left the door ajar and ran on, the shrieking of the klaxon wiping all thought from his head.

He came to a circular intersection, through the middle of which grew a strange glass pipe like the one he had seen in the underground. There were hallways ahead and to his left, and a doorway on his right. He tried the door; it opened onto a stairwell, this one cramped and made of metal, the walls lined with wires and pipes. He took the stairs two at a time, his prosthetic foot wobbling dangerously.

The klaxon was even louder in here. It pounded against Mero's head until he thought he would faint. He climbed a flight, turned, climbed another, turned, climbed a third, turned again. Ten flights later, the stairs were still climbing, and Mero worried that his movements had become predictable. He threw open the next door he found and dove through it.

It was an intersection identical to the one he had left behind: paths leading off in three directions, a glass trunk growing in the middle. For a second Mero froze entirely, wondering if he was going insane. Then he darted down the corridor to his right, sprinting as fast as his prosthetic would let him.

Another large room, drenched in red, the klaxon vibrating off the metal shutters covering the windows. The room was round and high-ceilinged, its floor dominated by a large, circular depression. Mero swept the room with his eyes and found nowhere to hide. Even if he had, he wouldn't have stopped. He did not feel safe anywhere in this building. The alarm came from every direction at once, malice seeping from the very walls. He leapt down the stairs leading to the sunken section of the floor, climbed those on the far side, and passed through another door.

Without the sky or any landmarks to go by, he couldn't tell which direction he was headed. Every room he entered looked the same: red walls, red floor, red furniture, windows shuttered tight.

Finally he opened a door onto an airy room filled with crisp, clinical furniture. In the corner twined a spiral staircase, terminating at a bright red door. Mero mounted the stair and tried the door. Instead of a latch, it had a thick metal bar running horizontally across its width. Mero thrust his weight against the bar and it yielded with a mechanical *chunk*.

A blast of cold air met him as he fell through the threshold. The wind was up, and it carried a greasy, chemical smell. Mero was outside. He rose to his feet and glanced around.

He stood atop one of Uron's black spires, dizzyingly high up—he hadn't realized just how high he had climbed. Even so, yellow lights shone down from every direction. It was a dark, cloudy night, and the shapes of the spires melted against the sky, leaving only those winking lights bearing down on him like the eyes of gods. Mero was awestruck by the size of the city. Climbing one of Uron's shorter spires gave him a new appreciation for the incredible height of its tallest.

The red door swung shut behind him, muffling the sound of the klaxon. In a daze Mero stepped to the waist-high wall lining the roof's perimeter. He peered over the edge and was met with a stomach-swooping view that ran down the face of the building all the way to the street below. Lights filled the world from bottom to top, liquid in the misty air. Walkways of metal and glass spidered between the dark spires, turning the entire city into a single integrated megastructure. It was a breathtaking display of wealth and power that must have taken thousands of men generations to build.

And now all of it was empty.

Mero took a moment to catch his breath. The air was cool and full of moisture, but it left a greasy taste on his tongue, and his throat burned after only a few breaths. His skin itched, and his eyes stung. He fumbled for his lenses and mask and pulled them on.

Resting his left hand on the parapet, he walked the perimeter of the tower's roof, getting a sense of Uron's layout. It was easiest to use the towers themselves as landmarks, for while many of them were indistinguishable columns of stone and glass, others stood out by virtue of their design. One had the shape of an enormous letter X and was trimmed with bright violet lights that hurt to look at. Another twisted like a wrung-out cloth, each successive floor tilted ten degrees off from the last. One looked like a sorcerer's tower from a children's fairy tale: its roof was decorated with four enormous claws that reached skyward, and it was lit with a deep red light like the fires of hell.

Halfway along his tour around the roof, Mero's steps faltered, the hand skimming the parapet coming to rest. His eye had fallen on a tower two or three miles deeper into the city, where the black spires grew even taller and closer together. It was a giant among giants, a column fit to support the weight of the firmament. It was dressed in thousands upon thousands of dazzling yellow lights, describing a shape like a spraying fountain. Its summit was lost, beheaded by the pall of cloud hanging over the city.

As Mero beheld the tower, an invisible hand hooked a finger into his ribs and yanked. The sensation was so strong that he instinctively braced himself against the parapet to keep from tumbling over the edge. In that instant Mero knew that he and the gaudy tower were connected by fate—that this tower, *not* the city of Uron, had been his destination the entire time.

A sound interrupted Mero's stream of thought: a low, rhythmic whirring, as of air being displaced.

WHUP-WHUP-WHUP-WHUP—

Mero realized he had been hearing the sound long before he noticed it. It had been growing steadily since he spotted the fountain tower. It was a familiar sound—where had he heard it before? An image of Lia flashed in his mind's eye. She made a ring with her second finger and thumb and held it up to her eye like a telescope. They were hiding under her cloak together, hiding from—

The silver birds.

The instant the realization struck, the whirring rose to a crescendo, and one of the silver birds appeared before Mero, sliding upwards into his line of sight. Buzzing loudly, it hovered in the air beyond the parapet, just out of arm's reach. From this distance it did not look like a bird at all, but a glass eyeball the size of a man's fist, kept aloft by a whirring halo of motion—wings beating so quickly they couldn't be seen.

The eye inside the glass casing was a lurid, glimmering purple like the heart of an amethyst, its pupil a squiggle of pink esophagus.

Mero's limbs seized up. He could neither move nor blink. A roaring sound filled his stomach. The eye pointed directly at him, pinning him in place.

The bird made a strange chirruping sound. Lights flickered down its sides, blue and green.

Mero swung Sheathless in a savage horizontal cut. His blow connected with the floating eyeball, and a jolt traveled up his arm. There was a *POP*, a *SNAP*, a spark, and the silver bird tumbled from the sky, trailing smoke, its buzzing frantic and high-pitched.

WHUUMwhummwhUMMwhummmMMM—

The sound faded. The quiet of the city crept in. But Mero's mind was a cacophony, thoughts trying desperately to arrange themselves while a growing sense of panic scattered them like birds. In the end only one thought made it through, a thought that reverberated in his mind with the steadiness of a heartbeat.

He saw. He saw.

He knows.

The sand was falling.

Mero turned from the parapet and ran for the door.

69

orgol the giant had not returned to Palta since trying and failing to harvest Mero's *dama* on the beach. He had a hundred excuses. He told himself he was merely stretching his legs for a few days before returning to his responsibilities; that he was reacquainting himself with the eastern countryside, which he had not visited in years; that his travels had given him a taste for the open road and that he owed it to himself to indulge it.

His initial disappointment upon discovering that Mero had no *dama*—at least, none that Gorgol could find—had been acute. He certainly thought it unfair that he should go unrewarded for such an excellent performance. The thrill of the hunt—*that* had been missing from his visits to the village in the grasslands. Stringing the brash young traveler along had been tremendous fun, and to have it all spoiled at the eleventh hour left a sour taste in Gorgol's mouth. He wandered listlessly across the wastelands, unable to shake the irritating sensation of business left undone.

"Oh, well," he told himself, several times a day. "Such is life. We can't all be winners all the time, can we? Besides, you got that good-for-nothing in the end. He learned his lesson, oh yes."

As time wore on, however, he discovered to his supreme vexation that this sense of incompleteness was growing rather than shrinking. It was like a piece of gristle caught in his teeth, and no matter how much he tried to ignore it, it loomed larger and larger in his mind until there was room for little else. No matter that he had successfully harvested thousands of *dama* in his time—all he could think of was the last, that which he had lost. He grumbled and ground his teeth as he walked, lashing out at anything that caught his eye: plants, animals, even odd formations of rock. He uprooted trees, swatted birds out of the sky, and stomped on animal dens until their denizens were crushed under the earth. Whenever he found a larger animal—a grazer or a wild dog—he would catch it, break its legs, and stick his nails up its anus, pretending it was Mero and searching for the *dama* he knew he wouldn't find.

"Aha!" he would say, though there was nothing between his nails. "*There* it is! You thought you could keep it safe, little Mero, but you can't outsmart old Gorgol!"

Eventually he would tire of this game and crush the animal in his fist, its ribs cracking one after the other, its guts spilling between his fingers in steaming coils. And Gorgol would smile in deepest satisfaction, though the piece of gristle remained.

His stomach started to ache, cramping while he walked and gurgling most unpleasantly every time he lay down to rest. It didn't matter what he ate or didn't eat; the vipers nesting in his gut wouldn't go away. His mood deteriorated further, and he began to rage aimlessly up and down the countryside, snuffing out life and beauty wherever he found it.

"*Mero*," he snarled through his teeth, clutching his gut as he tried to sleep. "*Mero! What have you done to me?*"

Gorgol's hair grew tangled and wild. His body was covered in bruises and scrapes from the times he had inadvertently injured himself while doing violence to the world around him. He tore up the earth and bellowed at the sky. He smashed, punched, kicked and scratched everything he saw, turning his rage on himself when no other target was presented to him. All the while a single face haunted his dreams, and a single name climbed his throat like acid.

"*MERO!*"

Then a pair of lights flickered in the corner of his eye, blue and green. Gorgol froze.

Slowly he turned his face to the east.

His mouth opened wide—wider—forming a perfect dish. His head was split nearly in two, his eyes pressed back, blank and unseeing. The back of his throat vibrated like a frog's.

Minutes passed. Gorgol no longer seemed angry or even alive. He might have been mistaken for a tree, the ends of his hair swaying in the breeze.

Gorgol's mouth hinged shut. His eyes, which had gone dull and dark, regained their inner glow. For a moment he stood silently, chewing his lip.

It can't be.

Mero was dead. Gorgol had watched it happen, had felt the final shudder of his heart through his nails.

So why was he alive and well in Uron, swatting one of Gorgol's eyes out of the air?

Volcanic rage swelled in his breast. Rage, and another emotion that was as alien to him as frustration had been a month ago: fear.

Fear for his secret.

Fear for his life.

MERO!

Gorgol clenched his fists and loosed an inarticulate roar. He dug his feet into the earth, then kicked off, his mighty legs working like pistons, arms pumping at his sides.

With murder in his heart and Mero's face fixed in his mind's eye, Gorgol made for Uron.

70

The alarm still blared inside the building, but Mero was no longer frightened of it. The worst had already come to pass: he had been spotted by one of the floating eyes. He didn't think it mattered that he had killed it. The damage had already been done. All he could do now was make for the fountain tower as quickly as possible.

While standing on the roof, Mero had spotted several glass walkways leading from his own building to those adjacent. The closest of these was about ten floors down and ran from south to north, meaning it would bring him one step closer to his destination. He located the service stairway and galloped down it, counting doors as he went. The eighth door he flung open and stepped through, turning right as soon as he did to search for the walkway. Failing to find it, he returned to the staircase and tried the next floor down. He repeated this process two more times, at which point he noticed a new hallway leading off from what had previously been a dead-end room. This hallway was blocked, too, though only by a metal fence rather than the heavy shutters that sealed off the windows. Mero hacked at the fence with Sheathless until he had opened up a gash wide enough to squeeze through. It was hard work—the metal of Uron was incredibly strong and doubtless would have thwarted any other weapon. Mero, in his haste to push through the opening, caught his prosthetic on one of the broken bars and fell face-first on the glossy floor, slicing his ankle open as he did. Cursing, he untangled his boot from the fence and rose, his limp more pronounced than ever.

The walkway ran unimpeded into the gut of the next building over, this one blessedly silent. Few lights were on, and its interior was a maze of shape and shadow. Mero set off with strong intent, but soon lost himself among the endless hallways and stairwells and antechambers. Pushing into a side room, he found a window and peered through it, careful not to touch the spotless glass. He couldn't see the fountain tower, only the violet glow of the X-shaped building. Closing his eyes and recalling the layout of the city, he realized he was facing south instead of north or east. Leaving the room, he turned right, then left again once he could go no farther.

Eventually he found himself in some sort of huge indoor market-place. Over twenty levels of interconnected pathways looked down on a tall, narrow fissure at least a quarter of a mile long. Hundreds of shops lined the walls just as they had in the underground city, each preserved behind its own pane of glass.

As Mero passed the first of the shops—a sleek, minimalist storefront picked out in white and sterile blue—there was a loud *CLACK*, and the lights inside flared to life. Tinny music played from within, sounding as though it was being piped in from some distant location. Mero's curiosity was aroused, not because he wondered if a band of musicians was held captive inside the store, but because he knew there wasn't. This was merely another illusion of life wrought by the city, a reproduction of a piece that had been played centuries before, or possibly never by living hands. Mero wondered how the trick worked. The scholar had been fond of claiming that anything that could be produced could be reproduced, but had never managed to create a device that could replicate the sounds it heard.

But there was no time to stand here and listen to music. Driven by the hiss of sand through the glass, Mero turned to leave—then stopped short, frozen in surprise.

A woman stood before him. She wore a short blue skirt, a matching jacket, and a sunny, welcoming smile. Her hair was pinned back, her shoes polished to a mirror sheen. Seeing Mero's eyes on her, she folded her hands and bowed demurely.

"Who are you?" Mero croaked, both hands on Sheathless.

Beaming, the woman spoke. Her voice was strong, her enunciation flawless, but her words meant nothing to Mero. Inclining her head, she gestured towards the white-and-blue store. The music swelled as if in response.

Mero eyed the woman warily. Something about her reminded him of the images he had glimpsed through the idol's window.

"You want me to go inside?" he asked.

The woman spoke again, contriving at all times to keep the smile plastered on her face. Mero stepped to one side and her eyes followed him, yet she seemed to be looking through him rather than at him.

Mero put a hand through her face.

His arm disappeared into the woman up to the elbow. He met no resistance but a faint sensation of warmth. The woman flickered, blue fire riding the contour of Mero's bicep. Then, in a wink of light, she disappeared, only to reappear a few feet away wearing the same smile as before.

Bile rose in Mero's throat.

"You're not real," he said to the woman. "You're just another lie."

She bowed and gestured him into the store. Mero didn't bother responding. He stepped through her and carried on his way.

71

The marketplace was far from finished with Mero. Each storefront had its own strategy for beckoning customers. Some lit up; others played music; others still wafted delicious smells into the aisle. Once the very floor beneath Mero's feet began to move, funneling him towards a door that slid open of its own accord. Legions of phantoms flickered into existence, clamoring for his attention. Some were still images, pointing arrows or dancing text. Others were far more bizarre. There were strange beasts and bumbling caricatures that laughed and sang. Once an entire forest glade grew up around Mero's feet, giggling fairies circling his head while invisible birds tweeted and chirped.

Most of the illusions were of beautiful women dressed in provocative, outlandish costumes. Some, like the first, wore a veneer of modesty. Others pouted, crooked their fingers, squeezed their breasts together, and blew kisses that floated through the air and popped against Mero's cheek like soap bubbles. He brushed them aside, shutting out the din of their wheedling voices.

Eventually he found a balcony that offered him a view of his progress. The fountain tower was closer than before, but he still had a few miles to go.

As well as approaching the fountain tower, he had also come closer to the ground. This gave him more options for moving between the buildings: at ground level, most of them ran together in a single, uninterrupted maze. There did not seem to be such a thing as an outdoor street in Uron. If one had ever existed, it had been roofed over and built upon as the struggle for space became more and more desperate. It meant Mero could travel through the city without breathing its burning air—the buildings had some way of keeping the pollution out—but it also meant the threat of getting lost was constant. Mero oriented himself using windows and balconies as often as possible, but found no straight path to the fountain tower.

Despite the urgency of his situation, the repetitiveness of Uron wore on Mero's spirit. As he limped down the endless halls and arcades, he worried that he was running in circles, or even that the city was shifting around behind his back so as to keep him lost forever. His paranoia was not completely unfounded, for Uron did seem to have a will of its own, as though the souls of those who had perished here had seeped into the very walls and were struggling to make themselves known. Mero climbed a flight of stairs, only for the steps to start flowing downwards beneath his feet. He bounded up the stairs two at a time like a fish climbing a waterfall, but the effort left him exhausted. Doors opened and shut of their own accord; lights flickered on and off; illusions chased him from room to room.

One of the most frightening incidents occurred when Mero was crossing what had once been an outdoor street. The road was brick instead of poured stone, and the storefronts facing onto it sported awnings and decorative façades. One such storefront caught Mero's eye. It was lit from inside with warm yellow light, and shadows passed back and forth in front of the window as though the store was packed with people. Upon seeing this, Mero shrank into a corner and watched the shadows for fully a minute before deciding this was merely another lie. He crossed the street, threw open the door, and discovered that he was right. The store was barren but for a few sticks of furniture scattered about. The shadows were just that, projections of no depth or substance that lived inside the glass. Mero considered smashing the window, then thought better of it.

His arms and legs were getting heavy, as though they were slowly turning to stone. Still the sight of the silver eye haunted him.

I'm running out of time, he thought.

Out of time, the goddess answered.

72

Mero emerged onto a rooftop promenade and was greeted with a view of the fountain tower, directly ahead and closer than ever. He was awestruck by the size of it. It was simply the biggest thing he had seen in his life, a palace fit to house tens of thousands of people. He wondered who had owned it, who had commissioned it to be built. Sanja Al-Sat could only dream of such wealth.

A road led out of the fountain tower like a long black tongue, the first straight road Mero had seen since entering the city. It was several floors below him, but if he were to find a way down to it, he could follow it all the way to his destination.

He searched the rooftop and found no easy way down, nor any doors other than that from which he had emerged; but the next building over featured an outdoor balcony a couple floors down from his own. The two buildings were squeezed tightly together, no more than ten feet of space between them. Mero bobbed his head up and down and side to side, gauging the distance. Leaping onto the balcony would have been easy had he possessed both of his feet. As it was, the prospect made his testicles shiver.

Mero considered his options. He could turn back and look for another way down—one that might not exist—or he could risk his entire mission on this jump. Looking at it that way, the choice was obvious. Yet even as he thought this, he found himself clambering onto the ledge facing the balcony, fixing his eyes on a platform no larger than his bedroom in the junk city had been. Sheathless rattled against the stone railing as he climbed up. Balancing on the parapet, he made a few practice swings, then tossed the blade onto the balcony. It sang through the air and landed with a clatter.

Now I have no choice, Mero thought.

No choice, said the goddess.

His right leg would need to do all of the work; involving his prosthetic would only make him lose his balance. He squatted down and gripped the railing on either side, coiling his body like a spring. He would kick off with all his might and stretch his arms through the air. With luck, it would be enough. He visualized the jump in his mind, adjusting his stance so the edge of the railing rested under the ball of his foot.

NOW!

He leapt. It was heavy and sluggish. Horror crawled over him as he realized he didn't have the distance. The balcony rushed towards him, but it was still too far away.

Wind roared in his ears. He wasn't going to make it. He was—

His shins struck the balcony's metal railing, and his legs exploded in agony. His palms slapped down on the ground, followed by his chin. His teeth snapped shut on his tongue and his awareness shattered into a million aching stars. He curled into a ball, squeezing a pitiful moan from his chest. And yet through all the pain roared a fiery tide of triumph. He had made it after all.

73

He limped the length of the balcony until the worst of the pain had subsided. His shins throbbed with every step; it was possible he had fractured one or both of them. His palms were scraped raw and he had sheared off the tip of his tongue, but his leap had brought him closer to the fountain tower than he had dared hope. After smashing the glass door leading inside from the balcony, Mero located a flight of stairs that took him all the way down to street level. He pushed open a heavy steel door to find himself outside once again, on a flat, featureless road running west to east. There were no phantom women or flashing signs out here, only gray, rain-stained buildings sneering down at him. Mero donned his lenses and mask, then turned right down the road. If he kept moving east, he was bound to cross the road to the fountain tower.

Mero's boots scraped against the ground as he walked. He could no longer be bothered to lift his feet any more than was absolutely necessary. The atmosphere of this city weighed on him like a shroud. He had expected Uron to resist his infiltration, to present him with obstacles, danger, monsters like that which the golden idol had promised. This bleak emptiness was somehow worse. It was as though some power more subtle and complete than any earthly terrors had chased all lesser evils from Uron's streets. Mero felt small and insignificant, a mite squeezed between the pages of history. The people of Uron had perished. The city alone endured, a vessel unaware of its own emptiness, a song sung to an abandoned amphitheater.

It's no wonder we've stopped moving forward. The past is too heavy. We can't throw it off.

As this strange thought fluttered through his mind, he slipped between two buildings and emerged onto a wide, empty road running south to north, sloping gently upwards as it did. At the end of the road was the fountain tower, glittering like the gates of heaven.

Mero swayed on his feet as he contemplated the tower. It was ridiculous, really. Humans were not giants. They had no reason to build so high. His awe drained away as the absurdity of it all sank in. Was he supposed to be impressed? Even Menahem's obsession with death had been more worthy of praise.

Dragging his feet, he set off towards the tower.

74

arricades had been erected across the road, turning the arrow-straight highway into a zigzagging maze of barriers. The barricades were made of poured stone reinforced with steel, topped with loops of razor-sharp wire to prevent the industrious invader from climbing over. It seemed the fountain tower had served its owner not only as a castle, but as a keep. The barricades bore slashes, burns, and pockmarks. Some had been torn down and hacked to rubble. Mero slipped between them, using Sheathless to cut a path through the wire when no other option presented itself. That earned him several nicks on the arms and cheeks, but he didn't feel them, and they did not bleed.

His world narrowed. Already it was difficult to look at anything but the fountain tower. All around him Uron melted like a sandcastle swallowed by the tide, the lines between the spires and the pall of cloud overhead blurring into insignificance. Mero wondered dimly if the whole city was an illusion, one that would flicker and disappear the moment its purpose was served.

Light glinted atop one of the barricades ahead. Mero froze, holding himself still as only a dead person could. It was a silver bird like the one that had spotted him earlier, its amethyst eye pointed down the road. It was as still as Mero himself. He couldn't tell whether or not it had spotted him.

Moving one muscle at a time, he squatted and grabbed a piece of rubble from the road. The silver bird twitched, making a faint whirring noise.

Mero rose to his feet, adjusting his grip on the chunk of rock. His shins no longer hurt, and his legs were steady. He judged the distance between himself and the bird, then lunged forward with his prosthetic, sending energy up through his hips and into his arm, and hurled the rubble as hard as he could.

The bird's wings hummed to life, but the missile was already on its way. It struck with a *CLANG*, and the bird tumbled to the ground. Mero sprinted after it, rounding the barricade on which it had sat. The sight that awaited him was a pitiful one. The bird spun in circles as it tried to fly, sparks flying from its damaged body. Its wings were not really wings at all, but a circular fan like the blades of a windmill.

Mero cut down with Sheathless, severing the spinning blade from the bird's body. It continued to squawk and spark, its lurid eye rolling in its casing. Mero struck again, and the eye exploded in a shower of glass. But the instant before Sheathless came down, it had looked directly at Mero, and in it he had seen a bottomless well of malice.

His body shook uncontrollably. He limped towards the fountain tower, as quickly as his injured legs could manage.

75

marble staircase the width of a thoroughfare climbed to the fountain tower's door. It must have been at least a hundred stairs. Mero contemplated this final barrier, then heaved a sigh and started to climb.

It was like wading through sand. He leaned heavily on Sheathless as he climbed, his breath coming in big, heaving gasps. He hoped and prayed that his intuition was correct, and that the fountain tower was indeed the end. If not, his mission was doomed to fail.

Mero was a quarter of the way up the stair when he realized someone else was climbing beside him. He wore a robe of rough, homespun wool and the top of his head was shiny and bald. His beard was long and white and his hands were covered in liver spots, but his eyes twinkled with youth.

"We never finished our conversation," the scholar said.

"You'll have to remind me what we were talking about," Mero responded. "It's been quite a while."

"That it has." The scholar cleared his throat. "I was telling you about the most frightening monster man has ever conceived."

Mero nodded. "I remember."

"Do you remember what he was called?"

A name bubbled up from the depths of Mero's memory.

"Dracula," he said. "But that name doesn't mean anything to me."

"I wouldn't expect it to. He comes from an age of man many cycles past. It's a testament to his influence that any record of him exists at all."

"What makes him so frightening, then?"

The scholar grinned and held up four knobby fingers. "I'm delighted you asked. There are four reasons."

Before he could say any more, however, the wind changed, and the vision of the scholar faded, his white robe blown to tatters. With the wind came a foul smell, a stink of putrefaction strong enough to penetrate Mero's mask and activate his dulled receptors.

Mero froze. Slowly he looked over his shoulder, down the stairs and past the barricades, to the place where the black road was swallowed by the gloom of Uron.

His spine turned to ice.

"What are you doing in my city, little Mero?" said Gorgol the giant. "I don't recall sending you an invitation. Don't you know it's impolite to wander where you don't belong?"

His mane was wild, his belly distended, his grin a white gash. And his eyes—how they glowed.

"I believe you have something of mine," Gorgol said.

Mero ran. He turned and scrambled up the stairs, employing his hands when his legs started to wobble. A roar drummed against his back, the earth shaking as Gorgol gave chase. Mero took the stairs two, three at a time, but the door of the fountain tower seemed to be getting no closer. He was trapped in a nightmare, climbing through air as thick as molasses. The CRUNCH of Gorgol's footsteps grew louder every second, the earth quaking to such a degree that Mero thought he would lose his footing and tumble into the giant's arms.

The wind howled. Mero felt Gorgol's breath on his neck. He stuck Sheathless in the ground and vaulted up the stairs, fighting gravity, fighting the resistance of the air, fighting the treachery of his own body.

Suddenly he was at the top of the stair, facing the great doors of the fountain tower. They were sheathed in metal, fifteen feet high and half a foot thick. These, too, bore signs of attack, but the story told by the myriad of scratches and scorch marks was one of failure. The doors had stood firm against the assault, just as they now stood against Mero.

He swept his eyes over the tower's façade in desperate search of a weakness. A dark panel set into the wall at waist height caught his eye. It was about a foot on the side and had a glossy depth to it that reminded Mero of the idol's ring. He put his palm on the panel and pushed. There was a buzzing sound, and a red light flickered from within. Mero stared at the panel, then reversed his grip on Sheathless, braced its pommel with his off-hand, and drove it into the glass with a surge of his shoulders.

The black glass shattered with a popping sound, darkling shards spilling over Mero's fingers. Metal grated against metal as Sheathless sank into the wall, the panel shrieking as though in rage. A jolt of electricity snarled up Mero's arms, sinking into his muscles and making them spasm and twitch. His teeth slammed together and the cords of his neck turned to iron, but he pushed Sheathless deeper and deeper, sawing the blade up and down. The panel spat sparks at him and shone red lights in his eyes, but Mero wasn't paying attention: he was looking at the tower doors. As he dug Sheathless into the panel's guts, the metal barricade started to sink into the ground.

"WHAT DO YOU THINK YOU'RE DOING?" Gorgol roared.

Mero glanced back. The giant had reached the cluster of barricades and was plowing through them with terrifying ease, casting the stone barriers aside with great sweeps of his arms.

The doors were half open. Mero's arms were numb with shock and sparks burrowed into his cheeks. He pressed his entire weight into the panel, watching the doors grind open with agonizing slowness.

"The first reason," said the scholar, "is that he disguises himself as a man."

He stood to the left of the panel, his hands folded, the hems of his robe stained with earth. Mero didn't answer. He was struggling to breathe.

"Most monsters are easily recognized as such," the scholar went on, unconcerned with Mero's lack of response. "They have scales, fangs, hideous faces. They announce their presence with rancid smells or bowel-shaking roars, and how fortunate for those they terrorize! Because if a monster can be recognized, it can be fought, even if the battle will be hard-won.

"Dracula extends his prey no such courtesy. When he steps out, he wears a man's skin. He walks and dresses like a man. He is mannered and urbane. If you met him on the street, you would never guess he was a fiend in disguise. To combat him, you must be able to see him for what he is. And for many of his victims, that realization comes far too late."

There was a moment of breathless silence, then an earth-shaking *CRASH.* Gorgol had jumped the last of the barriers, and was crouched at the bottom of the stairs like an enormous toad. He started to climb, leading with his hideous grin, his nails digging into the marble.

"MERRROOOO!" he bellowed.

The metal barrier was down, revealing flimsy inner doors of glass and golden filigree. Mero yanked Sheathless free of the panel and it vomited sparks and wiring onto the ground. He wobbled like an anemic, and red, root-shaped scars crawled up his forearms.

The inner doors were locked, but Mero smashed the glass with Sheathless and staggered over the threshold. The atrium of the fountain tower was everything he had expected it to be, a cavernous hall of impossible ostentation. The floor was marble polished smooth as glass. Columns the size of ancient trees buttressed a ceiling as distant as the sky, from which hung a chandelier that looked as though someone had melted down the crowns of every earthly king that had ever lived and cast them into a single piece. In the center of the floor stood a golden fountain decorated with hundreds of sculptures of creatures of every kind: dogs, cats, birds, deer, fish, whales, beetles and mice. At its top stood an idealized man, his genitals modestly covered with a single leaf. One of his legs was extended, one hand upraised. He seemed to have been captured in the act of plucking an apple from a tree.

There was a staircase at the far end of the chamber. Mero limped towards it, but suddenly the glass behind him exploded inwards and a huge, hairy arm lunged into the room. Fingers as hot and hard as red iron curled around his waist and lifted him from his feet. He heard his ribs crack.

"GOT YOU!" Gorgol cried.

Mero raised Sheathless and plunged it into Gorgol's finger. The blade sank in to the hilt. Gorgol howled in pain, his palm springing open. Mero fell to the ground, pulling Sheathless loose with a wet, sucking sound. He dashed for the stairs, sparing a single glance behind. Gorgol was on his hands and knees, trying to shoulder his way through the doors. His arm flailed, spraying the atrium with blood. His bottom lip dragged on the ground.

"VILLAIN!" he roared. *"BASTARD! SCOUNDREL! I'LL PAY YOU BACK FOR THAT, OH YES! I'LL PLUCK YOUR GUTS OUT ONE BY ONE! OH, JUST YOU WAIT! JUST YOU WAIT UNTIL I GET MY HANDS ON YOU!"*

76

Mero rounded the fountain, headed for the back of the room. As he did, he noticed that the golden man was not holding an apple after all, but a globe—a miniature model of the planet. The statue's grip on the planet was firm, as though he was about to crush it in his fist.

The stairs beyond the fountain were carpeted in red. Mero wobbled up them, his vision swimming. Halfway up the stairs split left and right, and he chose the rightmost path simply because he was already leaning on the banister. At the top of the stair stretched a long hallway trimmed in gold. Its left wall was inset with a number of gold-and-glass tubes interspersed with glossy black panels. Mero had learned enough of Uron to guess that these were lifts, and though he hadn't yet been able to operate one, now he simply walked up and impaled one of the panels with Sheathless. Sure enough, the doors of the tube nearest to him slid open even as the panel whined and belched sparks.

This time, when Mero pulled his sword free of the wall, he noticed that he could not uncurl the fingers of his right hand. It smelled of charred flesh; the skin of his fingers and palm had melted and fused with Sheathless's hilts.

Once Mero would have been horrified to discover this. Now he merely reckoned this was long overdue. He stepped onto the lift and the doors slid shut behind him, muffling the sound of Gorgol's raving.

77

On the lift's inner wall was a panel covered with dozens of yellow buttons, each marked with a different glyph. Though he could not read the language of Uron, Mero recognized the glyphs as numbers counting up.

He pressed the button in the top-right corner of the panel and the lift immediately started to move. It accelerated at an incredible rate, the floor pushing against Mero's feet, the skin of his cheeks dragged down. Even so, it was utterly silent inside the small glass box. The floor was carpeted and the movement of the lift was smooth. Mero allowed himself a moment to collapse against the wall and recover his strength.

"The second reason," said the scholar, "is that he feeds on the blood of men to survive. He does not sow, he does not make. He doesn't even have the decency to defecate. In short, he puts nothing into the world, only takes parts of it out. And this he does with such subtlety that his victims often do not even realize they have been taken advantage of. They blame their failing health on the stresses of work, a sudden illness, a change in the weather—never realizing that their misfortune is not a natural consequence of life but a deliberate act of malice. So they carry on their daily lives while the parasite grows fat on their essence."

The lift slowed and stopped, and the doors opened to reveal the hallway beyond. The scholar melted into nothingness, and Mero lurched into the corridor. He doubted he was even halfway up the tower. He would need to find another lift to take him further up.

He stalked through the darkened rooms, his sense of urgency mounting with every step. His nerves and muscles were fraying, dead tissues coming apart under the stress of his flight from Gorgol. He couldn't tell how much longer he would be able to pilot the marionette of his dead body, only hope it would be long enough.

He found another lift and stabbed the panel next to it, electricity crackling up his arm and smoke issuing from his clothes. Each time he attempted this trick he worried that it would no longer work, yet the lift doors opened obediently. He staggered inside, collapsing against the wall. He thumbed the topmost button with his left hand — his right was now little more than a blob of flesh with Sheathless at the center — and again the lift slid upwards.

78

Mero sank to the ground, cradling his wounded arm. It was charred and smoking, curling against his chest. His right hand was irreversibly fused with Sheathless's hilt, the blade growing out of his forearm like an exposed bone. His breath came in hitching gasps. His eyes closed and he couldn't muster the strength to open them again. The last thing he saw was the scholar hunkering down next to him, the thongs of his sandals creaking.

"The third reason," he said softly, "is that he turns ordinary men into copies of himself. You see, whomever Dracula bites is destined to become a monster just like him, a bloodsucker that preys on the very people it once wished to protect. And thus, from a single individual, the curse spreads from hearth to hearth and hamlet to hamlet, until the whole world is infected. The reign of Dracula is a plague deadlier and more virulent than any earthly disease, and once it begins, it is almost impossible to eradicate."

Mero's eyelids fluttered. He struggled to form his lips into words.

"I'm sorry," he mumbled to his chest. "I'm sorry I killed you."

"Oh, I'm not bothered," said the scholar. "Death is just the other face of life." When next he spoke, his voice was inches from Mero's ear. "Would you like to hear the final reason?"

79

The doors opened. Mero rolled onto his side, stuck Sheathless's point into the ground, and pushed himself to his feet. But no matter how hard he tried, he couldn't get his eyes open. Finally he peeled back an eyelid with his left hand, and in so doing was able to find his way off the lift.

This chamber was not like the others. It was vast and stark, with no signs of gilt or statuary. A path was marked out on the floor in strips of cold blue light that hurt the eyes. Lining the path on either side was a series of glass tubes, each glowing with its own internal light. At first Mero thought these were lifts like the ones he had ridden, but as he passed the first and peered inside, he realized it was some kind of specimen jar, filled with a viscous, translucent liquid.

Inside the jar was a human child.

It was a girl no more than eight years old. She was naked, and her head had been shaved. Wires extended from her wrists, her chest, and the sides of her head, disappearing into the upper portion of the device. She floated as though suspended in space and time, eyes closed, seemingly sound asleep.

Mero rested his hand on the glass, his eye once again sliding shut. As he swayed suspended in a manner reminiscent of the girl, her awareness tickled his palm, as though a spark of thought had passed from her to him. And what he sensed through that connection was not the languor of sleep but the silent, eternal scream of the enslaved.

Mero's eyes opened with a jolt. For an instant he thought he was looking into a mirror. Then he realized the girl's eyes had opened as well.

She stared at him in frozen horror. He stared back, too stunned to do anything else. Then, in the space between one moment and the next, the girl's eyes flickered to the left.

Mero followed her gaze. Ahead, the lighted path climbed a short flight of stairs, then terminated at a set of double doors. As his eyes fell upon the doors, a hundred ghostly hands pressed into his back, urging him onwards. He could no more resist that feeling than the tide could resist the calling of the moon. His hand slipped from the girl's jar as he headed for the stairs. He passed other jars as he went, some holding boys, others young women of about Lia's age. All were beautiful despite their shaved heads, their skin free of blemishes, their youth eternally preserved.

"The final reason," intoned the scholar, "and the most insidious of all, is that Dracula does not die. Death is the great equalizer; so long as death exists, we may take solace in the fact that no evil can endure forever. But Dracula, rather than fearing the passage of time, is able to use it to his advantage. Illness and age have no power over him. Unless he is brought low by deliberate, conscious effort—unless those he has terrorized find their strength and come together to banish him from their lives—he will persist until the end of time, free to work his evil on every fresh generation of man. And if he is ever hunted, wounded but not killed, he can retreat to his catacomb, to his refuge under the earth, and sleep the ages away until his face is forgotten. And that, my friend, is why the terror of Dracula is unmatched. Because his only reaper is his prey—feeble, fearful, forgetful man."

Mero climbed the stairs and put his hand on the double doors. At that moment there was an explosion of glass behind him. Shards of it peppered Mero's back, slicing into his clothes and skin. A hot, bitter wind boiled into the chamber. Mero collapsed against the doors, his vision split double, his ears ringing. With difficulty he rolled his head around.

Gorgol stood inside the chamber, framed by empty sky. He had burst through the room's back wall, which was made of nothing more than panes of dark glass. His nails were long and hooked, his hands covered in blood: he must have climbed all the way up the outside of the tower. Steam rose from his skin and the wind whipped his mane into a crazed halo.

He sighted Mero and a terrible grin split his face. He seized the capsule containing the girl and ripped it from the ground. Fountains of sparks rained down, and alarms blared deep in the walls.

"*Now, Mero,*" Gorgol roared, drawing back his arm, "*you DIE!*"

He hurled the capsule. Mero hurried to open the doors, but he was too late. The capsule clipped him on the shoulder. There was a sensation as though he had been slapped, then the air was full of glass and freezing liquid and Mero was sent spinning through the doors and into the chamber beyond.

80

Mero landed hard, sliding and rolling on the smooth, cold floor. He was dazed, his world spinning. Freezing liquid oozed into the corners of the room, soaking his clothes. By the time he got his hands under him and rose to his knees, he was shivering badly.

The floor shook, and Gorgol reached an arm into the room just as Mero scrambled to his feet. The giant seized one door and then the other, pulling them off their hinges and tossing them into the room behind. He tried to mash his face through the opening, heaving on the frame as though meaning to pull the entire wall down.

Mero looked around frantically. The room was circular, the ceiling high, the walls choked in a rampant growth of pipes, wires, and panels. A single specimen jar stood against the back wall, emitting a ghostly blue light. Mero dragged himself towards the jar, splashing through liquid and crunching glass beneath his feet. His skin was flayed, his muscles failing, but his eyes burned with passion, a righteous rage he had inherited from his goddess.

The jar's occupant was a man of fifty or sixty years. He was pale and grossly fat, rolls of blubber engulfing his stomach and legs and arms. He was bald and naked like the rest, his penis poking out from under his belly like the head of a baby mouse.

"*YOU,*" Mero snarled.

"*DON'T YOU DARE!*" Gorgol screamed. "*DON'T YOU DARE LAY A FINGER ON THAT MAN!*" As the giant bellowed and pawed at Mero through the door, the muscles of the man's face and hands twitched faintly.

With a wordless roar Mero raised his right arm and smashed Sheathless's point against the glass. The surface rippled but did not crack. Mero struck again, driving his weapon directly at the fat man's head. This time a hairline crack appeared.

"*NO!*" Gorgol ripped a chunk from the wall and tried to shoulder his way into the room. "*STOP THAT! DON'T YOU KNOW WHO I AM?*"

Alarms were blaring, the room swathed in blood-colored light. Mero smashed at the glass again and again, feeling his arm coming loose at the shoulder, his shinbones cracking, his vocal cords snapping like harp strings. The crack in the jar widened with every blow, Sheathless's peerless edge gnawing at the resilient glass.

"*NO! YOU CAN'T! IT'S NOT ALLOWED—I FORBID IT! I AM MASTER, I AM IN CONTROL! THIS WORLD BELONGS TO ME! IT BELONGS TO—*"

Sheathless came down. As its point struck the glass, the blade snapped cleanly in half, with a sound like wind howling through a distant valley. At the same time, the cracks in the glass widened, split, widened again, in a chain reaction of structural failure. Fluid spurted from the jar. Suddenly it exploded outward, jettisoning its entire contents onto the floor. The fat man came sliding out feet-first, buffeting Mero to the ground. He slipped in the fluid gushing from the container and fell sprawling to the floor.

Gorgol howled.

Mero rolled on to his back, watching in horror as the giant was seized by some kind of fit. Gorgol clamped his hands down on his head, then began tearing out great chunks of his mane. His legs shook, and he fell to his knees. Foam poured from his mouth. He raked his nails through his own skin, opening deep rivulets in his arms and chest. He threw his head back, howling, his eyes rolling in their sockets. He stuffed his hands into his mouth and prized his jaw open, as though trying to rip off the top of his own head. His stomach heaved, and he vomited, a green-blue slurry spilling over his lips and down his chest in a steaming torrent. Gorgol made a choking sound, clawing at his own neck. Then, suddenly, his arms went limp, falling to his sides. He teetered for a moment, then listed sideways and fell to the floor with a *CRASH*.

Mero wobbled to his feet. Something glinted in his peripheral vision. It was the last two feet of Sheathless's blade, lying among the shards of the fat man's jar. Mero stooped and picked it up, then stepped over to the fat man and rolled him onto his back. The man's eyes were wide and staring, yet even as Mero watched, they twitched ever so slightly in his direction.

Mero sank to his knees, clutching the shard of Sheathless to his chest. He drew a deep breath, blew it out, then drove the point into the man's heart. He left it there, quivering like a silver flower, as he staggered out of the chamber and down the stairs.

81

Dawn was breaking over the black lake. Though Uron was still shrouded in fog, the eastern horizon was clear. It paled now from a dingy gray to the cool blue of a new day.

The faceless girl sat on Uron's shore, that featureless ramp of poured stone, and watched the sky with her knees hugged to her chest. Her tiny form was silhouetted by the rising sun. A faint breeze tugged at the hems of her dress.

From behind her came the sound of footfalls, an uneven gait like that of a man with one wooden leg. She didn't bother to turn around; she knew the owner of the footsteps would be joining her in a moment.

Sure enough, a figure soon drew up next to her, though he didn't sit down right away. He stood with one hand resting on the bone of his hip—his other had fused into a claw of metal—and watched the sunrise in respectful silence. After a minute he sighed and sank to the ground with a grunt.

"Did you find what you were looking for?" the girl asked him.

Mero stared at the faceless girl in surprise. Only she wasn't faceless anymore. Her profile revealed not a stretched canvas of skin, but a brow, a nose, a mouth, a chin—a pair of dark, serious eyes that now turned in his direction.

Me, he thought, in a moment of rapturous clarity. *Me, if I were a woman.*

"My name is Orem," the girl told him. "Thank you for finding my face."

"I only did what you told me to do," Mero said.

The girl shook her head. "I never told you anything."

Mero fell silent, considering this. The girl shifted closer to him, so that their arms and thighs touched.

"What happens now?" he asked.

The girl couldn't help but smile. "Whatever you want."

"Whatever I want?"

"It doesn't matter." She nudged him gently. "This is *our* time, you know. The only time we'll ever meet face-to-face."

Mero bit the inside of his lip, a slight quaver entering his voice. "Does that mean I'm dying?"

"Mero, you've been dying since before you were born. I was there with you in your mother's womb. There is only one power in the universe, and that is me. I'm in every candle flame, every budding flower, every dawn and every dusk. To love me is to love me in *all* of my forms, and to reject me is to smash the mirror that reflects your own existence. Do you reject me, Mero? After all this time?"

Tears trickled down Mero's cheeks.

"No," he whispered. "No, I can't. But I'm afraid. I'm so afraid."

"Then be afraid," said the goddess. "I won't stop you. I brought you out of the void, just as I brought every other creature who walks the face of the earth. And very soon I will guide you back to where you belong. What you do until then is entirely up to you."

"Then it doesn't matter?" Mero said. "It really doesn't matter how we spend our lives?"

"Not to me. But that doesn't mean it can't matter to you."

Silence fell. Mero watched the sun. Eventually his shoulders started to shake. He wept for a long time, thinking of the pitiful life he had led, of all the years he had wasted in fear of the very goddess who had given those years to him. The goddess only sat by his side, never speaking, never judging, letting his grief run its course. By the time his tears subsided, the sun had breached the horizon, and tomorrow had begun.

"Mero," said the goddess. "Your tide is coming in."

He closed his eyes, feeling the sun on his cheeks. "I'm ready."

She reached out and took his hand. And together, they went.

www.ingramcontent.com/pod-product-compliance
Lightning Source LLC
Chambersburg PA
CBHW030552170726
48283CB00002B/293